BROKEN ROAD

BROKEN ROAD

MELISSA HARDY

Exile Editions

Publishers of singular books
Fiction, Poetry, Drama, Translations, Nonfiction and Graphic Books

2009

Library and Archives Canada Cataloguing in Publication

Hardy, Melissa
    Broken road / Melissa Hardy.

ISBN 978-1-55096-121-8

    I. Title.

PS8565.A63243B76 2009   C813'.54   C2009-904868-X

Design and Composition by Active Design Haus
Cover Photo by Les M.C. Glasson / iStockphoto.com
Typeset in Garamond, Copperplate Light and Cochin fonts at the
  Moons of Jupiter Studios
Printed in Canada by Gauvin Imprimerie

The publisher would like to acknowledge the financial assistance of
the Canada Council for the Arts and the Ontario Arts Council, which is an
agency of the Government of Ontario.

Published in Canada in 2009 by Exile Editions Ltd.
144483 Southgate Road 14
General Delivery
Holstein, Ontario, N0G 2A0
info@exileeditions.com
www.ExileEditions.com

Canadian Sales Distribution:
McArthur & Company
c/o Harper Collins
1995 Markham Road
Toronto, ON M1B 5M8
toll free: 1 800 387 0117

For
Martha Nell Hardy,
Beloved Mother, Actress, Teacher, and
Weaver of Baskets,
With profound gratitude

CONTENTS

PROLOGUE

My name is Sophia Sawyer and I am long dead. Indeed, the last thing I remember doing while I was still alive was hiking up my skirts and wading into the Oconaluftee River at Saligugi, Turtle Place, where the children used to swim on hot summer days. I was carrying a silver-headed cane in one hand and a battered old dream catcher in the other and my pockets were filled with stones lest I change my mind or fear change it for me. August 16, 1838. The date sticks in my mind, like a bone in the throat. The date of my death.

One thing I have learned: death does not extinguish our souls nor does it instantly banish them to some point beyond our imagining. No, souls just linger on, and, as time passes, fade like all worn things. People expect much from Heaven, but it is only this – diminished presence, gradual dissolution. I think that this must disappoint many – the missionaries with whom I cast my lot as a young woman put such store in an Afterlife – when we are but time travelers relaying our handful of messages across the centuries in shifts. And I am content with this, for I have much to remember and reflect upon. I have my stories.

Let me explain.

Pretend, if you will, that I am a bear and have a coat and stories are burrs that stick to it. As I passed through life and beyond to this place of dream catching, many stories have stuck to me. Over time, some of these story-burrs have fallen off on their own accord or caught on some other passing thing and so have been carried away. I can no longer remember them. They are elsewhere and someone else's property.

Other stories continued to stick until the passage of time and the force of movement has woven their rough prickly parts and the parts of me they cling to into a tight mat of fur and burr that encases me and protects me and keeps me warm.

Still others I have cut carefully out of my coat. These were, for one reason or another, binding or too painful to bear with me through life and beyond: the general lack of enthusiasm which my entrance into this world excited, the way the society in which I was raised set me aside as too tall and gawky and enthusiastic to be of reproductive use, for example; the way the Missionary Society finally sent me packing – that I could cram a heart into a satchel! Unstable, they said. In Boston, they said that I wrote far too many letters, made too many demands; in Tennessee, that I was wild and unpredictable and a danger to myself. And later, the Removal. All those dead, the Nation divided, everyone blaming everyone else for the loss of their homeland. The bloodshed and the fighting. But I get ahead of myself. That was later, much later, and stories must begin at the beginning. That is their nature.

Over the years I have become one with my stories. For this reason, they are not past but always present. And if they have not once happened to me, they do now, for they are part of my fabric and exist alongside me, forever present tense. And so it is with the story I am about to tell you – the story of a magic stone, a transparent or ulunsuti as it is called in Cherokee.

But first I must tell you the story of how such a stone came to be.

THE GROUNDHOG'S MOTHER

ONE

A long time ago, the deep places of the river, where it is green and dark and cold, were inhabited by uktenas – great, spotted or sometimes ringed snakes, as big around as the oldest trees in the forest. These uktenas had horns on their heads, their scales glittered like stars and a bright crest like a diamond blazed from the middle of their foreheads.

These crystals – for that is what in nature they resemble – measure about two inches in length and are perfectly clear except for a blood-red streak running through their center from top to bottom. In addition to perhaps a half dozen crystals that fell into the hands of men and were passed down, generation to generation, conjuror to conjuror, the rutile quartz, which can be still found today in the mountains of western North Carolina and eastern Tennessee, constitutes the only intact remains of uktenas, whose bones, being liquid heat, dried to a glittering dust within moments of the monsters' deaths and blew here and there. It is this bone dust that causes granite to sparkle in the sunlight and the leaves of certain plants to grow variegated and the eggs of certain birds to be speckled in the nest.

That their remains have not remained distinct, but have instead peppered the earth with light, is the reason white scientists discount uktenas as myth, while acknowledging the existence on the earth of such fantastic creatures as dinosaurs. That, and because it was the Cherokee who first told the story of the uktena – Indians who knew nothing. White men only believe natives when they tell of gold . . . over there, beyond the mountains. If one is to believe what the red man tells the white, that is where gold has ever lain. Over there. Beyond.

Three centuries ago, the white men who were my forebears were only peculiarly wan strangers with unusual goods to barter, newly come to live to the East of the *Ani Yunwiya*, or Real People, as the Cherokee called themselves. At that time, the Cherokee were more concerned about other Indian tribes, traditional enemies like the Shawano or the Creeks, than white men. White men seemed more a novelty than a real threat. Then the Cherokee held great tracts of land – from the head streams of the Kananwha and the Tennessee southward almost to where Atlanta stands today, and from the Blue Ridge on the east to the Cum-berland range on the west. Just north and west lived the Shawano, and so the two tribes fought over the land that stretched between – green, rolling Kentucky, which means in Cherokee Our Hunting Grounds. War between the Shawano and the Cherokee took the form of periodic raids in which few were killed and others captured. The man at the center and beginning of the old story I am about to tell you was just such a one – a Shawano captive, taken as a boy of perhaps ten winters by the Cherokee. He was called Aganunitsi, which means the Groundhog's Mother.

The Cherokee were, as a rule, kind to their captives – they embraced the concept of letting bygones be bygones. Once seized, abducted and perhaps roughed up just a little, so as to impress upon them the direness of their straits, captives were generally and genially adopted into the tribe. In time, they grew to think of themselves as Cherokee and became, in most cases, indistinguishable from their captors. So it was with the Groundhog's Mother, who was welcomed as a boy into a Cherokee family of farmers living in the village of Qualla, which lies in the shadow of Atsilawo-i, Where-the-fire- comes-down or Rattlesnake Mountain, as the white man calls it, and Nugatsani, where the Nuhnehi live. At this time the Cherokee Nation was divided into three geographic areas: the Middle Towns in the Smoky Mountains of western North Carolina; the Lower Towns in South Carolina and Georgia, there around the head-waters of the Savannah; and the Overhill Towns in Tennessee, on the far side of the Smokies. Qualla was one of the Middle Towns, like Cowe or Tuckaseegee or Kituhwa.

The Groundhog's Mother grew up short and stocky with one bowed leg and one withered and a slight hunch to his back. Did I mention that he was somewhat deformed? Not sufficiently that one would notice straight away. More . . . skewed, out of line, like a chair in need of re-glueing. In addition, one of his shoulders was not only noticeably larger but also somewhat higher than the other. All these factors combined to make his gait a rolling one with a slight hitch at the end like a lurch. Despite all this, he was surprisingly adroit. Finally, there was his left eye, which wandered strangely in his face and sometimes twitched violently, and his speech, which was as thick as hominy, so that he was understood only with some difficulty.

But what was most noticeable about the Shawano captive was his extreme restlessness. He was dream-driven and twitchy – like a dog which dreams, as soon as it closes its eyes, of the hunt and, which, because of the peculiar intensity of this dream, never fully awakens. Let me say that the fact that the Groundhog's Mother should be two people, or even several persons, wrapped tight in the skin of a single individual, surprised no one, for the Shawani were widely known to be a nation of conjurors and wizards. As the name Yunwiya means the Real People, so Shawani means the Southerners, but also perhaps the Salt People. The Shawani used to make salt by boiling water from salt springs; this they traded with other tribes who would, quite naturally, cry, "Sewan! Sewan!" upon seeing them: "Salt! Salt!" The magic inherent in salt is well known.

The Shawani were also great travelers, unlike the Cherokee who had inhabited the land defined as theirs since before memory. They drifted over the continent like a cool breeze, settling now on the banks of the Savannah River, which takes its name from them, now in the hilly Cumberland region . . . .

In the course of all these migrations, the Shawani had come to sit around many fires. They had dwelt in many sacred places. Magic is like pollen. It rubs off on all that brush past it. It travels like burrs and ticks and on the wind. And so, with the passage of time, the Groundhog's Mother's people grew in knowledge and power.

There are two worlds – the world of waking and the world of sleeping. There is also the world of Over There, but one cannot go to that world without dying or, at the very least, without being on a mission of some sort, and the Cherokee today do not go as often as their forefathers did . . . or, if they do, they rarely make it back across the dream divide. All creatures that are alive spend roughly equal times in the Waking World and the Sleeping World, and it's a peculiar phenomenon that, when we are awake, we tend to think the World of Waking is the real world and the World of Sleeping of no account, but that, when we are sleeping, we think the opposite. As a result, every creature that lives has two sets of realities and two sets of priorities.

These two worlds do not have a tight seal on them. This is why we sometimes remember dreams when we are awake. It is also why, when we are asleep, we tend to people our dreams with those we know and situations and events that are familiar to us from the other side.

Of course, everyone is different. Some people's seals are tighter than others, and some are less. The man who steers his consciousness with an easy expertise between Dream World and Waking World, like the man who paddles a canoe into an underground cavern, open-eyed and with his wits gathered close about him . . . he is likely to become a conjure man, someone with great medicine.

But the man who slips crazily between worlds and cannot tell which is which becomes a madman and is lost. There are places in the river, whitewater eddies, where one goes round and round and can never get out. This is the kind of madness I mean.

When the Groundhog's Mother was a boy on the brink of manhood, he began to have a recurring dream. At first, he thought that it was a series of different, perhaps even unrelated dreams. Then, one night, right in the middle of the dream, he realized that he had been in that place before, that he knew the dream's layout: what had happened before and what would happen next . . . these were as familiar to him as the inside of his adopted parents' cabin after a long winter spent indoors or the arrangement of Qualla, the village in which he lived.

This realization was like a thread that he could follow back through a labyrinth of dream tunnels, each one feeding onto the other. Over the many nights during which he walked with sleep steps the byways down which his dreams fled, he learned their configuration and how best to track them. The warm moons passed and the cold moons came. A year came and went, then two, and, during this time, the Groundhog's Mother became an increasingly skilled hunter of dreams, catching little ones, letting them go, ever on the trail of the big one that continued to elude him.

By now, the Shawano had also realized that a dream is not a sequence of events so much as a place, and that states of consciousness, of which dreams are one, are also places to or from or through which he could travel almost, if he could but get the hang of it, at will.

The problem was this: he forgot all he did and knew while inside the dream the moment he awoke, save this one thing: that he had forgotten something momentous, something that no one else knew. This is how it happened that the Groundhog's Mother, his nights full of heady revelation, his days misspent in futile attempts at remembering just what that revelation had been, and all this over a period of years, became alternatively listless and highly agitated, taking to his pallet one moment, then leaping to his feet and rushing from his adopted father's house out into the forests and the mountains the next.

At length, his family sought the aid of the village's conjure man in treating the Shawano's curious condition. He, being old and wise, suspected that confounding dreams lay at the root of the Groundhog's Mother's condition. This was a common enough diagnosis. So he decided that he would prepare for the young man something new, something a Creek who had traveled far towards the Darkening Land in the West and returned from there to live over yonder in Tanasee had once told him of. The Creek had called the thing a dream catcher. A dream catcher consists of a rough circle, about a hand span wide, twisted from a length of grapevine. The thinnest sinew is then attached to the hoop at more or less equidistant points around the circle and from these strands are woven a web which resembles that of a spider. The conjure man strung onto one of the pieces of sinew making up the web a piece of rutile quartz crystal into which a small hole had been drilled. When the web was completed, this crystal hung close towards its center. A wild turkey feather hung down from the dream catcher, attached to it by another length of sinew onto which beads had been strung. The conjure man used a red and a white bead on the Groundhog's Mother's dream catcher. Red signifies success and triumph, while white means peace and happiness, that which is achieved when a person's dreams are always good.

The night air is filled with both good and bad dreams. The function of a dream catcher is to capture and filter the dreams of its owner. The good dreams it allows through to the dreamer; the bad it holds in its web until the first light of day causes the tangled dream to perish. Good dreams know the way through the web and so are able to slip through its center hole and to drift down off the soft feather to the sleeper below. The purpose of the crystal in the center is to enhance the good dreams so that they might be better remembered the next day.

Bad dreams are, however, by their very nature, confused. They do not know about the central hole in the web and, by their struggle to escape, become hopelessly entangled in the dream catcher's web.

And this is what happened. The morning after the conjure man had given the Groundhog's Mother the dream catcher and the Shawano had hung it over his pallet, he awoke and remembered everything: the hunting and the catching, the fact that the dreams were one and that they were this:

The Groundhog's Mother dreamed that he was high up in the mountains where he had never been before, picking his slow way across a sloping field jagged with jumbled boulders. A rock-strewn stream cut through the field to his right, flanked by gray-barked white ash, silver bell and basswood. On the moist, mossy rocks that rode the stream, sore eye trailed idly finely tapered fronds in the cold, oddly transparent water. The water made a curiously hollow sound as it flowed, as if it was an echo rather than the sound itself, and the sky was a soft, palpable, unwieldy pinkish haze. He moved through it with difficulty, as though through still water.

Something was watching him.

Thus far it made no sound; it did not in any way displace elements within the environs so as to set up vibration and therefore to generate sound . . . no, that was not how the Groundhog's Mother knew that something was there. He knew it in the same way he had known an enemy waited for him in his Shawano family's cabin the day he had been taken captive by the Cherokee. A small boy, he had wandered into the little log house from the forest about midday, looked about the windowless room and thought how strange it was that his mother and grandmother were not there, preparing the big meal. A split second later he had frozen before the hearthstone, sensing in the thick, portentous darkness the crouching warrior covered in their blood. He could not see him, but he knew he was there.

He thought that the thing, whatever it was, followed him across the rocky outcrop, though he could not hear footfalls or turn quickly enough to see it coming close behind him. In his dream, he became frightened and began to run, haltingly at first, a lurching lope because of his shriveled limb, along the bank of the stream – there were fewer boulders here than in the field. Then, miraculously, he could run faster. As he continued to run, his withered limb was transformed, first into the leg of a strong runner, then into that of a swift, powerful animal.

Just as he came to the edge of the field and was about to enter the shaggy, deciduous wood beyond, he saw what he had sensed. Behind turned into before: the creature materialized, lifting up out of the stream in a great, sinuous arc, shedding sheets of water like green light – a monstrous spotted snake, as large around as a tree trunk, its forehead ablaze with an ulunsuti, a transparent. Then he knew that it was an uktena of which he had dreamt all these years.

The uktena spoke to him. *Aganunitsi*, it said in a voice, which he heard not with his dream ears – the creature's mouth had not moved – but inside his head. It was a silvery voice, which did not articulate the syllables as much as chimed them. It knew his name. *Come to me*, it said in its no-voice. *I seek my own death at your hands.*

Then the Groundhog's Mother blinked and opened his eyes to find himself on his pallet, in the village of Qualla, on the other side of reality. He knew that the dream was a good dream, a dream of calling – otherwise it would not have slipped through the center of the dream catcher's web – and he knew that, if he were ever to be more than a hunter of dreams, he must do as the uktena bid him.

TWO

Over the long centuries, the Cherokee have formulated and redrafted a History of the World told in tales and worn smooth by repetition. They have theorized, postulated and analyzed. They have critiqued their culture and that of the whites and the blacks and the Shawnees and the Creeks and then turned their critique upside down and so shaken it that all their ideas have come tumbling out in a heap, like puzzle pieces from a box, all mixed up. Then, with infuriating patience, they put the puzzle back together again. Methodically. Painstakingly. Each time it turns out slightly different, because, in the interim, this or that had happened, and altered perspective or shaved expectation or weighted a previously unsubstantiated opinion with the ballast of experience. The Cherokee spin history, and each time they weave, it is a web which grows so complex that, in the end, it becomes too heavy to cling to that which must support it and so must fall away in fragments and be re-spun . . . and it is, for the spiders are ever vigilant.

According to the stories told me by the old ones around the council house fire or in the wattle and daub lodges shaped like beehives which, together with a few log cabins, made up the town of Qualla during the dozen or more years in which it was to be my home, nothing in this world of ours remains quite the same as it started out. Either it has a short tail when once it had a long one or a long tail when once it had a short one. Or maybe it talked long ago, but now doesn't, or had a topknot and now is bald. This principle – that nothing remains the same – holds true for uktenas: all the uktenas who are, or have ever been, started out as men disposed to anger. It is a rare transformation – from man to snake – and uktenas are, accordingly, few in number, having been reported in only four places within the Cherokee nation: in Nantahala, the deep valley between the heads of the Tuckasegee and the

Little Tennessee Rivers, in Citico Creek in Overhill; in the Tallulah River in Clay County and in the Cohutta Mountains of northern Georgia. What follows is the story of how a particular uktena – the uktena central to my story, that of the Cohuttas – came to be in the water. This is that story.

Every day as Sun was climbing along the sky arch to the west, she would stop off at her daughter's lodge for dinner – Sun's daughter lived at high noon, right in the middle of the sky. Now Sun was the sourest old woman, easily displeased, and she had taken a strong dislike to the people of the earth early on. "Every time they look up at me, they screw up their faces," she complained to Moon, who was her brother. "They are so ugly."

But Moon was altogether more easygoing than Sun. "I don't know," he said. "It seems to me that they are very handsome. They always smile pleasantly when we meet." Of course, Moon's beams were soft, not hard like old Sun's.

But Sun hated the people of the earth, and, over time, her hatred and irritation festered to such an extent that she decided she would kill them all and so be spared the sight of their grimacing faces. She hit upon a plan by which she might accomplish this:

Just as she reached her daughter's home in the middle of the sky, she would send down such hot rays that they would burn people up.

She carried out her plan and, indeed, her rays were so hot that some people did die of the heat, and everyone feared that he or she would be next and soon there would be no one left on earth.

So the people of the earth went to Soco Gap, where the Yunwi Tsunsdi, the Little People, lived. The Little People were famous for their magic.

"Sun is an unreasonable old woman," said the Yunwi Tsunsdi. "There's no talking to her. The only thing to do is to kill her." The Little People are a notoriously ruthless lot and, though they have a lively sense of justice, they are also pitiless.

Once everyone had agreed that Sun must be killed, the Little People changed one of the men who had come as emissaries from the people of the earth into a Spreading-adder and the other into a Copperhead and set them to watching near the door of the daughter of Sun. The plan was this: when Sun came to dinner on the following day, the two snake men would bite her and so she would die.

The next day came and, with it, Sun, walking the sky arch as has ever been her wont, but, unfortunately, when she was drawing near the house of her daughter, the Spreading-adder was blinded by her bright light and could only spit out yellow slime, as he does to this day when he tries to bite.

"You nasty thing!" Old Sun called him and went back into the house.

The Spreading-adder crawled off without trying to do anything else. He was that demoralized.

So the people of the earth continued to die from the heat and, if they didn't die right away, they got spots on their skin, which then, over time, grew and consumed them.

Finally, in desperation, they traveled to Soco Gap once again and once again sought help from the Little People.

"What? You again?" the Little People asked. "You big people can't do anything right."

However, after some grumbling, they agreed to help the people of the earth again. This time they changed a warrior into a rattlesnake and another into a serpent that had never before been seen, a great uktena with horns on its head. These lay in wait for Sun beside the door to the house of her daughter. However, this plot worked no better than the first, because the rattlesnake is so quick and eager by nature, that, when Sun's daughter opened the door to look out for her mother, he sprang up and bit her and she fell dead in the yard. The uktena was so angry at the rash stupidity of the rattlesnake that it fell from the sky in a dark fury, with the rattlesnake side-winding its way down through the clouds behind him, begging the bigger snake's forgiveness, but with no success for the uktena would not so much as speak to it.

Once it had returned to the village of the people of the earth, the uktena grew angrier and angrier all the time. It seemed as though, having become a reptile, its human side had eroded and it could not check its burgeoning wrath. At the least provocation, it became very dangerous, hissing and lashing its powerful body. And every once in a while, in a fit of pique, it would eat someone's old grandmother or dismember a child.

At length, the people of the earth called a council and decided that the uktena had simply become too volatile to live alongside them, even though it had once been of their number and had undertaken a dangerous mission on their behalf. Full of regret and remorse at having to exclude it, yet knowing there was no other way to solve their problem, they sent it up to the Cohutta Mountains to live in the deep waters of the river that courses through that wild range.

As for the Little People, they were quite disgusted with men's efforts to save themselves from Sun. "They can't do a thing right," they complained. "They are incapable of sticking to even the simplest plan."

The Little People made a transparent cloud and placed it between the earth and the sun to protect the people from Sun's evil rays. The Sun did not even notice them doing this, so distraught was she over her daughter's violent and untimely death. And until recently, when the people of the earth began to shoot holes in this cloud with chemical arrows, it continued to protect them against the rays of Sun.

And this, according to the old ones, is how the uktena of the Groundhog's Mother's Dream came to be living far away in the Cohutta Mountains where, as must happen with uktenas, its rage grew until it crystallized into the powerful ulunsuti which it wore in its forehead. For that ultimately is what is an ulunsuti – pure rage in crystal form – and there is nothing so powerful in nature than one of these rare stones.

(Oh, and this is also how red men came to be red . . . from the time when hateful Sun burnt them.)

THREE

Of course the Groundhog's Mother had heard the tale of men's attempt to do away with Sun many times. Because of this, he knew that the place he dreamt of must be in the Cohutta Mountains.

According to the elders, the Cohutta Mountains are also called Gahuhdi, which means, "The Finishing Place." The range is located far to the east and south of Qualla – in Murray County, Georgia, about seven miles east of what is now Chatsworth. The Groundhog's Mother had to walk many miles and many days to get to the place the uktena lay in wait for him – it was during Hunger Moon, and snow covered the high places – and then he had to search carefully throughout the Cohutta Mountains for the monster. This is a small range, but the search took him the better part of two days, as he restricted it to daylight hours and these were fewer during the cold moons. He did this because he wished to keep safe those members of his family who had remained alive after the Cherokee raid in which he had been taken captive six years before – these included his two elder sisters, whom he had dearly loved. To come across an uktena asleep would be to doom his sisters to death.

Late in the afternoon of the second day, he was returning to his camp below the rock wall across the southern face of the mountains, when suddenly he came upon the field of jumbled boulders split by the rock-strewn stream of his dream. His heart pounding, he had turned to leave the place – it was too close to dusk for his ease – when he saw the glittering monster lying coiled in sleep on the edge of the field nearest his camp.

(Far to the north, in what is now Ohio, one of the Groundhog Mother's two sisters began to choke as she was cooking meat in a pot, as though something were caught in her throat which could not be dislodged, while the second sister, who was in the throes of labor, the moment her brother's eyes fell upon the sleeping uktena in the Georgia forests, expired and her baby too, the chord having suddenly wound itself around the infant's neck.)

The Groundhog's Mother heard these deaths in his heart and that organ swelled in his breast and beat like a bird attempting to escape its cage of ribs. He was angry for he thought suddenly that the uktena must have dreamt him the same way he dreamt the uktena all these years and so had known of his coming in advance. Therefore, it had planted itself thus so as to bring about the death of the Groundhog's Mother's sisters. So furious was the Shawano youth that he decided to not wait until morning to attack the monster but to kill it then and there.

To this end, he dug a trench around the beast and filled it up with the pine cones that grew in abundance in those coniferous woods. He then positioned himself so that he would be well placed to shoot the monster with a single arrow – luckily the light which flashed from the ulunsuti in its forehead shed an almost phosphorescent glow on the darkening wood – and, taking careful aim, he let fly an arrow which found its true mark in the beast's heart.

Poisonous blood spattered everywhere as the great snake reared from the ground in agony, twisting towards its slayer on the arrow locked in its heart. As it did, one drop of its blood flew from its wound straight and sure as an arrow shot from the bow of a hunter and hit the Groundhog's Mother in his forehead. It stung like cold, liquid fire, and the Shawano's hands flew to his brow to contain the pain. The next instant, however, the youth remembered his plan and, dropping to his knees on the bank of the trench he had dug, he ignited with hands that shook so badly from fear and pain that he could barely hold the flint the dry pine cones in the trench . . . . If the monster charged, the ensuing fire might cut off its attack. The pine cones were dry with the season and took the fire easily.

The fire lit, the Shawano knelt on his hands and knees, staring at the ground through tear-filled eyes, then, slowly, he peered up through the shimmering wall of flame and the gauze of wood smoke at the dying uktena.

You came, the uktena said to him. It spoke in its no-voice. Its mouth did not move, yet there the words were, inside his head. *It is good. Now, at last, I can die. I have lived in exile far too long. It has been so lonely all these centuries, in this mountain fastness where no man ever comes.*

"Why did you trick me so that my sisters might die?" The Ground-hog's Mother was full of bitterness.

I am man gone snake, the uktena reminded him. *Not kindly. And not used well, Shawano. I too need revenge. But, mind you! Take you my ulun-suti, for he who possesses such a stone is assured of success in hunting, love, rainmaking and anything else he might wish to undertake. Blessed . . . or cursed, for success in all things can be an intolerable burden and he who can make rain is only welcome some of the time.*

The Groundhog's Mother, feeling something on his forehead, lifted his hand to his brow. From it a small snake, the length of one of his fingers, dangled, fanged and hissing softly, like a wind low through the grass. He withdrew his hand in horror.

But now the uktena was fading, shifting shape. Its outlines softened. Its solidity fell to liquid as its green and glassy color drained from it onto the patch of earth on which it lay, darkly staining the ground beneath and around it. In the end what remained of the creature bore the same messy resemblance to the uktena as might its decomposed body, its features puffy and distorted. Only the ulunsuti remained the same – a flashing, hard jewel in a melting setting.

"Dead?" asked the Groundhog's Mother.

Not quite, said the voice inside his head – a smaller voice this time and closer. *Never entirely.*

He knew then that the uktena lived on in him, in the snake that grew from his forehead. He tore at it but could not rid himself of it. He reached for his hunting knife.

If you cut me from you, you shall bleed to death and nothing can stop the flow. Not cobwebs. Nothing.

The Shawano, beside himself, seeing no other way out, called out to the birds of the forest in his desperation, "Come! Come eat this monster." Then he returned to his camp at the rock face to brood and despair until the birds should have done their work.

And the crow and the raven and the dark-eyed junco and even the ruffled grouse and the wild turkey came, and over the seven days that followed, they pick-picked the bones of the uktena clean. The weather was dry and chill over that same period and the air soon dried the bones. Once dry, they sifted to a fine, glittering powder that the wind blew here and there.

In the meantime, the Groundhog's Mother waited, waited in his solitary camp with only the snake growing from his forehead to keep him company. The spot at which it joined his skin stung like a fresh scrape, something outside that more properly belonged inside, and the incessant murmur of the drooping snake's bell-like voice inside his head made him almost distracted at times. At other times he listened to it, as though it was a haunting melody heard in a dream.

Seven is a sacred number, according to the Cherokee, time enough for most things. Therefore, on the seventh night following the death of the uktena, the Groundhog's Mother left his camp on the rock face and went to the rocky meadow of his dream. What with the birds and the wind, he could find no trace of the monster. Then, he saw a pulsing, greenish light waver from one of the twisted yaupon trees which stood on the edge of the meadow, near to the trench he had dug around the uktena. He came closer and discovered the creature's ulunsuti, a crystal the size of an egg, caught in a fork of one of the yaupons. A raven had plucked it from the cranium of the uktena but had found it too large to carry far and so had dropped it here. Working with care, the Groundhog's Mother disengaged it from the place where it had come to lodge. As he pulled it free, it lit up the night and then flashed like lightning. Remembering its utility, he wrapped it carefully in buckskin and began his journey back to Qualla.

The Groundhog's Mother became, in time, so great a conjure man that his name was remembered many years after his death. As for the ulun-suti, it was passed down to the Groundhog's Mother's son and his son's son and his son after that, until, at length, it passed into the possession of a hunter named Dayunisi or Beaver's Grandchild.

DAYUNISI

ONE

In the year my people call 1736, Dayunisi's young wife Salili saw the marks smallpox had left upon her pretty face and promptly hung herself from the branch of a tree down near Turtle Place. Turtle Place is a deep hole in the Oconaluftee River near Ela where a giant monster turtle is reputed to live; it is a favored place for suicides. This caused Dayunisi to take his and Salili's only child, a baby girl named Tsikiki, and move far away from Qualla to a place called Adagahi, or Gall Place. Dayunisi had several reasons for this radical relocation. In the first place, his heart was broken; he had loved Salili dearly. In the second place, he wanted no further contact with white men; it was they, after all, who had brought smallpox to the Middle Towns. Finally and perhaps chiefly, he feared that others might conspire against him to steal the ulunsuti, which had come down to him from his great ancestor the Groundhog's Mother and was the key to his continued success as a hunter. For the ulunsuti is both boon and bane; it exerts a powerful hold on the one who possesses it and Dayunisi, being by nature suspicious and quick to take offense, perceived threats when there were perhaps none.

Gall Place is located westward from the headwaters of the Oconaluftee on the northern boundary of what is now Swain County, between the heads of Bradley's Fork and Eagle Creek. It lies within a very wild section of the mountains, heavily populated by spirits of one kind or another, so that the very trees seem to listen and to move with purpose. The Cherokee know that Gall Place lies in this general vicinity, but, despite this knowledge, only a few have seen the medicine lake. That is because the path to this place is so very difficult and strange that only the animals know the way and their knowledge seems inherited, for even very young animals, when orphaned or wounded, will make their way towards it, as if instinctively.

If a hunter becomes lost in the woods and comes by chance near Gall Place, he will instantly know where he is by the tremendous whirring sound of the thousands of wild ducks that fly about the lake. On reaching the source of that turbulence, however, he will find only a dry flat, without bird or animal or blade of grass, unless, of course, he has first sharpened his spiritual vision by prayer and fasting and vigil. To one who has prepared himself in this manner, the lake at daybreak might appear as a wide-extending, but shallow sheet of purple water, fed by springs spouting from the high cliffs which surround it, and in its water he may glimpse all kinds of fish and reptiles and, swimming upon the surface or flying overhead, great flocks of ducks and pigeons, while, all about the shores are bear tracks that cross in every direction. This is because Adagahi is a medicine lake for birds and animals. Whenever a bear is wounded by hunters but not caught, it attempts to make its way through the woods to this lake and to plunge into its water. When it comes out the other side, its wounds are healed. For this reason, Gall Place is a refuge for animals, and they prefer to keep it invisible to most hunters, only privileging a few select men. That Dayunisi was able to not only see the lake but to come and go at will was testimony to the tremendous strength of his ulunsuti medicine. Few men have ever done this and none but Dayunisi had ever proven capable of not only finding it, but also finding his way back time and time again.

When Tsikiki grew to be a maid, she became restless and longed to live among people, despite the beauty and abundance of Gall Place. There were several reasons for this, chief among them the fact that, from the time she could accommodate him, Dayunisi had lain with her as he would a wife. Tsikiki did not like this very much at all, for the things he did to her hurt and he was always calling her by her mother's name – Salili. At those times she felt she didn't exist; that it was Tsikiki who was a ghost and not Salili and this both angered and frightened the girl.

Finding a husband for Tsikiki would not have been difficult. There were many young men who would have courted the girl for the respect and, indeed, awe, in which her father was held throughout the Middle Towns, as well as for her rare and fragile beauty, for, like the mother who had slain herself over the loss of her smooth face, Tsikiki was lithe and quick-footed and gentle featured. But these would-be lovers could not find their way to the post and wattle cabin at Gall Place without undergoing a strenuous vigil and this was why Tsikiki, who could not be made aware of their interest in her in the usual ways girls come to learn such things – through the carefully directed gossip of old women or the chatter of friends – thought herself well-enough served when, on one of their rare visits to Qualla, a man called Edahi or He Goes About proposed that she exchange a basket of her own weaving for the leg of a deer killed by him and so become his wife, this despite the fact that he was closer in age to her father than to her and not a very good hunter. And so they were married, though it caused Dayunisi great grief, and together had one child, a lame little boy called Young Squirrel. This was a very common name. Many little boys were named Young Squirrel.

While He Goes About was fond of, even foolish about his pretty, young wife, it was clear to everyone in the settlement that she cared little for him. Moreover, she had not lived long within the settlement before she figured out that she could have made a much better marriage for herself than she had. Consequently, she made her husband's life far from comfortable, demanding much and yielding little, even after her son was born. The townspeople had little sympathy for her plight. Not having been reared in society, she had few social graces. She spoke her mind and did her will with little regard for what her townspeople considered proper. This alienated the older women just as her beauty alienated those girls who might otherwise have been her friends. Young men continued to find her attractive, but she was the wife of another and, besides, she was strange. According to tradition, adulterers had their ears cropped close to their skulls. Was the peculiar daughter of Dayunisi worth such disfigurement?

The result was that Tsikiki soon grew as lonely and as dissatisfied in Qualla as when she had shared her father's bed at Gall Place.

Then the white trader came.

TWO

George Kinnahan was a Scotsman who built his factory, as he called it, in the fertile valley down from Spillcorn Creek, there in that smother of elderberries and sweet bays where the squirrels bark and woodpeckers are forever puncturing the air with their staccato tattoos. He built it carefully, squaring the logs like bridge timbers, joining and notching them closely, smoothing the puncheons, which he had riven from heart pine, as if they were planed, using mortar instead of clay, as the Cherokee did, and there he kept the coarse cloth, bone buttons, knives and hatchets he traded for ginseng and furs and beeswax.

George was a tall man, with a fierce red beard, and eyes so pale a blue that they seemed almost transparent. The old women called him the Moon-eyed One and spoke of a time before this latest influx of white people, when the Cherokee coming to this land out of the Northeast had encountered a race of absolutely white moon-eyed people on this soil. The Cherokee had waged an easy war on these strange and vulnerable people, who could not see in the daylight, driving them to the mouth of Big Chicamauga Creek. There the adversaries entered into a treaty – the moon-eyed people would remove immediately to the west, if permitted to depart in peace. And this they had done many years before.

Dayunisi would not deal with white men. His initial contact with them had cost him his young wife, after all, and he bore grudges like scars cut deep into his soul – he was a man who forgot nothing. Accordingly, he brought what he trapped to his daughter Tsikiki in Qualla and had her trade the shaggy hides of wolf and the soft dun rabbit skins and the stiff pelts of gray possum and red fox and black bear for knives and scrapers and other things he fancied. Sometimes Kinnahan threw in something for Tsikiki – a length of calico or a copper kettle or a little glass in which she could see her face; it was miraculous, that glass, as though she were gazing at her reflection in the water, only clearer. Of all the women in the village, Tsikiki seemed to George to stand alone and apart, to be in need of a friend. After he learned that the name Tsikiki means Katydid, he began to call her Katy; it was easier for him to pronounce than Tsikiki.

And it was not long before the young wife began to visit the trader even when she had nothing of her father's to barter, and people began to talk among themselves.

Later George gave Tsikiki a spindle and a loom with heddles and treadles and taught her to spin and weave and dye cloth and then bought homespun she made to sell in the factory. First he taught her how to shear his sheep – he kept four sheep, a horse and a cow. Then he instructed her in picking, washing, carding and spinning the wool: linsey for underwear and dresses, jeans cloth with chain of cotton, filling of wool for men's clothing. He taught her to dye cotton using indigo for deep blue, madder root for red and maple bark for purple. He also showed her how to use the hulls, roots and barks of walnut, sumac berries and laurel leaves and taught her that roots and sprouts were best got on the new of the moon. "Then you skin them," he told her, "boil them three hours, then boil them again together with the wool, outdoors, to let the odor free. Afterwards you hang it the sun to dry and darken further."

George Kinnahan was a man who knew many things, and his teaching her how to make cloth meant that Tsikiki spent a great deal of time with the Moon-eyed One.

❧

The Thunder Moon had almost turned and the time was drawing near for Selutsungitisti, the two-week-long thanksgiving celebration that coincided with the ripening of the first corn. At this time it was customary for enemies to be forgiven, home fires extinguished and a new fire kindled by Old Tobacco, the Adawehi or conjure man of the village. From this new fire all other fires would subsequently be lit.

By this time, Tsikiki and George Kinnahan knew enough of each other's language that they could communicate without much difficulty, half in English and half in Cherokee.

"Tell me about your religion," asked George.

"What do you mean by religion?" Tsikiki did not know this word.

"Your gods."

"There are so many. There is the Sun God and a Red Fire God, but there is also Sun who is an old, cranky woman and her daughter who is a Red Bird as well as being Sun's daughter . . . . But she was killed by a rattlesnake. There are other peoples too, the Little People who live in caves in the mountain slopes and those who, like the Thunderers, cause things to happen, like rain and lightning. There is also Moon. He is friendly. And star men who fall from the skies and get caught in trees. There are ghosts and Raven Mockers and dream catchers. There is the terrible Spearfinger. There is Long Man the River."

"Who reigns over them?" George wanted to know. "Who is their Master?"

Tsikiki shrugged. "No one that I know. Sometimes a conjure man can make them do his bidding. If his medicine is powerful enough."

"The white man has one god," George told her. "His name is God. And that God has a son, Jesus Christ, who is also a God. And He has a great enemy, the Devil, who is an evil spirit."

"How do you know about this God?"

"His Son told us about him. A long time ago."

"How do you know about his great enemy?"

"Sometimes he comes to me." George's face darkened and he looked briefly away. "I know him well enough, Katy."

"The Little People came to my father's house once," said Tsikiki conversationally. "I did not see them, but one rarely does. They left bean bread."

"Tell me about the Green Corn Dance," said George.

Tsikiki smiled. "During the two weeks in which the harvest is celebrated, the first ears of corn are deposited in the council house for the poor. This way the poor have corn for the winter too. On the main day no voices are heard until nightfall. Then the whole town comes together to hear Adawehi pay homage to the new harvest and thank the earth for its bounty and to pray for the spirits to bless the corn and meat during the year. Then everyone eats, goes to water and returns to the council house for dances. We do many dances – the Groundhog dance and the Pheasant dance . . . ."

"Do you like to dance, Katy?" asked George.

"Yes, I do."

"The white men do many dances too. Shall I teach you one?"

"Oh, yes!"

"This is a reel," said George, and there in the deserted factory he took her in his arms.

⁂

It must be said that Tsikiki liked the white man's reel far more than the dances she had performed hand in hand with the girls of the village – soft voices, advancing and retreating as the skin drum beat time and the gourd rattle shook and the deer leg flute piped airy discords, the dim square of the ceremonial ground lit by flickering torches . . . .

She liked it much, much more.

Tsikiki grew to feel affection for George Kinnahan. She felt none for He Goes About, and, as time went on, her little lame Young Squirrel, whom she had loved once, began to look strange to her, as if she did not quite recognize him. "It is because he is the fruit of an imperfect union," she reasoned.

Wishing to impress the white trader, Tsikiki told him that her father was a charmed hunter and that he had in his possession an ulunsuti that had been handed down to him by his great-grandfather and his grandfather and his father after him.

"I would like to see this magic crystal." George had never seen such an object and thought that what Tsikiki had described to him might turn out to be a rare jewel of some kind. You could dig rubies in these mountains. Rubies fetched a good price down on the Coast.

Tsikiki shook her head. "That would bring disaster to my father. The elders have told us that no white man must ever see an ulunsuti."

"That is a made-up story," George told her. "The elders just want to see that the stone stays among your people, that it is not stolen or sold. What possible harm would it do just to have a look?"

"I don't know," said Tsikiki. "Perhaps you are right."

"Bring it to me then."

"What if I cannot?"

"Then I shall say that you are useless."

Tsikiki sighed, her heart suddenly heavy. She could not bear to lose the trader's affection. "It will be very hard," she said, "but I will try."

೩೨೨

During Harvest Moon her father came to visit, bringing pelts for trading. Tsikiki asked to be taken back with him to Gall Place for a few days before winter set in. "It is so beautiful there," she told her father, "that I have been missing it every day." Being without powerful medicine, she was unable to find Gall Place on her own.

Dayunisi, who had been very lonely in the absence of his daughter, was filled with joy and agreed at once that she should accompany him on his return journey. They set out the following morning. Tsikiki carried in her pack a bottle of whiskey that George Kinnahan had given her – this was for her father.

The journey through the mountain fastnesses was tiring and they slept well the first night home, not as before her departure on the same pallet, but on separate ones, as befitted her married state.

It was on the evening of the second day that Tsikiki gave her father George Kinnahan's whiskey. Dayunisi had only tasted whiskey a few times in the past and was suspicious of the white man's medicine, but, after a few drinks, he lost all his caution and, by the time darkness fell, he had drunk most of the bottle. It was then that he insisted that Tsikiki bed down with him as before, for she reminded him of the wife he had lost, he said, and he was a lonely hunter living far removed from his kind within the confines of a magic place and why? Because it was his fate to protect the ulunsuti that had been handed down from his great-grand-father and this was a tremendous task and one which required much sac-rifice from him.

Not wishing to anger him or arouse his suspicions, Tsikiki con-sented to lie with him. Afterwards, when he had rolled off of her onto his side asleep, she got up, his seed sticky between her thighs, thick, like blood, and, drawing a blanket around her shoulders, made her way out of the house to the *unwadali*, the storehouse. This was a small conical building supported by eight posts about seven feet tall, well daubed with loam both within and without, to keep out insects. Dayunisi stored his beans and corn there and, hanging from one of the posts, the ulunsuti, stored in a brittle, stained buckskin pouch, drawn closed by a length of sinew. It was a very old pouch, having been made from the buckskin in which the Groundhog's Mother had wrapped the ulunsuti after dis-lodging it from the yaupon.

She placed the bundle under her blanket and started forth into the night. She knew her drunken father would not awaken easily. When she had come to the lake and gone some little way around it, so that there was no danger that she would be seen, she took the ulunsuti from the buckskin. It flashed a greenish light so powerful she knew she would have no trouble finding her way back to Qualla, despite the fact that the night was moonless. As she made her way through the trailless jungle of heath thickets, dense with masses of dog hobble intertwined with trunks and branches of dripping rhododendron and laurel, she passed perhaps a half dozen wounded animals – a bear and a night-prowling bobcat and a white-tailed deer, a coon and a rabbit and a painter – as they struggled towards the healing waters of the enchanted lake and redemption.

She arrived in Qualla shortly after daybreak and, though she was dirty and disheveled, her clothing torn, her hair tangled, she did not stop to pause at He Goes About's house, but went straight to George Kinnahan with her prize. She found the trader in his factory, bundling pelts for conveyance south. He was going down the Savannah, to the port at Charleston with an ox cart piled high with beeswax and comb honey and ginseng and furs.

"I got it," she told him breathlessly. "The transparent. I took it from its place in my father's storehouse while he lay sleeping. Our plan worked." She did not tell him that she had lain with her father – the Moon-eyed One would not want to hear that.

George straightened up immediately and turned to her, wiping his big hands upon his aproned flanks. "Let's have it, then."

Carefully, with trembling hands, Tsikiki opened the buckskin pouch and pulled from it the ulunsuti – at first light she had returned it to its pouch, so afraid was she, with her father's fear, that someone might see it and attempt to take it from her.

To her surprise, the crystal that had lit her way home like intermittent lightning just a scant hour before no longer emitted any light at all. Instead it resembled nothing so much as a mineral spar – a dull, milky-white chunk of quartz shot through with a single streak of vibrant red.

George took it from her and held it up so that the light from the doorway shone through it. "This is no ruby," he said after a moment. "It's nothing at all." He handed it to her and turned back to his work.

"But it is an ulunsuti," breathed Tsikiki. "The flashing stone plucked from the brow of an uktena."

"It's a piece of quartz, Katy. Just a piece of rock."

Stunned, Tsikiki replaced the ulunsuti in the pouch and started to turn away. Surely she had lost his esteem.

But George had thought of something. "Never mind about your crystal," he said. "I've got to go down to the coast with these furs. You come with me."

At that, Tsikiki forgot all her disappointment and clapped her hands. As she did, the pouch containing the transparent fell to the sawdust floor.

♨

Tsikiki slipped away from Qualla the following day before sunrise and went over the mountains and into the steamy south lands to the coast with George Kinnahan. They traveled through pines and palmettos and yellow jasmine and passed by swamplands where trees, with vines for hair, leaned on one another like drunken men at a gathering. She saw wondrous things – villages made of stone, so big that a body couldn't see where they began and where they ended, and ships with sails that were like big wings. And in Charleston George Kinnahan bought her a length of the prettiest yellow and red calico she had ever seen and said it was a present to her.

Later they were married by a circuit preacher and settled down not in Qualla, to which Tsikiki would have been loathe to return, but near Settico, one of the Overhill towns in the land called Tanasee. They had many children. Some died, but others lived and Katy Kinnahan, as she came to be known, and her white husband did well enough with his new store for many years.

♨

Dayunisi, waking to find Tsikiki gone and the sun high in the sky, decided at once to go in search of her. But first he staggered, head throbbing and belly full of knives, to his storehouse to get the pouch containing the ulunsuti, for he went nowhere without the transparent. That was when he discovered that it had been stolen.

Desperate now, he started off after Tsikiki, but found the woods that lay between his house in Gall Place and Qualla, which he had so often traversed without difficulty, suddenly strangely unfamiliar. He became lost and only reached the village on the day after his daughter had left it, weak with hunger and half-mad with the losing of his prize.

In despair now of finding the ulunsuti, he attempted to return to Gall Place but found only a barren plain to mark the lake where he had lived for so many years. He no longer possessed the magic to see the place where animals come to heal themselves.

Once more he made his way back to Qualla, where his daughter's abandoned husband He Goes About took the once-famous hunter into his home.

꿍

As for Young Squirrel, the little son of Tsikiki and He Goes About, the one with the twisted foot, his father had sent him to the trader's factory in search of his mother on the day of her departure and there he had found upon the sawdust floor a buckskin pouch. The thing within the pouch glittered and flashed erratically. He could see light coming through the seams of the pouch. His heart beat rapidly – was this what he thought it was? Taking the pouch, he opened it and saw that it contained the transparent. He recognized it at once, of course. Many times he had asked his grandfather to see it, and several times the old man had consented to show him it, but not kindly, for no one had much use for the crippled boy who could not run and hunt like the others. Looking quickly about him to see if anyone observed him, Young Squirrel slipped the pouch under his shirt and immediately bore it off to a safe place in the forest – a hollowed-out tree of which only he knew. There he hid it away.

I shall be the great man now, he thought, returning home to watch his grandfather slowly die.

Young Squirrel

ONE

Away and away, we're bound for the mountain.
Bound for the mountain, bound for the mountain.
Over the mountain, the hills and the fountains,
Away to the chase, away, away.

This is a song that Young Squirrel had heard George Kinnahan sing many times as the white man sat on the stoop in front of the door to his factory, cleaning with oily rags the fine Kentucky rifle with the thirty-five-inch barrel and brass trim that he called the Bucksmasher. This was before the trader had run away with Tsikiki, Young Squirrel's mother.

Once the boy had asked the white man what the song was called.

"The Deer Chase." George Kinnahan replied. "Oh . . . ." and, because he was drunk, he proceeded to favor the boy with a verse:

"We heed not the tempest, the toil nor the danger,
As over the mountain, away goes Ranger,
All night long, till the break of dawn,
Merrily the chase goes on."

Who was the Ranger? Young Squirrel wondered, but did not ask. He did not like to ask too many questions, for people tired of him when he did and shortly afterwards told him to go away. Young Squirrel remained, quiet, on the edge of things. In this way, he saw much and came to his own conclusions. (One thing that Young Squirrel had observed was that, when you do not ask questions, people will often explain themselves spontaneously. Silence combined with a presence draws conversation just as tobacco will draw the poison from a bee sting.) In truth, he, like his mother, had been drawn to this foreigner in the Nation, to the strangeness of his ways. Like the mother, the boy was always about. The difference was that no one noticed. Young Squirrel was like one of the invisibles – he had that quality of presence that does not obtrude.

> Now we're set just right for the race,
> The old hound dogs are ready for the chase,
> The deer is a-bounding and the hounds are a-sounding,
> Right on the trail that leads o'er the mountain.

Young Squirrel had memorized the words when no one thought he was even listening.

୧୬

There was the matter of hunting. Kinnahan did not hunt like the Cherokee. He did not use a bow and arrow. Instead, he shouldered the Bucksmasher and took with him to the woods a big buck knife and a shot bag filled with something like wood ash called Thompson's powder. Often he drank whiskey before setting out. This "keeps the eyes skinned," he told the boy. It also kept the trader's walk unsteady and his trigger finger twitchy. No one in the village dared go out when the white man was hunting – he shot at everything that moved and some things that didn't. There were trees in the surrounding forest, beech and birch and sugar maples, with big, black holes blazed in them.

Young Squirrel also noted this surprising thing: the trader shot whatever it was he wanted or could and did not stop to thank that which he had killed for yielding up its life to him. He seemed to do this without a thought, as if nothing in the forest held life but himself, as if

34

it was his right to take. As if there would be no retribution. No kneeling afterwards to pray to the spirit of the animal killed, no burial of propitiatory beads, no fire built in the path behind him, so that the spirit chief of his prey might not be able to follow him home and there attack him and the people of Qualla with whom he traded.

Young Squirrel observed one thing further, that the trader seemed to believe that he must take, must fight the forest for his food, must conquer in order to live. There seemed to be no truce between all other things and the trader, as there was between the Cherokee and the creatures with whom they shared the earth, but instead a war without cease fought in daily skirmishes. Victory, in this war between the trader and the world, was measured out in the white man's continued survival.

At first, Young Squirrel thought that the white man was rash indeed, and foolish. He believed that the Elders were right on this score, that if hunters did not perform the proper rituals, animal spirits would afflict them with diseases like the Crippler, which white men call rheumatism. He took some comfort, after the departure of his mother, in thinking of George Kinnahan twisted like a yaupon, crabbed like a crawdad. Later, he grew less sure. Bad things rarely happened to white men.

After his mother ran off with George Kinnahan, Young Squirrel was full of hate. In his own, different way, he, like his mother, had been fascinated with George Kinnahan. Now he hated him. This hatred was much worse because he had once found the trader of such keen interest. Unrequited love is a terrible bond.

He also hated his mother, but his hatred for her was more complicated. He wished all manner of evil for her, and he wished to be there to see her afflictions. Finally, he wished to be able to save her from that which afflicted her, to be her rescuer.

As for his grandfather and father, his contempt for them grew proportionately with their increasing weakness, for truly the one dragged the other down, until, by the time Dayunisi succumbed to death a little more than a year after Young Squirrel had found the ulunsuti cast aside by his mother and hidden it in the hollow of a tree, He Goes About hunted no more but had grown dependent on the gifts of beans and venison from more prosperous villagers. They despised him, but without saying so, as a have-not and one who had lost his wife to the Moon-eyed One. So did Young Squirrel. A man should at least be able to keep his wife.

Because of all his hatred, Young Squirrel had difficulty sleeping at night. He would lie awake, staring at the ceiling of his father's house for hours on end. The ceiling consisted of low beams, darkened with wood smoke, from which hung dried strings of yellow and red pepper and field corn and leather britches, things plucked by his mother's fingers and hung there which no one would ever eat now. Stared at long enough through the swimming eyes of an exhausted boy, it came to resemble a still place in a river, an oxbow clogged with marsh grasses and alive with frogs. The frogs cried in unison for their mates, so many of them that the air quaked with their love call. *Tsikiki! Tsikiki!* rasped the katydids.

Perhaps Young Squirrel was not awake at all when the ceiling seemed to him not itself but the marshy slope of a river. Perhaps he slept and dreamt and did not know it, but sometimes he thought he glimpsed his own face, hollow cheeked and ravaged, staring back at him from beneath the clouded water with eyes washed in blood. This face of his always frightened him and, upon seeing it, he would close his eyes.

"Oh, Brother . . ." the apparition would call out in a hollow voice like water draining.

However, Young Squirrel would block his ears and shake his head, hissing, "No! No!"

Then, one night he did not close his eyes or cover his ears or shake his head. Who can say why? Perhaps he had decided that the apparition was not going away, that he might as well negotiate with it. So he spoke back to his image, acknowledging the hideous presence: "Brother?" he asked tentatively.

"Yes, brother." replied the phantasm.

From that time on, Young Squirrel was never without his terrible brother. The peculiar apparition was by his side, day and night, whispering in Young Squirrel's ear and, in general, inciting a quiet sort of mayhem.

જ્

Shortly after the death of Young Squirrel's grandfather Dayunisi, a full eighteen months after the departure of the trader and his mother for the headwaters of the Savannah, a new trader came to take Kinnahan's place. From now on, there would always be a trader in Qualla, but not just for those Cherokee who wished to exchange pelts for the white man's goods. The Scotch-Irish, Germans, Huguenots and English had been crossing into these mountain fastnesses for nigh onto two decades now, one or two or three families at a time. They came in ox-drawn wagons, through Soco Gap, along the broad valley of the Oconaluftee. Many went south to Georgia or east to Tennessee, but others stopped because of sickness or a broken wagon axle or because they liked the look of the country or were too worn out to continue. They needed iron, powder and reading matter. And families from North Carolina, Regulators who had cut the Yellow Mountain Road between Marion and Spruce Pine, began to spread eastward from their cluster of homes on the Watauga River to the valleys of the Holston and Clinch and Powel and French Broad Rivers. From the valleys they spread into the mountains and along the fertile bottoms. They needed bullets, muskets and paint.

The new trader, Henry Matlock, was a stout, middle-aged man with a game leg like Young Squirrel's and a temper as ragged and sharp as a rusty saw blade. He took little interest in anything but his business. This lay in amassing an inventory of pelts – beaver, buck, bear, wildcat, fox, coon and mink – loading it onto an oxcart and driving it south two or three times a year, to return with axes, auger bits, hunting knives, blankets, coverlets, pots, pans and gourds of salt. Because his customers

37

included whites, Matlock's stock was more varied than Kinnahan's had been.

In turn, seeing what was now available to them at the store made the Cherokee wish to buy even those things they had either once made or didn't need. They traded for spoons of tin and pewter when once they had carved their eating utensils from deer horn. They forsook the bow for the Pennsylvania rifle or Brown Bessies, the British smoothbore muskets. A rifle cost twenty-five skins, bullets forty a skin. Why chip flint for arrowheads when a man could shoot many more deer with a rifle? The women also brought in items for exchange: beeswax, wool, herbs and nuts. Matlock made money and he used that money to buy land.

Two years passed. Young Squirrel now had eight winters.

Listen to the hound bells, sweetly ringing,
Over the mountain the wild deer's springing,
All night long till the break of dawn,
Merrily the chase goes on.

No one noticed when Young Squirrel began to help Matlock at the trading post. In truth, Matlock scarcely noticed. Certainly it was a slow process. At first there the boy was, hanging around the place, not in the way. Young Squirrel was careful never to be in the way. Then one day perhaps the trader had said, "You there! Boy! Give me a hand with this!" and the child had shyly complied.

At first Young Squirrel swept up and helped Matlock, if the task was more than one person could handle. For this he received a sweet.

Then Matlock set the boy to taking stock, which led to his doing inventory. For this he received a small wage. The trader thought him a likely lad, and so he was; he knew enough English to talk to white customers. Like his mother, Young Squirrel was quick, even though the trader did occasionally catch him muttering to himself as if to a ghost who walked beside him:

"Let me see you do it!"

"No!"

"Come on! I dare you!"

"Will you shut up?"

As for Young Squirrel's father, he rarely moved from his house anymore, unless it was to sit with other have-nots on the benches outside of the Ceremonial Square. There, in the shade of the thatched umbrella that shaded the dancers, they complained and reminisced.

"You should be learning how to hunt," He Goes About told his son. "Hunting is how a Cherokee man makes his way."

But Young Squirrel only sang:

"See the wild deer, trembling, panting,
Trembling, panting, trembling, panting,
Only for a moment for hunger standing,
Then away on the chase away, away."

"That is a white man's song. You shouldn't be singing a white man's song," He Goes About scolded. "You forget who you are. You are a Cherokee."

"The white man's song is the song to sing." In truth, Young Squirrel cared little what the old man thought.

෨෨

One cold morning during Long Night Moon, He Goes About awoke to find that he could not move his legs or even stand. Tsa lagayu-li, or Old Tobacco, the conjure man of the village, came to see the old man. Wizened and toothless with disproportionately big hands and squinting, bloodshot eyes, he wore a turban of the deepest indigo and carried with him wherever he went a large gourd rattle – the badge of his great authority. The guardian of tradition, the recognized authority who officiated at the Green Corn dance, ball-play and other tribal functions, Old Tobacco was also a healer and hunted for herbs barefoot and when the snow was deep. He knew well how to uncurl the rheumatic with ferns, the tightly coiled young fronds which unroll and straighten as the plant develops to full size, and how a lover might be made to adhere to his sweetheart through a love potion made from boiling the roots of certain tenacious burrs.

"A malicious spirit visited you during the night and stole the life force from your legs," was his diagnosis of He Goes About's condition. He suspected that the malicious spirit lived alongside He Goes About in the person of his strange, crippled son, but said nothing. He quickly ran through a few formulas and directed Young Squirrel in the concoction of a fomentation. "This medicine has the virtue to dissipate and dry up the gross and viscous humors," he advised the boy. It consisted of lye mixed with oak leaves, a little vinegar and a half a handful of salt.

Young Squirrel went through the motions of preparing the fomentation but, upon his invisible brother's suggestion, left out the most important ingredient – the vinegar. The truth was that neither the real nor the unreal brother wished to see He Goes About's condition improve. Nor, indeed, did it.

From that time on, He Goes About lay in his house day in, day out, receiving what few visitors came. It fell to Young Squirrel to take care of him when he was not working at the trading post, for the old man had outlived his other relatives.

In this way more years passed until Young Squirrel owned twelve winters.

"You should not be working for the white man at the trading post," He Goes About complained to his son. "You should hunt. Then you would not be gone so much and I would eat the food my son has brought me and not what everyone else leaves."

"I have a crippled leg, Father," Young Squirrel reminded him.

"Your mother's ancestor, the Groundhog's Mother, had a crippled leg," He Goes About told him, "and he was a great hunter."

"The Groundhog's Mother had the ulunsuti," Young Squirrel reminded his father. It gave him enormous pleasure to know that he possessed his grandfather's ulunsuti when his father thought it was lost forever, taken by Tsikiki when she fled Qualla with George Kinnahan. "If you have an ulunsuti, it does not matter if you have a crippled leg." As soon as he felt himself able to protect it from those who would take it, Young Squirrel planned to remove the transparent from its hiding place in the forest and bring it here so that all its blessings might fall on him. "Anyway, soon there will be no more animals left to hunt. The Cherokee are killing all the animals there are in the woods with the guns and bullets the white man gives them in exchange for goods. I know, Father. I see the pelts, as many as the forest has leaves."

"It is not true," He Goes About insisted. "There are many animals. They are just hiding. The white man will grow tired of living in our woods and go away. Then the animals will return. Now, tell me a story, boy. One of the old ones, for the constant tedium of my life is unbearable."

Young Squirrel often told his father stories. After all, his father lay about all day with nothing to do and such people are often told stories to amuse them. Young Squirrel only pretended to want to amuse He Goes About, however. That is why his stories tended to take the old man along roads that began pleasantly enough, being broad and well traveled and well lit, but that soon diverged from the main road and grew narrow and dark to twist and turn through increasingly rough and dangerous terrain until at last they ended, faltering breathlessly on the very brink of steep and treacherous precipices.

Initially they resembled stories the elders had told, generation after generation, stories that He Goes About had heard long ago, and there is comfort in that. But Young Squirrel had not learned these stories from the elders. Instead he had learned them from his mysterious brother and his brother dwelt, as dead men do, in a dark place. Needless to say, these dark and terrible stories never failed to upset and frighten the old man but, lonely and tedious as his life was, he could not resist the going-somewhere of them and so each time chose to forget the effect they had on him.

"All right," said Young Squirrel with a touch of slyness, for playing with truth is like juggling balls of flame, a matter of some delicacy. "I will tell you the old story of the Wild Boy." And he hunkered down beside the old man's pallet.

"I believe that I once knew this story," He Goes About sought tremulously to assure himself that the story was a familiar one, that it held no surprise, "but I have forgotten it. You have a fearfully strong memory, my son, to hold all of these stories in your head. Yes. Go on."

"Long ago," Young Squirrel began, "soon after the world was made by a water beetle, a hunter and his wife lived at Tsuwateldunyi, which white men call Pilot Knob, with their only child, a little boy. The father's name was Kanati, which means the Lucky Hunter, and his wife was called Selu, or Corn. That is like our family, Father. You were a hunter, and you and my mother had one son."

He Goes About sighed. "Ah, yes, but I was not a *lucky* hunter." At first Young Squirrel's stories provided a springboard for conversation between father and son. This tended to reassure He Goes About and make him feel less apprehensive and, indeed, this sort of discussion was common enough, for the Cherokee will chew over old stories the way white men discuss the Bible. Later, however, as the story progressed, He Goes About's interjections would become less and less frequent; finally he would fall silent and only listen. That moment, however, was yet to arrive. "As for the famous mountain Tsuwateldunyi, your grandfather Dayunisi once traveled there, if I remember correctly. He told me that the faces of its cliffs present a peculiar appearance under the sun's rays, as of shining walls with doors, windows and shingled roofs – like those of the white man's house."

"Tsuwateldunyi is, indeed, a magical place by all accounts," agreed Young Squirrel wearily, for his father's insistence on polite chatter bored him. "There on the high peaks where no timber grows, the Nunnehi, the People Who Have Always Lived, have their townhouses and it is said that inside of the mountain there is another country where one may live if invited by the inhabitants."

"Under Mountain," He Goes About named the place. "Yes, I have heard of this country and would like to have gone there. Truly, if something interesting is to happen, it would be on this special mountain."

Young Squirrel continued the story: "The reason they called this hunter the Lucky One was this: whenever he went into the woods, he never failed to return with game. It was Selu's job to cut up this game and prepare it for cooking. She did this by first washing it in the nearby river."

"This is why we always build our villages near a river, to wash game, but also so that we can fish and Go to Water more easily," said He Goes About. In order to purify themselves or to ready themselves for some great endeavor, Cherokee bathed themselves in a river; this was called Going to Water. "Truly, a river is a necessary thing," he said. "What is a village without a river?"

"Well, the son of Kanati and Selu used to play down by the river every day," said Young Squirrel, "and one morning the couple thought they heard laughing and talking in the bushes as though there were two children there." He thought of his own late-night conversations with his secret brother, hushed so that the old man would not hear. "When the boy came home at night, his parents asked him who he had been playing with all day. 'He comes out of the water,' said the boy, 'and he calls himself my elder brother. He says his mother was cruel to him and threw him into the river.' That was when Selu and Kanati knew that their son's playmate was not human, but had sprung from the blood of the game that the woman had washed off at the river's edge." He paused and, for the first time, He Goes About did not seize the opportunity to make a comment. Young Squirrel could see that the old man was growing apprehensive. "Every day when the little boy went out to play, the other would join him, but, as he always returned to the water, Kanati and Selu never had a chance to see him," said Young Squirrel. "At last one evening Kanati said to his son, 'Tomorrow, when the other boy comes to play, get him to wrestle with you and when you have your arms around him, hold on to him and call for us.' Well, the boy promised to do as he was told, so the next day, as soon as his playmate appeared, he challenged him to a wrestling match. The other agreed at once, but as soon as they had their arms around each other, Kanati's boy began to scream for his father. The hunter and his wife came running down to the river. Imagine their surprise upon seeing that their child's playmate looked exactly like their own child, though more hollow-cheeked and, of course, naked. In fact, the two boys were as alike in every way as twins." Young Squirrel looked carefully at his father to gauge his reaction. The old man was stiff, silent and pale. Clearly he did not like this idea of a phantom twin, composed of the blood washed from game. Young Squirrel pressed on: "As soon as the boy's friend saw Selu, he struggled to free himself and cried out, 'Let me go; you threw me away!' But the boy held on until his parents managed to seize the boy and wrestle him down. They took him home with them and kept him in the house until they had tamed him, but he was always wild and artful in his disposition, and was the leader of his brother in every mischief. They called him Inageutasunhi (He-Grows-Up-Wild) and he possessed magic powers."

"Stop! Stop!" cried He Goes About and shuddered. "A boy born of blood? That is a terrible story, Young Squirrel. A boy born of blood and wild . . . with magic powers! A boy who resembled in virtually every way his brother born of the woman Selu! It is not a thing I wish to think on. It cannot be. Can it, Young Squirrel? No! No! It troubles me grievously. I do not remember the elders telling me this story. How could I have forgotten such a story? No. I will sleep, Young Squirrel. Leave me now." He turned away from the boy, hitching his rough blanket up so that it covered him to his chin and made a show of shutting his eyes tight.

Young Squirrel stood slowly and turned towards the door to leave. Usually he took pleasure at his father's discomfort, but not tonight. Did the degree of anxiety exhibited by He Goes About mean that he might know about the secret brother who dwelt increasingly within and beside Young Squirrel? After all, the parallels between the old story and his were striking. For example, had not Tsikiki, like the Wild Boy's own mother, thrown her son away, washed her hands, perhaps not of blood but of him, of Young Squirrel?

Oh, he would have his revenge, his retribution, not on the trader Kinnahan – for he was far away now, beyond the reach of Young Squirrel – nor on his wayward mother, but on his weak, ineffectual father, for permitting Tsikiki to be stolen away.

That Young Squirrel vowed.

TWO

A year went by, then two, and, as the different moons came and went, it became clear to Young Squirrel and the blood brother who dwelt no longer in the dark recesses of the ceiling but, alternately, inside and beside him and whom he called after the blood brother in the tale He Grows Up Wild, that their father was not as he once had been in the head. His thoughts had begun to hop here and there like a rabbit, his memory was punched full of holes, he took exaggerated fright at the slightest thing, and, once frightened, could be easily reduced to a word-less, wide-eyed, sweating panic. All these symptoms increased over time.

"It is easy to see that, when the malicious spirit was about stealing the strength from his legs, it also stopped to siphon off some of the power from his mind." Old Tobacco's diagnosis.

As time went on, Young Squirrel came to know his secret brother better and better. Together they now shared many secrets and made many extraordinary plans. Young Squirrel had no other intimate in the village, not even his employer. While friendly, Matlock never gained Young Squirrel's confidence nor Young Squirrel, his.

He Goes About grew increasingly querulous: "I long for venison," he fretted. "Why will you not bring me venison?"

"There are so few deer in the woods these days," Young Squirrel told him. "Some Cherokee say that the white man has locked all the game up in the earth, and that they will be released if only the conjure man can find the right formula." He shook his head. "I say it is the Cherokee who are to blame. They kill all the deer they can so that they can trade meat for the white men's goods."

"There are as many deer in the woods as there are stars in the sky," insisted He Goes About. His speech was slurred; his words sounded run together, as though they had been stirred up inside his head with a big spoon. He peered at Young Squirrel with unfocussed, swimming eyes. Suddenly a look of alarm gripped his features. "Who are you?" he whimpered.

"What do you mean, Father?" Young Squirrel asked impatiently. Truly, the old man grew more tiresome each day.

"I mean: who are you *now*?" He Goes About whispered. When Young Squirrel only stared at him, He Goes About continued in a quavering voice. "You . . . You and your brother . . . *You* are responsible for allowing all the game to escape so that the white man could capture them and keep them inside the earth."

"Don't talk nonsense, old man," Young Squirrel said, attempting to mask his growing alarm with curtness. "My mother had but one son!"

"I curse your mother! Do you hear? Ungrateful whore! As for you, you have a brother, all right! I have seen him in your voice. He is . . . right there." He pointed.

"Where?" asked Young Squirrel, bluffing, for his brother was indeed there, beside/inside of him.

"There," insisted He Goes About. "And you shall be punished, the two of you. Bad, bad boys!"

క్రిస్

Young Squirrel and his brother decided that, as their father clearly knew more than they had suspected, they must kill him.

That night, as He Goes About slept his fitful, mumbling sleep, Young Squirrel and his blood brother took Young Squirrel's pallet and, folding it in half, pressed it over their father's face. It was not as easy to kill the frail old paralytic as they had thought. He struggled vigorously, drawing on resources of strength that they had not expected him to possess. At length, however, he grew quiet and then still.

"*Ha! Yu!*" cried Old Tobacco, upon viewing the corpse in the morning. "First the power from his legs, then from his mind . . . now the malicious ghost has snatched his spirit entirely. Most likely a Raven

Mocker passing through." For it is quite true that Raven Mockers are always about in these mountains, scavenging for souls.

✍

Two nights after his father's burial, Young Squirrel proceeded to the place where he had secreted the ulunsuti and, hiding it beneath his shirt, brought it to He Goes About's house. When he removed it from the buckskin pouch, it gave off an intermittent flash of the same metallic green light a firefly emits. He felt himself strengthen in its presence.

"From now on, we may live here together in this house," he told his blood brother. "There is no one to know anymore."

"It is good," replied his brother approvingly. "Or, at least, it is how it should be."

That night, Young Squirrel could not sleep. It was not hate that kept him awake, as it had all those years before when his mother had run off with the white trader. It was a slight itch, annoying, not strong but comparable to a tickle in the throat which never quite leads to a cough. He turned to He Grows Up Wild. "Can you sleep, Brother?" he asked.

"No," said his brother. "It's like there are bugs under my skin."

"Mine, too. It must be our father's curse on us. He Goes About must have been stronger than we thought."

"His influence will pale, and his ghost will grow less substantial with time," He Grows Up Wild assured him.

"In the meantime this itch will drive me mad." He looked carefully at his brother. In the sickly light flashed by the ulunsuti, the Wild Boy's face appeared ghastly, his skin hung as slack on his bones as a bear's at winter's end; and the whites of his eyes were tinged with pink. Then he seemed to turn watery, transparent. Young Squirrel could make out the dark shapes of the room through him – the bench, the table.

"You are already mad," the Wild Boy told him in his voice of water draining, a gurgling, hollow sound. "Have you not noticed, Brother?"

THREE

Because he continued to be afflicted with the terrible itch long after his father's death, Young Squirrel sought out Old Tobacco for a cure. "Please help me, Adawehi," Young Squirrel begged. "Since the death of my father, vermin crawls beneath my skin. I cannot see them, but I can feel them. I can tolerate the itch no longer."

"Such an itch is uncommon but not altogether unknown." The conjure man looked Young Squirrel over with a practiced eye. The youth's skin, particularly around his swollen, patchy face, was cross-hatched with scratches the size of welts. These puffed along their length and then dripped a watery, blood-tinged fluid, so that his face was as streaked as though he had been weeping sad, bloody tears. He appeared strangely raw, like one who is being flayed in fits and starts – patches of new skin scattered among patches of raw and glistening flesh. Old Tobacco wondered what secret crime against the spirits Young Squirrel had committed to deserve such a punishment. "Yes, I have seen such a case . . . but only once or twice."

"Is there a cure?"

"Sit down." Old Tobacco indicated a rough stool beside the table. Young Squirrel perched on the stool. "There is a treatment. Watch carefully while I tell you of it, for you must perform this treatment often and must know how it goes together. I cannot say when you will cease to need it. Perhaps you will always need it." Searching among the herbs and roots that hung drying from his ceiling, scowling with concentration, he selected first one and then another bunch of roots and laid them on the table in front of Young Squirrel. "You see this?" He pointed to the bunch of roots on his left. "This is burdock root. You take one mess of burdock root, like so. This much. See?"

Young Squirrel nodded.

The conjure man went over to the fire and removed an iron pot from its hook over the hearth. He set it on the table in front of the youth and, taking a buck knife from the leather sheath he wore strapped to his leg, cut the burdock roots into seven pieces each and dropped them into the pot. He picked up the remaining bunch of roots. "This is yellowdock root. Add to the mess of burdock root one mess of yellowdock root." He cut each of the yellowdock roots into seven pieces. "Seven is the sacred number. If the remedy is to work, the roots must be cut into *seven* pieces. Not eight. Not six. *Seven.*" He dropped the chopped yellowdock root into the pot. "Be sure to keep the green tops on them, Young Squirrel. There is good medicine in these green tops." Lined up next to his hearth were rows of bladders and gourds filled with river water. Old Tobacco selected one, then another, then reconsidered and settled on a third bladder. Carefully he poured the water it contained over the roots in the pot. "Long Man the River, speak to these roots and tell them what they must do," he instructed the water. "Water to cover," he said to Young Squirrel. He replaced the pot on the hook over the fire. "The water must boil for a while. In the meantime, we will sing."

Old Tobacco and Young Squirrel sang for a long time. During that time, He Grows Up Wild entered the room. He had a way of seeping into spaces, like wind through a chink in the wall, and then reconstituting himself bit by bit. Once he had reassembled himself, he squatted near the fire – gaunt, nearly transparent and intent upon the proceedings. He, too, was covered with suppurating wounds; he shared Young Squirrel's torment. "Why did you not fetch me?" he asked Young Squirrel, half-indignant, half-plaintive. "Don't you know that you cannot go from me without my knowing?"

But Young Squirrel did not answer. He did not wish by his behavior – either through sudden speech directed seemingly at the air or through the movement of his eyes – to alert the conjuror to the presence of his blood brother. Conjure men were reputed to be far more sensitive to unseen presences than common folk, able to smell a witch, and yet, so far as Young Squirrel could see, Old Tobacco did not appear to have noticed either the Wild Boy's arrival in his house or his continued presence. Young Squirrel inferred from this that his brother must be a very powerful spirit. He felt at once proud and a little afraid – was there to be no help for him should he decide to disburden himself of his malevolent sibling? *I would not have been smitten with this plague of invisible vermin had it not been for my brother*, he thought. *I, by myself, would not have conspired to kill our father. It was the Wild Boy's urging that led me to suffocate He Goes About and so seal our fate, his and mine . . . .* For Young Squirrel was convinced that the persistence of his skin condition was the result of his father's curse and the work of his avenging spirit.

At last, the conjure man stood, went to the hearth, examined the mixture in the pot and then removed it from the hook over the fire. "It has boiled enough. Now we will strain the mixture." He set a large clay bowl on the table and handed Young Squirrel a length of loosely woven homespun. "Hold this over the bowl as I pour," he instructed the youth. Young Squirrel did as he was told. Old Tobacco gingerly tipped the pot and allowed the boiled root mixture to seep slowly through the cloth.

"Now for some bear oil." He fetched an earthen jar and scooped a quantity into the bowl with a large wooden spoon. "Hog lard works just as well, but there was that big he-bear Siwasee killed last autumn. Lots of fat on him." He turned to a wooden shelf on the wall and took from it two stone-glazed jars. He removed the lid of one. "Now add to this powdered sulfur, two shakes, quick, like this, and a couple of ladles full of spirits of turpentine. Can you remember that? Two shakes of sulfur . . . a couple of ladles of spirits of turpentine?"

Young Squirrel nodded. The smell arising from the mixture was so strong that it made him light-headed. He sat back on his stool, away from the smell.

"The proportions are very important."

Young Squirrel nodded, chewing on a hangnail – the urge to scratch was almost overpowering. The skin around his nail was gnawed raw, as were his knuckles.

"You must pay careful attention to the proportions," Old Tobacco repeated his caution. (Should one of Old Tobacco's remedies not work, he would always say, "The proportions – they must have been off.") "Next, we boil the mixture until it is the consistency of tar. While it is boiling, we will go to the sweathouse and tell stories as the elders did. It is this that binds us together as a people. Stories and blood. Come on, then!"

The sweathouse was a conical lodging across the way from Old Tobacco's house, excavated to a slight depth and covered with dirt. Many people in the village had a sweathouse – often it was used as a place for sleeping during the winter months because it was easy to heat. Old Tobacco's sweathouse was, however, more esteemed, because the conjure man had used it in his cures for so many years that it was deemed a sacred and powerful place. Needless to say, when Young Squirrel and Old Tobacco arrived inside the structure, He Grows Up Wild was already there, hunkered down beside the river rocks, which, when heated, provided warmth.

"I shall tell you the story of how the deer's tail became turned up," Old Tobacco announced. "And what transpired thereafter."

Young Squirrel glanced sharply at his brother, knowing the story and its purport, wondering if the phantasm had influenced the old man's mind. His brother talked to him inside his head. In how many other people's heads did he talk?

"It begins thus," said Old Tobacco. "There was once a hunter named Kanati who had a wife Selu and two boys, one of whom was a Wild Boy. Now, whenever this Kanati went into the mountains, as he did almost daily, he always brought back a fat buck or doe, or maybe a couple of turkeys. It never failed. And so those who knew him considered him a very skilled and lucky hunter.

"One day the Wild Boy said to his brother, 'I wonder where our father gets all that game, for surely we have never seen so much when we go walking in the forest. Let's follow our father the next time he goes out and discover for ourselves what secret place he goes to.' The next day, Kanati took a bow and some feathers in his hand and started off towards the west. The boys waited a little while and then went after him, keeping out of sight until they saw him go into a swamp where there were a great many of the small reeds that hunters use to make arrow shafts. There on the edge of the swamp the Wild Boy changed himself into a puff of bird's down (which he could do because he was a Wild Boy and, strictly speaking, not quite human) and the wind lifted the puff up and bore it along a little ways, before letting it fall upon the shoulder of Kanati, who was cutting reeds. The old man cut reeds for shafts, fitted the feathers to them and made some arrows, and, when he had finished, he came out of the swamp and, once again, headed out to hunt. The wind blew the down that was the Wild Boy from his shoulder and it fell onto the ground. As soon as his father was out of sight, the Wild Boy took his right shape again and returned to where his brother was waiting and told him what he had seen. Following their father but being careful to keep out of his sight, they followed him up the mountain until he stopped at a certain place and lifted a large rock. At once out ran a buck, which Kanati shot and then, lifting it upon his back, he started for home again. 'Ah!' exclaimed the boys, 'he keeps all the deer shut up in that hole, and whenever he wants meat he lets one out and kills it with those things he made in the swamp.' For Kanati was the first hunter and, before him, there were neither arrows nor the knowledge of how to make them. The boys hurried and reached home before their father, who had the heavy deer to carry, and he never knew that they had followed him. A few days later the boys went back to the swamp, cut some reeds and made many arrows, and then started up the mountain to where their father kept the game. When they got to the place, they raised the rock and a deer came running out. Just as they drew back to shoot it, another came out, and then another and another, until the boys got confused and forgot what they were about. In those days all the deer had their tails hanging down like other animals, but, as a buck was running past, the Wild Boy struck its tail with his arrow so that it pointed upward. The boys thought this hunting good sport, and when the next deer ran past, the Wild Boy struck its tail so that it stood straight up, and his brother struck the next one so hard with his arrow that the deer's tail was almost curled over his back.

"The deer carries his tail this way ever since." Young Squirrel was very tense. It was all he could do to not scratch, particularly as He Grows Up Wild seemed to be making no attempt to suppress his own urges. Still squatting by the river rocks in the center of the sweathouse, the Wild Boy moaned, low, like an incessant, whining wind, as he clawed at phantom welts with long, jagged nails that drew from the sores a reddish, milky fluid.

"Yes," Old Tobacco agreed, "but there is more to the story than that. The deer came running past until the last one had come out of the hole and escaped into the forest. Then out of the hole ran droves of raccoons, rabbits, and all the other four-footed animals – all but the bear, because there was no bear then. Last came great flocks of turkeys, pigeons and partridges that darkened the sky like a cloud and made such a noise with their wings that Kanati, sitting at home, heard the sound like distant thunder on the mountains and said to himself, 'My bad boys have got into trouble; I must go and see what they are doing.'"

Young Squirrel flinched. Wasn't that what He Goes About had called him and his brother – "My bad boys?"

"So Kanati went up the mountain," Old Tobacco narrated, "and when he came to the place where he kept the game locked up in the mountain under the rock, he found the two boys standing beside it and all the birds and animals were gone. Needless to say, Kanati was furious, but, without saying a word, he went down into the cave and kicked the covers off four jars in one corner. Out swarmed all manners of vermin – bedbugs, fleas, lice and gnats – and they flew and crawled and crept all over the boys – even under their skin. The boys screamed with pain and fright, Young Squirrel, but it was no use."

Old Tobacco fell silent. He poked absently at the cold rocks with a stick. After a few moments had passed, Young Squirrel, squirming, asked, "Is that the end of the story?"

"Yes," said Old Tobacco.

"I tell you he's onto us," hissed He Grows Up Wild.

"Shhh!" insisted Young Squirrel.

"What?" Old Tobacco asked.

"Nothing," Young Squirrel assured him. "A sudden chill, that's all."

"In this heat?" Old Tobacco shrugged, then, stood stiffly and slowly straightened his limbs. "Well, come on, then. By this time the medicine will be ready."

Young Squirrel also stood. "Old Tobacco," he began suddenly. He knew he shouldn't ask, but he couldn't help himself. "Why did you tell me that particular story?"

Old Tobacco met his gaze steadily. After a moment's pause he said evenly, "To pass the time."

They returned to Old Tobacco's cabin.

"This is the ritual which must accompany the use of the salve," explained the Conjure Man. "Go to the river and wash all over. After that, rub the mixture in well. Do it standing by the fire just before going to bed. The heat helps in the absorption by the skin of the salve. Repeat this process three times, Young Squirrel, then change your clothes. And keep clean. You must keep clean. And don't scratch if you can help it. If you do all this, if you get the proportions right and do things in the proper sequence, this skin condition may even go away. With time."

"It will not go away at once?" Young Squirrel asked, clawing his arm, his heart heavy with despair at this plague of vermin he must endure.

But Old Tobacco was noncommittal. "That depends," was all he would say. As his *ugista ti*, or payment, the conjure man took a quantity of red calico from the store. "Your brother can also use the salve," he told Young Squirrel upon his departure.

FOUR

Old Tobacco's salve did not entirely cure Young Squirrel and the Wild Boy's torturous skin condition, but it did serve to ameliorate the terrible itching somewhat. So that he and his brother might always have a supply of the medicine, Young Squirrel arranged with various Cherokee women for there to be a steady supply of green burdock and yellowdock in exchange for trade goods. Matlock always stocked sulfur and spirits of turpentine at the trading post so they were easily to be had. Every day Young Squirrel bathed in the river – even on the coldest days of the winter when snow covered the roofs of the village and the Oconaluftee was sluggish with churned ice. Every night he applied the salve to his skin three times before the fire.

In time, his wounds healed to scars. These were so universal upon his person that his skin as a whole became exceedingly tough, leathery and immobile, glossy with scar tissue like that of someone who has survived a fire and stained yellowish from the sulfur. It looked less like human skin than the slick carapace of an insect. Also, because his skin had lost its mobility, Young Squirrel's face became largely expressionless.

As for He Grows Up Wild, he followed Young Squirrel's regimen only when he could be bothered.

As the years went slowly by, the Wild Boy became increasingly unsteady and intemperate. He drank whiskey that Young Squirrel bought him under protest from Matlock's store and refused to wear clothes even in the coldest weather or to eat or bathe or dress the matted, filthy hair that hung halfway down his back. Because he did not eat from one day to the other, but only drank, he grew very thin but did not lose his essential stringy wiriness. He crouched by the fire like an animal for days at a time – he had never had any bodily functions that Young Squirrel was aware of. Sometimes he muttered to himself. Much of the time Young Squirrel couldn't understand him. He spoke in a tongue that was neither Cherokee nor English.

More time passed. He Grows Up Wild began to fade. By the time Young Squirrel had turned twenty, his blood brother had faded to such an extent that he had become difficult to see. Sometimes Young Squirrel had to look twice in the dim light to even know he was there. Sometimes he had to blink. Often, he would enter the cabin at night and know his brother was there only by the cross-hatch of dripping wounds that congealed into a human-like shape before the fire – his brother had come to resemble nothing so much as a shadow composed of weeping sores.

Weeks and months and years passed. The two brothers rarely communicated any more save by bouts of occasional silent and, at times, murderous wrestling. There, before the fire, at night when the village was quiet, the two scarred, itching youths, then later the same two youths become men would wrestle on the dirt floor, naked and covered in salve. The Wild Boy always won. "Ha!" he would exclaim, his foot on his brother's neck. Then he would shift his weight onto that foot for a long moment, until Young Squirrel choked and sputtered and begged for mercy or death as darkness swam around his eyes and threatened to engulf the fire's golden light. Only then would He Grows Up Wild remove his foot from his brother's neck, smile and shudder before turning, lurching the few steps to the stone hearth before dropping down onto his haunches to squat once more before the fire.

This affliction of Young Squirrel's, this terrible itching, shaped his existence from the time of his father's death onwards. It determined his character and dictated the course his life would take. He became at once irascible and capable of great concentration. Because he had continually to master the urge to tear at his flesh, his will hardened like a muscle strengthens with use and burden and pain; he grew capable of extraordinary focus. Always on his guard against scratching, he never relaxed, but held himself stiff and tense, feet planted wide apart, arms held slightly away from his body, fingers spread and curved into claws.

As a result of this constant tension, Young Squirrel was quick to rage and even quicker to control and master that rage. He seemed to wrestle always with demons – they left their stink upon him, said the white settlers who traded at the store, for Young Squirrel was to smell all his life of rank sulfur and spirits of turpentine, "of brimstone," the settlers said.

Because of the ulunsuti, hidden away in a dark corner of the run-down cabin he shared with the Wild Boy and the vengeful ghost of his father, Young Squirrel prospered in a strange way. Both Cherokee and the scattered white settlers who inhabited the coves and hidden valleys of the region brought him hides of deer, cow, and hog; skins of bear, painter, wildcat, rabbit, raccoon, mink, muskrat, otter; fox and rat; hams of pork and venison; ginseng for the China trade; pinkroot and snakeroot. He, in turn, sold them dry goods, hardware, gunpowder and whiskey. Matlock's trading post was the only source for supplies within a radius of a hundred miles, after all.

Moreover, the Cherokee had a head for figures, an eye for what would sell and an ability to persuade that owed a great deal to an ability to intimidate, due to the peculiar, leathery horror of his countenance. In fact, his ability was such that, as time passed and his gout worsened, Matlock made a partner of the boy who had once swept up his frontier store and sold candies to the other children at so much a pull of ginseng.

Finally, Young Squirrel thought of ways to make money that had simply not occurred to others of his race, such as translating his profits into land – rich bottomland, as Matlock had done. Twenty cents an acre was the going price. He took some of that land as payment for debts; other parcels he purchased at sheriff's sales for unpaid taxes. It was a novel concept, buying land.

"Why buy land when you can have it for nothing?" the Cherokee wondered. They laughed. "Why not buy air . . . or water?"

Young Squirrel must have heard them laughing, for, in time, he bought water as well as land – a shallow piece of the river up around Ravensford and the bank on either side of it. On the Qualla side, he built a house, set back a little, to accommodate spring flooding – it was a one-story log cabin, stripped of bark and notched at the corners, plastered with tempered clay, then roofed with the bark of a chestnut tree. However, this house was not for him.

The Cherokee were puzzled. "Why would you build a house, if it is not for you or your family?"

"It is not the house that is important," explained Young Squirrel. "It is the river."

"What about the river?"

"I own that bit of river."

"What kind of crazy man thinks that he can divide Long Man the River into pieces?" Among themselves, they said, "Truly, Young Squirrel could use a new house, even though this new one is small and mean, for that of his father is old and falling down. Surely Young Squirrel goes the way of his poor father and his bad mother." They shook their heads. "It is sad to see."

Young Squirrel engaged a young man, one of the ball players, to live in the cabin beside the river. "Your job is to collect money from white people wishing to cross the river at this point." He gave him a flintlock. "Shoot anyone who doesn't pay."

The Cherokee of Qualla were amazed. What a strange idea! Who would have thought up such a thing? Paying money to cross a river? "No one will do such a foolish thing. Not even white people. It is true that the waters are calm up around Ravensford, but crossing is not so hard at other points. Just wait and see. People will go down river a bit and cross there. Young Squirrel has wasted his money."

However, to their considerable amazement, the white men came. And paid. "Where's the ford?" the men would ask, stopping at the store to pick up provisions.

"Up at Ravensford," Young Squirrel would tell them. "Follow the river north and you will soon come to the place."

They never asked the villagers, who would have told them, "The ford is wherever you think you can get across."

Fifty miles of river, and the white men went to Ravensford to cross. "They are like sheep," said the villagers.

"Golden sheep," replied Young Squirrel, and bought more land.

During the spring of the year he established the crossing, the river rose, flooding its banks. Young Squirrel had a large raft built, which Matlock called a ferry, and he moored this ferry next to the house by the river. He announced that he intended to charge for the use of this ferry – seventy-five cents for a six-horse freight wagon, fifty cents for a five-horser, thirty-seven and a half cents for three- and two-horse wagons, twenty-five cents for a one-horse cart, six and a half cents for each traveler on horseback, two and a half cents for every horse without a rider, two cents for one head of cattle and one cent per sheep or hog. It cost more to ride the ferry than to cross on one's own.

"No one will stand for it," said the Cherokee.

But the Oconaluftee runs shallow in most seasons and is full of rocks and rapids, so the white people came to Ravensford and thought nothing of paying for passage across. Young Squirrel made more money and this money he used to buy more land.

On one of these pieces of land, he built the first mill in the region, diverting water from a fast-flowing feeder of the Oconaluftee down a wooden sluiceway. A white miller happened to be passing through Qualla on his way to Tennessee. Young Squirrel hired him to supervise the building of the mill and to work it. The miller's name was Lemuel Parrot. On one day Lemuel Parrot ground wheat into flour. The next day he ground corn into meal. Young Squirrel sold the flour and the cornmeal in his store. The Cherokee said that they would never buy flour and cornmeal ground in this way. Why do that when you can grind your own using a wooden beater (*ka no na*)? But the *ka no na* took so long! Eventually they came and bought flour and cornmeal at the store. Young Squirrel made more money.

By the time he was thirty years old, Young Squirrel was a wealthy man by the standards of his neighbors, yet he was a poor man by many people's standards, for he had no woman and lived in a mean place and shared his wealth with none, which made it suspect. His one indulgence were the fine, soft clothes in the English style that he had made for himself in Charleston out of either deerskin, prepared for him by a local woman, or linen. These sat softly on his tortured skin and gave him a displaced look in the mountain village.

Throughout his third decade, Young Squirrel never ceased to be mad. The Wild Boy was his madness. Sometimes the blood brother stayed at home, plucking at invisible lice with transparent fingers. Sometimes he trailed along behind his brother as he made his solitary way from store to mill to ferry. His appearance was singular on these occasions. He Grows Up Wild loped like a loose-limbed wolf, his long, large tongue lolling out of his mouth and his eyes rolling wildly. No one could see him but Young Squirrel, except possibly Old Tobacco – the brothers were never sure on this point – but they could smell him. Of course, everyone thought the smell came from Young Squirrel. There was a great deal of speculation as to how anyone who bathed with the regularity of Young Squirrel could smell so horrible:

"Something inside of him must have died a long time ago," was the conclusion people reached, and, in it, that they would have been correct.

FIVE

The trader Matlock developed gout in his bad leg, which worsened over time, despite his attempts to treat it by applying buds from the balm of Gilead to the afflicted parts and drinking quantities of a concoction of hemp and spignut, steeped and mixed with a bottle of sarsaparilla syrup. The trips by ox cart to the coast became difficult for him, then impossible – all that jostling over bad or nonexistent roads, from Qualla to Keowee and the Lower Towns of the Cherokee up to Congaree Fort, past the Eowtaws along the Santee to Monks Corner and on up to Charleston Neck. From the age of thirty, therefore, Young Squirrel made the trips alone, conducting business on behalf of the trader.

One spring, Young Squirrel arrived in Charleston to find that one of the factors with whom Matlock had traded for years had died of a fit over the winter. The tavern keeper recommended a man named Pringle in his stead.

"I've been selling cotton for trade in Cherokee country for over twenty years," Pringle told him, as he wrapped bolts of calico in brown paper and tied them with string.

"Who do you trade with?" Young Squirrel asked.

"A number of fellows. Rough men, all of them. A man named Cheslock. Another called Handy. George Kinnahan was another, and MacGregor, Sandy MacGregor . . . ."

The blood rushed to Young Squirrel's head. "You knew . . . George Kinnahan?" His throat closed like a fist around the words. He felt light-headed.

"Twenty years," replied the cloth merchant. "How'd you come by old George Kinnahan, anyways?"

Young Squirrel turned away. He pretended to examine some French cotton, so that the factor might not see his face, contorted with emotion. "Oh," he said, "he lived in my village. Once. It was a long time ago."

"As far as I can recollect, he was somewheres in those North Carolina mountains to start off with, at the farthest end of the Indian trail . . . . Hey, Chief! You want this blue with the flowers?"

Young Squirrel lifted his hand in confirmation, but remained with his back to the factor.

"Then he up and moved to Tennessee. Some trouble with the Indians . . . ." The factor paused, peering at the Cherokee. "Are you all right?"

Young Squirrel nodded, wordless.

Pringle shrugged and returned to his wrapping. "Run off with an Indian princess," he said. "Saw her myself. Just the once. He brought her to the store to buy some calico just after they made their getaway. Sort of a present for her. I remember that calico. It was yellow. Yellow and red. Kind of gaudy, I thought, but you people like that, don't you? I got me a memory for cloth. Yessir. I can remember every bolt of fabric I've ever handled."

She always did like yellow and red, Young Squirrel thought. How had he remembered that? He had been so young when she left – six or seven? Gripping the counter, he took a deep breath.

"A pretty little thing that could speak English not half bad, as I recall. A lot of these traders marry Indian women, I guess. Helps to make them at home in the community, I suppose . . . and ain't no decent white woman going to live with a bunch of Indians. You didn't happen to know his wife, did you? Her people?"

"Whose?"

"The Indian princess?"

Young Squirrel was barely able to speak. It was as if all his organs of speech had twisted up. "I was a boy when they left Qualla," he croaked.

"I reckon." The factor looked at him, trying to gauge his age. Because of his scarring, it was difficult to be certain. "The last couple of years, George hasn't been around. The rheumatiz got him pretty bad, I hear. Well, we're all getting old and that's a fact. He sends his son."

Rheumatism! Young Squirrel thought. *The Crippler!* "His son?"

"Real bright young fellow for a half-breed. George Junior. Twenty-five, thirty."

Young Squirrel was stunned to learn that he had another brother, not one born of blood but of flesh. "Do you know whereabout in Tennessee they're living?"

"Up Hiwasee way. Up Unicoy Road."

Young Squirrel left the man's shop in dazed haste, stumbling over the threshold into the street as if he were drunk. Once there, he stood in the sunbathed thoroughfare like a man who had woken up from a dream to find himself in a place he did not know.

What should he do now that he knew where his mother was? Go to her? Should he go now? At once? But he had not finished half his trading. The cart would be half-empty. He couldn't do that. He mustn't. If he did, he would lose money. Young Squirrel never lost money, he told himself. Young Squirrel *made* money.

A lady gave him a pointed look and then a wide berth, pulling her skirts to one side as she sailed around him, and he realized that he was in the way of pedestrian traffic. Embarrassed – for he had always prided himself on decorous behavior when among the whites – he began to walk. He neither knew nor cared where.

You must be strong, he told himself. Vigilant. You must not let this great news affect you.

Oh, Mother! I have dreamed of this day, the day when I should find you. But what shall I do now? Must I kill you, Mother? Must I kill him? I am no longer a boy. Once I was sure what I must do. Now I don't know.

He struggled to keep his face impassive. He had reached the waterfront, crowded with ships, smelling of fish and rank seawater and rotting hemp. Black slaves filed from one of the ships, their legs in chains. They smelled powerful and hot from their months in the hold; their purple-black skin was ulcerated. They moaned softly in their native tongues, looking as broken as broken-down horses.

You left me and you took him with you . . . . All I loved and you left me with two old men and a terrible child not of my making. If it were not for that, I would not have suffered from this terrible plague of unseen vermin all my life, so that to live is torment and no woman will look on me and all I can do is work, work, work or I shall go insane.

He touched his tapestry vest. A pocket in its satin lining held the ulunsuti. It felt warm through the rich fabric. How could something so cold feel so warm?

Yet, if you had not left, he reasoned, *I would have never got the ulunsuti. Dayunisi might be alive today. Those who possess the ulunsuti live to be over one hundred years in most cases. And, even if he had died, he would never have passed the talisman onto me – the grandson he despised for my clubfoot and my apparent weakness . . . . Perhaps you might have had another son with my father. He might have been strong and received the ulunsuti in my stead. And if my blood brother and I had not killed my father, I might not have been afflicted with the plague of vermin. That is the curse that befalls the son who kills his father. That I am so tormented is not, perhaps, your fault.*

Thinking along these lines, Young Squirrel reasoned that his mother's departure had perhaps worked to his advantage. Indeed, it had so shaped the entire course of his life that he could not imagine what he would be like under other circumstances – the crippled boy of an undistinguished man and a withdrawn and depressed mother.

I hate my life, Young Squirrel realized, *but even more would I have hated not having had that opportunity for power that circumstances have afforded me.*

So with great effort, he controlled his emotions, using the same mechanisms he brought into play to keep his tormented fingers from digging beneath the skin to where the vermin were, to the place of crawling maggots and budding larvae, that kept him, in short, from flaying himself alive. *I am strong,* he thought. *I can master this. .*

He turned and directed his feet once more towards the Exchange.

I will conduct my business. I will sell my goods, buy my trade items and return to Qualla, he thought. *Then I will make the journey to Overhill.*

Before he met with his next supplier, he returned to Pringle's shop where he purchased a length of the finest English cotton – bright yellow with little red flowers and soft as silk. It would be his gift to his mother.

SIX

It took Young Squirrel a week on horseback to reach the Overhill Country from Qualla. I imagine him pressing on, day after day, while behind him – out of sight, but always following, steady-paced as any wolf, the Wild Boy loped. Young Squirrel must have thought that he had left him behind, but he was wrong. Not even Young Squirrel was aware of the extent to which the Wild Boy was ever with him. At least, this is what I imagine.

At last he arrived in the town of Hiwasee, nestled in a fertile bottom at the base of the mountains. Young Squirrel passed fields along the river where corn, potatoes, squash, beans, pumpkins and melons were grown, where horses and cows grazed. Pigs wandered freely, identifiable by the notching of their ears, and hens picked at dirt yards. Hiwasee was a town of about fifty houses, all one-story log cabins, stripped of bark and notched at the end and plastered with tempered clay, as was typical of most Cherokee homes.

He passed the council house, a large rotunda accommodating several hundred persons, and came to a house some distance outside the village that was almost identical to Matlock's store, only somewhat bigger. Like that store, it had been built by George Kinnahan. A man sat on the porch in a twig rocker; there was a Kentucky rifle trimmed with brass laid across his knees. Though it had been many years since he had last seen it, Young Squirrel recognized the Bucksmasher at once. The man's beard was long and faintly pink in color. His leathery skin was wrinkled. He was stoop-shouldered and slighter than of old, but Young Squirrel could read the younger George Kinnahan in the old man's features.

Kinnahan peered at the stranger with a combination of curiosity and hostility. Young Squirrel must have been an unusual sight – clearly an Indian, but dressed in the clothes of a white man of some prosperity.

Then there was his scarred face. . ."What you be doing in these parts, Stranger?" asked George. The rasping voice was saw-toothed and rusty, a little shrill.

Young Squirrel did not answer right away. Slowly he dismounted his horse and hitched it to the porch railing. He climbed up the steps to the porch. Because of his deformity, his walk was uneven, lurching.

"I say, who be you, Stranger? What brings you to Hiwasee?"

"You do not know me?" Young Squirrel's hands were clammy. His voice was trapped in his throat like an animal in its lair. Was this Kinnahan? This old man? How could he hate what he could barely recognize? Ah, but he had killed other old men. It was not so hard.

"Never seen you before," said Kinnahan. "Wouldn't forget a face like your'n. What happened to you, anyhow? Fire?"

"Acid," replied Young Squirrel, and, turning, he went into the store.

There, resting her elbows on the counter, a faraway look in her eyes, stood his mother. The store was dim. The only light came through the door that he held open and what managed to straggle in through the chinks in the log walls. In the dimness, Tsikiki appeared to have changed very little except that she looked smaller and slighter than Young Squirrel remembered her and her long hair, pulled back in a bun, had turned a hard, iron gray. She had her teeth and her figure still, although her body had lost some of the tense erectness it had had in her youth. Because of that tension, she had always reminded him of a deer.

The deer is a-bounding and the hounds are a-sounding
Away! To the chase! Away!

She would have been a little over fifty years old.

Tsikiki winced into the light that flowed through the open door into the dark place. Lifting her hand to shade her eyes, she stared at the stranger. With his back to the light, she could make out little save his unfamiliar form and the cut of his fine white man clothes. "Help you with something, Mister?" Her English was flat and toneless, but perfect in its ease. She had taken him for a white man.

Young Squirrel did not know what to say. He took off his wide-brimmed hat and held it in his hands.

"'Spect you're headin' out towards Brainerd. We had another one of you missionary fellows through the other day." She stepped out from behind the counter.

"I'm not a missionary."

Tsikiki squinted at him. "No. No, you're not."

"I am Cherokee."

"Mighty dressed up for a Cherokee," she commented with a dryness that Young Squirrel remembered.

He smiled, but the expression barely registered on his leathery face. "I am a trader."

"You're not from around here."

"The Middle Towns. From the back of beyond."

Tsikiki looked at him sharply, then cast her eyes down. She turned from him to step back behind the counter.

"I am from the village of Qualla," he said.

"Never heard of it." Picking up a rag, Tsikiki began to wipe the counter.

"Perhaps you've heard of me. My name is Young Squirrel."

Tsikiki paused for just a second, the length of a quick breath, then continued wiping, but more slowly, as if the surface were covered with sap and resisted her efforts at cleaning. "Where I come from many boys are named Young Squirrel."

"Don't you remember me?"

She shook her head. "I've never seen you before. I don't know what you're talking about."

"You are my mother."

Tsikiki stopped wiping the counter. She looked at Young Squirrel. "I had a son back there. It is true. His name was Young Squirrel. That it also true. But it has been so long that I have forgotten him. It is as if he was never born."

"If you speak of him, you cannot have forgotten him."

Tsikiki shook her head. "He was a boy and you are a man. I remember the boy and he is no more. The boy is dead."

"Not dead. Grown."

"He was weak. He would not have lived to grow up."

"I am your son," insisted Young Squirrel. "You are my mother."

"I have two other sons and a daughter besides. Together they have replaced the other boy. I could not love the other boy anyway. He was crippled and, besides, I hated his father."

"He Goes About is dead, Mother. Many years now."

"Don't call me Mother," Tsikiki warned him. "And He Goes About was not your father. Dayunisi was your father."

Dayunisi? His grandfather? Young Squirrel dropped back a step. His stomach twisted.

"I never let He Goes About into my blanket. Dayunisi I could not keep out."

"I did not know."

"Be glad of it. He Goes About was a fool and not a drop of his blood runs in your veins. Dayunisi, at least, was no fool."

"I killed He Goes About," confessed Young Squirrel in a rush.

Tsikiki covered her ears with her hands. She shook her head. "Do not tell me these things. Please. I am not interested. It no longer has to do with me."

Young Squirrel looked long at her. Her former beauty hung to the bones of her face in remnants, like ruined petals to a stalk. "Why did you leave me, Mother?"

Tsikiki shrugged. "I did not leave you. I left everything. And why? Well, why not? The door was open."

"Why didn't you take me with you?"

"We had to travel fast."

"No one chased you."

"We had to travel fast," Tsikiki repeated. "What of my father?"

"Dayunisi?" asked Young Squirrel. "Dead these many long years. He chased you. He came to Qualla to find you and he never left. Without the ulunsuti he could not find his way back to Gall Place."

"Then it is gone," Tsikiki said. "Gall Place, I mean."

"It is there," said Young Squirrel, "for anyone who can find it."

"Who would want to find it?" Tsikiki shuddered. "A beautiful place, but so alone and wild. The memory of it makes my heart cold, and yet I think it must be like the Heaven the white missionaries speak of – a terrifying place of beauty and peace. No, you must have the ulunsuti to find your way there and it is gone. I don't even know what I did with it now. George said it was no good, and he knows everything. So I believed at the time. I threw it away."

"And I found it."

Tsikiki regarded him. "Ah, yes. I can see that."

"It has made me strong."

"You lived when I thought surely you would die."

"I am a powerful man in the village. I own much good land. I own a mill and a ferry. I run the trading store."

"You wear fine clothes. But what has happened to your face?"

Young Squirrel shrugged. "A plague of vermin. A punishment. It does not matter now. What matters is my wealth. All of it comes from the ulunsuti. Like my father and his father before him, I am a hunter, but my prey is different. Whenever I go hunting I too bring back game. Not venison and turkey. Profit and land. I want for nothing, Mother. See." He held out to her the bolt of yellow cotton wrapped in paper and tied in twine. "This is for you."

Tsikiki took the bundle and untied it. She shook the fabric out of its folds and looked at it for a long time.

"It is the finest cotton in all of Charleston," he said.

"It is fine indeed." She lifted it to her face and held it to her cheek. "Yellow and red . . . . But I shall give it to my daughter Nancy. I am no longer pretty enough for such fine cotton. Nancy will look pretty in a dress of this."

"As you wish."

"It grows dark. You may stay the night, Young Squirrel, but only on the condition that you tell no one who you are. I will tell them that you are Tall Walker, a distant cousin of my mother's from a village near Qualla. Otherwise perhaps my sons will kill you. George might tell them to do that . . . out of fear. Tomorrow you must go and not return."

"As you wish," repeated Young Squirrel, bowing his head.

SEVEN

The Kinnahans had not grown so prosperous as the trader Matlock had. Overhill was more densely populated. There were, as a consequence, more traders, more general stores than in the mountains. And in the Kinnahans' case there were three children. Although the fact that they worked might be considered an advantage, they also ate and required clothing. The family lived in a house which was almost identical to the log cabin that George had built at Qualla, save that it was partitioned into two rooms and had a lean-to to the back. In one room were the beds; the other was the eating room. It was there that Young Squirrel met his half-brothers and sisters – George, who was about five years his junior, Abel, who was in his late twenties and Nancy, the youngest. She had just turned twenty and was engaged to be married to a white settler – Charley Butler – who lived at a distance of about twenty miles.

The three siblings had an olive darkness to their skin and brown, straight hair; it is a shade of brown that only half-breeds have, a sort of dusty, grayish color. Their eyes were hazel, verging on yellow. They had the features of white men, but the grace and litheness of the Cherokee – the sense of being cats in a strange place, alive to sound and moving with a degree of exaggeration that made their movements seem choreographed and graceful; Nancy in particular, with her windblown hair and her body light as a child's. She looked to Young Squirrel strikingly like his mother as he remembered her, but with this strange new coloring. She was much more forthcoming to him than the girls he was accustomed to.

"Why were you named Tall Walker?" she asked Young Squirrel as soon as Tsikiki introduced them.

Young Squirrel fumbled for an explanation. "When I was a child learning to walk, it must have seemed to my mother that I was tall," he said at last, lamely. "What does it mean . . . the name Nancy?"

"I don't know," said Nancy.

"White names don't mean anything," George Junior cut in.

"They meant something long ago, but what that was is now forgotten," their father corrected him.

"What is the use of a name if its meaning is forgotten?" asked Young Squirrel.

There was no meat for dinner. The boys had gone hunting, but had caught nothing.

"The game is scarcer than it has been," Old George commented. "Used to see buffalo in these parts and elk too. No more." He shook his head.

The family ate knee deeps and leather breeches cooked with salt and grease, ramps, creases and sochani, and large pones of sweet bread made with honey from Tsikiki's bee gum. They drank whiskey from the store and milk from the cow.

"She's a good cow," said Old George.

When the sons offered to share their bed with Young Squirrel, he thanked them but asked to sleep in the shed across the dooryard instead. "Sometimes I am up half the night," he explained. "I am used to it, but you would be tired for your work tomorrow." Whiskey made him wakeful, and he had learned so much that was new that day that he wished to sit up a while to think it over. Besides, insomnia had become habitual with him. Those who possess the ulunsuti need less sleep than others.

Needless to say, when he entered the shed, he found his brother He Grows Up Wild waiting for him, hunkered on the floor in his usual manner, half naked.

"You found our mother," The Wild Boy observed.

Young Squirrel shrugged, annoyed. Where had his brother come from? He had not once glimpsed him on the trail; he thought he had lost him for once. He unrolled the pallet and laid it on the earthen floor of the shed.

"Such great news! Why didn't you tell me?"

"She is more my mother than yours," Young Squirrel pointed out, sitting down on the pallet and pulling off his leather boots. "Besides, what is the point of telling you what you already know?"

"She is every bit as much my mother as she is yours!"

"That is not true, He Grows Up Wild. She bore me."

"Well, she cast me off. For that matter, she cast you off."

"She does not know you exist."

"Are you so sure of that?"

There was a tapping at the door. Young Squirrel was startled. He hesitated, then, glancing sternly at He Grows Up Wild, he placed his finger over his lips. Standing, he crossed to the door and opened it.

His half-sister Nancy stood outside holding a pewter plate on which there rested two ears of corn. "Mother sent you corn." She did not see the Wild Boy although he was in plain sight. No one ever did.

"Thank your mother," said Young Squirrel stiffly. He took the plate.

"I brought you something as well." Reaching into her apron pocket, Nancy drew out a little earthenware pipkin and thrust it at Young Squirrel. "Here. It is an oil made of witch hazel tea and rose leaves. I made it myself. For your . . . for your skin," she said hastily. "I use it too, Tall Walker. It soothes against chapping and such."

Young Squirrel took the pipkin from her. "I am grateful." Then, because he did not know what else to say to his half-sister, he said, "Good night, Nancy," and shut the door.

"Two ears of corn!" The Wild Boy laughed triumphantly. "Two! See, Brother? Our mother knows that I'm here."

"One person may eat two ears of corn," Young Squirrel objected. "That she sent two means nothing."

How well and truly sick of his brother he was! As long as He Grows Up Wild existed, Young Squirrel could never be truly alone, and didn't a man have to be alone sometimes?

"And where did she get corn so ripe and new?" asked the Wild Boy. "It is but May. The harvest is not for months. I tell you, our mother is a witch. Do you remember the story that Old Tobacco told you of the Thunder Boys and Kanati? Do you know how it ended?"

"I wish to be quiet now, He Grows Up Wild. Let there be no more talking."

"Do you know the story of how there came to be corn?" the Wild Boy persisted.

"I do not know the story, and I do not wish to."

"I will tell you it then, since you do not know it."

"He Grows Up Wild!" Young Squirrel objected. "I said, no more talking!"

But the Wild Boy persisted. "After Kanati had lifted from his sons, the Thunder Boys, the curse of lice and maggots and vermin that was their punishment for having let all the game loose on the mountain, he sent them home. It was such a long way home! By the time they arrived at the cabin on Pilot's Knob, they were tired and hungry. They said to their mother, 'We are hungry.'

"But she said, 'There is no meat, boys, but here. Sit down by the fire and wait a little while and I will get you something.'"

"I am not listening to you," Young Squirrel informed him. He picked up an ear of corn and began to eat it.

"Their mother took a basket and started out to the storehouse," the Wild Boy continued. "This storehouse was built upon poles high up from the ground to keep it out of the reach of animals, and there was a ladder to climb up by, and one door, but no other opening. Every day when their mother got ready to cook the dinner, she would go out to the storehouse with a basket and bring it back full of corn and beans. The boys had never been inside the storehouse, so naturally they wondered where all the corn and beans could come from. After all, the storehouse was not a very large one. Accordingly, as soon as Selu went out the door, the Wild Boy said to his brother, 'Let's go and see what she does.'"

"I wish you would stop," Young Squirrel interjected. "What has this to do with us?"

But the Wild Boy pressed on. "The boys ran around to the very back of the storehouse, and, reaching up, knocked out a chunk of clay from between the logs, so that they could peer in. The light was dim, but they could just make out Selu. She was standing in the middle of the room with the basket in front of her on the floor. Then, leaning over the basket, she began to rub her stomach – so . . ." And He Grows Up Wild pantomimed rubbing his stomach. ". . . And suddenly the basket was half full of corn! Then she rubbed under her armpits – so . . ." He Grows Up Wild made as though to rub under his arms. ". . . And the basket was full to the top with beans!" He paused and laughed. "Our mother gives birth in so many ways. Surely such a woman is dangerous."

"Our mother is not dangerous. She is only an old woman."

The Wild Boy paid him no heed. "The boys looked at one another and said, 'This will never do. Our mother is a witch. If we eat any of this corn and beans, it will poison us. We must kill her.'"

"I do not like this story!"

"That does not matter! When the two Thunder Boys came back into the house, their mother took but one look at them and knew their thoughts. 'So,' she said, 'you are going to kill me?'

"'Yes,' they answered. 'You are a witch.'

"Their mother was resigned to her fate. 'Well,' she said, 'when you have killed me, make sure that you clear a large piece of ground in front of the house and drag my body seven times around the circle. Then drag me seven times over the ground inside the circle and stay up all night and watch and in the morning, you will have plenty of corn. There, I have done my duty by you. Now, kill me if you must.'"

"So the Thunder Boys battered their own mother to death, using clubs, and they cut off her head and put it up on the roof of the house with her face turned to the west and said, 'Look for your husband now; he comes soon.'"

"I cannot live by stories any longer," Young Squirrel told He Grows Up Wild. "I have eaten the corn my mother sent and it will not poison me. My mother is not a witch, but a woman, and I find I can no longer judge her actions. She was driven by her heart to leave and that is a kind of madness. As for you, Brother . . . I begin to suspect you do not even exist."

"What kills exists. I can kill."

"Only with my hands."

"I can drive you mad."

"I know of you only because I am mad."

He Grows Up Wild shook his head. "A madman does not know he's mad. It is impossible."

"It is the ulunsuti," said Young Squirrel. "It gives me the power to think at the same time as I am mad. Ah! Do you know, Brother, it has just now given me the idea of killing you?"

"You cannot kill me," protested He Grows Up Wild. "I'm not alive in the same way you are. Therefore, I cannot be killed in the same way you can." He tried a different tact. "If you are not to kill our mother, Brother, at least steal our sister away with you. I can help. She is very pretty and fresh, I think, and will remind us of our mother when we are far away."

"Do not speak further to me of this," said Young Squirrel. "I'm busy thinking of how I shall kill you."

At this the Wild Boy fell silent and only sat hunkered by the door as Young Squirrel undressed and lay down on the pallet. Chewing on raw knuckles, rolling them in his mouth as though he were chewing the last kernels off a cob, he watched as his brother lay down on his pallet and drifted into a troubled sleep, tossing and groaning as he rode out dreams that roiled and eddied like whitewater. The Wild Boy could just imagine those dreams. Talking inside his brother's head, he planted them like seeds of corn:

Rise up, go forth into the night, and burn down George Kinnahan's cabin. Take Bucksmasher from the wall and shoot them all. Our mother too. Rape Nancy first.

This is what the Wild Boy wished Young Squirrel to do. This is what, talking inside his brother's head, he advised.

However, Young Squirrel did not do as his brother wished, but only groaned and tossed and slept on. Finally, towards dawn, He Grows Up Wild gave up trying to influence his brother's dreams. Instead, he pondered the previous night's conversation. What if Young Squirrel could kill him? What then? Would he do it? If so, when? The truth was that He Grows Up Wild understood little about the nature of his own existence or how, indeed, it had even come about. Of course, he had formulated theories. They were as diverse and as many as the stars in the sky.

Early in the morning, just after daybreak, Young Squirrel rose and took his leave of Hiwasee. He Grows Up Wild followed his brother on foot, loping along as usual, like a half-wild dog, but much diminished and barely visible even to Young Squirrel.

From that time on, Young Squirrel, having exerted his will over that of his brother, grew less tormented. His skin did not itch anymore, though he would be scarred for life. His mother he no longer saw as evil, his father's identity he knew and George Kinnahan he saw now as the old man he had become, twisted with rheumatism as punishment, Young Squirrel realized with satisfaction (for knowledge that the universe is an ordered place, bound by rules, can be a source of satisfaction), for the reckless and ungrateful way the white man had hunted.

As for He Grows Up Wild, he degenerated into the kind of fool that goes muttering to himself about the village, except that none but Young Squirrel could see him – none, that is, of whom they were aware. "Then we set to work to clear the ground in front of the house," he would mutter to himself, retelling over and over again the story of Selu the witch-mother and the origins of corn, "but, instead of clearing the whole piece, we cleared only seven little spots. This is why corn now grows only in a few places instead of over the whole world. Oh! Oh! Oh!" He would wave his thin hands distractedly in the air. "We dragged the body of Selu around the circle, and, wherever her blood fell on the ground, why, there the corn sprang up. But instead of dragging her body seven times across the ground, we dragged it over only twice. My brother and I are so lazy. Ha! This is the reason the Indians still work their crop but twice. Come, Brother, let us sit up and watch our corn all the night and in the morning it will be full grown and ripe. Come, Young Squirrel. Come!"

But his brother never came.

The Wild Boy planted a small field of corn down next to the river and tended it so assiduously that, in season, the brothers had as much corn on their table as anybody else. The villagers were amazed that Young Squirrel could work at Matlock's store all day and night and never be seen to be tending such a productive field.

"How does he do it?" the villagers asked. In the end, they agreed, "There is something about him."

EIGHT

Towards dusk on a hot, hazy day early in the Thunder Moon, Nancy Kinnahan Butler, the daughter of George Kinnahan, the white trader for that territory up around the Hiwasee River where it joins the Tennessee, was returning home from a visit to the Zants, a family of Pennsylvania Dutch come recently to settle eight miles down river with their several children – Nancy and her new husband Charley were living with her parents until such time as Charley could clear enough trees to build them a cabin on the land hard by the forks, which he had laid claim to the winter before.

Although Nancy was used to walking such distances – her mother Katy, or Tsikiki as she was called in her native tongue, was a Cherokee, after all, and Cherokee are great walkers – the visit to the Zants had proved a tiring journey, what with the heat and the fact that Nancy was some few weeks pregnant and still in the sleepy, swooning stages of that condition. Frequently she had stopped along the way to draw off her heavy wooden shoes and rest in the scant shade provided by some tall, indifferent tree, dreaming, as women who bear children do, fingers for her child and eyes and the beaded necklace of cartilage that would become his spine. Nancy in repose looked almost like a child herself. Small-boned and light, she wore her straight hair long and loose. It was that dusty brown that only the hair of half-breeds is and her hazel eyes, in certain lights, verged on yellow.

"Several's the times I've near shot my Nancy with the Bucksmasher," her father used to say, "for in the dark, you'd as like take her for a bobcat as a lass."

The day had been a still one, but now, with the coming of evening, a slight breeze had lifted off the river that caught her father's land in the crook of its elbow, rattling the dry leaves of the trees overhead. Nancy peered upwards. Birds, too oppressed by the day's long heat to budge from their perches, now stirred, ruffling their feathers and muttering, and the cicadas started up their murmuring vibrato. Frogs spoke from the marshy places around the river and, in the bushes, fireflies twinkled like green stars.

Her long walk nearly ended, her mother's hearth close by, Nancy's step lightened and quickened and, as she walked, she sang a song that her husband had taught her, an English song, which he called "The Fourth Day of July":

> *"O the cuckoo . . . she's a pretty bird,*
> *She warbles as she flies . . . .*
> *She never hollers 'cuckoo'*
> *Till the Fourth Day of July."*

In the song the object of the singer's affections was called 'Willy,' but for 'Willy' Nancy always substituted the name of her husband: 'Charley.'

> *"Gonna build me a castle*
> *On the mountains so high . . . .*
> *So I can see Charley*
> *As he goes on by."*

Then the refrain:

> *"Oh, the cuckoo . . . she's a pretty bird . . . ."*

"The cuckoo!" her mother had snorted when first she heard Nancy singing the song. "Did you know that the Cherokee call the cuckoo the Deceiver? Put some of that corn into the *ka no na*, Daughter." They were grinding corn for meal.

Carefully Nancy poured some corn from a keg into the hollowed-out wooden stump her mother called the *ka no na* – to Nancy's knowledge, there was no English word for the device. "No," she said. "Why?"

"Oh, there is a good reason." Her mother took up the paddle to grind the corn. "I will tell you how it is: a bird leaves its nest unguarded. Along comes the wily cuckoo. It pushes and prods an egg over the edge of the nest until – oh! – it tumbles to the ground and cracks and the tiny bird within it dies. The cuckoo lays its own egg in its place and flies away. Back comes the other bird. It cannot tell one egg from another. It is not so cunning as the cuckoo. Instead it sits upon the cuckoo's egg and hatches it and raises the changeling as though it were her own."

"The cuckoo is a murderess?"

"Well . . ." her mother equivocated. "Here." She gave Nancy the paddle and lowered herself gingerly onto a log. "You beat for a while. My wrists ache." Tsikiki was ever noncommittal. It was her way. After a few moments, she had this thought: *To behave in this manner is the way of the cuckoo and so, perhaps, she cannot be blamed for it. Indeed, in that she goes to such lengths to avoid the tedium of child rearing, she is more subtle than her fellows and so perhaps deserves our admiration.*

Cherokee like to take a thing and say, Yes, without a doubt it should be so, then turn it upside down so as to get a different angle on it. "Cherokee prefer many paths around to one way through," Tsikiki often observed.

Remembering the discussion, Nancy smiled and sang the song's next verse as she turned off the path into the door yard:

"Jack o' Diamonds, Jack o' Diamonds,
I know you of old.
You robbed my poor pockets
Of silver and gold."

There was her old father sitting in his accustomed place on the falling-down porch, the Bucksmasher on his knees – over the past few years, his rheumatism had made him a virtual prisoner of the old twig rocker situated near the cabin door. Nancy lifted her hand to greet him and was on the point of crying out, when, suddenly, she stopped with her hand half raised in the air and her lips parted.

Her father's body slumped in his chair, his head drooped to one side, and there was something about his head . . . . It was as though its top had been lifted clean off. From where she stood she could just make out, through a glinting black and mobile veil of flies, the fleshy membrane which wrapped her father's skull. There was blood everywhere.

The breath was squeezed from Nancy's lungs; she could not scream. Invisible walls pressed her tight between them; they edged closer and closer together. She could not move. Even her heart seemed unable to find space in which to beat; she had a dizzying sense that it might rupture from the pressure of not contracting.

Suddenly a jagged sound ripped through the silence – a dog's frantic, high-pitched barking. Turning, she saw Nero, her father's old black hound, slink around the corner of the house and stand, blinking with wonder at her a moment before it began to bark again, greeting her with a raucous, deranged joy. It loped disjointedly towards her, side winding like a snake, stumbling like a drunk, its snout covered in dried blood. Upon reaching her, it wrapped itself around her feet as she squatted down in the dust to embrace and cling to it and whisper frantically, as though the dog might find its tongue and tell her what it had seen, "What happened, Nero? What?"

Later, accompanied by the dog, Nancy rose and went into the house. There she found the scalped bodies of her mother and her husband Charley. Her brothers' bodies she located out back by the corncrib and on the crooked path leading to the cool dampness of the springhouse. The dog nosed them anxiously and whimpered. There was little Nancy could do. The bodies were heavy with death. She was too weak to move them. Flies hovered about the corpses like a crowd collects at the scene of an accident – busy, avid in their attention. She swatted at them but only succeeded in breaking their ranks momentarily. In despair, she turned from them towards the house.

As she stumbled past the shed, the solitary cow kept by her mother turned her tethered head to look over her shoulder at Nancy. The cow bawled plaintively, insistently. She had not been milked that day. Why hadn't the men who had murdered her family taken the cow? Raiders usually took livestock. She shook her head helplessly. Was there any telling? The cow was the only one that Nancy could help, so she drew up the rickety three-legged stool and, numb with anguish, milked her until her udders yielded no more. She placed the full pail away from the cow's back feet so that she would not kick it over and started once again for the house. Eagerly Nero rushed forward and lapped at the warm milk in the pail.

Returning to the porch, Nancy found that she was unable to muster the courage to re-enter the house where the bodies of her mother and husband lay. Sinking down on the step, a few feet in front of her murdered father's feet, she stared out into the woods. After a moment, she thought she saw something flicker in the near darkness. Gasping, she started to her feet and dropped back a step.

But it was only her father's white, notch-eared pigs moving between the trees beyond the dooryard, shiningly visible at this darkening hour. By day, the pigs hunted grubs and roots in the forest. Come nightfall, Nancy's brothers filled the trough out back with slops for them. Now, however, fearful of the blood smell that hung over the devastated homestead (for the smell of blood strikes terror into the heart of a pig, and more blood had flowed on that day than at any Fall pig sticking), the wary animals were reluctant to move beyond the safety of the forest. Instead they lingered, caught about the edges of the homestead like ghosts on the periphery of a living world.

Nancy could feel their terror. It hung all around her, as thick and heavy, as palpable as the thick air of the Tennessee summer. She wanted to scream, to shout, to laugh . . . anything to break the portentous silence in which murder had wrapped her father's house. To run . . . but there was nowhere to run. Nowhere safe. Nowhere her shaking legs could propel her before night closed in around her like a fist. She pried the Bucksmasher out of her father's death grip. Why hadn't the murderers taken it? Didn't they usually take weapons? Once more she sank down onto the stoop. If only she had been here, she thought, her terror would now be over.

Off in the distance, a cuckoo cried its monotonous call from the trees beyond the house – *cuckoo*!

Now Nancy, desperate for sound, strained to hear the cuckoo's call: faint, muted, incidental. A bird's small brain cannot encompass tragedy nor, indeed, she thought, its own inherent evil. For it there is life, terror, fragments of joy, then a death it neither anticipates nor comprehends. It wears out the long summer like a fisherman with low expectations who seats himself on a riverbank and casts out his line. *Cuckoo!* The bird calls, casting idly about for love or conversation.

As the sun set, Nancy wondered if the men might come back, after all.

ຂາ

What had happened at the Kinnahan homestead was this:

Chief Attakullakulla, whom the white men called Little Carpenter for his skill at fashioning treaties, had a fierce son whose name was Tsiyu Gansini or Dragging Canoe. This warrior was as tall as Attakullakulla was short and hard lean in his powerful body. His long face with its strong, big features was badly scarred and pitted by the smallpox he had contracted from a white man as a child, but from which he did not, like so many of his village, die. For this and for another reason Dragging Canoe's heart was hardened against the alien race that had come to dwell alongside the Cherokee – it was clear to him that, no matter how much land the Cherokee ceded the Long Knives through all his father's many treaties, they would always want more.

"Such treaties may be all right for men who are too old to hunt or fight," he was reported to have said in council. "As for me, I have my young warriors about me. We will have our lands."

So Dragging Canoe withdrew from the Cherokee nation. He went to the Chickamauga district in Overhill and founded new towns where his people lived in the old, good way that was easy to understand, depending on the hunt for food and their well-tended fields of corn and squash and beans, and wearing no clothing made from the traders' calico or linsey woolsey, but only the knee-length buckskin shirts of their ancestors, sewn with the dried sinew of animals, and, beneath these, for the men, loincloths – for the groin is the seat of much mystery and must be kept safe.

From these lonely places in Overhill, Dragging Canoe waged a war against the white man using not rifles, but the old weapons of the Cherokee – ball-headed war clubs, spears, bows and arrows. This is why they did not take the Bucksmasher – the rifle was a white man's weapon, of no use to them. This war went on for nearly twenty years and consisted principally of this activity: murder. It was very simple. Whenever Dragging Canoe found a white man on lands he considered Cherokee, he killed him. He killed him like a chicken – which means, indiscriminately. He then took his scalp and sold it to Henry Hamilton, at that time the Lieutenant Governor of Canada. This was the Cherokee name for Henry Hamilton – the Hair Buyer – because he was always eager to acquire more rebel colonist scalps for his collection. One of the white men that Dragging Canoe murdered in this way was the grandfather of Davy Crockett . . . but that is a different story.

In this year of 1787, then, in this month of July, as it was inevitable that he sometime must, Dragging Canoe found the white trader George Kinnahan living among the Cherokee near Hiwasee, the Overhill town in which he and his Cherokee wife had long resided, and killed him like a chicken, together with his white son-in-law, Charley Butler, his two sons by Tsikiki, and the woman herself.

Actually, killing Tsikiki had been an accident. Dragging Canoe had come upon the old woman in the store, which, lacking windows, was too dimly lit for him to make out her Cherokee features. This was irrespective of the fact that she had cried out to him in Cherokee, *"Doe-yust had-do-nay?"* "What are you doing?" White men always know some Cherokee phrases, as Cherokee know some English – Dragging Canoe was one of those. For example, "I am killing you, old woman!" he had replied to Tsikiki's question, using white man words, and then he had slit her throat and, with a second slice of his knife, parted her scalp from her head.

Later, stepping out of the store and onto the porch, he held up Tsikiki's scalp in the fading light and found the hair to be that black that a white man's never is. The gray mixed in told him his victim's age.

"What is it, Dragging Canoe?" his men called to him.

"A ga yv li ge i!" "An old woman!" *"Tsa la gi!"* "Cherokee," exclaimed Dragging Canoe bitterly. He shook his head with exasperation and sorrow. He did not like to kill Cherokee. What was the point of that? Yet it happened. Cherokee women should not take up with white men, he reflected, hooking the scalp onto his belt. Dropping down off the porch, he strode across the yard to where his horse and men waited.

"E li se!" one of the warriors said, shaking his head.

"Someone's grandmother!" said another.

The warriors also shook their heads and made low sounds connoting sorrow in their throats. Well, they thought, pulling up on their reins and tapping the flanks of their horses with their heels in preparation for the ride home to Chicamauga, it is too bad about the old woman, but mistakes happen.

"I am just glad there were no babies," somebody observed as they were turning their horses onto the path.

At this, everyone nodded his agreement. Nobody liked to scalp babies. In the first place, the Cherokee were very partial to little children in general. In addition, the soft spot in a baby's head beat like a second heart once the scalp had been lifted off – persistently – and kept on beating until the infant died. Such a sight was unsettling and most disturbing.

❧

The retreat of Dragging Canoe and his men had been observed by George Kinnahan, whose hairless, bloody-pulp-headed corpse perched precariously on that front porch twig rocking chair where he had taken up residence over the past decade after his rheumatism had gotten so bad that he could scarcely rise to walk to the cowshed. He had been slaughtered as he sat, protesting his astonishment at his fate while the geese in the dooryard honked and the guinea hens ran here and there. His long pink beard was caked with gore and he stared with eyes that have gone wide, then blind from the howling nothingness they look upon. A fact known to those who have passed over . . . . As the hair and fingernails of a corpse continue to grow after death, so the rods and cones of the eye continue for some little time to translate visual stimuli into pictures for a consciousness in retreat from life. At first these pictures are as clear as when we are alive, then our vision begins gradually to tunnel until it's as if we peer down a kaleidoscope towards a bright chaos that is the light.

❧

The night she discovered her family murdered, Nancy Kinnahan Butler spent crouched in the woods with the pigs and the dog Nero and the Bucksmasher. The next morning she, the dog and the cow walked the long miles back to the Dutch family's homestead. She carried the rifle over her shoulder and led the cow by a rope, knowing that the animal would buy her refuge for a time – a cow was rare enough in these remote parts and worth something.

She would have taken the pigs had they not been so hard to lead. Pigs are intelligent animals and have their own notions as to where they must go and when.

NINE

Towards the end of the Harvest Moon of that same year, Young Squirrel made his way down to Charleston to barter. Now he made such trips twice a year, once in the spring and once in the early autumn, leading the way on his sorrel mare. A boy from the village drove the slow oxcart, piled high with pelts and beeswax and comb honey and the bundles of ginseng roots, which Young Squirrel bartered for guns and iron pots and calico. Matlock had died five years before, leaving Young Squirrel the store and all his lands. As a consequence, the Cherokee trader had grown even richer than before.

Young Squirrel was in his mid-forties now, a man in his prime, seemingly in control of his divergent selves. The plague of vermin beneath his skin that had been his supposed father's death curse upon him and his mysterious brother had long since ceased to torment him, though he bore the marks of that struggle still. His face was stiff with scar tissue and appeared tortured, as though the flesh had been torn and yanked and then left twisted and misshapen to heal as best it might.

As for Young Squirrel's terrible brother, he had not quite disappeared, but lingered about the edges of the trader's life like an unruly will-o-the-wisp – having so far deteriorated as to be little more than wisps of mist that vaguely congealed into the shape of a human body and sometimes not even that. He Grows Up Wild accompanied Young Squirrel on this as on all his trading missions, loping along beside the ox on the slick brown pine needles and the soft sand. He was like an old dog which has in him one last trek. Young Squirrel caught sight of him now and then – the way one may glimpse a spider web stretched between the branches of a tree if only the light is right – but the trader tried, by and large, to ignore him. He had learned through experience that his blood brother fed on attention, growing more substantial, and difficult to control if acknowledged.

It was Pringle the cloth merchant, the same man who, ten years before, had informed Young Squirrel of his mother's whereabouts, now told him of her murder and the slaughter of her kin at the hands of Dragging Canoe. "Oh, by the by, that George Kinnahan fella, the one you knew . . . . Him and his whole family . . . murdered by Indians!"

The news acted upon the trader the way a spider's poison will act upon the nervous system of its victim – it paralyzed him. Hung in the web of the brightly lit shop, surrounded by bolts of dusty cloth stacked up to the ceiling, Young Squirrel listened, his chest as empty of air as if he had been hit in the gut, his throat tight, his eyes blazing dry, to the factor's third-hand tale of mayhem.

"Scalped 'em too. Savages! Blood everywhere was what I heard."

Young Squirrel supported all his weight on the counter with the heel of his hand. If it had not been for the counter, he would have stumbled and fallen to his knees. The trader had not seen his mother for close to a decade. She had been dead to him since his childhood thirty years before, yet the possibility of her love, the possibility of her presence in his life had existed so long as she lived. Her death was the death of his hope for him and her, a hope he had nurtured the way a village will its Constant Fire – what was there in the beginning, what will be there always. Now it was gone, destroyed.

"No, now, I'm wrong," Pringle corrected himself, deftly winding cloth onto bolts. "One of them did survive."

"Which one?" asked Young Squirrel.

"The daughter, I think it was."

"Nancy?"

The factor, surprised that Young Squirrel knew the girl's name, eyed the Cherokee with curiosity. "Well, yes. She was away when it happened. You know her then?"

"I know of her," Young Squirrel replied. "Where is she now?"

"North Georgia. Up around Spring Place. Some Dutch folks come down from Pennsylvania took her in and the whole lot of them got scared and pulled up stakes and headed south pretty quick after the massacre." He laughed, smiled, showing broken teeth. "Figured as to how they'd like to keep their yellow hair."

❧

Young Squirrel walked slowly along the quay, staring out to sea to where cargo ships from Europe destined for harbor bobbed distractedly on the horizon.

Spring Place, he thought. *Not that far from Qualla.*

The day was still and the glare of the mid-morning sun off the sea made the cloudless sky seem almost overcast, heavy.

Just drop down towards New Echota, he figured, then take the federal road from Carmel north and east.

Further down the quay naked black slaves shouted to one another in Gula as they unloaded ships and the gulls screamed, equally incomprehensible, and swooped.

He Grows Up Wild lurched alongside his more substantial brother, struggling to keep up. Bits of him tended to become inoperative at times, necrotic. At present, it was his right leg. He dragged its dead weight after him like a sack of stones, now and then stopping to pick it up and heave it forward with an exclamation of exasperation and disgust: *"Hu!"* He Grows Up Wild began to speak, as Young Squirrel had known he must eventually do. (Actually, he had been speaking for some time, but Young Squirrel had not heard him. The Wild Boy's voice had grown so thin and high pitched that what he said was sometimes lost in the shriek of the gulls or the throbbing of the waves against the quay – this was all right with Young Squirrel, as He Grows Up Wild was prone to endless repetition.) "She so resembles our mother," he said in his sibilant, singsong whistle. "Oh, come, Brother. I know you have not ceased to think of her since the day you saw her first. Nor have I. No. How could I? How could you? A pretty thing. A beautiful thing. We must go and fetch our beautiful sister home, Brother."

"It is no good," Young Squirrel told him gruffly. "She does not know us. She would not come."

"Tell her you are her distant kinsman. Of her mother's clan. That is what our mother told her. Nancy will not know better. Our mother will not have told her more."

Young Squirrel stopped and looked at his brother with surprise. "How do you know that?" he asked.

He Grows Up Wild set his leg down and half straightened from his crouch. "Owh!" he exclaimed softly, then, "It is simple, Brother: our mother would have been ashamed."

Young Squirrel frowned and started walking again, faster, so that He Grows Up Wild would have difficulty keeping up.

"Wait!" cried He Grows Up Wild. "Wait, Brother!"

Young Squirrel did not wait. He Grows Up Wild would catch up with him later. He always did. The Cherokee trader could walk away from his troublesome blood brother, but he could not rid himself of his company for long. To make it worse, his blood brother was right – when it came to obsession, He Grows Up Wild was always right. The trader would go to fetch his sister home and he would go soon.

"Before the snow," he said aloud.

He Grows Up Wild might have lagged far behind, but he heard his brother's words as clearly as if he had spoken them out loud to himself. He stopped where he was and, tilting his head to one side, laughed his loon laugh.

TEN

"Gonna build me a castle
On the mountains so high . . ."

The sound of a woman singing. Sweet, high and thin. Faint. A breeze that smelled of peaches brought it to Young Squirrel's ears – the sound came from the direction of the orchard.

"Is that . . . Mrs. Butler singing?" Young Squirrel asked the blond boy seated on the steps to the front porch. The child was not much older than seven or eight and small for his age, like a fruit that grows wormy and hard. In one hand he held a blowgun; he had been playing at being an Indian.

"Yessir," said the boy uncertainly. "Why you be asking?"

"Where is she?" Young Squirrel ignored his question.

"What you'd be wanting her for?" asked the boy, standing. "I reckon my Pa would like to know that."

"Take my horse." Young Squirrel handed the mare's reins to the boy. "See that she gets some hay and water. I'll pay you for your trouble." He started off in the direction of the voice.

"Pa!" The boy turned towards the house, the reins slack in his small fist. "Pa!" he bellowed.

❧

"So I can see Charley
As he goes on by."

Nancy stooped to pick the last few windfall peaches from the ground – carefully, for she was now advanced in her pregnancy and her

94

back had begun to pain her – and gently placed the bruised fruit in the big basket that her mother had double woven from the vine of a honeysuckle. It was one of the things which she had taken with her from the Hiwasee homestead when she and the Zants had stopped on the road to Spring Place to bury her people, soft, pungent mounds of decomposition by the time she had returned with the Dutch family, that needed to be shoveled into their graves. That and the Buck-smasher.

One peach had rolled a little down the slope and caught in the gnarled roots of a tree. Nancy knelt on the ground and bent low so that she could retrieve the fruit. As she did, she heard the sound of a footfall and, before she could twist around to glance up, a voice, low and flat in its intonation. "Mistress Nancy Kinnahan Butler?"

At the sound of the unfamiliar voice, Nancy's breath caught in her throat. Ever since the massacre she had frightened so easily. She turned around and rose up onto her knees. A man stood ten feet away with his back to the late afternoon sun and his planter's hat in his hand. It was impossible to make out his features.

"What . . . who are you?" Her hand rose to grasp her throat.

Young Squirrel stared at his half sister in shocked surprise. It was not so much that she was far gone with child, although he had, of course, not been prepared for that, but her hair, formerly a dusty brown, was now as white as an old woman's. It had turned white the day she had returned to her father's homestead to find her family slaughtered, and white it had remained.

"Nancy?" he asked again, suddenly unsure that it was she.

Where was Gerard Zant? Nancy looked this way and that in panic. Young Hans? Had this man murdered them that they had not come to protect her?

"Nancy?" He took a step forward.

"Oh!" she cried, sitting back onto her heels.

Realizing then that he frightened her, Young Squirrel stopped in his tracks. "Do you know me?"

"No," whispered Nancy, shaking her head. At first she had taken the stranger for a white man. He wore white man's clothes – sweat-stained, rumpled linen, a jacket and a hat. Now she saw that he was Cherokee. "No, I do not know you."

"Ten years have come and gone since we met." *She is still beautiful,* he thought. *Despite the white hair. Like my mother, she has maintained her beauty despite age and sorrow.*

Nancy peered hard at the scarred, immobile visage, cocking her head to one side. There was something about his face . . . . "Yes," she said after a moment. Truly it was a face that would prove hard to forget, and yet . . . . "I may have met you once." She came forward onto her knees again and started to rise. He offered her his hand. She took it and let him pull her to her feet.

"I once spent the night at your family's homestead," Young Squirrel reminded her. "You were but a girl."

At his mention of her family, Nancy turned her head away and lowered her eyes to the ground. The thought of them was a knife's quick stinging prick on the very tissue of her heart. "My family is dead," she said and, placing the handle of the fruit basket on her arm, she turned from him and started to walk back to the house.

"I slept in the shed." Young Squirrel started after her. "You brought me corn . . . and a pipkin of ointment. Do you remember?"

She stopped.

"The ointment was for my skin. It was very kind of you to give it to me."

A scrap of memory fluttered in her mind, like a torn bit of flag tossed on a breeze. "It seems to me I do," she said. There was something . . . . "Yes. Mother gave me corn and said . . . ." She stopped, trying to fit this oddly shaped piece into the puzzle of memory. Of course! How agitated her mother had seemed. That had been unlike her. Katy was always so composed, almost detached.

"I heard of your trouble. I . . . ." He was unused to conveying sympathy; he could not find the words. "I was sorry to hear of it."

Nancy stared at the ground, her throat constricted, her eyes filled with sudden tears.

People die all the time, often violently. Their deaths leave chasms down which the living sometimes slip. Nancy had slipped down such a chasm. Part of her was dead; the other part was dying. Everyone saw it. "It will not be long before she goes to the Darkening Land," the Cherokee of the region said among themselves. "She is between worlds."

As for the Zants, they hoped Nancy would move on. She did what work she could, but Dragging Canoe's massacre of her family had left its mark. Once sanguine in temperament, she had become nervous, prone to sudden terrors and fits of weeping alternated with periods of deep despondence during which she would neither eat nor speak nor so much as move from her bed, but only lie, staring for hours at the wall. Moreover, her continued presence meant an extra mouth to feed in a family where there were already four children and another on the way; if Nancy's baby lived, there would be six children for whom the Zants must provide.

"Perhaps she will die in childbirth and the baby too," Ann Zant told her husband quietly when she thought Nancy could not hear. Of course, Nancy was just outside on the porch at the butter churn and so heard perfectly. "With all that she has been through, that would be a blessing," Ann had concluded.

"What brings you here, Stranger?" Nancy lifted her chin and blinked back her hot tears. She must not cry so much, she thought, angry with herself. She was weary of these tears that came so quickly and from nowhere. She lived in their constant thrall.

"It's . . . . I . . . ." He did not know how to begin this. "Your mother . . . she was not from Hiwasee."

"No." Nancy wondered how he knew. "She was from the mountains, I think."

"Do you know what village?" Young Squirrel guessed that she didn't . . . hoped that she did not.

To his relief, Nancy shook her head. "No," she said slowly. "My mother did not talk about her village. I think it troubled her to remember it. Perhaps something bad had happened to her there. Some sorrow. I don't know."

"And your father?"

"He was from Scotland. Glasgow, he called it."

"Did he ever mention your mother's village?"

Nancy frowned, trying to remember. She shook her head.

Secure now that she would not know he lied, Young Squirrel drew a deep breath. "Your mother was a kinswoman of mine, though not of my clan," he told his half-sister now. "She was of the clan of my father's mother and lived in Kituwah. It is a village which is no more. Smallpox killed many of the people who lived there and, because it had become such a sad place, those who lived there went elsewhere. Up river. There is no one from there now, only a mound, but I know of this village and its fate from my father."

"I seem to remember my mother saying that you were kin," said Nancy. "But your name . . . ."

"I called myself by a different name when first I visited you," said Young Squirrel. "Tall Walker. Your mother knew who I was. She did not want your father to know."

"Why?"

Young Squirrel shrugged. "Perhaps her people did not want her to leave. Perhaps it was your father who made her go."

"What is your real name then? Who are you, and where do you come from?"

"My name is Young Squirrel. I am a trader in the village of Qualla, one of the Middle Towns."

"You are not white . . . . How can you be a trader?"

"I worked for the white trader for many years and learned from him. I learned very well. I am a rich man, Nancy, even by white standards."

"You dress like a white man. I thought you were a white man when first I saw you, with your back to the light and your face in shadow."

"I wear the clothes of the white man and follow his ways because that is the path we must follow," Young Squirrel told her heatedly – this he fervently believed. "We have no choice, Nancy. We become as they are or they will kill us."

Nancy shook her head. "Dragging Canoe killed my family because we were half-white." She started back down the hill again.

"Dragging Canoe is a fool," Young Squirrel insisted, starting after her. He caught her by the elbow and turned her around. "Dragging Canoe thinks he can drive the white man from the land, but he does not know the white man. The white man cannot be stopped, and he has no reverence for what he kills! This I know."

"My father was a white man and he is dead," Nancy protested. "My husband was a white man."

"Their deaths will be avenged more times than you can count," Young Squirrel told her. "It is almost over for the Cherokee, but it is not over for me . . . and it is not over for you if you come with me."

Nancy stared at him, incredulous. "What?"

"I have come, to take you back, with me. That is why I have come."

"Back?" Nancy was amazed. "Back to where?"

"To Qualla. To my home."

"But why?"

"You are kin, Nancy. You are of my blood."

"What's going on here?"

Young Squirrel turned around to see a tall sun-burnt white man standing in the path. The fingers of the white man's right hand gripped the curving curly maple stock of an old flintlock. His voice was gruff and his manner assertive, but it was clear he was frightened. The small boy to whom Young Squirrel had spoken earlier stood a few feet behind him, holding the Bucksmasher.

"Nancy?" the man demanded.

Nancy looked at Young Squirrel and then at the white man. "It is all right, Gerard," she said. "It is only Young Squirrel. He is kin to my mother. Do not worry."

The white man lowered his gun. "I'll leave you, then?" he asked uncertainly, hopefully.

"Please," replied Nancy.

✒✒

Jack o' Diamonds, Jack o' Diamonds,
I know you of old.
You robbed my poor pockets
Of silver and gold.

✒✒

Nancy thought this: *why not go with this strange man? What life is there for me in this place? True, I might find another husband, or, more likely, the Zants might find one for me, to be rid of me once and for all. What kind of man might he be? Who can tell? Whatever the frontier turns up. Such a man might be rough. Such a man might prove unkind. I might not care for him.*

This man, on the other hand, is strangely familiar to me, though he frightens me too. Something about the way he carries himself . . . . That hideous face . . . . He is Cherokee and my father and husband would not have liked that. Then again, he wears the clothes of a white man and speaks the white man's English . . . .

When it came down to it, her thought was: *could what he might bring me to be worse than this, less bereft of hope?*

She thought this, knowing that the hopelessness was in her heart, that she bore it like a child that will not be born but only lingers in the darkness half-formed and poisonous, that she would carry it with her wherever she went. Still there is that urge to walk away, to leave behind that which cannot, will not be abandoned. Movement outward from the center. Escape beyond the pull of the heart.

I often have wondered
What makes women love men,
Then I've looked back and wondered

෧ඈ

Young Squirrel, watching her, his body beneath the cumbersome, linen suit stiff and damp with perspiration, but alive, *alive*, thought this: *it was a mistake to come. You were wrong, He Grows Up Wild, to convince me to come. Before, I had a choice. Now that I have seen her again, I have no choice. She must come. She has to come. If she will not, I will have to take her.*

He fought to keep his expression neutral as he watched the woman turn and walk a little ways away. Resting her hand upon the gnarled trunk of a peach tree, she leaned her weight against it, the palm of her right hand pressed into the small of her back to counter the backache caused by the straining forward of her belly. She bowed her head.

From disparate bits of this and that floating in the air, He Grows Up Wild amalgamated into something resembling a human shape. Circling around his brother, he crossed to his left and, leaning over, whispered in his ear: "Shame, brother! Are you in love with her?"

"Quiet!" Young Squirrel hissed beneath his breath, his face hot and rigid. "Go away!" He lifted his hand to swat his brother, but lowered it quickly when he saw that Nancy had turned and was taking a step toward him.

"When do we leave?" she asked, her beautiful face suddenly bright.

ELEVEN

Young Squirrel built a new house for Nancy. He thought the house of He Goes About was too poor, too miserable a place to bring her. They lived in a tent until the house, which was very fine, shingled with oak, with a stone chimney, puncheon floors cut from yellow poplar and a porch just like George Kinnahan's, was ready. It took six weeks to build and was completed just before the first snowfall.

Nancy's son (and Charley's) was born in that tent just as the leaves were turning and the last bees dying and the mountains looked all over afire with the change. She named the boy George after her father. The house was a ways from the village – a half-hour's ride down river at Ela. Young Squirrel wished to keep his half-sister away from the other women of the village. He feared that she might deduce from their idle gossip who she was to him.

Nancy lived in this house peacefully enough for a number of winters. It was pretty up Ela way, prettier than dusty, hot Hiwasee. By day she could see Rattlesnake Mountain from the porch and, by night, through the lookout cut into the logs next to the chimney, she could spy a whole sky full of stars. She had her work to do, a house to run; her kinsman was prosperous and generous. She did not want for the wherewithal to do her housekeeping or, indeed, for anything. Her boy kept her occupied. Also, there was her heart that required healing.

However, as time wore on and winter passed into summer and into winter again, Nancy became increasingly aware . . . and finally acutely aware . . . that she was lonely. The handful of white women who lived in the Middle Towns region were scattered far and wide on isolated homesteads and did not think of a half-breed woman dwelling with a Cherokee relation as their peer, while the Cherokee women of the village seemed shy of her, skittish and perhaps suspicious; at any rate, they took no steps to be friendly. Isolation breeds isolation. Just as Tsikiki had been isolated as a young woman, so too was her daughter.

Oh! Nancy missed her mother.

It was not that Young Squirrel was unkind. It seemed to Nancy that he wished to please her, but the habit of secrecy is a hard one to break and the trader was unused to company, particularly a woman's company. He kept his own counsel, so much so that, upon occasion, she had even observed him speaking with vehemence to himself as though he were engaged in a struggle with someone who had greatly annoyed him. Every once in a while he would break his customary silence to tell her – with peculiar urgency – of some new scheme he had devised to make money. Apart from such mundane observances as, "I am going out now," or, "Here is that flour you wanted," his only conversation consisted in these occasional, fervid outbursts. He had lived so long alone and unto himself that he was not easy with other people except . . . and this intrigued her . . . when he was selling them something. Then his whole demeanor altered. Then he seemed to come to some sort of strange life. She had seen this happen in the store. In the presence of customers, he became suddenly almost overly animated; he reminded her of a panther she had once glimpsed crouched high up in a tree in the Tennessee woods – as lithe, keen and ready as that.

As she pretended to weigh the merits of one bolt of calico against another, she observed out of the corner of her eye that her peculiar kinsman was a man who could talk anyone into anything, who could bend wills and desires as if they were green wood. It was a wondrous transformation she observed – before her eyes he turned into a man she barely recognized and, when she thought of it, as she often did in her isolation, she could not figure out for the life of her where this other man resided or whence he came.

As for Young Squirrel, he did not like Nancy coming to the store and told her so.

"You distract me." Then, because that sounded harsh, "Besides, it is a long way into town. All you have to do is tell me what you want and I will bring it to you."

What he did not tell her was that her presence made him nervous. He saw how people looked at her. He watched the sideways glances and knew what people said when he was not listening:

"Who is this half-breed woman?"

"Where does she come from?"

"Is she Young Squirrel's woman? Surely she must be."

"He calls her kin, but kin to whom? His mother or his father? Both He Goes About and Dayunisi were from Qualla. Their fathers and mothers too . . . yes, and their grandparents before that. Where would a kinswoman to Young Squirrel come from if not from Qualla?"

"Surely she is his woman, fetched up from Charleston or one of those distant, far places he goes. He has fetched her back like any other goods, like a fine English rifle or a new set of clothes. But if so, why hide it? She is a pretty woman and Young Squirrel is a rich man. He may have a wife if he chooses without calling her kin."

"But why is her hair white? It is as white as an old woman's!"

Then, as he watched, he thought he saw something different in the glances of the old ones. He thought he saw them compare Nancy's face to their remembered image of his mother's beautiful countenance. He thought he saw them remember that Tsikiki had left with the white trader at least as many years ago as Nancy was old. He thought he saw them figure it out. Thought, though, of course, he could never be sure.

Then it was not that he wished to keep Nancy from the people so much as he wanted to keep the people from Nancy. He did not want her to know that she was, in fact, not a distant cousin but his half-sister. This was because he loved her, had since the first time he saw her, and she had replaced his mother in his thoughts and in his dreams and he thought that he might one day live with her as with a wife. As long as the truth of their relationship could be kept from her, he reasoned, what would be the harm in that?

So Nancy stayed away from the village, by and large, and had little to do with its inhabitants, relying on her son and her strange and taciturn kinsman for what company she had and a King Charles spaniel which Young Squirrel had bought her on the coast to replace the dog Nero who died of old age when Nancy had been in Qualla two years, whom she trained and loved dearly and called Willy.

Children, however, slip more easily through the interstices between worlds than adults. As Nancy's son George Butler grew older, he came upon other children, Cherokees, living in hidden away places up Ravensford and Grassy Branch. While his mother sat slowly rocking on the twig rocker that was like her father's, looking out towards the long spiny ridge of Rattlesnake Mountain with her dead eyes that saw only those things that have happened and not that which is before them, these children and George played at hunting in the deep woods and at other things as well. In this way George became acquainted with an old grandmother named Toineeta.

Toineeta lived up on what the white folk called Madcap Branch, upriver from Ravensford and to the west. Most Cherokee lived in the settlement, but some had always lived outside, building their houses hard by their fields, like white men. Toineeta's family was among these. Old Toineeta had a peach orchard and a field of beans and corn, and she lived alone these days, though her children and grandchildren and others from the village were frequent visitors, for the old woman's ability to heal was at least as good as Old Tobacco's and she knew a few dark things besides.

The source of Toineeta's knowledge was this: cataracts had half blinded her for close to forty years. The layers of milky glaze that looked like gristle had begun to coat her eyes when her first grandbaby was born and this condition had first given rise to and then sharpened her second sight. Through the deep, white fog through which she must ever peer, she could discern shapes that others could not and movement of things unseen. For example, she had long been aware of He Grows Up Wild, who sometimes streaked through her bean field, baying like a dog. So she was curious about the little, mostly white child whom her grandson Inadunai, or Going Snake, brought to her door to beg bean bread or to her orchard to steal peaches. He trailed a mystery behind him like a comet drags its tail across the sky.

"I want to see your mother, boy," she told George one day. "Send her to me. Tell her that I have special medicines for her. And a story."

So early one morning, during the Harvest Moon, when Young Squirrel was down in Charleston on a trading trip and due back any day, Nancy, guided by Georgie and Going Snake and accompanied by the dog Willy, made her way up the tangled path that forms the bank of Madcap Branch to Toineeta's far cabin. Nancy's house was in order, the cow was milked and the chickens fed and the corn husks laid out in the sun to dry for bedding and she had nothing pressing to do. Besides, she had learned from her mother that an offer of medicine from a woman wise in such matters should never be passed up. Where there is medicine, there is often magic, and there was no telling when a body might need either cure or curse.

The air was fresh and chill. The dew hung from the waxy leaves of the mountain laurel that overhung the path in beads as viscous and darkly glowing as droplets of mercury. Overhead, high, white clouds sailed on a blue sky like schooners grazing the surface of a glassy sea.

Toineeta waited for them out beyond the cabin by the bean field. She sat on a log rolled there for that purpose. Between toothless gums, she clenched a corncob pipe, snorting the acrid smoke out through her nostrils. She was hump-backed with age, tiny, and the eyes that stared straight ahead as though they actually saw something were as slick as marbles and streaked with milky white.

Gingerly Georgie reached over and lifted the old woman's limp hand from her lap. He guided it over to his mother's arm and let the fingers brush against her skin. Then he let it go. Toineeta did not drop her hand. Instead her fingers encircled Nancy's arm.

"Don't you think I can hear you coming?" she asked Georgie. "Come winter, I can hear a squirrel piss in the snow a way up there on that Knob!" She pointed in the direction of Fox Knob. "Now, go play with my grandson. As for you," she said to Nancy, squeezing her arm before releasing it and patting the log beside her, "sit you down."

"My name is Nancy Butler," Nancy told her. "I've come for the medicines. That is . . . Georgie told me . . . ."

"I know what you come for," Toineeta told her. "I'll get them for you by and by. In the meantime, sit you down."

Reluctantly, Nancy sat beside her on the log. She felt uneasy. The old woman frightened her, with her white eyes and abrupt manner.

Toineeta sucked on her pipe for a moment, then, "You're not from this village?"

"No."

"I take it you are the wife of Young Squirrel?"

"I am his kinswoman," Nancy said carefully. She herself was unclear about the nature of their kinship, Young Squirrel having always proved somewhat vague on this point.

"Um." Toineeta, too, was noncommittal. "Let me tell you a story, Young Squirrel's kinswoman. It is an old story . . . ." She seemed to sense the younger woman's impatience. "Don't worry, Nancy." She waved her pipe in front of her and beamed with her toothless gums. "It is not a long story." Clearing her throat, she began. "A widow had but one daughter. *Yu*, she had no son and this was very hard on the widow, for a man is good for sharing the work and she was an old woman with a bad back and such a bad hip that she limped when she walked. For this reason she was always after her daughter, saying, 'We need a man in this family, someone who can hunt and help in the field when my back is hurting me, and it is your job, daughter, to find one for us.'

"One day a young man came courting. He was a very peculiar-looking man, with a long, beaked nose and strange bright eyes, but still he was a man. The daughter, being a dutiful child, told the young man, 'I can only marry you if you are a good worker, because my mother is much in need of help.' The young man assured her that he was a very good worker, and so they were married.

"The morning after their wedding, the widow gave her new son-in-law a hoe, sent him out to the cornfield and returned to the cabin to make breakfast. When it was ready, she went out to call the son-in-law, but he was nowhere to be found. She saw a small circle of hoed ground but that was all. Away in a thicket she could hear a huhu calling.

"Do you know what a huhu sounds like, Nancy?"

"A huhu?"

"Like anything it cares to mimic," Toineeta told her. "It is like the mocking bird in this respect. It is a deceiver."

Oh, the cuckoo, she's a pretty bird . . . .

The words to the old song blew through Nancy's thoughts like a dry leaf.

Toineeta continued her story. "The son-in-law did not come in for breakfast and he did not come in for dinner. When he returned home in the evening, the old woman asked, 'And where might you have been all the day long?'

"He replied, 'Hard at work.'

"'Well, why didn't I see you when I came to call you to breakfast?'

"'Oh,' said the young man, 'most likely I was down in yonder thicket, cutting the sticks I need to mark off the new field.'

"'A man must eat,' observed the old woman. 'Yet you did not come in for dinner either.'

"'I was too busy working,' the young man told her.

"'You see what a good worker he is! Truly he is a fine husband for me!' exclaimed the daughter, who had fallen much in love with the beak-nosed man and had thought of nothing but his return all day.

"So that was the end of it. They had their supper, but the old woman remained uneasy.

"The son-in-law started off early the next morning with his hoe over his shoulder, bound . . . or so he said . . . for the corn field. Once again the old woman went to call him to breakfast and once again she found no sign of him, only the hoe on the ground and the field un-hoed. She did notice, however, a huhu. Over in the thicket, it called, 'Sau-h! sau-h! sau-h! hu! hu! hu! hu! hu! hu! chi! chi! chi! – whew!'

"'Humph!' said the old woman and returned to the house.

"That night, when at long last her son-in-law sauntered through the door, she asked him, 'Just where were you all day long when you were supposed to be in the field hoeing?'

"'Do not disturb yourself, Mother-in-law,' he assured her. 'I was working hard.'

"'Leave him alone, Mother!' cried her daughter, throwing her arms about the man's neck. 'My dear husband is tired from all his labor.'

"'Hah!' snorted the widow. 'I came after your husband and he was nowhere in sight, no, nor any work done. My back and my hip may be bad, but these old eyes can still see.'

"Then it was clear that the young man felt uncomfortable. He shuffled his feet and glanced away. 'I was just over in the thicket, visiting my kinsfolk,' he said in a low voice.

"The old woman looked at him sharply. 'The thicket?' she demanded. 'There's nothing lives in the thicket but huhus.'

"At that, the son-in-law hung his head, and she saw for the first time that he had no ears but only holes in his skull where, were he a man, ears might be. She also saw that his skin was as prickly as a pullet's. In fact, he was no man at all but a huhu who had seen the daughter from the thicket, fallen in love with her and mimicked a man's form in order to win her. 'That's it!' declared the old woman. 'I want a man for my daughter and not a lazy huhu. Out with you!'

"With no more ado – for it is bad luck to have birds in the house – the widow drove the deceiving huhu from her door with a twig broom, while her daughter screamed and wept and tried to wrestle the broom from her mother and stamped her feet when she couldn't, for her mother was stronger than she appeared."

Toineeta turned her gristly, unseeing gaze in Nancy's direction. "That is the end of the story."

"What happened to the daughter?"

"That's another story."

A silence descended between the two women, like a cloud settling between mountains. Toineeta re-lit her pipe and puffed quietly away on it. Nancy picked burrs out of her dress. Then, after a bit, Nancy asked, "Why did you tell me that story?"

"So that you might know that all is not what it may seem."

Toineeta gave Nancy three medicines and explained their uses. "A poultice made by withering single daisies on a hot shovel and then bruising them . . . . To strengthen your eyes so that you might see more clearly. A decoction of sage, rosemary, thyme, lavender, chamomile flowers and meliot stewed in red wine. To strengthen your legs and feet, for the journey ahead is a long one. An infusion steeped in white wine of the sawdust made from a pitch pine knot and the pulverized tops of vervine and agrimony. To strengthen your heart so that you might have resolve."

Nancy thanked Toineeta for her trouble and her gifts and was just standing to leave when the old woman waved her hand absently in the air and said to the bean field, "By the way, Nancy Kinnahan Butler, I think I knew your grandfather. Yes, I'm sure of it. He lived in Qualla long ago. Did you know that? And died here. There is something of him in you, I think. Yes, the two of you displace light in a similar way."

Old women, like the biggest trees in the forest, seem to have been around forever. Was there any time when they were not? Yet, in a year no one can remember, including Toineeta, this hump-backed old woman sitting on a log up on Madcap Branch, puffing on a corncob pipe, was the most tender of girls and, later, in another year, a pliant woman bending before every wind. But that was long ago and long forgotten and Toineeta occupied this place on the hillside like an old tree whose extended roots spread deep and wide. Her great wisdom, accumulated slowly over time and made up of facts and observations, experience and connections, girded the tender, vibrant core within like hard, woody rings gird the green, living interior of a tree. It kept her safe and strong.

TWELVE

Nancy returned to Young Squirrel's cabin perturbed. She did not hasten to the house immediately, but sent the boy and Willy ahead to see if Young Squirrel had, by some chance, returned earlier than expected. Certainly he was due home shortly. For some reason that she could ill define, she did not wish to see her kinsman just yet. Instead, she sat on a fallen tree and waited impatiently and full of dread for Georgie's return.

Unbeknown to her, He Grows Up Wild kept her company on the fallen tree. She could not see him, but she felt his presence. It was not the first time that she had experienced the urgent restlessness that was the affect of her kinsman's strange brother, but she had always thought that this troubling disquietude arose from her own heavy melancholy and not from without.

Her conundrum was this: How could her grandfather have been from Qualla?

The question had not occurred to her until after she had left the old woman's cabin far behind; then it had struck her with great force. Young Squirrel had said Tsikiki was from Kithuwah. Had he lied? Had Tsikiki been from Qualla instead? Then why would he have told her she was from Kithuwah?

It became dusk and still Georgie had not returned. Sighing, restless and chilled, concerned that the boy had not come when he had been told to, Nancy took her leave of the forest and returned with trepidation to the cabin. No matter how much time had passed since the massacre of her family, she could not help but think, every time she returned home alone, of the bloody scene that had awaited her at her father's homestead that hot day in July when she had found her people murdered.

However, there were no signs of mayhem about her kinsman's house. All was still and quiet, but not as it had been on the day of the massacre, a silence laid thick over screams, just ordinary. Chickens wandered haphazardly about in the twilight, picking at corn kernels, big pigs jostled one another, peering speculatively into an as yet empty trough, the milk cow lowed from her crib – it was a sound that bespoke indifferent contentedness rather than pain. As Nancy passed the shed where Young Squirrel stabled his horse, she noted that the roan mare was not in her stall and breathed out her caught-up breath with relief. Her kinsman was not yet home . . . but where had Georgie gotten to?

She rounded the corner to the house. There, on the porch, she saw Georgie sitting on the twig rocker. Willy lay at his feet. She could see that the boy was holding something. At first glance, she thought it might be a very small lantern, perhaps three inches long. However, the glow flashed by the strange object was not the yellow light typical of a lantern but a kind of harsh yellow green, like the color of lightning. Both boy and dog were staring so raptly at the object that it was only when she stepped closer and cried, "Georgie!" that her son looked up and the dog jumped to its feet and, leaping off the porch, ran, barking with joy, towards her.

"Mama!" Georgie exclaimed. Then, standing and holding out the object to her, he said in a hushed voice, "Look what Willy and I have found under our kinsman's bed."

✍

Nancy made the boy a supper of ramps and hominy, fried up with some back bacon. As she was putting him to bed, she took the stone from his hands – for that was what it appeared to be, a spar of quartz, a rough crystal – and laid it on the table beside the bed.

"It is an ulunsuti," Georgie told her excitedly, "a transparent. It is the crystal that sits in the forehead of a river monster called the uktena.

Toineeta told me and Going Snake all about it . . . . It knows the future, Mother. It can make rain, and the hunter who owns it always brings home game." The boy's hands seemed to Nancy unusually cold, as though he had been holding something frozen.

"There, there." She chafed his hands between her own warm ones to dispel the chill. "I will keep this strange stone for you and think of what we must do." She tucked the transparent into her apron pocket and, taking up the lantern, for it was quite dark by now, she walked out onto the porch. Setting the lantern down beside the twig rocker, she dropped down the steps which led to the door yard and, looking up, surveyed the black vault of sky.

No, she thought. Even if Young Squirrel were in the region, he was unlikely to return tonight. There was no moon and the route over hill was made treacherous by night goers and other spirits besides – for who knew what life-forms these woods held beyond those one could see. No, she thought, Young Squirrel would not catch her with his treasure tonight. Returning to the porch, Nancy sank wearily down into the twig rocker and took the crystal from her apron pocket. The dog had followed her outside. Now it flopped its soft body at her feet, sighing.

To be sure, this was no ordinary stone. The boy had called it an ulunsuti; he spoke of a river monster. Nancy thought that she had heard of such a crystal, such a monster once before . . . from her mother. However, that was many years ago, when she was a small child, and then her father had come along and said, "Stop telling the girl rubbish, Katy. You and I know there was never such a thing as a magic crystal." Nancy held the stone before her eyes. Yet, magic it must be. Why else would it flash so? And what was that vein of ruby red that pulsed within like a heart encased in ice?

Suddenly the dog's ears pricked up and it started to its feet. A second later, it began to bark frantically.

"Willy!" Nancy spoke sharply, for the dog had frightened her. "What's gotten into you? There's no one here."

It was then that she heard the voice . . . if voice it could be called. It was more like the wind than a voice, toneless, breathlessly sibilant, like the dry flowing of a snake through leaves. "Hello, Sister," it said. "I see you've found the transparent."

THIRTEEN

Nancy thought, *Am I going mad that I seem to hear words and a voice speaking to me?* She stood, holding the ulunsuti aloft. Its green and almost queasy light illuminated the far end of the porch and the tangle of mountain laurel beyond.

There, standing beneath the arched boughs of laurel, was He Grows Up Wild.

Nancy stared in disbelief. She took a tentative step forward.

Certainly she saw something that resembled a man in shape . . . but what was it? A reddish swirl of tattered vapor, facial features a smear . . . .

It is a night gore, she thought. *A misplaced spirit.*

In terror she drew back, her hand at her throat. She was just turning to flee when the creature spoke again.

"I was wondering when you'd find it," the apparition continued conversationally. "I would have thought you'd found it long ago. I must say, you've taken a long time. Years."

Nancy turned back. For a moment she said nothing, then she whispered, "The boy found it."

"The boy is more inquisitive than you." It hauled something vaporous resembling a leg onto the porch, using two misty hands.

Nancy gasped.

"What?" The creature looked over towards her and laughed. "Don't tell me that you are afraid of your own brother?"

"Are you . . . are you George Junior or Abel?" Nancy asked tentatively. "I do not recognize you, Brother, now that you have passed over."

"No, not George nor Abel either. I am yet another brother, one you do not yet know about. And you have another still."

"I do not understand. Who are you?"

"He Grows Up Wild is what I am called. I was born of the blood of animals our mother washed in the river, and I exist because Young Squirrel sees me. Yes, and several others. Old Tobacco, for one, and your good friend Toineeta .... Lately it seems I can't turn around but there's that old woman, staring at me." He laughed and shook his vaporous head. "And now you. You see me because you hold the ulunsuti. It was pried from the forehead of an uktena by a raven, you know, and found by our mother's great-grandfather. Its magic is very great."

He stepped up onto the porch. It seemed an effort. He held his hands out from his sides as if uncertain of his balance.

Nancy shook her head. "I don't understand. I can barely make you out. What do you mean, 'born of blood?' Are you a ghost?"

He Grows Up Wild riddled her: "I am both dead and alive. Sometimes I am more dead than alive and, other times, more alive than dead. Now, for example – yes! – is one of those times."

"When you are more alive than dead?"

"Yesssss," he hissed.

"You said 'our mother.' Who are you talking about?"

"Well, Tsikiki, of course! Or Katy, as you would have known her. As the white man called her." He Grows Up Wild swayed and then toppled off to one side, grabbing hold of a post in an effort to remain upright. "This bad leg of mine!" he said by way of explanation. "I'm talking about our wayward mother, of course. Yours and mine and Young Squirrel's."

"My mother was the mother of Young Squirrel?"

"Of course!"

"I don't understand .... Young Squirrel is my brother?"

"Your half-brother. As I am. Do not forget me!" The creature seemed put out. Its smear of features took on a cast that appeared both aggrieved and hurt. "Of course, you might also say that, as well as being your half-brothers, Young Squirrel and I are also your uncles. For you see, our father was Dayunisi, the father of your mother. Of course, for many years, Young Squirrel and I believed our father to be an old hunter whom we murdered. I am speaking of your mother's first husband, He Goes About."

"My mother was married to another man?"

"Married to her father *and* to He Goes About. She left them for the trader. She left Young Squirrel and myself behind as well, although I, being shy and, well . . . transparent, had not yet made myself known to Young Squirrel. That was to happen later, in the wake of her flight. We missed our mother sorely, I can tell you. Her abandonment has left scars, as you can see." He turned on his heel so that she could see the wounds carved upon his remnant of a back.

"My mother married . . . . And to her father? I don't understand, strange brother-uncle! Why hasn't Young Squirrel told me this?"

"Because he is in love with you. Yes, Nancy, he loves you as he loved our mother. It was not the love of a son for a mother . . . or perhaps it was." He Grows Up Wild shrugged. "Being all but alive I find I cannot know these things for certain. My thinking on the matter is simply this: perhaps you will marry Young Squirrel, if you do not know that he is our brother. Perhaps you will not marry him, if you do."

"But I do know," Nancy pointed out. "Now I know."

"And how do you know?"

"Why! Because you have told me!"

"And you believe me?" He Grows Up Wild shook his head. "Such an insubstantial creature as myself! How do you know I even exist?"

"Why are you telling me all this? You must have a reason."

"How is this for a reason? Young Squirrel has tried to banish me. He has tried to diminish me. I have little love for my brother and would thwart his plans if I could. There." He paused. "And do you believe that?" he asked.

"Yes," said Nancy evenly. "I can see that such an existence as yours must be is a painful one. I can see that you are composed of hatred and envy."

"And love, sweetest sister." He Grows Up Wild was wistful. "Love too."

"And love," Nancy conceded, bowing her head under the weight of this new knowledge.

> *I often have wondered*
> *What makes women love men,*
> *Then I've looked back and wondered*
> *What makes men love them.*
> *O, the cuckoo, she's a pretty bird . . . .*

The cuckoo, Nancy thought. The Deceiver.

Lifting her head, she stared into the darkness beyond the porch, but He Grows Up Wild had dissolved like blown smoke. He was not there and there and everywhere and nowhere all at once, and she realized that, from now on, wherever she went, he would follow at her heels like a repellant, but faithful dog.

Nancy took the ulunsuti to bed that night. She lay with her hands folded at her bosom. In one hand she held the ulunsuti tight; the other she folded over top of it, to keep it safe. She lay awake a long time, not thinking so much as riding internal rapids of sensation mixed with thought. At no point was she in control of either; she struggled to keep herself from capsizing, from being swept away. Partly this was due to her new knowledge; partly to the nature of the crystal. It imparted to her a kind of a strange, pulsing energy, not unlike that peculiar radiant heat experienced by women at the end of their childbearing season. She was aware that her senses were more acute, her hearing sharper, her eyesight more capable of reading shapes in the deep dark of the cabin than usual. At the same time, she perceived there to be a light ringing in her ears, as though she inhabited a cavernous place, and a gray dance to her vision that fell just short of fibrillation. Her heart was affected as well. Its slow beat was so grounded that each beat seemed to rock her body. Her blood was hot. Yet, despite the increased acuity of her senses, she also felt separated out, as distinct from her surroundings as the yolk of an egg is from the white in which it swims.

When at last Nancy fell asleep, she dreamt of a place a day's walk away, where a cabin stood in some disrepair beside a calm lake the pearl-gray color of a dove's wing. No one lived at this place, only animals. It was the most peaceful spot she had ever seen and she thought she might feel happy there.

Later, when she woke, it was to that leaden darkness that precedes the dawn and to cold and to a choking sense of isolation.

FOURTEEN

Young Squirrel returned from his trip to the coast three days later. By that time, Nancy and the boy had replaced the ulunsuti in the brittle buckskin pouch in which Georgie had found it and returned it to its hiding place underneath their kinsman's bed, below an unsecured plank of flooring.

Young Squirrel bore in the breast pocket of his coat an opal ring which he had bought in Charleston. On the night of his return, after they had eaten their supper and the boy had gone to bed, Young Squirrel showed the ring to Nancy. "This is for you," he told her.

"It is very pretty, Kinsman." Nancy trembled a little as she took the ring from him.

"It is what they call an opal. And these are rubies on the side. And this is gold. The white man who sold it to me told me that his people think opals are unlucky, because they resemble eyes blinded with cataracts."

Nancy, remembering Toineeta's white, omniscient eyes, shivered.

"I said to him, 'What is unlucky for the white man must be lucky for the Cherokee, so I will buy this ring from you.' The white man does not know that those with cataracts have special vision and can see things others can't. Besides, there is fire in this stone, Nancy. See." And he pointed out the iridescent markings of the stone.

"It is a fine ring," agreed Nancy in a faltering voice.

"Well?"

"What?"

"Aren't you going to put it on?"

"Of course." Nancy slid it onto her right ring finger.

"When white people marry, the man gives the woman a ring, like that band you wear."

Nancy glanced down at the ring finger of her left hand. She still wore the ring her white husband had given her . . . how long ago had that been? Long enough that their son was half grown. "Yes. It is the custom among the whites to exchange rings."

"It is a good custom, I think. The Cherokee man gives the woman he wants to marry the leg of a deer. Such things don't last as well as gold and sometimes are hard to find." He laughed awkwardly. "I myself am no hunter." He cleared his throat, then stood and moved over to the fire. He made as though to warm his hands before the blaze, although the night was not so cool and he was sweating from fear. What would she say when he asked her? How would she react? More troubling: how much of the truth had she managed to guess by now? They had been together for so many years now. Seven? Eight? True, she gave no sign of knowing what he was to her, but she was a quiet woman, artful perhaps. He could not tell. What did he know of women? Although he had kept her apart, she was not bound to the house. Someone might have told her something, some gossip he did not know about, and she, not wishing to jeopardize her position in this house and the boy's (for where would she go if he turned her out?) might have kept her silence so long as he stayed where he was, so long as he made no move towards her.

"So, it's come to this, has it?" A voice from the shadows to the right of the chimney. Young Squirrel glanced sharply in its direction. There squatted He Grows Up Wild, matted and filthy. "It seems that we are an inbred family. Father and daughter. Brother and sister . . . ."

"Silence!" Young Squirrel snapped.

"What?" Startled by the outburst, Nancy rose to her feet.

"Nothing. I . . . sit down, Nancy. Please. I was only . . . thinking aloud." Young Squirrel turned from the specter of his brother and, crossing to the table, sat opposite her.

He was speaking to the ghost brother, Nancy realized, sinking back into her chair, to the one born of blood. "We have lived a long time in this house, you and I," he began afresh.

"We have, Kinsman."

Young Squirrel rapped the table with his fingers. After a moment, he bowed his head. "I would like you to marry me and live here as my wife, Nancy."

Nancy inhaled sharply.

"Well. . . ? What do you say?"

"You . . . you surprise me!"

"That is what the ring means."

"Please, Young Squirrel, allow me time to consider this."

Young Squirrel raised his head to look at her. "How long must I wait?"

"Not long."

"How long?"

"When you return from Sugarlands," she said in confusion. "Then you shall have my answer."

❧

Young Squirrel journeyed to Sugarlands once a month to go over the miller's accounts. He was gone a day and a night, for it was a ride of twelve miles, and it is a difficult task to find one's way by night through the mountains, when there is no moon.

On the morning of the day that Young Squirrel saddled up his horse and left, when the boy was playing at blow guns outside, Nancy got on her hands and knees and crawled under Young Squirrel's bed. She lifted up the piece of loose flooring and removed the ulunsuti from its hiding place, hanging the buckskin pouch in which it was kept from a string around her neck. Then she threw open her cupboard doors and gathered together a bundle of clothing, both hers and the boy's, together with some food and bags of seed. She was just choosing what medicines she would need when she became by slow degrees aware of a presence other than hers inside the cabin. Turning, she saw He Grows Up Wild, crouched in his accustomed spot next to the cold chimney. "Where are you going, Sister?"

122

"I don't know what the place is called, but I have seen it in a dream," she told him. "I believe I can find it, though I don't know how."

"The place you dream of is Adagahi, Gall Place, and the ulunsuti will take you there." He Grows Up Wild sighed. "If I had hands that could grasp, I would have stolen it from my brother long ago and become real, but it is not within my power. My fingers pass through it, as if it were not solid."

"That is because you yourself are not solid," Nancy told him. "You will not tell him where I have gone, will you, Brother-uncle?"

He Grows Up Wild shrugged and dragged a nearly transparent elbow across his nose. "I cannot predict what I will do. It is my nature to be inconstant. So you must run, Sister. Run and hide. Go far away. Or near, for that place you dream of is both far away and near. Near for the approaching, far for the arriving. The transparent makes it all possible. Yes. Yes. And we shall be alone once more." He began to weep noisily.

And Nancy wept too, for she thought that she might have loved Young Squirrel well enough to marry him and be his wife, had only she not known the nature of their relationship. She wept for what could never be and for the isolation in which she would soon find herself and wished that Dragging Canoe had waited until she had returned to her father's homestead before murdering her people, seeing that this was what her life had come down to.

After a time, she dried her tears and, ignoring He Grows Up Wild's histrionic lamentations, walked onto the porch and called for the boy and the dog.

When they came, she explained that they were going on a journey – not far, but they might be gone overnight. She took one bundle, gave the boy the other and put the Bucksmasher over her shoulder (the Kentucky rifle was one of the things she had brought with her from Spring Place) and together they started out over the mountain in the direction of Gall Place.

GEORGE BUTLER

ONE

"Rattlesnake, O' rattlesnake.
What makes your teeth so white?
I've been in the bottom all my life
an' I ain't done nuthin' but bite, bite.
Ain't done nothin' but bite."

As she washed the blood from a rabbit caught in one of her son George Butler's snares, Nancy sang the old song that her daddy had taught her back in Hiwasee – young George's namesake had played a banjo tolerably well and the guitar too. How many years ago was that?

Bending forward at the waist, she dragged the skinned carcass through the cool, thick waters of Adagahi, the medicine lake. The rabbit's blood blew after it in slippery strands, like red ribbons riding a light breeze.

Going onto thirty-five it must have been. She had been just a slip of a thing at the time. And the tune had just come back to her that moment, intact and whole, as though she had heard her father sing it but the day before. Testing her powers of recall, she tried a second verse:

"Muskrat, O muskrat.
What makes you smell so bad?
I've been in the bottom all my life
till I'm mortified in my head."

Whatever did that mean – *mortified in the head?*

Smiling, for it was nothing if not a silly song, one that had made her brothers and her laugh as children and clap their hands, Nancy straightened up and uttered the requisite words out loud: "Thank you, Great One, for the gift of our brother rabbit" – the departed spirits of rabbits are among the most punctilious observers of the protocol that governs the relationship between hunter and prey; they take umbrage easily and their capacity for revenge is quite disproportionate to their size. This fact and more besides Nancy had learned over the dozen odd years since that autumn morning that she and George had fled the house of her half brother and, guided by the ulunsuti, had come over the high mountain and through the tangled, snaky bottoms to the medicine lake that lay between the headwaters of Bradley's Fork and Eagle Creek.

It was a different autumn now and close to dusk. The season was near enough summer that the day had been a warm one, full of bees and bright colors. The ground was littered with fallen leaves, their spines as brittle as the bones of insects. They crunched under her feet. Before, in Hiwasee and later at Qualla, the coming of winter would have made Nancy fearful, but at Gall Place they never wanted for the wood that meant fire or the game that meant food. Everything was plentiful here and for the taking, provided the proper observances were made.

Lifting her head and shading her eyes with her hand, Nancy gazed over Adagahi's gray, choppy surface towards the dense forest on its far side and the blue heave and swell of mountains beyond. She was looking for her son who had been away these seven days – on a hunting trip, he said. She knew, however, that George sometimes visited the village of Qualla, for occasionally he would bring her back things from Young Squirrel's store – a pewter spoon once and, on another occasion, bright blue ribbons for her long white hair. The youth's foolishness, coupled with his gallantry, had made her laugh then and shake her head as she turned away from him, for Nancy Butler was no longer a young woman interested in such trifles as ribbons and beads, but old – forty-four winters by her best figuring and, hidden away in an invisible place from which she had not once ventured in all these years, a walking ghost locked inside a sacred perimeter, which she may not leave, beyond which there is only bright chaos.

Nancy worried that someone in Qualla might recognize George and tell Young Squirrel who his youthful customer was. She worried that Young Squirrel himself might recognize the boy who had shared his home for eight years in the rough young mountain man who came trading furs and the ginseng she gathered and the pinkroot and the snakeroot or the distinctive Kentucky rifle that accompanied him everywhere he went. George carried the ulunsuti with him on his hunting trips – this was to ensure his success and also to enable him to return to her across that which divided this dream terrain from the world they had fled. She also feared that her son might be recognized and the ulunsuti stolen from him. What would happen to her in that case? Not knowing his fate, she would wait for him . . . and wait and wait. It would be like being buried alive, an eternal solitude.

George reassured her. "I was a child when I left Qualla. I am a man now. Besides, white men are flooding into the Middle Towns – more every year. To the villagers, I am just another white man, and, when I am with them, I call myself by another name – I call myself John Bliss. As for Young Squirrel, he stays in his house all the time, Mother. He has for years. No one ever sees him. They say that that he never got over your leaving, that he hates everyone and has no friend and talks sometimes to people who aren't there. They say he drinks too much and that he is always drunk. He still owns the mill and the store and the ferry. He's rich enough. I've heard that he sleeps upon a mattress stuffed with American money. He owns a tavern too, near the council house . . . . That is new these past five years. But he almost never visits his businesses. He leaves their management to other men, strangers, white men, who grow rich stealing from him. I think it is a shame."

George glanced quickly at his mother, trying to read in her face what he had never understood – why they had left Young Squirrel's house in such a hurry, taking with them only what they could carry . . . why they had lived so long in this hidden, faraway place. Unlike her,

George had no intention of remaining at Gall Place forever. He did not wish to hunt and snare and fish all his life and live alone in his great-grandfather's ramshackle old cabin with only his old mother for company. He had met a girl in Qualla and thought that she would marry him and that they would have a fine life. But for that he needed money. His kinsman Young Squirrel was the richest man in Qualla, rich enough to make George rich if the trader but knew his identity. Why should other men who shared no blood with Young Squirrel share his wealth and not George Butler? But the young man could read nothing in Nancy's impassive face; she held her secrets tight.

George also brought his mother bright calicos of red and yellow and green back from Young Squirrel's store. Nancy wore out the cold moons by quilting. After thirteen winters in Gall Place, she had many quilts – Snail Track and Cat Track, Soldiers Return, Weaver's Pleasure, True Lover's Knot and Young Lady's Perplexity were some of their names.

There was a mystery here. Nancy's Cherokee mother Tsikiki had not known how to quilt; she had been unfamiliar with European needlework. And there were no women hereabouts to show Nancy the patterns they made and handed down to their daughters or shared with the woman on the next farmstead, and the names by which they called these patterns, yet somehow Nancy knew. She just *knew*. In her mind's clear eye, she saw the quilts that other women made elsewhere; she heard the names they called them; sometimes she even dreamed quilt patterns and remembered, upon waking, how the squares fit together. She had pondered it at great length and come to the conclusion that it must have been the effect of the ulunsuti, which affected different people differently and imparted different kinds of knowledge to those who possessed it. The ulunsuti, Nancy divined, gave its owner what that person needed.

The water of Adagahi reflected a sky the color and sheen of lead. The wind was picking up and a thunderstorm was building, dark cloud upon dark cloud. Soon the Thunder Boys will play, Nancy thought, and the Red Man of Lightning. She shook her head. Once she had thought like a white woman. No longer. Living so long beside the medicine lake had leached the white from her.

And still no George. Nancy was not overly concerned. The ulunsuti would keep him safe enough. In many respects, it was like a fierce dog. Probably it was the girl who was keeping him so long. For Nancy knew that George was seeing a girl from Qualla. Oh, yes! She knew a great deal. When George was not away from Gall Place, the crystal was in her keeping and it taught her much. She wondered if her son would bring the girl to Adagahi. She would like a daughter-in-law to pass the time with. As for leaving Gall Place, the very thought of venturing outside this sacred refuge to a place where violence was random, and there were many people whom one couldn't trust, terrified her. Here, at least, she was safe from those things that cannot be foreseen.

Once again and to set the rabbit's chilled flesh, she dragged the body through the cold water, singing:

> *"Groundhog, groundhog,*
> *what makes your back so brown?*
> *It's a wonder I don't smotherfy,*
> *Living down in the ground, ground."*

She laid the rabbit's cleaned, bluish carcass in the dry grass beside the water, wiped her hands on the front of her long deerskin shirt, and, placing one hand in the hollow of her back, gave her spine a little shove. Like her father, she inclined to some stiffness in the joints, a condition that she treated with buckeye and a tea made from witch grass roots – a plant that grew abundantly in these strange parts, as did all useful plants. Still, it troubled her somewhat. Raising her voice – for she liked the sound of it, high and clear and true – she sang the next verse of the Rattlesnake Song. It is a wonderful thing, to be alone and to sing as loud as one pleases.

"Rooster, O rooster.
What makes your claws so hard?
Been scratchin' this gravel all my days.
It's a wonder I ain't tired."

There, she thought, *that's all I can remember. That must be the end of it.*

Stooping, she picked up the rabbit and was just turning towards the cabin when she heard a voice come from behind her: "Stop! There's another verse besides!" The voice was as toneless and sibilant as the wind; it might have been the wind, Nancy reckoned. But then it sang in a high-pitched shriek, very rapidly:

"Jaybird, O jaybird.
What makes you fly so high?
Been robbin' your corn patch all my life,
It's a wonder I don't die, die."

Willy the spaniel staggered through the half-opened door of the cabin. He squinted in the direction of the lake for a moment with his bleary eyes and then began to bark as frantically as his great age and decrepit condition would allow; he tottered with the effort. (Creatures lived beyond their normal span at Gall Place and each time Willy had fallen ill, Nancy, who could not bear the thought of losing her beloved pet, had washed him tenderly in the cool and healing waters of the lake and so preserved his life.)

With a leaden feeling of fear, Nancy turned slowly around.

About ten feet from shore, in water up to its waist, stood, or rather lingered, suspended, a vaporous, shifting form painted red by and dripping with the blood she had washed from the rabbit. Through it she could just make out the opposite shoreline.

TWO

"He Grows Up Wild," said Nancy flatly. She had not seen Young Squirrel's peculiar blood brother since the night George had discovered the ulunsuti and the specter had told her that she and Young Squirrel were children of the same mother. "What are you doing at Adagahi?"

"Are you not glad to see me?" He Grows Up Wild wafted towards her, extending phantom hands. "Ah, Nancy! You have not said so."

"Willy, be quiet!" Nancy ordered the dog, whose barking had disintegrated to soft yelping. Exhausted by the effort, the dog lay down on the lintel again, as if grateful that it might still possess the wherewithal to discharge its duty and relieved to be done of it.

"You have no business here," Nancy told the apparition. "You are Young Squirrel's problem, not mine. Go away." Turning her back on him, she started once more for the cabin, walking swiftly this time.

"But it is about Young Squirrel that I come," He Grows Up Wild called after her. "Sister! My errand is serious."

Nancy halted.

"There! Good! Stay where you are." He Grows Up Wild clambered onto shore with some difficulty. The points at which his nebulous limbs joined his spurious body were slowly dissolving and he was at some pains these days to coordinate their efforts or even to keep them coupled. "I am coming apart and water is more difficult to pass through than air for me," he explained. "It drags more." After a moment, in which he realigned and reconnected the confused parts of himself, he observed, "I could not help but notice that you still wear my brother's ring."

Nancy turned to face him. With the index finger of her left hand she touched the opal in its gold and ruby setting. "And why not? It is a pretty ring and Young Squirrel bought it for me. I still wear my wedding band and Charley has been dead these many long years."

"Ah, yes, well . . . . But you were married to Charley."

Nancy flushed. In truth she did not know what her feelings for Young Squirrel had been, or even what they were at present. When he had plucked her from the Zants in Spring Place so soon after the murder of her family and her husband, she had been like one who only appears to live. The years in which they shared a roof she remembers as lonely ones, yet, over the course of those years, she had begun once more to live. Fire will leap from one branch in the forest to another when the woods are dry and the season has been one without rain. So too will love. Learning of Young Squirrel's affection, Nancy felt that she might have come to return it, at least in part, given time. She was loving by disposition and saw that her kinsman was a kindly man, deserving of at least as that measure of happiness that befalls most men in their lifetimes. However, she had learned of his love for her in the same breath that she learned what he was to her. For this she was at once grateful to He Grows Up Wild and resentful. In her confusion and, yes, for this is how she named her purpose in her heart, her cowardice, she had fled, had come to this magic place. Now she was old and much altered. She hung her head. "Whatever it is you seek, He Grows Up Wild, I cannot help you."

"On the contrary. Only you can help me, for you see, Young Squirrel is turning blue."

"What?"

"The spirit of the North is blue. Blue means defeat. Trouble. Turning blue is a very bad thing."

"What has that got to do with me?"

"Don't you see? If he does not stop turning blue, he will turn black. The spirit of the West is Black. Black means death. Young Squirrel is dying, Sister. Every day he is dying more."

Nancy flinched. Then she shrugged, half turning away. "Everyone must die."

"It is before his time."

"How do you know? Young Squirrel is not young."

"Not young, but not old either. It is the white man's whiskey that has done this . . . ." His expression turned cunning. "And the loss of the ulunsuti. I know you have it, Sister. Give it back."

Nancy stiffened. "It has passed on. It is the nature of the ulunsuti that it changes hands. It was mine to take but it is no longer mine to give back. It is Georgie's now. Besides, how has our brother become a drunkard? He never used to drink whiskey. He said a Cherokee could not afford to be at a disadvantage."

"The ulunsuti made him strong. Now it makes you strong. Without it, Young Squirrel has grown weak and now blue. He lies in bed all day, Sister. He will not rise. He says he will be glad to die if it will mean that he is rid of me for well and good."

"I will not give the ulunsuti back. I cannot." She could not imagine being without its power. She was accustomed to seeing much; how could she accept limitations on her vision? It was bad enough Georgie being gone these seven days. Already she felt light-headed and a little queasy.

"Come and see him then." It was clear from the Wild Boy's expression that he despaired. "He speaks of you often, Sister. He cannot hurt you now."

"No!" Turning her back on He Grows Up Wild, she started to walk away from him again. Then she stopped. "I cannot leave here," she said, as if realizing this for the first time. "I couldn't if I wanted to. Don't you see? I am not . . . capable of it."

"Your Grandfather Dayunisi traveled where he wished. Your boy walks in and out of here at will."

"What?" She was surprised that he should know this of Georgie.

He Grows Up Wild barked in sharp laughter. "Oh yes, Nancy, I see him in Qualla half a dozen times a year. He calls himself by another name, but I know he is George Butler. He courts the daughter of Tsinawi, a girl called Tuti, Snowbird. Soon he will make you leave Adagahi, or you shall have to live alone in this lonely place with only an old dog for company – and I warn you, the dog will die too, one day."

"How do you know all this?"

"To the eye that does not see, I am invisible. And I've nothing to do all day long. I track human beings for pleasure, like an idle dog left to its own devices. Besides, it is in my best interest to know where you and he are and how you fare."

Nancy considered this. "I thought you hated your brother, He Grows Up Wild. Why do you seek to assist him now?"

At this He Grows Up Wild tore at the remnants of the long, tangled stuff that seemed to emanate from his head like hair, but which more closely resembled the sort of weeds that tangle at the bottom of ponds. Lifting his face to the heavens, he howled like a wolf. The sound was so loud and so dismal as to be alarming.

"Stop! Stop!" Nancy covered her ears. She would have shaken him, had there been anything to shake.

"Don't you see?" Bloody tears coursed down the apparition's face. He wrung vaporous wisps of hands. "If Young Squirrel dies, I fear I die too."

"Why should that be?"

"I am . . . connected to him somehow. How, I don't know, but I feel it, Sister. I have always felt it. Young Squirrel turns his face towards death and, as his head turns, so does mine. It is as if our chins are joined by some invisible thread thought I cannot break, though I would wish it. He is like the man who, drowning, becomes stronger than he was before and throws his arms around the neck of his rescuer with such vigor that, together, they are drawn down into the watery vortex. We are like those brothers who are sometimes born joined together. If they are cut apart, one dies, perhaps both. If one dies, the other dies of fright. I do not want to die, Sister."

"Every man must go to the Darkening Land, where he might meet relatives who have gone before or other ones from his village," Nancy reminded him. "I have often longed to go there . . . to see my mother and my dear Charley."

"It is different with you," He Grows Up Wild said sullenly. "What is may die and be again as a spirit with those others of his tribe. What is already spirit may die and become . . . what? Perhaps nothing! I cannot be nothing, Sister!"

But Nancy had grown weary of this interchange with the wind. "As far as I am concerned, you are nothing now! And there is nothing I can do for you or for Young Squirrel." She started once more for the cabin.

"There is wrong to be righted!" He Grows Up Wild pleaded. "Justice to be served. Young Squirrel has had neither friend nor wife, but lived alone and to himself, and, when he fell in love with you and took you away from a place where you were not wanted and put a roof over your head and over the head of another man's son, you took the source of his strength from him and fled from him to this place."

"I am his sister!" Nancy objected. "My son is his nephew! He wanted to make his sister his wife!"

He Grows Up Wild brushed her objection away with a disdainful gesture. "Eh! And now our poor brother poisons himself with the white man's whiskey and, little by little, the men who work for him rob him and grow rich on the crime. You did this to him, Nancy. You . . . and . . . our . . . mother . . . ."

But He Grows Up Wild had begun to dissipate, like the fog that sleeps the night away in the deep clefts of the mountain valleys – this is the fog which the sun eats upon rising. As he disintegrated, he sang the last verse of the Rattlesnake Song once more. It was the ranting of a lunatic:

> "*Jaybird, O jaybird.*
> *What makes you fly so high?*
> *Been robbin' your corn patch all my life,*
> *It's a wonder I don't die, die.*"

The words *die, die* were barely audible. The lips that uttered them were no longer there.

THREE

George Butler did not return to Adagahi that night.

Or the next.

Or the next.

He was gone all that long, long winter of 1808 . . . or was it 1807? Or 1809? Time passed differently in Gall Place than elsewhere. It passed as dreams do; it was as interminable as a dream and as swift. That is because the coil that is time begins its spiral in Adagahi. Adagahi is the navel of time, the source, and the river is always different at its source than it is downstream. The present at Adagahi was like a whirlpool, a hole in the river, which sucks in the past and spins out the future until there is no telling which is which, until there is only the swift rush and the heady circling of the now.

Nancy did not worry about George while he was gone. She knew full well where he was, who he was with. He was in Qualla, with the girl He Grows Up Wild had called Snowbird, and, in time, he would return. She did what she always did in winter. She quilted. The winter that she was alone, she made three quilts, start to finish. Now, that was something. Blazing Star was the name of one and Flower of the Mountain . . . and another besides.

The worst thing was growing accustomed to not having the ulun-suti nearby. Although she had recognized that the crystal charged the air in a certain way and had, over time, an effect upon moods, sensations and perceptions, she had not recognized the extent to which it had affected her. In the weeks following George's departure, Nancy felt light-headed and unsteady, she experienced sudden attacks of vertigo, her hands trembled and there was a faint ringing in her ears which distorted her hearing and made her head ache. At length these symptoms subsided, but the process had affected her like an illness would – it left

her weaker, diminished. At night she piled her bed high with quilts –
she was always cold now – and laid down next to a half-dead bag-of-
bones dog to dream her solitary dreams.

෴

One night in mid-March of that same year, when the green ice was
all broken up on the lake, and here and there a shoot of something
living poked up through the red clay earth and great flocks of honk-
ing geese filled the sky over head, flying in formations which looked
like the head of an arrow shot north, Nancy dreamt an uktena's
dream. That she should do so was not unusual. Ever since the ulunsuti
had come into her possession, she had dreamt many uktena dreams,
and this was to be expected – an uktena's ulunsuti, set as it is in the
monster's forehead, is the place where its dreams are stored and whence
they issue. At first these dreams had frightened her, for they were dark
and terrible, the dreams of an angry creature. But gradually, she had
become accustomed to them, to the point that she often failed to distinguish between her own dreams and those of the huge snake from
which the crystal had come. Her son and she had not spoken of this
– there were many things Nancy and George did not discuss – but she
knew that he sometimes dreamed the uktena's dreams too. She had
heard him cry in his sleep before and swear and thrash; he thrashed
like a snake. She thought that Young Squirrel must also dream these
dreams. (Once a person has dreamed a snake's dream, it is difficult to
stop.)

What was different about this particular dream was that it did not
issue from the monster slain by the Groundhog's Mother in the Cohuttas, but from a different uktena altogether – whether from the uktena
of Nantahala or Citico or the Tallulah or from some unknown uktena
she could not say. Perhaps all uktenas communicate with each other
through dreams; surely it is not impossible that such solitary creatures as
these, despised and feared, might in this way seek each other out. In any

136

case, her dream was of how this uktena had ceased to be a boy and become a monster and it went like this:

There was a boy who used to go hunting birds every day. All the birds he caught he gave to his mother. She was fonder of him than she was of her other son, for he was her firstborn and her favorite for more reasons besides. This made her second son and also her husband very jealous and they, in turn, so mistreated the favorite son, that, one day, he swore to his mother that he would run away from home, but that she should not mourn him.

The next morning he refused to eat any breakfast, but went off to the woods, hungry. When he returned home, he brought with him a pair of deer horns and went directly to the hothouse, where his anxious mother was waiting. He told her that he must be alone that night, so she got up and went into the house, where the rest of the family was eating supper.

At daybreak the mother went once more to the hothouse and there she saw an immense uktena instead of her boy, so big that it filled the entire hothouse. It had horns on its head and an ulunsuti blazed in the middle of its forehead, but, as yet, its snake tail had not developed. Instead it retained two human legs on the feet of which were the moccasins that she herself had beaded, using sea shells bought from the coastal Indians. These legs and feet were all that was left of her son; the rest had changed into an uktena. The monster spoke to her in a voice, which sounded like her son's, but was, at the same time, not quite human and told her to leave him. Frightened, horrified and grieving, she obeyed.

When the sun was well advanced in its trip across the sky, the uktena began to wriggle out of the hothouse, forcing its huge body through the little door, inch by slow, painful inch. This was no easy matter. In fact, it was such a tight squeeze that it was noon before the monster managed to force itself all the way out.

And all the time it was squeezing through the door, it was making a terrible hissing sound of displeasure so that everyone who heard it, except for the mother, fled in fear of their lives. As for the mother, she stood a little distance away and wept and wrung her hands, crying, "Oh, my son! My poor son!"

Once free of the hothouse, the new uktena reared up on its two little boy legs and proceeded to stagger through the village like a human boy carrying a rolled up carpet that is too heavy and unwieldy for him to manage. On its trek, the uktena pitched from side to side and occasionally toppled over, landing with a loud crash on looms, which the women of the village had set out in front of their houses so they might weave at the same time as they gossiped with their neighbors, or the poles on which they had set hides to stretching and the pots in which they simmered their stews of squirrel and groundhog.

As for the people of the village, they wisely hid inside their houses while the snake made its riotous departure.

Finally the uktena reached the Oconaluftee, shook the beaded moccasins off its boy feet and dove into the river. As its body broke the surface of the water, the legs, which were all that remained of the boy, snapped off. They were found later downstream by people who wondered what they were and where they had come from. These people saved the boy's severed legs for several days and then buried them.

The poor mother picked up the moccasins and took them home. She grieved for her boy, even though he had told her not to, and would not give either her second son or her husband the moccasins, which were very fine. This made them extremely angry.

"If you think so much of that good-for-nothing son of yours, why don't you go stay with him?" they asked.

So that is exactly what she did. One morning, a short while after her eldest son had turned into a snake, the mother walked through the village to the place where the uktena had entered the water. She did not hesitate, but walked directly into the river, just as though it were not water but dry land, and disappeared. She had gone to join her son, of course.

She took the moccasins with her so that neither her husband nor her second son might have them. As she sank to the bottom of the river, the moccasins became snakes and, breaking free of her, swam away. This is how there came to be water moccasins swimming in the river.

FOUR

Nancy was outside, soaking walnut shells for dye and skinning corn when she heard a gun shot and looked up to see George on the far side of the medicine lake, hoisting the Bucksmasher in greeting. She straightened up and raised her arm above her head in reply; at this distance, he would not hear her cry. She stood thus, with her arm stretched over her head, until the canoe he and she had burnt out of a tree with live coals years ago was halfway across the lake. Then she cried, "George!"

"Mother!" he called back and waved his hand.

From where Nancy stood, she could just make out the buckskin pouch that hung from a piece of sinew around her son's neck. Already she could feel the ulunsuti's warmth, its tug; it came to her from across the water like a hot wind.

✑

"You didn't want for anything," he asked later, after she had made him supper of ash cake and gritted bread.

"Company," she told him. She was making lye. "Give me the lye bowl."

He handed her a bowl – it was a special bowl, with a hole in the bottom.

"My traps . . . . You knew where they were?"

"I ate rabbit all winter. Squirrel too. Groundhog once." Carefully she spooned ashes from the hearth into the bowl. She had been burning hemlock and maple – hardwood. Hardwood made for the best lye ashes.

"I'm sorry I was gone so long, Mother."

"No matter. Hand me the gourd." She was thinking that he looked different. Older. More like a man now than a boy. It was what came of having a woman. And how old was he now, anyway? Twenty-two? Twenty-three?

George handed her a hollow gourd. She balanced it below the bowl; despite the gourd's relatively flat bottom, this was a tricky job.

"One thing had led to another, and suddenly there was all this snow . . . ."

"I know. There was snow here too." Taking a skin of water, she dribbled it over the ashes – slowly, for she did not want to tip over the gourd, which was intended to catch the lye drippings. "There!" she said when she was finished; she stepped back and wiped her hands on her shirt. "We'll let that sit for a piece." Her heart was big with the pain; there was scarce room left for breathing. George was working up to something. She knew it, and she knew what it would be. The uktena's dream had taught her that.

"Mother, I have something to tell you."

Nancy sighed, smiled. She shook her head. "I know you do."

"I have a wife."

"I know. See?" She went to the cedar chest at the foot of her bed and extracted a quilt. She unfolded it for George to admire. "I have made this quilt for my daughter-in-law. It is called Steps to the Altar."

George examined the quilt, which was executed in neat, small patches of white and green cloth. "It is a beautiful quilt. Snowbird will like it." He paused. "Mother."

"Yes?"

"There is something more."

"What is it, Georgie?"

Taking her by the arm, George turned her towards him. "Listen to me, Mother. Soon I will have a son. A son or a daughter. Well, before the Green Corn."

"A grandchild. That is good!" She knew what he was going to say next. She did not want to hear it. It was the last thing she wanted to hear.

"I've come to fetch you back, Mother."

"Oh, Georgie . . . ."

"No," he said firmly. "I have thought about it. We have hidden away long enough. Now we must return to Qualla."

"But Young Squirrel . . . ."

"Young Squirrel is a sick, old man," said George firmly. "I don't understand why we had to run away in the first place . . . what he did to drive you from him, but I am a man now. I will protect you."

"What happened was long ago and is of little consequence," Nancy said, realizing, as she spoke, that this was so. "Or so it now seems," she said, marveling at the change.

"What is Young Squirrel to us? I have often wondered, Mother."

"Your grandmother Tsikiki was mother to us both." Nancy sank down into a chair. What difference did it make now? Why keep the nature of her and Young Squirrel's bond a secret any longer? "He is my brother and your uncle."

"Your brother! My uncle! All the more reason to reconcile ourselves with him! He is a rich man and we are his only kin. I don't have it in me to be a farmer and I already have a wife to support and soon a child." He knelt before his mother and took her hands in his. "Say you'll come with me, Mother. "

Nancy squeezed his hands tightly and glanced away towards the fire that burned on the hearth. She knew that in the end she would agree, that she, like the mother of the boy who became the uktena, would follow him into the world that he had chosen, for he was her good boy, her child, all that remained to her. "But I am so frightened."

"Mother! Mother!" George reassured her. "It is just the world."

FIVE

On a morning in mid-April, 1809, George announced to Nancy, "We must pack our things, now. It is time to go."

Over the month since his return to Gall Place, he had gathered many pelts – enough to fetch a good price at the trading post and satisfy his new wife and his father-in-law that his absence had been a profitable one.

The cold winter had made for a cool spring. Despite the advanced season, snow still capped Beck's Bald. Looking south from Adagahi, Nancy could just make out the mountain's white knob. She was worried. Willy was so old – twenty-four that Spring and as frail as a hundred-year-old granny who has shrunk to half the size she was in her prime, yet still her heart beats and there is life in her eyes. Would the little dog be able to survive the journey from Gall Place to Qualla?

After packing what she and George would take with them, she wrapped the old dog in one of her favorite quilts, the one she kept always on her own bed. Roses and Pinies in the Wilderness was its name and it was a pretty piece of stitching.

"What are you doing?" George asked her.

"I am carrying Willy."

"He has legs," objected George. "There are other things to carry."

"Then the horse must carry them," said Nancy firmly. On this point she would not budge.

On the journey across Adagahi and through the mountain passes into the tangled bottoms, Nancy cradled the little dog tenderly in her arms, as though he were a sickly child that had not grown. He felt as hollow-boned as a bird and his breathing was so shallow that she could scarcely feel his brittle ribcage through the cloth and batting of the quilt when he breathed in and out.

Then she became distracted by the effort required to walk away from Gall Place. Adagahi was possessed of a force akin to gravity that so tugged at her that, for much of that first morning, she felt as though she were walking into a strong headwind that only diminished with distance. Having never before left the medicine lake, she had not been prepared for this.

"Didn't I tell you?" George asked her offhandedly when she spoke of it. "I am quite used to it now."

In the bush beside the trail, she noted traces of fresh blood and paw prints headed in the opposite direction from that in which they traveled. Once they crossed paths with a wounded deer whose punctured side leaked blood and who, with stunned eyes, sought the lake's healing waters. As her pelt was ruined, George did not shoot her, but let her stumble on in the direction of Adagahi. "It's a pity, that," he said. "Her pelt would have fetched a good price."

Then, towards noon, when the walking had become somewhat easier and George and she were coming down along Bradley Creek, Nancy began to be apprehensive about Willy. Her burden seemed even lighter than before, as if, with every step she had taken away from the medicine lake, more of Willy's small store of life had drained from him.

Finally, when they came to the place where Bradley's Creek ran into Chasteen Creek, it seemed to her as if there was no longer anything inside the folded quilt at all – nothing that lived and breathed. Not wanting to know for sure just yet, wishing to postpone her pretty pet's death one last time, she did not call out to George to stop, but trudged on, her heart sick with foreboding.

At last, when they paused to rest at Smokemount, she laid her bundle down and unwrapped it with fingers that fear and grief made thick and clumsy.

Willy lay still and cold inside the dainty quilt, crumpled like a broken thing. As Nancy had known in her heart, he could not survive outside the sacred perimeter of the medicine lake.

"You see?" She turned angrily to George. Hot tears started to her eyes. "I knew we would not be able to survive outside! You ask too much of me, George, and I have given too much!"

"Don't be foolish, Mother," George told her shortly. His eyes were cold. "You are not a little dog who has lived beyond your time." He continued as she tore at her hair and wept, "Whose fault is it if not yours, Mother? You should have let him die years ago. What? Did you think that Willy would live forever?"

George buried Willy, wrapped in the quilt in which Nancy had carried him, where the Chasteen feeds into the Oconaluftee. George had not wanted to bury the quilt. "It took you months to make that, Mother," he argued. "If you care so little for your handiwork, Snowbird will gladly take it for our bed."

But Nancy insisted. "Willy must sleep in a bed he knows," she told her son angrily. "I will not walk another step with you, or live with you and your wife in your house, but will die in these woods if you do not do what I say!"

While George dug out a shallow grave for Willy, Nancy sat on the ground nearby, her arms wrapped around her knees. Her head tilted to one side, her cheek resting on one knee, she watched her son work. As he bent over, the ulunsuti in its buckskin pouch swung from the sinew he wore tied around his neck – a heavy, unwieldy amulet but, in appearance, no different from those worn by many Cherokee, who fill similar pouches with certain stones or feathers or the root or bark of some tree or plant, to bring luck or love, or to ward off evil or disease. How different the contents of George's pouch!

Her son's reaction to Willy's death had shaken her and, despite her angry threat, had left her fearful. It was as though, with his brusqueness, the young man had reached inside of her with a cold hand. How could he have been so unfeeling? So harsh? Willy had been the companion of his youth; for many years, the only companion. Surely he mourned their dog? Over the month since he had come home, she had noticed certain differences in her son. Changes. *George is not the same,* she thought to herself, rocking gently, tightly, back and forth to ease the grinding pain deep in her gut. *It is the snake in him, always the snake.*

❧

Nancy and George Butler had fled to Gall Place in 1796. They returned to the village of Qualla thirteen years later. Much had changed in that time. Now there was a road running along the Tuckasegee River from the Kituhwa mound, past Agisiyi, where spirit people were once seen washing their white clothing and drying them upon the bank, past Ela and Turtle Place, where Tsikiki's mother had hung herself, and on through Qualla towards Ahalunuh-yi, or Ambush Place, which white men call Soco Gap. It was a muddy, rutted thoroughfare wide enough to accommodate a wagon and seemed, to Nancy, to split the village apart and send it flying in different directions. The presence of the road, coupled with the raucous shouts of the white men who drank in Young Squirrel's tavern and then spilled out into it, made the once compact village, centered about its ceremonial ground and its seven-sided council house, appear strange to Nancy, noisy and disjointed, as though Qualla had been taken over. And so, in a way, it had. The drunken white men that roamed the road seemed to her like dogs that are too hungry. She shrunk from them when they veered her way. When they were angry, she observed, they were like yellow jackets whose nest has been set fire to.

Despite the fact that George's new father-in-law possessed a white man's skill, the wheelwright Tsinawi kept the old ways. His family lived in town close to the river and near the communal corn fields in an old-style Cherokee house made by driving four poles into the ground, placing and then tying river cane between them – so that the walls were like those of a tightly woven basket – and then plastering the whole, inside and out, with red clay. The roof was made in a similar fashion to the house, then thatched over, with a hole left in the center to let the smoke out. It was a large enough house by the standards of the Cherokee, but too small for the wheelwright, three grown sons, Snowbird and her husband and now her strange, sad mother-in-law.

Tsinawi's wife had gone to the Darkening Land many years before, and so it had been Snowbird who tended the family's corn and beans, Snowbird who ran, in a haphazard but dictatorial fashion, Tsinawi's home. As young as she was –she had turned fourteen just that winter – Snowbird was used to being the woman of the house. Pretty, with bright, sharp eyes and tiny as a small child with little hands and little feet, she was nevertheless sharp-tongued and hard-mouthed like some horses and opinionated as well. She soon let Nancy know that she did not think that she would like to be ordered around by someone such as a mother-in-law.

So Nancy retreated to a corner, or, when the weather turned fine with the coming of summer, sat outside the house on a log and worked on a quilt that she thought might be called High Cricks Delight – at least, that was the name that had come to her when she pieced it out in her mind.

When Snowbird complained loudly and long to all that would listen that her mother-in-law was lazy and not worth the food she ate, Nancy pretended she didn't understand Cherokee and tried not to listen. Then it was as though she were back at Spring Place with the Zant family more than twenty years before, lying on her pallet with her face turned to the wall and her nostrils full of the odor of death (a sweet, hot, heavy odor when new), trying not to hear when Ann Zant spoke of marrying her off to the first man that came through the settlement or the blessing it would be if only Nancy would die in childbed. Oh, had she only done that, she would have spared herself all the pain and grief to follow!

And then she would think, for a fleeting moment, of the man who had taken her from Spring Place to this village. She remembered her first glimpse of him, standing with his back to the sun in the peach orchard, wearing his white man's crumpled suit, his white man's broad-brimmed hat in his hand – Young Squirrel – and the thought was almost unbearably sweet. It made her throat constrict to think of it and her eyes fill with sudden hot tears. It was true that he had not told her who he was to her, but it was also true that he had been a steady man, unwavering in both his attentions and his affection. And lightly, without looking, almost without thinking, she would touch the opal and ruby ring on her finger.

✌✌✌

By high summer, relations between Nancy and her daughter-in-law had worsened to such an extent that they did not speak to one another, but directed their conversation through another person.

For example, Snowbird would say, "Would you respectfully advise my mother-in-law that, if she wouldn't take all day grinding the meal, we might have our dinner before sunset!"

Or she would ask George, "Would you inform your mother that it is not fitting that an expectant mother should go without so that an old woman might stuff herself with food she took little part in preparing!"

Like a dog often whipped, Nancy took to spending as much time apart from Snowbird as she could and flinched whenever she heard the girl's sharp voice.

"Why did you bring me here?" she asked her son bitterly. "Your wife has nothing but contempt for me, and I am allowed to do nothing. Take me back to Gall Place. I was happier there alone than I am here among so many people who have no use for me."

But George reassured her. "There is a use for you here, Mother," he told her in great earnest. "Make your peace with Young Squirrel and you will have more than earned your keep." He was nervous because Snowbird and Tsinawi and his sons and all the men who came to Tsinawi to get wheels for their wagons and all Snowbird's girlfriends wanted to know where it was that Nancy and George had lived before and all the story of their past lives and why George always found game when he went hunting and why Nancy knew so many quilt patterns and sewed with such a neat, tight hand . . . . He did not dare to tell them of the ulunsuti for fear that it might be stolen from him by night . . . and all his good luck with it. He could scarcely sleep at night for the vigilance required to keep watch over it.

If, however, his connection to Young Squirrel were to become public knowledge, people would deem him lucky by virtue of birth, rather than by magic . . . for anyone could see that Young Squirrel was an extremely lucky man. A poor Cherokee by birth, the son of a worthless man, he had nevertheless amassed much wealth, to the extent that he had actually become like a white man in many respects.

Besides, George did not wish to live in Tsinawi's little house for the rest of his life, crowded in with his wife's family, hunting game the way the Cherokee had before the coming of the white man . . . . For one thing, there was not nearly so much of it in the forest as there once had been and even less as the years wore on and more white men came into the country – white men shoot at anything that moves.

No, George longed to be like Young Squirrel, to have what he had, and the best way to get that, George figured, was for his mother and the trader to reconcile and for him to take over the running of Young Squirrel's businesses and become his heir. Then he could kill him or not, as he saw fit and when he saw fit.

All these things George had pondered long and hard, lying by Snowbird in the dark, with his hand covering the buckskin pouch that lay on his chest, the ulunsuti pulsing like a second heart.

❧

One day in the Moon of the Green Corn, Snowbird, who was in a particularly peevish mood, had a fit of weeping, then said tearfully to her husband in Cherokee, "Tell your lazy mother that I want that pretty ring she wears! The one that looks like old Toineeta's blind eyes. You have given me no wedding ring like white men do. Tell your mother that she must give it to me for my wedding ring. Then I will be happy."

149

George hesitated. He knew his mother was partial to the ring that his uncle had given her. To his knowledge she had never taken it off since the night Young Squirrel had placed it on her finger, just before he and she had left for Gall Place. He had often seen her stop and gaze at it when she did not know he was looking, turning her hand this way and that so that the blood-red rubies that flanked the opal might catch the light.

"George!" insisted Snowbird.

George found his pretty wife's bad moods hard to endure. Like her father and her brothers, he had acquired the habit of appeasing her. Reluctantly he turned to Nancy. "Mother. . ." he began.

But Nancy would have none of it. "Tell your wife that she may not have my ring."

Snowbird gaped. "What did she say?"

"Here." To George's great surprise, Nancy proceeded to yank at the plain gold band that his father had placed upon her finger so long ago. After so many years, it had worked its way into the flesh of her finger and she was able to twist it off only with difficulty. "There!" Wrenching it free at last, she handed it to George. "She can have this."

"But, Mother . . . ."

"No, Georgie." Nancy's voice was calm; her tone firm. She did not know where this sudden resolve had come from, but she felt strong and sure. "Snowbird may have the gold band for a wedding ring. Not the other."

"But my father . . . ."

". . . is dead," she finished for him. "Young Squirrel, on the other hand, is alive." And, with that, she turned away from her son and daughter-in-law, walked out the door of Tsinawi's house and headed down the path along the river toward Ela and the house that Young Squirrel had built for her two decades before.

SIX

Young Squirrel sat in the twig rocker on the porch, his legs stretched out before him and his feet placed carefully on top of a wooden barrel. Even from the distance at which she stood – just this side of the porch, where the narrow path through the forest gave way to the partial clearing in which the house was built – she could see that her half-brother's legs were badly swollen and wrapped tight in soiled rags. He stared fixedly ahead into the door yard where tattered hens plucked in a desultory fashion at a few corn kernels and sunflower seeds scattered here and there. On the floor beside the trader a glass half-filled with yellow whiskey glowed gold like a lantern.

Beyond that, He Grows Up Wild hunkered, transparent arms wrapped around transparent knees, as naked, unkempt and emaciated as ever. Catching sight of Nancy, the specter gasped audibly, even theatrically, drew his ragged hair from before his eyes and slowly stood, staring in her direction. Puzzled by this action on He Grows Up Wild's part, Young Squirrel turned to squint into the forest. Seeing Nancy standing in the shade of the big trees, he flinched, then leaned forward, peering into the gloom. "Nancy?" he asked in a voice as jagged as broken glass. "Is it. . . Nancy?"

"It is."

Young Squirrel seemed smaller to her than when she had seen him last, mounted on the roan mare on his way to Sugarlands, turning to wave goodbye to her once before he was gone – the gesture of a lover. He seemed diminished.

"Yes, it is Nancy," she repeated and stepped out into the clearing. Strange, she thought, gazing around her at the familiar outbuildings, the house. All the years that she had hid away from him in Gall Place and these past months when she had lived in such fear that he would discover her in Qualla . . . . Now that she was here, at his and her home, she felt no apprehension at all. Rather a sense of peace . . . and dullness. *It is a pretty place,* she thought, almost absently. *Look at Rattlesnake Mountain – old friend!*

"Take off your bonnet." Young Squirrel was gruff. "Let me see your hair."

Nancy laughed. It had been a long time since she had laughed – not since she had come to Qualla from Adagahi.

"By now my hair would have turned white with age in any case," she reminded him.

"Nevertheless," he said sternly. He did not smile.

She untied the ribbons that held the poke bonnet in place and re-moved it.

He gazed at her fixedly for a moment, then looked away. "It is not so much the color," he said by way of explanation, "as the way it falls. Yes." He leaned stiffly to one side, his hand groping for and then closing around the glass of whiskey. Straightening back up, he raised the glass before him in a kind of toast. "It is Nancy, come at last," he advised He Grows Up Wild. "How long have we waited for this day? Long enough that I had ceased to hope for it." He drank.

"No!" insisted He Grows Up Wild. "Now that she has come you must stop drinking."

Young Squirrel stared hard at him, then looked away. "I thought I heard a voice a moment ago," he told Nancy. "But it was only the wind."

"I do see him, you know. The Wild One."

Young Squirrel considered this. "You do?"

Nancy nodded.

"Well, well!" Young Squirrel shook his head. "What a lot of secrets we have, Nancy! But I don't feel like talking to him right now. Sometimes you have to shut him out. Otherwise he grows tiresome."

"Brother!" objected He Grow Up Wild. "Nancy!" He turned to Nancy.

"What's wrong with your legs?" she asked.

But Young Squirrel, his face contorted, did not answer her question. Instead, "Where did you go? And why, after so long, have you returned?" he demanded. Then, as swiftly as he had given way to anger, he regained control of his features, of himself. He had always been like that – quick to anger, quick to control that anger. "Gout," he said stiffly, dismissing his swollen, outstretched legs with a wave of his hands. "I am afflicted by gout."

"At Adagahi I learned how to treat gout," said Nancy quietly.

"The ulunsuti!" Now he laughed, but with bitterness and rue. "It teaches men to hunt and women to cure. It taught me how to make the white man's money."

"It is very powerful. I know."

"So . . . ." He spoke in a low voice, squeezing the words out between his teeth. "You still have it?" Despite his efforts to dissemble, Nancy could hear the excitement in his voice. It was like a light in a dark place.

"It has passed on," she told him. "That is its nature. It is no longer mine nor yours, but my son Georgie's."

"Kill the boy!" cried He Grows Up Wild. "Get the ulunsuti back!"

"Georgie's!" Young Squirrel echoed Nancy's words. "Little Georgie?" He took another drink of the whiskey, then closed his eyes. Clearly her words brought him pain. All these long years without the ulunsuti, yet he could still feel the sickly sense of power that its possession had imparted to him – the small, lame boy visiting his treasure in the hollow of a tree only he knew about, the green, queasy light within. "Little Georgie's and not mine!"

"The ulunsuti is a kind of curse," she told Young Squirrel. "No one who owns it can live as others do. It disposes one to extremes. It is unpredictable. One can not say what it will do. Our sadness now is only this – to live as others do. In truth, it is my son I fear for."

They were all silent for a moment, even He Grows Up Wild. Each thought of the ulunsuti with a longing that tugged at their bowels. Nancy was the first to break the silence. She crossed the clearing to stand in the door yard in front of Young Squirrel. "Willy is dead."

"Willy?" Young Squirrel was incredulous. "The little dog I gave you?"

Nancy nodded. Sudden tears started to her eyes. "Coming back from Adagahi. He was a very old dog." She bowed her head. Tears rolled down her cheeks, although it had been months since the dog's death. She cried soundlessly.

Young Squirrel leaned back in his chair. He shook his head with wonder. "Last spring? I gave Willy to you after Nero died. I brought him up from Charleston in my jacket pocket. How could a dog have lived so long?"

Nancy shook her head. "I don't know. The waters of Adagahi are healing waters." Rolling her knuckles along the line of her cheekbones, she wiped the tears from her face.

"Adagahi!" Young Squirrel reflected. Gall Place. Where the man whom he had thought was his grandfather had lived in isolation, where his mother had been reared. "I might easily have gone there, but I never did."

"It was a safe place."

"You were safe here."

"No," she corrected him.

"Nancy, I am not a monster."

"But you are my brother."

Young Squirrel was silent a moment. Then, "You knew."

"He Grows Up Wild told me." Nancy sat down on the bottom step of the porch, looking up at the trader.

Young Squirrel turned to He Grows Up Wild, who defended himself. "I cannot lie! I am not wise! I cannot bite my tongue! I have no tongue to bite!" He tore at his spectral flesh; he pulled apparent hair. "Oh, I have brought such sorrow on myself, and now I must die! Die! Nothingness! Blackness!"

Young Squirrel turned back to Nancy. "I have one question. Would you have consented to marry me had you not known?"

"Yes," said Nancy.

They sat for a moment in silence. It was a densely packed silence, not empty, but full of all the things that might be said, but never will or, indeed, ever can be. This kind of silence is like a graveyard in which many babies are buried.

Finally it became too much for He Grows Up Wild. He began howling like a wounded dog, panting loudly and rushing about the door yard until, at last, he dashed crazily off into the woods and disappeared from sight.

"What is wrong with him?" Nancy asked Young Squirrel.

"He is insane." Young Squirrel shrugged. "In time, he will return. He always does."

"I will treat your gout." Nancy rose. She started to turn away but Young Squirrel reached out and grabbed her arm.

"You did not tell me why you came." His tone was urgent. "After all these years?"

"The same reason as before. I am not wanted by those with whom I live."

"I want you here."

"I know you do." She set her bonnet on her head and tied the strings.

"But where are you going?"

"*Shhh*, Young Squirrel!" Nancy laid her hand upon his arm. "I will come back this time. I am only going to get my things."

Nancy plucked buds off the plant white men called balm of Gilead and steeped them in alcohol. This was for a salve for Young Squirrel's afflicted limbs. In addition, she picked up a bottle of sarsaparilla syrup at the trader's store and mixed in with it one ounce of queen of the meadow roots and equal parts of hemp and spignut and let the mixture stand for a day and a night. Then she removed the soiled wrappings from Young Squirrel's legs and rubbed the balm of Gilead salve over the swollen limbs. As for the sarsaparilla mixture, she made him drink a ladle's worth of it. "None of this will do any good unless you stop drinking whiskey," she advised him.

"Listen to her, Brother! Listen!" He Grows Up Wild pleaded.

But Young Squirrel had no plans to stop drinking whiskey. "I do not care whether I live or die," he told Nancy. "It is a matter of great indifference to me which world of shadows my spirit inhabits."

Yet he seemed happier and would sometimes smile and even laugh.

When Nancy moved back to Young Squirrel's house, George and Snowbird remained behind with the wheelwright. This was not in accordance with George's wishes or Snowbird's, for that matter. Young Squirrel had a fine house by the girl's standards, and the trader was rich and respected for his money if not for his character or his habits. Snowbird had not married George for nothing. George was half white and related to a rich man. She hoped through her marriage to live as white people do and to be well off enough to have an orchard of peaches and a four-poster bed and a golden locket and a music box and one of those clocks from the coast.

However, Nancy had made it clear to Young Squirrel that she would on no account share a roof with her demanding and spoiled daughter-in-law. Young Squirrel acquiesced quickly enough to her wishes in this respect. Indeed, he had lived alone too long to wish his home to be too full of life. Nancy had always been a quiet woman, speaking only when necessary and moving with such economy of grace that she occasioned little sound. Snowbird, on the other hand, chattered constantly and loudly, screamed with laughter, yelled when she was angry, banged pots and accomplished everything she did with a noisy vigor. True, Young Squirrel harbored hopes of getting the ulunsuti back, but he figured that he could always speak to George sometime on his own and effect an exchange. Perhaps George would take the mill for the ulunsuti . . . or the tavern.

As for the townsfolk, Nancy no longer made any secret of her and the trader's relationship. "I am Young Squirrel's half-sister," she told them, and, to be sure, after some initial wonderment, no one thought a thing about it. They remembered how Young Squirrel's mother had left with George Kinnahan long ago and how Nancy had come to Qualla and then left and then returned. It seemed natural enough to them – this coming and going and coming back again. It used to be that no one went and everyone stayed, but that was no longer the case in Qualla.

As for where Nancy had been all those years, the old ones thought it likely that she, like Dayunisi, had hidden herself away at Gall Place, which was well known if seldom glimpsed; the younger people thought the medicine lake a place that existed only in stories. Already white missionaries had advised them that the stories told by the old ones were simply that – stories, and that they must exchange the sacred places of the Cherokee for others in a distant land with names like Bethlehem and Gethsame. Perhaps Nancy had gone to Tennessee, they thought, or south to Spring Place. Or perhaps she had gone to some of the white man's sacred places, to that town they call Rome, or to Jerusalem.

Despite the fact that Young Squirrel continued to drink whiskey, his gout improved to the point where, using a staff and leaning on Nancy's arm, he could walk a little without too much pain in his joints. Perhaps, though he did not stop drinking altogether, he drank a little less.

SEVEN

Snowbird got her birth pains about suppertime on an evening in the late autumn when the Cherokee of Qualla were busy firing the woods around the village. They did this every autumn to clear out the undergrowth that impeded travel through the woods during the remainder of the year and served as tinder for random sparks from a fire started or a gun shot off.

Tsinawi fetched Toineeta down from Madcap Branch – despite her incredible age, she was still the Granny Woman in these parts – and George came down to Ela to fetch Nancy back to his wife's childbed, it being her duty to assist her daughter-in-law in bringing her grandchild into the world.

The air was cold and acrid with smoke. A hot wind blew off the fires that burned steadily away to either side of the winding path that led to the village, eating the low growth with a rasping, chewing sound. The fires looked like rivulets of ember and flame, and the woods about were mantled with soft ash.

George and Nancy held their forearms pressed over their mouths as they walked. The smoke made their eyes sting and water; and the firelight made their shadows dance against the darkness. As they walked through the dusk, Nancy prayed to the Provider in her heart that her grandchild, in being born, might kill Snowbird, whom Nancy hated with an intensity that was new to her, but which grew with every day that passed. If only that would happen, she would take the child to stay with her in Young Squirrel's house and raise it and George could live there too. The mother-in-law's prayer was so dark that she felt her smooth face to be a mask behind which evil crouched, while the hand that held her medicine pouch seemed to her as crabbed and clawed as the talons of an eagle or a hawk, which will pluck the heart from the breast of its prey. Or so it is said.

When they reached Tsinawi's house, the wheelwright was standing outside the door with his three sons. Their hair was thick with ash and their faces were smoke-blackened. They had been outside since Toineeta had banished them from the hut in which Snowbird lay screaming and shouting imprecations, just shortly after George had been sent to fetch his mother.

The old Granny Woman met Nancy and George at the door. She was even smaller than Nancy remembered and so bent over and hump-backed that her head appeared to grow from a point in her chest instead of her neck. The old woman's skull glowed through the scraps of sparse white hair that remained to her and her milky eyes stared sightlessly out of a face as cross-hatched as if the tines of a fork had been pressed at random into its soft dough. "You, George Butler, go away!" Toineeta barred George's way into the house with her body. "Only women can do this serious work!" She turned to the wheelwright and his sons. "Go! All of you! Sit with the other men in the village and be useless together. I will send for you when the time has come."

The men shifted their weight from foot to foot and looked at one another. They appeared momentarily uncertain, but the Granny Woman had great authority and births, particularly first births, are known to be a long process. Tsinawi gave a curt nod and, taking George by the upper arm, gently propelled him forward. The men trudged off, heading towards the council house.

When they were out of earshot, Toineeta asked Nancy, "They are gone?"

"Yes," Nancy assured the blind woman.

"Good. There is a lot of blood. I did not want them to see it." Stepping aside, she allowed Nancy to enter the house.

Snowbird lay on her side on a pallet on the floor, her knees drawn up towards her big belly. The pallet was drenched with the blood that ran fresh and red from between her legs. Where she had touched herself – on her face, on her stomach – there were bloody handprints. Her face was drawn and pale, distorted with pain, and the brown eyes that had watched her mother-in-law's every move so jealously were dull now and unfocussed. They barely registered Nancy as she knelt beside the pallet, laying her medicine pouch on the floor beside her.

"It is bad." Toineeta spoke matter-of-factly. "This girl is too small. She has been at it a long time already. Half the day. There is nothing for it but to frighten the baby out. Otherwise both she and the baby will die." The old woman shrugged. "Probably they will die anyway."

"Can't we stop the bleeding?" The sight of so much blood made Nancy queasy. The smell in the house reminded her of a pig sticking and that reminded her of the massacre at Hiwasee.

"It is the afterbirth coming first. Very bad. It means there's no stopping the bleeding. Here. Prop her up for me. She should be sitting when I do this. You! Snowbird! Do you hear me? Pay attention, girl! Sit up now!"

With some difficulty, Nancy half shoved, half pulled a resisting Snowbird into a sitting position and, squatting in front of her, gripped the girl's shoulders to keep her upright. Toineeta took a position behind her.

"Listen!" the old woman intoned in a loud, shrill voice. "You, little man, get up, now at once! There comes an old woman! The horrible old thing is coming, only a little ways off! Listen! Quick! Get your bed and let us run away. *Yu!*" Having uttered these words, she blew a decoction of something that looked like yellow root through pie-weed onto the top of Snowbird's head.

"What are you talking about?"

"It is the formula used in such cases," Toineeta explained. "A boy is always afraid of an old woman because she might live until he grows up and force him to marry her, old and shriveled as she is."

She repeated the formula three more times. After the first repetition, she blew the decoction on Snowbird's breast instead of her head. After the second and third repetitions she blew it first on the palm of her right hand, then on the palm of her left hand. Then she made her drink the rest of the decoction.

"How do you know it's a boy?" Nancy asked. "What if it's a girl?"

"We wait to see if a boy comes out. If nothing happens, it must be a girl. Then I try the formula for a girl." Toineeta sat down near the fire. After a few moments, her head began to nod. She had fallen asleep.

Some time later, Snowbird's labor became less sluggish and her contractions increased, then grew more intense. Nancy woke Toineeta, and, working in tandem, they managed, at length, to drag from Snowbird's convulsing body the afterbirth.

"This is a big afterbirth. Like a buffalo's liver." Toineeta placed it carefully in a tin bucket.

"Can't you say the formula for a girl?"

"No, no." Toineeta dismissed the suggestion with a wave of her hand. "The baby must be turned around wrong. Feet down, instead of head. The formula will not turn it around, no matter what it is. It's useless anyway. Now that the afterbirth is born, the baby cannot live long. Perhaps it has already strangled on the chord."

"We can do nothing to save it?" Nancy's heart was full of pain. She wished Snowbird dead, but she wanted the baby.

Toineeta shrugged. "We could cut Snowbird's belly open. If the baby is still alive, it might survive."

Nancy shuddered. "But what about Snowbird?"

"Sometimes the mother survives. If the wound doesn't go bad. As for Snowbird, she has already lost too much blood."

"I shall ask George what he wants us to do." Nancy stood wearily – standing was a chore for her on account of her rheumatism – and walked outside. It was that still time of the night when the moon has long since set and the darkness is as thick as tar and sticks to everything it comes in contact with. A gray mist lay on the river's silver body, as heavy and immovable as a sleeping drunkard, and all that was left of the brush-eating fires that had, that day, cleansed the surrounding forest of a season's growth were embers that glowed like red jewels or red eyes and hot wind and air that smelled of wood smoke.

Then she remembered that the men had gone to the council house. That had been hours ago. Probably they had gone to someone's house for the night or they had been invited to sleep in someone's sweathouse. It would take her twenty minutes to walk from Tsinawi's house to the council house. It would take even longer if they had gone elsewhere and she had to search them out.

She went back inside the house. "We will cut the baby out," she told Toineeta, speaking in a low voice and glancing, as she spoke, towards Snowbird.

The girl stared fixedly ahead, her dark eyes glazed. Her blood-streaked face was beaded with sweat and her teeth chattered audibly. It was an inhuman sound – like a timber rattler that shakes his vertebral tail in warning.

Toineeta slipped Nancy a hunting knife, quickly so that Snowbird might not see it. "I cannot see to make the cut," she whispered. "I will hold her down. Don't worry. There is much blood, but a knife in the belly hurts less than in other places. You will cut where I show you."

Toineeta moved over to the pallet. She rolled Snowbird over on her back. Then, taking a cotton rag that had been soaking in water from a nearby kettle, she wrung it out and mopped the girl's forehead. Folding the rag into a rectangle, she laid it over Snowbird's eyes like a compress and held it there with one hand. With the other she traced a line in the girl's blood across her swollen abdomen. She nodded to Nancy.

Nancy knelt at Snowbird's feet and retraced the line Toineeta had drawn with the sharp point of the blade. Bright blood bubbled along the line. Snowbird gasped with surprise and pain, pulling her knees up towards her stomach. Nancy pushed them down again. "Stop it!"

"Deeper!" insisted Toineeta. "You've only cut the skin! You must cut through the muscle to the baby."

Snowbird screamed now and tried to sit up, but loss of blood and the long labor had so weakened her that Toineeta easily forced her back down on the pallet and, kneeling over her, held her wrists pinned against the ground so that she could not grab at the knife.

In desperation, Snowbird attempted to roll over to her side and draw her knees up to her belly to protect it, but Nancy rose slightly from her crouched position and then knelt again, this time on Snowbird's quivering legs. She placed the knife's point on the line she had drawn with the blade and, leaning into it, managed to push it through the taut girdle of muscle and abdominal wall. Gripping the handle with both hands, she hacked along the incision. The skin made a sound like heavy cloth being ripped and blood welled from the wound in sheets, like a tide that flows, soaking Nancy from her thighs down.

When finally she had finished and Snowbird lay, swooning, her stomach a gaping wound, Nancy flung the bloodied knife from her and covered her face with bloody, shaking hands. She had cut open many animals in her time, but never another human being.

Toineeta started to her feet and felt around the earthen floor until she had found the knife. Clamping it between her teeth, she crouched down next to Snowbird and reached with both hands inside the bleeding hole at her center. After feeling carefully around for a moment, she lifted out a baby and, taking the knife from between her teeth, sawed through its umbilical chord. It was no bigger than a squirrel, thin and bluish. With deft fingers the old woman unplugged its tiny nostrils and, laying her mouth over its face, breathed her ancient life into its fragile honeycombs of lungs. The baby squalled fitfully. Its limbs wobbled in a feeble effort to express its indignation.

"Is it. . . ?" Nancy began.

"Hush!" Toineeta admonished her, handing her the baby. "I am not done here." Reaching once more into Snowbird's opened womb, she lifted out a second infant. "I thought the afterbirth was too big." With one hand she groped at the infant's genitals. "A boy!"

"Both boys," exclaimed Nancy. "Twins!"

But Toineeta was busy unplugging the second infant's nostrils. "There!" she said when she had gotten the baby to cry. "Now you must wrap both babies tight. They are too small to stand the cold. I will see to Snowbird."

Nancy did as she was told. She wiped the two infants clean and swaddled them tightly. They felt limp, toneless. It was as though all their bones were broken. She placed them on a pallet and tucked around them the Steps to the Altar quilt she had made for George and his bride during her last, lonely winter in Gall Place.

In the meantime, Toineeta sewed up Snowbird's split stomach with a horn needle threaded with sinew and wiped her down with white vinegar. Then Toineeta took Snowbird under the arms and Nancy took her feet and together they lifted her up and onto a clean pallet. Nancy took one end of the bloody pallet on which Snowbird had lain and dragged it outside and away from the house towards the river. She folded it over on itself, struck the piece of flint she kept in her pocket and set fire to it. Burning, it smelled like game roasting. It was the blood that made it smell like that. She returned to the house, where Toineeta had finished dressing Snowbird's wound with a poultice made of the chewed bark of the alder tree. They covered the girl with four quilts. Still she did not stop shivering.

Nancy knelt beside the babies. Gently she cupped their heads with her hands. "Will they live?" She did not care about Snowbird.

But a good conjure woman is always noncommittal. Toineeta shrugged. "They are too small and they are undercooked. They might live. Maybe not. As for Snowbird . . . . She has lost much blood. Perhaps too much, perhaps not. Who can say?"

EIGHT

It was dawn before George returned. Nancy heard his footsteps; she met him at the door. "You have two sons. Twins."

"Two?" He was surprised. "And Snowbird?"

Nancy hesitated. "Snowbird is sick, Georgie. She lost so much blood. I didn't know how much blood there was in a person. That you could lose that much and still . . . ."

George seized her by the arm. "But she will live?"

Nancy glanced downwards. In truth, she did not trust her face to hide the pleasure that she felt at the prospect of Snowbird's imminent demise.

George tightened his grip on her arm. "Mother, answer me! Will she live?"

Toineeta, seated on a chair by the hearth, spoke up. "We do not know, George Butler. Snowbird has a fever. She is weak."

"Let me see her!" George released Nancy's arm and pushed past her into the house. He dropped to his knees beside his wife's pallet. "Snowbird!"

Snowbird did not answer, but only moaned. It was a moan like a sigh – light, full of air. "Ahhh!"

George lifted the pile of quilts from his wife's stomach. He stared at the angry gash bisecting it.

"We had to cut her open." The words were hard for Nancy to say – they stuck in her throat like bones. "To get the babies out. There was no other way, Georgie! She would have surely died if we hadn't . . . and your sons too. Don't you want to see your sons?"

George shook his head. Sinking back onto his heels, he buried his face in his hands for a moment. Then he stood and started towards the door.

"Where are you going?"

"To borrow a horse or a mule."

"Why?"

George glanced in Toineeta's direction. He shook his head. Taking Nancy by the arm, he drew her close and whispered, "I must take my wife to Adagahi. I must bathe her in the medicine lake . . . as you did Willy when he was sick! I love her too much to let her die, Mother!"

In his distress, he had forgotten that the absence of sight made Toineeta's hearing doubly acute. Out of the corner of her eye, Nancy noticed the old woman's face, without expression but alert in its repose, like that of a dog that has just that moment smelled something on the wind. "The journey is too rough," she replied in a whisper. "Up mountain and through the bottoms, and the chance of an early snow . . . . She would not survive the jolting, Georgie."

George released her arm and turned away. "You are right." He hunkered down for a moment and considered the situation. Then he removed the ulunsuti from the buckskin pouch that hung from his neck and placed it beside Snowbird's pallet.

"*Hu!*" Toineeta cried softly, gazing about her with rapt, sightless eyes. "What strange magic is this, Nancy Butler? I see light and dark and light and dark, and there is a feeling to the air . . . . As it is before a storm when the Thunder Boys mutter under their breath and circle one another in the sky, ready to fight." Lifting her old nose, she sniffed the air. "Ah! And the sharp smell of lightning!"

Nancy laid her hand on Toineeta's and squeezed it hard, crushing the crabbed fingers together. At this signal, the old woman's blind eyes widened slightly and she said not another word – for George had drawn his hunting knife from its sheath and, despite Nancy's shaking her head *No*, would have killed the old woman had she but said aloud what she was thinking: that in this flashing light and smell of ozone was the explanation for George's prowess as a hunter. For Toineeta was old enough that she had known Dayunisi when he still lived in Qualla, before his wife had hung herself over the loss of her beauty and he had taken his daughter Tsikiki and moved to a secret place. That had been before so many white men had come, when everyone knew everyone else – for, in truth, who else was there to know if not the people of one's village? And everyone in Qualla had known that Dayunisi possessed the ulunsuti, that it had been handed down to him by his great-grandfather. What they hadn't known was what had befallen the crystal upon the great hunter's death. She turned to Nancy. "Tell your useless son that he must fetch fresh cobwebs to staunch the bleeding. Tell him that the wife of Suyeta will have some."

George hesitated.

Once again, Nancy shook her head. Her lips formed these words: "She suspects nothing!"

George replaced the knife in its sheath and, turning, rushed from the house.

"Do not let on that you know!" Nancy advised Toineeta, when she was sure her son was out of earshot. "He fears thieves. He wishes no one to know."

"The crystal is very powerful," Toineeta warned. "Sometimes it will cure; at other times its power is too strong and it will kill those who are exposed to it. It depends on the disposition of the uktena in question and uktenas are most unpredictable creatures."

"But this uktena is long dead," Nancy objected. "Before the time of your grandmother and even before that. There is no telling how long ago it died."

"An uktena can never be completely killed. Trust me, Nancy Butler; it is contained within its ulunsuti in a way not easily understood. Take the babies to my granddaughter's house and tend to them. Leave me here to see to Snowbird and we will see what is to be."

So Nancy took the babies to the house of Toineeta's granddaughter and tended them there, feeding them on barley sugar water dripped from rags into their sucking mouths, while Toineeta remained in Tsinawi's cabin with Snowbird for three days and four nights. At length,

Snowbird regained consciousness and began slowly to heal. Her wound did not go septic.

To Nancy, Toineeta confided, "It was the ulunsuti which saved her. She was beyond my curing."

To George she said, "See, George Butler. The old medicines are good. They have saved your wife."

Satisfied that she did not know his secret, George kept his knife sheathed and did not kill the old woman as he had thought he might, but instead paid her for her trouble in game and let her return to the old cabin up by Madcap Branch.

NINE

"What will you name your boys?" Nancy asked.

George shrugged. These things did not concern him. He was thinking of how to better his lot, now that he had two sons and a wife whose insides were all mixed up – it seemed that Toineeta, in her haste, had not put them all back in their right place.

"I want English names," Snowbird insisted. "Which I don't care, for all English names are ugly. However, I wish my sons to grow up and live as white men do and having English names will make that easier."

"Then you must name them, Mother," said George, "for I was not raised among white people."

"Joseph," decided Nancy, "for that is a name I once heard and thought good-sounding . . . . And Charley, after their grandfather." The word *grandfather* spoken in connection with Charley Butler made her heart ring and then ache like a soft tooth does when struck. Charley had been George's age when he died, a boy really. No years for him, no grief, no despair, no loneliness. Only a momentary terror and an instant of pain. Then soft oblivion. Some of us are condemned to die, she thought, and others to live.

"Joseph and Charley," Snowbird repeated. "What do these names mean?"

"I don't know. They meant something once, but what that was has been forgotten." Suddenly Nancy remembered a visitor to her father's home – this would have been many, many years ago. When told what she had just told Snowbird, the visitor had asked, "What is the use of a name if its meaning is forgotten." The visitor that was . . . Young Squirrel. And in that instant she remembered whole and in all its parts the trader's visit to Hiwasee, the first time she had seen him. And then she had brought him corn in the hot house and a pipkin of ointment . . . . She smiled to think that this memory must have been inside her head all this time, just hidden away, as things are on the moon's dark side.

"What is the use of a name if its meaning is forgotten?" Snowbird was complaining now. "George! *Yu!* All these people! This house is too small. We need a bigger house!"

TEN

After George's twin sons were born, he began to negotiate with his uncle. Nancy did not know of this, nor did Young Squirrel or He Grows Up Wild tell her, for they knew that she was adverse to the ulunsuti changing hands and that was what they hoped to effect through their discussions with George – the return of the transparent to Young Squirrel's possession. Young Squirrel was convinced that the stone would make him whole and well again, and, besides, the crystal obsessed him. He could not rest easy until it was back in his hands.

At first, Young Squirrel offered his nephew the tavern in exchange for the ulunsuti and George agreed to this trade. However, he insisted that Young Squirrel sign a document, assigning the property to him and he took the added precaution of having the trader's signature witnessed by a lawyer who, by chance, was staying in one of the rooms over the tavern. The lawyer was a man named Mueller from the town of Salem, far away in the Piedmont. He had come to the mountains to negotiate the purchase of land for a Moravian mission.

Nancy knew of the transaction but thought that Young Squirrel was gifting his nephew with the tavern, that affection for the man who had been a boy in his house and his own advancing years and ill health had predisposed the trader to make new business arrangements advantageous to his nephew.

That was in the last week of February. Days passed. A week. Still, George did not come to the house up towards Ela with the ulunsuti, as he had promised he would.

Young Squirrel sent Nancy into town for him, saying, "There are matters concerning the tavern and its operations that I must discuss with him," and, after a delay of several days during which George pronounced himself too busy to see the trader, the new tavern keeper rode into the door yard of Young Squirrel's house on a gray gelding, which his newfound prosperity had enabled him to purchase from a white settler. "I have been thinking, Uncle," he told Young Squirrel. "The tavern is a poor exchange for an ulunsuti. A man will have a glass of whiskey on the day he comes into town, but he eats bread every day. So that the exchange will be worth my while, I must have the mill as well."

Young Squirrel objected to this. "That was not our agreement."

"You do not need the mill if you have the ulunsuti," George pointed out. "Besides, you have plenty of money already."

"I do not!" Despite Young Squirrel's efforts to remain composed, his voice quavered. "That is nothing more than gossip." He did not like people to know about the American money sewn into the ticking of his mattress. There were so many strangers about these days, and it was an isolated spot – no one around but him and Nancy. He feared that thieves would come into his house at night and rob him. "Except for my property, I am a poor man. These last years I have only seemed to prosper."

George paid no attention to these protestations. "I will not give you the ulunsuti until you sign over the mill to me." Getting on his spotted horse, he rode back to Qualla.

Three days passed, then Young Squirrel called George to him once again.

"You may have the mill," he told him when, at last, he came. "But, before I sign it over, I must have the ulunsuti in my hands!"

"Don't think that you can give me orders, old man. You want the ulunsuti more than I want the mill. You are not in a position to dictate conditions to me."

Young Squirrel was angry. "Do you think I am a fool that would give away all he has for a promise?" Once again he sent him from him. Once again he waited. He waited a week, then said to himself, "I have already lost the tavern. If I do not get the ulunsuti now, I will have given it away for nothing." Besides, he wanted the ulunsuti so much. For months, it seemed, he had watched with dreamer's eyes as an uktena rose from a stream in a great sinuous arc, shedding sheets of water like green light and singing to him in a no-voice, *"You have allowed my crystal to be stolen. Get it back. Do what you must,"* before the dream shattered into a thousand pieces and he woke in a cold sweat to stare wide-eyed into the darkness. He could not endure this terror night after night. He feared that his heart might stop, or that he would go mad and become He Grows Up Wild entirely. He had to get the crystal back, whatever sacrifice that entailed. He sent George another, urgent message by Nancy: the young man should come and quickly; he was willing to make him a deal.

Once again, George had the trader sign a document assigning the mill to him. Once again the lawyer Mueller witnessed both George's and the trader's signature.

"Now," Young Squirrel said to George, when Mueller had strolled out onto the porch for a smoke on his pipe, "give me the ulunsuti!"

"I have hidden it away for safekeeping, so that the white lawyer would not become suspicious. I will bring it to you tomorrow."

"You are my nephew and I expect you to honor your word."

"Have no fear, Uncle." George called to Mueller to mount up and rode back to town with the deed to the mill in his pocket.

"He is not to be trusted," He Grows Up Wild advised Young Squirrel. "You should have killed him while you had the chance."

"I know, but Nancy would not forgive me if I murdered her son."

"We could do it secretly . . . hire assassins!"

"How would we find the ulunsuti if we were to kill him? Mark my words. He has hidden it, the way I hid it in the hollow of the tree so that Dayunisi would not find it."

"He is lying. He wears it around his neck in the buckskin pouch when he is in town. I have seen him. He only takes it off when he comes here. He's afraid that we might leap upon him and take it from him. And so we should, for it is ours. I tell you, Brother, we should kill George Butler before he kills us."

But Young Squirrel was reluctant to act against his nephew if he could avoid it, and so the next day came, and the next and still George did not return with the ulunsuti as he had sworn to do.

A month passed. Then, one day, Young Squirrel stopped drinking. It happened this way: he picked up a bottle of whiskey, stood, and, using his walking stick, which was cut from a stout length of hickory, went outside onto the porch and emptied it into a tangle of rhododendron. Nancy, who was sitting in the twig rocker on the porch at the time, sat back from her quilting frame and stared after Young Squirrel with amazement. She had been after him to quit drinking ever since she had moved back, but he had remained adamant in his refusal even to discuss it. "I must have my wits about me," he explained to her now. Then he shuffled back inside the house and lay down on his bed.

He didn't get up for a week. This was because, at first, he was very ill. His hands shook and he broke out in cold sweats and saw more things that weren't there than He Grows Up Wild. Once, he thought that locusts fed on his flesh, jaws crunching as their heads swiveled this way and that; once, that he ran, stumbling and falling towards the river, his body engulfed in flames; once, that his swollen legs were logs of dead wood, riddled with termites . . . that chunks of them kept breaking off, soft and dry with rot and swarming with pallid insects.

Nancy treated this delirium with a concoction for nervous affections made by mixing in four quarts pure rain water, one ounce each of lobelia seed, cayenne, Solomon's seal, blue violet roots, spignut, and two of yellow poplar, along with a handful of beech drops, the same quantity of Indian pipe and four pounds of molasses.

Later, once his bouts of delirium had eased and then altogether ceased, he suffered from waves of vertigo and nausea so overwhelming that he could barely sit up in bed without vomiting gouts of blood and yellow bile. Nancy fed him as much Poland starch as he could take, but it wasn't until the second week that he could hold even broth down.

After that, Young Squirrel's health steadily improved. He sat up in bed. Then he moved to a chair. The swelling in his joints eased so that he moved with less pain and could even walk a little on his own, with the aid of his walking stick. He began to eat again and put on flesh. Oh, there was that about the drinking that he missed – the softness in which it had wrapped his days and blunted his consciousness, the unconditional sleep. There was nothing now to take him away, nothing that permitted him to hide and rest. He had become the hunter once again, no longer that which merely wakes to watch and sleeps to dream.

ELEVEN

In late April Young Squirrel told Nancy, "You must go to town and fetch George back with you. I have business with him."

"You have much business with my son lately," she complained good-naturedly. She had to go into town anyway. She was making a new quilt – Acres of Diamonds, she called it – and needed a spool of thread from the trading post and a paper of needles and tallow besides.

George did not return with her that day; in fact, it was going onto two weeks when he finally rode into the dooryard. Nancy met him at the door. "I must speak to my uncle alone, Mother," he told her and so she remained outside on the porch while he went inside, intending to work on her quilt. As she pulled a needle from her pine needle basket, however, she changed her mind. The Planting Moon had just turned and the crabapple trees and the peach trees and the cherry trees were all in pale, sweet flower. The air was filled with floating blossoms and the cry of bees. It struck her that it was too beautiful to sit up under the porch roof when she could be walking in the woods. She pushed aside her quilting frame. Today she would hunt herbs and roots in the forest. The new growth after the fires of the autumn was not yet so dense that she would have difficulty spotting the tender greens. Picking up her basket, she slipped its handle over her crooked arm and started down the steps to the door yard. Crossing it, she took the path leading to the river.

•

George closed the door behind him and stepped into the room. Young Squirrel sat facing him in a chair drawn up close to the table. His walking stick was propped up against it, by his side. "You sent for me, Uncle?"

Young Squirrel did not waste any time. "Don't try and cheat me, George." His voice was steady. "I gave you the tavern and the mill, and now you must give me the ulunsuti."

However, George only pulled up a chair and sat down opposite him. "I have been reconsidering my offer."

"What more of me can you want?"

"Isn't it obvious?" George leaned forward, across the table. "I want the trading post."

"I will not give you the trading post. It was the first thing I ever owned. I worked hard for it. It was willed to me by Matlock."

"It was built by my grandfather." George stood and crossed to the hearth.

"Your grandfather was a scoundrel." Young Squirrel spat the words out. "I hated your grandfather."

"That was only because my grandmother preferred him to your father . . . ."

"He Goes About was not my father!"

"Then who was?" George turned back to face him.

"Your great-grandfather, Dayunisi, was my father – the owner of the crystal before me. Your great-grandfather lay with your grandmother and so I came to be. I am Dayunisi's heir. Not you."

George snorted in surprise. Then he shrugged. "The ulunsuti passes where it will. It is mine now and I will not let it go." He crossed back to the table, and, resting his hands on the scarred oak, leaned forward so that his face was but a few inches from the trader's. "You may as well give me the trading post, Young Squirrel, for it is no good to you anymore and I will never give you the crystal."

The two men glared at one another. George, unprepared for the ferocity of Young Squirrel's gaze, was the first to glance away. The old man's eyes were clear, not glazed and unfocussed as before, and his speech was no longer slurred. Moreover, the trader's breath did not smell of whiskey. What was going on here? Was the old man actually sober? George did not know what to make of this new development. He had counted on Young Squirrel's continued dependence on alcohol to realize his plans – to take from his uncle all that the old man possessed. He felt momentarily confused, unsure of his course. Lifting his hands from the table, his wrists flexed and his palms flat as though to ward of a physical attack by Young Squirrel or to placate him, he stepped backwards.

Young Squirrel seized the knob of his walking stick and slowly, for standing pained him, started to rise.

"Hah!" George laughed. It was a contemptuous laugh . . . but it was also nervous. He had not thought the trader so mobile. Before he had been unable to stand without assistance. "What are you doing, old man?"

Young Squirrel did not reply. Scowling in concentration, he raised his cane.

"Are you going to strike me?" Reaching out, George grabbed the cane and, less easily than he would have suspected, twisted it out of Young Squirrel's grip. He flung it to one side.

At this, Young Squirrel's rage, so long contained, flowed from him in a torrent. Stepping forward, he shoved George's chest with such force that the younger man, unprepared, was thrown off balance and stumbled backwards into the lean-to where Young Squirrel had his bed, turning as he half fell onto it. He grabbed from beside the door an old ax Nancy used for chopping kindling and staggered into the lean-to after his nephew. He did not know where this newfound strength had come from or the sudden ease with which he seemed now to move – as though he were a young man again, with a young man's power and agility. His hatred of George and his fury were a fire which blew through his veins, devouring everything in its path – all his pain and stiffness. "The ulun-suti is mine," he shouted in a hoarse voice, crowding George as he advanced with the ax held diagonally across his chest, blade down. "It cannot be stolen from its master while he lives, George, and I am still alive!"

As Young Squirrel moved in, George reached out and seized the ax's handle with both hands. "Stop this, old man! This is foolish. You're not strong enough to kill me."

For a moment neither man moved; they stared at one another, eyes locked.

Then both tightened their grip on the ax's handle and George began to jerk at it in an attempt to gain control of the weapon.

"Let go!" he shouted, but the old man gave the ax such a violent wrench that it jerked upwards – the flat side of its blade struck him on the temple.

Stunned, Young Squirrel let go of the handle and dropped back a step. He touched his temple. It felt sticky and hot. He stared down at his hand. It was red with blood. He looked back at George in time to see his nephew raise the ax blade over his head, as though he intended to split the trader like a piece of kindling. Young Squirrel lurched to one side, knocking into a hutch and sending crockery crashing to the wooden floor. But George's swing was wide of its mark. It missed him entirely. The blade made a dull thud as it struck the floor and bounced once. Reaching down, Young Squirrel grabbed the ax just below the blade.

George howled in anger, then kicked at the old man and tried to throw him off balance by thrusting the ax at him. Young Squirrel responded with wrenching motions intended to jerk the handle out of George's grip. George moved his hands farther up the handle, trying to get some leverage.

Then Young Squirrel made his mistake: he leaned forward and tried to bite George on the knuckle in an attempt to make him let go. As soon as he was off balance, the younger man shoved the ax against his body with all of his might.

Young Squirrel reeled backward and fell sideways against the wall of the lean-to. As he struggled to regain his balance, his body turned away from George, the younger man once again raised the ax above his head and brought the blade down hard on the back of his uncle's head. The blow resounded with a hollow pop. Blood gushed from the wound carved into the back of the trader's head.

George dropped the ax and staggered backwards. Young Squirrel slumped towards the floor, blood pouring from his opened skull. George turned and lunged for the door. However, just as his hand closed upon its handle, Young Squirrel's body slammed heavily against the door, making escape impossible – it was as though his body was a sack of meal heaved there by some unseen hands.

Blood from the wound was now spreading thickly across the side of Young Squirrel's face. Looking down, George saw that his uncle had somehow managed to pick up the ax again. "Give me the ulunsuti," Young Squirrel whispered hoarsely. He was not six inches from George's ear, yet his voice sounded inhuman, like a wind come from far off. From the Darkening Land, George realized with terror. Was Young Squirrel dead or alive? He couldn't tell.

He grabbed at the ax once again and, once again, the two men executed their slow dance around the room, jabbing and pushing at each other with the ax that hung between them, Young Squirrel's split head dripping blood onto the floor until the yellow poplar was slick with crimson.

"Give up, old man! You're dying!" George wept with horror, but Young Squirrel did not say a word. Instead he grabbed a hank of George's hair and yanked him towards him, causing the younger man to lose his footing on the slippery floor. George lurched forward, falling to his hands and knees. As he struggled to regain his feet, Young Squirrel stumbled backwards and raised the ax, but the old man had grown weak from loss of blood. He could lift the ax no higher than his chest.

Twisting around, George grabbed Young Squirrel around the knees and pulled him towards him. The old man sprawled forward, falling almost on top of George. George shoved him hastily to one side, jumped to his feet and lunged towards the door again, but his hands were slippery now with Young Squirrel's blood. He couldn't get enough of a grip on the knob to turn it. He pivoted around just as Young Squirrel struggled to his feet and began to shuffle, weaving drunkenly, towards him. The old man was covered with blood. His eyes were glazed, unseeing. His lips moved silently, forming a word over and over again, "*E tsi!*" Mother!

"Die!" sobbed George. "You are supposed to die!" At this, Young Squirrel's glazed eyes widened and for one moment became strangely focussed, as though he glimpsed something just beyond George's shoulder.

"George Kinnahan!" He exclaimed softly, as if in greeting. Then his eyes narrowed again to slits and, placing one finger to his lips, he breathed out from somewhere deep in the back of his throat. "*Shhhh-hhhhh!*"

In a frenzy of fear, George seized the ax once more, wrapping both hands around the blade, and jerked violently at it, then leaned as far back as he could manage, breaking Young Squirrel's grip on the slippery handle. The old man reeled backwards a few steps, then regained his balance and rushed forward towards his opponent once again. As he did, George lifted the ax and brought it down across the top of the trader's forehead, piercing the skull with a hollow, cracking sound.

Young Squirrel threw his arms straight up in the air and shouted.

George raised the ax again and again brought it down on his uncle's forehead, once more cracking the skull.

Young Squirrel groaned and, doubling up, clutched his head. Fistfuls of his gray hair came loose in his clenched hands.

George struck a third blow, missing his uncle's head and slicing, instead, into his right elbow, snapping the bone. The old man's right arm dangled limply at his side. For a fourth time and a fifth, George swung the ax, turning the top of Young Squirrel's head into a red paste, carving deep gashes in his arms as the trader tried in vain to block the metal with his own flesh.

"Lie down! Lie down!" George insisted, but, though the old man's legs had begun to buckle, still he remained standing. His head bobbed and wove instinctively as he tried to avoid the next blow. His eyes rolled wildly in their sockets. If only he would lie down, then this would all be over. But Young Squirrel would not lie down.

Fear fueled George's frenzy. Was Young Squirrel a monster? A creature from the Darkening Land who would not die, no matter what?

What must he do to kill him? Anyone else would have been dead long ago.

He chopped and hacked and raised the ax again to swing again.

Finally Young Squirrel's legs became tangled with one another; he wobbled; one of his moccasins slid wetly across the floor, taking one leg with it. He swiveled in a half circle, knelt, and finally sat on the floor, his head slumped forward, his back to George. "Lie down!" George howled again. Rushing up behind him, he landed repeated blows to the old man's shoulders and the base of his skull. Then he struck him another time across the top of his head. Young Squirrel's brain seeped gray from the gash. He twitched once and lurched backwards, his bloody head thudding against the floor and landing between George's spread legs.

George screamed and swung again at the man who wouldn't die. He swung the ax at least a dozen times more, this time aiming at his uncle's face, his eyes until, at last, Young Squirrel's face was obliterated and the younger man's strength spent. Only then did George drop the ax and, wheezing for air, his heart pounding, kick it to one side. He turned away from Young Squirrel's body, not wanting to look at the carnage. His hands fell to his knees. He bent forward. His head drooped between his shoulders. He gulped for air until, at last, his chest ceased to ache and he could begin to breathe normally again. Then he straightened up again and walked hurriedly to the far end of the room. He crouched by the hearth, his arms wrapped around his knees. Though the day was a warm one and, moments before, he had been drenched in sweat, he now felt cold. His teeth chattered in his head; he shivered. Silently, he rocked back and forth on the hearthstone, staring at Young Squirrel's butchered body. There was blood everywhere. Much of it was not red, but black, or perhaps the blood was mixed with some other fluid that had flowed out of one of the gaping wounds carved into the trader's body. It was difficult to tell where one left off and the other began.

George smelled his hands. As a hunter, he knew that blood smell well enough, but, when he hunted, he did not hack his prey to pieces.

A single shot was often all it took and, when he skinned an animal, he was careful not to pierce its organs and taint the meat. Young Squirrel's neat house smelled of brains and the contents of intestines and severed glands. It was a pungent, fetid smell – hot, close and sickly. Smelling it now, George retched, gagging on the phlegm and bile that had collected in the back of his throat.

Vomiting up what there was in his stomach, he stood, shakily, and made his stumbling way to the door. After several attempts at getting the blood-sticky handle to turn, he seized a piece of Nancy's calico from the sewing basket beside the table and, placing it over the knob, succeeded finally in turning it.

He stepped out onto the porch. His mother was not there. How could she have been? All that shouting and the sound of the ax coming down over and over again . . . .

He stood, resting his weight against one of the posts which held up the porch, staring out at the door yard.

Then suddenly she was there, standing at the forest edge, with a basket on her arm and a look of horror on her face.

TWELVE

At the sight of her son standing on the front porch, covered with blood, Nancy's throat constricted like a fist squeezed shut. Her eyes widened. She parted her lips to speak, but could force no air through them. The silence seemed too huge to breach. She had heard this kind of silence once before – the day she had returned from the Zants to her father's homestead at Hiwasee to find her family murdered.

"Mother!" George stumbled down the steps, his bloody hands extended to her.

She dropped back a step and half turned, as though to flee. When she found her voice, it was thin and scratchy, like something that has not been used for a long time. "What have you done?" she demanded hoarsely. "Where is Young Squirrel? Where is my brother?"

"He tried to kill me!" George started towards her.

"Stop!" Covering her eyes with one hand, she held her other hand up, wrist flexed, to ward him off. "Don't come nearer, Georgie!"

George stopped half way across the yard. After a moment, he tried again. "He took the ax . . . ."

"I will not hear this, Georgie!" Uncovering her eyes, she glared at him. Then her eyes filled with tears and her face crumpled. "I cannot have this happen to me!" She turned away from him, shaking her head. "This has not happened! You have not done this terrible thing! Not my son! Not to Young Squirrel! No! No!" She crossed her arms over her breast and bent over at the waist, her body convulsing with nearly silent sobs. Then, after a few moments, she looked up again. Her eyes darted this way and that – she did not look at George. "I must leave here at once!" The words were barely audible. It was as though she were speaking to herself. "Yes! I must get out of here!" Hiking up her skirts, she wheeled first one way and then the other. Where should she go? Back to the river, or south, to the village?

George crossed the yard in two quick strides and grabbed her arm to detain her. She screamed and struck at him on the arm and chest with her fists. "Let me go! Let me go, murderer!"

"Stop it! Stop it, Mother!" George seized both her wrists, so that she would unable to hurt him. Just then a noise, coming from inside the house, made them stop and listen – a sound like wind howling up a narrow valley and, as they stood, riveted to the spot with horror, the sound grew louder, more insistent. George released his grip on her wrists. Together they turned and looked towards the house. "Is he not dead?" George shook his head, incredulous. "Surely he is dead!"

Nancy's hand rose to her throat. She took a step towards the house. George seized her arm. "Where are you going?"

"If he is alive, I must go to him!"

"But if it is not Young Squirrel? What if it is something else that makes this noise? Some evil spirit? A night walker?"

"Then let the night walker eat my heart and have the years that are left me! If Young Squirrel is dead at your hand, I have no will to live." She crossed the dooryard and climbed the steps to the porch. She hesitated for a moment at the door, bowing her head, then, straightening her spine, she opened the door and entered the house which Young Squirrel had built for her in the year of George Butler's birth.

Her half-brother lay face up, his head next to a front corner of the cabinet which stood to one side of the entrance to the lean-to. His legs, streaked with blood and criss-crossed with slender incisions, were stretched out rigidly; his knees locked. The rumpled linen suit he habitually wore was so saturated with blood that its grayish white color had gone brown. One arm lay in a pool of blood and fluid. The elbow of this arm had sustained a cut so wide and deep that, at first glance, it appeared to be severed. As for his face, all that remained of it was a mouth fashioned into a half grin, showing his front teeth, and one eye, the left, which stared down at his nearly severed arm. The rest was a red pulp, about which matted gray hair, tangled and soaked with dark blood, radiated in all directions. A few feet from his head was the heavy, wooden-handled, three-foot long ax she used to chop wood.

Kneeling beside her half-brother's body, she passed the palm of her hand over the ruined face as if to caress it; there was no touching him now. "Young Squirrel!" Tears leaked from her eyes in a constant stream, blurring her vision. They pricked her cheeks like pieces of broken glass. "Do you see?" she asked the ruined head. "I wear your ring still!"

"Aagghh!" A shrill, high voice that ended in a hoarse bray.

Lifting her head, Nancy turned and blinked in its direction. It was He Grows Up Wild, crouched in the corner by the hearth. He was very faint; she could hardly make out his contours. He lifted his chin and moaned and howled – it was the sound they had heard outside – a sound like the wind in the valley. "He is dead, Sister! Your Georgie has killed Young Squirrel, and now I too am dying!"

"What is that sound?" George stood tentatively in the doorway, peering into the house. He looked straight at He Grows Up Wild, but it was clear from his expression that he did not see his uncle's blood brother.

"Nothing," she told him shortly and turned back to Young Squirrel's bloodied corpse.

He Grows Up Wild moaned and rolled his eyes wildly. "He is dead, Sister! Tend to me and perhaps I will recover!"

"Go ahead and die! I shall be well rid of you!"

"What are you saying, Mother?" George could not believe his ears. Surely, no matter what he did, his mother would always love him! Hadn't it been ever so?

But, "Get out of here, Georgie! I do not want to see you. Go now."

"He was old, Mother! He was sick!" George defended himself. "I have two sons now. I must look out for them. Young Squirrel was my uncle, flesh and blood to me. He should have agreed to let me have the trading post."

"What?" Nancy exploded. "He had already given you the tavern and the mill! Did you want everything?"

"He wanted the ulunsuti. I couldn't give that up."

"Sister!" He Grows Up Wild lurched to one side and then tumbled over onto the hearthstone. He lay there for a moment, on his face. "I am coming apart," he muttered.

Removing his knife from the sheath strapped to his leg and thrusting Nancy to one side, George stepped gingerly over Young Squirrel's body and split his uncle's mattress down the middle. The sharp edges of new American dollar bills poked through the rent he had made in the ticking. He grabbed a fistful of dollars and stuffed them into the pocket of his breeches. Then he stopped. "There is too much," he observed, as though to himself. "I will need a bag."

"Have you killed your uncle for money, then?" Nancy demanded. "Have you killed my brother for land?"

He Grows Up Wild was growing even more indistinct. Sprawled over the hearthstone, he resembled a human being only to the extent that a cloud might remind a child gazing up at the sky of a ship or a cow. "I have always loved you, Sister! Always, from the first time I saw you. So beautiful. So like our faithless mother . . . . That was when I recommended to Young Squirrel that we rape you and carry you off . . . but he was always so reticent! What a fool he was, our brother! A most terrible, foolish fool . . . ."

Nancy sat on the floor beside Young Squirrel. She bowed her head and wept. George could not remember her weeping since Willy's death.

"Listen to me, Mother." Kneeling beside her, he placed his hands on her shoulders. "When you came to see Young Squirrel . . . when you moved in here, I thought, 'Good. Maybe now we will have something from the old man.' But there was nothing. All these months and nothing came of it. So I began to barter, using the only thing I had that he wanted – the ulunsuti – and I got the mill and I got the tavern and I would have gotten the trading post if he had not gone crazy like he did and tried to kill me. I didn't do it for me, Mother. I did it so that you and I and Snowbird and the boys . . . so that all of us could live and be well and rich."

Nancy said nothing.

George stood abruptly. He felt frustrated, angry. "What is the matter with you, old woman?" he demanded harshly. He strode to the door. "Would you rather Young Squirrel have killed me?" When she still did not speak, he stamped his foot in its heavy boot. "A lonely old man who loved no one and was loved by no one has died in his sleep . . . that is what we will tell everyone and what everyone will think . . . and now we have a house and a store and a tavern and a mill and money, Mother, lots of American money."

"What do I need with money?" Nancy spat the question out. "And Young Squirrel did love someone. He loved *me*!" She turned her head away. "And I . . . I loved him." Her voice so low that it was barely audible.

"At last she says it," He Grows Up Wild observed, but in a low-pitched voice that was not like his usual shrill – it was as though, in his final moments, Young Squirrel's released spirit had blended with that of his spectral blood brother. "Now, when there is nothing but darkness. Horrible. Tedious. Like being in a dark room and not knowing the way out." The voice became louder. "Nancy! Nancy! Bring a light!"

"I will go now and dig a grave," said George. "Together we will bury him. Then you will get water and soap and cleanse this house of blood." He turned to leave.

Nancy rose from a sitting position to her haunches. "I walked away from Gall Place for you, though it meant the death of Willy and I knew it. And I endured your wife for your sake and the sake of my grandsons, but I will not lift my hand to help you in this, George Butler!" She stood. "Give Snowbird a bucket and mop. Let her clean up after your murder!"

Startled, George stopped and, turning back, crossed to her. He took her by the shoulders. "The uktena's dream," he said in a low, urgent voice. "You must follow me to the water. You must come live with me in the river. There is no life for you without me, for you are my mother!"

"Like the angry boy in the dream, you have become a monster," said Nancy. "But I will dream the dream of monsters no longer."

George released her and stepped back. "As you wish, Mother!" he said angrily. "I will dig the grave now."

When he had gone, she gathered up a few things and tied them into a bundle. Then she took Young Squirrel's walking stick and, carefully wiped the blood from it. She would need a stout stick on her journey. Before leaving, she glanced once at the hearth. No spirit body lay sprawled across it, not even a shred of mist. He Grows Up Wild was gone, disappeared.

She walked out onto the porch, letting her hand fall lightly upon the back of the twig rocker which Young Squirrel had had made to resemble George Kinnahan's, thinking that this would make Nancy feel at home. The day she had found her father murdered, he had been sitting in the rocker on the porch at Hiwasee, the Bucksmasher on his knees, his scalp removed, his pate bloody, staring blind-eyed out into the woods beyond the door yard.

She could hear George now, out back of the shed. Digging Young Squirrel's grave. She sat down in the rocker and looked out towards the woods.

Once, she thought she saw Willy pass between the tall trees. Young Squirrel was with him.

Then her mother.

Then Charley.

The forest was full of ghosts.

At last she stood and, cradling her bundle as though it were a child, started down the steps and across the yard for the last time.

No one ever saw Nancy Butler again. George thought that she must have gone in search of Gall Place and died in the surrounding forest. He put such faith in the ulunsuti's power that he believed that no human being could approach the medicine lake without its assistance.

Toineeta up at Madcap Branch, however, remembered that such a feat was possible through fasting and meditation. When now and again she dreamed of Gall Place, as she had long been wont to do, she saw Nancy kneel by the lake and, standing, turn to walk with slow steps towards the weather-beaten cabin. In her dreams there were always many animals and birds about Nancy. She was not alone. The old woman did not tell George of this, for he had grown over the years to be a violent man, murderous in rage, and who knew how he would take news of the mother who had, at last, left him to his own devices?

BRAINERD ACADEMY

ONE

Have you ever noticed? History is a grid we lay upon the past for the purpose of a more general discussion – our coordinates are this or that war, this or that outbreak of pestilence, this or that treaty. However, we do not measure our own lives in such a useful, disinterested way. We say instead . . . .

"The year Mother died . . . ."

"When John went to war and never came home . . . ."

"After Elsbeth had the Scarlet Fever and we burnt every scrap of clothing in the nursery . . . . Yes, every toy and every blanket, and still the baby got it."

"The spring my heart broke and I thought I would die and did not . . . ."

We string our personal histories together like the women string beads on a thread, one event crowding close upon the other. Our memory selects what it chooses. To the extent that we feel pain, joy, longing, love . . . to that extent we remember and to that extent does the event become part of our history. Otherwise it slips from us to the floor and later someone sweeps it away – gone. Life is a long, slow dance. We chose some partners; others are chosen for us; and sometimes we must dance up through the pain to get to the other side, as when we must pass crouched through the gauntlet of a terrifying quadrille.

This is where I enter the story – Sophia Sawyer. I can't remember how old I was that autumn – my late twenties, perhaps, or possibly my early thirties – but, for all I knew of life and its dark dancing partners Sorrow and Death, I might as well have been pulled from my mother's womb the day before, so little did I know, so little did I understand.

✺

If you were a bird flying high in the sky, you would have seen this, looking down at our school – a vast expanse of forest and, carved out of this wilderness of random trees, a little clearing in which you might distinguish stables and storage rooms, a schoolhouse, dormitories, cabins for dining, sewing and weaving, little houses for teachers, male and female, and one for our Director, Reverend Cornelius, assorted outbuildings, a spring house and several acres cleared for planting, and there, on the steps leading up to the big log schoolhouse, with a psalter in one hand and a hymnal in the other, me, Sophia Sawyer of New Hampshire, on that autumn day when they arrived. I remember it so vividly. I had just turned to go into the schoolhouse when the white coach, stained red with Tennessee clay, came rattling through a crimson dust cloud which it had kicked up and which preceded it like one of the Plagues of Egypt, and shuddered and heaved down the rutted dirt road that led towards our version of sweet Salvation.

It was early October. Heat lingered still in the air, but the sun looked farther away in the sky than it had during high summer and more distinct and friendlier than the white smear of pulsating star which it had been for much of July and August. It had been my first summer away from New Hampshire and I confess that I had nearly perished in all that thick, swampy heat.

Now, however, there was an edge to the air like coolness and a smell of wood smoke from the hardby mountains, where, I was told, the Cherokee (whom it was our mission to deliver from General Evil) were firing the brush. This was their custom in the fall – to make of the vast forests that carpeted their land a canopied highway on which they might more easily travel throughout the coming winter.

As the coach pulled up in front of the schoolhouse, I saw that a man of middle years, tall and heavyset with broad, unwieldy shoulders, was seated on the coach's box beside the vehicle's Negro driver. Across his knees lay a Kentucky rifle. From the curious taupe color of his skin and the dull blackness of his hair, I surmised that he was an MB. That is how we categorized the students at the school among ourselves: MB for mixed blood; FB for full blood. Judging from his tightly fitted tan breeches and his dark green coat, he was a rich man as well. There were many rich Cherokee – MBs, the majority of them. They owned vast acreage and many African slaves and lived in fine brick and clapboard houses across the lawns of which peacocks strutted. Many had enrolled their children in our school, coming from as far as Georgia and northern Alabama to do so – it was the Rosses and the Ridges and the Vanns, the Hicks and the Scots, those with some English already and a smattering of learning, who tended to prize an English education. The FBs living in isolated mountain coves or away down the distant rivers were less tractable.

The driver gathered up the reins, pulling them tight as he did to bring the carriage to a full halt before the schoolhouse. He was coated all over with a layer of red clay dust. The man beside him leaned forward and spoke to me. "This is the Brainerd School?"

"Yes," I replied, thinking that his accent was a bit odd. Flat. I was not sure of his command of English.

However, it proved perfectly adequate. He turned to his coachman. "Let them out, Lehi."

The coachman laid the coiled reins on the seat and jumped nimbly off the box. He was as thin as something boiled and spry in the same desperate way a stray dog is. Yanking open the conveyance's door, he half handed, half hauled a tiny woman from the coach. She seemed to have some difficulty negotiating the descent on her own or, indeed, in standing on her own. She was no larger than a child and must have been quite pretty once, though now she looked worn. From her coloring and the cast of her features she looked to be an FB. Her silky black hair, streaked here and there with gray, hung straight and long down her back to her waist; combs of carved tortoiseshell held it back from her round face. She wore a voluminous red calico dress, not gathered at the waist, but worn loose, like the smocks favored by white women expecting a child in the last months of their confinement. From underneath the hem of the dress poked pale deerskin moccasins decorated with red beads. The little woman gripped the coachman's arm tightly, while the remaining two passengers, adolescent boys dressed awkwardly in best clothes a size too large for them, shambled out after her. These two boys resembled one another in every way, except that one was not quite as tall as the other and stooped and much thinner. It was apparent from his pallor and the way that he dragged one leg that he was not well. The more fit lad handed his mother and brother each a silver-headed cane from inside the carriage. Releasing the coachman's arm and planting the cane's tip firmly into the ground, the mother leaned forward, resting her weight upon it. They all proceeded to stare at me.

Feeling distinctly awkward, for I am not an easy person when it comes to social graces, I broke the silence. "I am Miss Sawyer. From New Hampshire. I am a teacher here at Brainerd."

"I am George Butler from Qualla. One of the Middle Towns," the man on the coach box explained. His voice was raspy; his tone gruff. "These are my sons, Joseph and Charley. This is their mother, Snowbird." As he spoke, I noticed the hands gripping the rifle for the first time. They were swollen and livid. Later his son would tell me that George Butler had once been quick to brawl and, in successive fights, had broken many small bones in his hands. Arthritis settled into the places where his bones had been broken, causing him almost constant pain. I also noticed the leather flask sitting beside him on the box.

"Do you wish to send your boys to our school, Mr. Butler?"

"We do," he replied. "Right now! Right away! You will teach them to be white men! You will begin this minute!"

"We will teach them to read and write and to do their numbers," I advised him somewhat stiffly – in those days I was still stiff. "We will teach them about our Lord Jesus Christ."

At this, George Butler's face became very red. "No *Jesus!*" he shouted, glowering at me. Seizing the flask, he opened it and drank. He was brutish in his manner and rather frightening.

"He does not like Christians," Snowbird explained hastily. "During the Cold Moon we thought he was dying. We thought an Utluhtu had got his liver for sure, so the Moravians came to the house and tried to tell him about that fellow Jesus. *Yu!* But George Butler jumped from his bed as alive as anyone and threw them from the house. You have never heard such a terrible uproar in your life."

"The Moravians talk about nothing but Jesus and Hell. I do not like it at all," said George. "They say I'm going to this Hell. I will go where I choose. Reading, writing and numbers. To learn the ways of the white man. That's what my boys need. Not Jesus."

"We cannot . . . neglect the children's spiritual needs," I faltered.

"George!" his wife implored. "Religion is a small price to pay for an education! Besides, you will not have to hear about Jesus if you don't want to. The boys will not mention him. Or Hell either."

"We won't say a word, Father," promised the lame son.

"We p-p-promise," the other son reassured him.

This seemed to mollify their father somewhat. "Good. For I will have no Hell and brimstone in my home, I assure you. Their bags!" He barked to the coachman. "Get down their bags."

The coachman removed two large leather valises from the carriage and placed them on the ground next to the boys.

"Get in the coach, Snowbird!" George instructed his wife.

"You will take care of them, won't you?" Snowbird pleaded with me. "They have only fifteen winters . . . they are men, but still boys. My mother-in-law cut me open with a big knife so that they could be born. She and an old woman who is a witch! They cut me in half and stitched me back together, but the old witch did it and she was blind. I grew back, but not the way I was before. Now I am all crooked and ugly and barely able to stand as you see, and, for this reason, I have no other children but my sons . . . ."

"The white woman does not want to hear about your trouble, Woman With No Middle," George Butler barked. "Get into the coach!"

Snowbird's chin sunk to her chest. Big tears rolled down her cheeks. She took the coachman's extended arm and climbed into the coach. The coachman shut the door and climbed onto the box.

Snowbird leaned out the window. "Look after Charley!"

"There is money enough in their valises for your price and their needs." George Butler was brusque. He nodded to the coachman. Lehi picked up the reins and slapped them over the backs of the horses. The horses whinnied and started nervously forward.

"He is sick!" cried Snowbird so that her voice would carry over the rattle of the carriage. "Charley has always been sick!" The carriage made a slow arc around the boys in front of the schoolhouse and started down the road again. "It's his hip!" By now, Snowbird had heaved herself half out the window and hung there, staring back at the boys. Then the red dust kicked up by the horses obscured her view of them and ours of her. George, I noticed, had not looked back at his sons once, but sat stiffly on the box, staring fixedly ahead at the road.

Taken aback by the abruptness of the Butlers' departure, I required a moment to collect myself. Then I said, very primly, "I suppose I had better take you two along to Reverend Cornelius."

But the boys did not seem to have heard me. Instead they stood in the road beside their valises, their mouths gaping, staring down the road in the direction the carriage had gone. They must have wondered what had just happened. I certainly did.

❧

Of the two Butler brothers, the stronger one, Joseph, showed sufficient progress (despite a slight stutter which no amount of shaming by the Director seemed to ameliorate) that, by the end of November, he had been selected by Reverend Cornelius to attend the school established in Cornwall, Connecticut, by the American Board for Commissioners of

Foreign Missions to educate and train heathen youth; as it fell out, an unfortunate Maori student at Cornwall had fallen ill with measles soon after arriving at the school and died, thereby creating a vacancy into which Joseph was able to step. At the time the boy went north to Connecticut, the missionary school included among its pupils Malays, Tahitians, Mauis, Hawaiians, Maoris, of course, and, from those Indian tribes which were neighbors to the United States, Choctaws, Monhegans, Oneidas, Tuscaroras, Coughnawaugha Mohawks, as well as the sons of several distinguished MB Cherokee families, such as John Ridge and Elias Boudinot and Charles Hicks.

The other brother, however, Charley Butler, did not prosper at Brainerd. Our physician Reverend Butrick quickly diagnosed his condition as a scrofula, which seemed concentrated in his left hip. "I can palpitate quite a sizable tumor inside the hip joint," Reverend Butrick explained in his sweet, light voice. David Butrick was a slight man, with wispy blond hair and a raw, red face. "It will probably become an ulcer and over time that ulcer will deepen, leading to the progressive destruction of the surrounding bone. That is the usual progress of scrofula." Judging from what Charley said of his illness, it was chronic; he could not remember a time when he had not experienced a painful itch in his hip joint or walked without a cane. Reverend Butrick went on to point out – delicately, of course, for our Director, Reverend Cornelius, was a somewhat prickly man, given to bombast – that the habitual dankness of the boys' cabin could only exacerbate Charley's already miserable condition. Those afflicted with scrofula were also prone to consumption, for example.

The Director, after some deliberation and consultation with his wife and, on the whole, rather ungraciously, agreed to have Charley moved for the interim into the garret of his own small house. "It will be your job to give Charles Butler his lessons," he informed me. "Brainerd is not a home for convalescents. If the boy's to stay, he must learn something."

That is how the small bit of my life that most closely resembles Heaven began.

TWO

Charley was so slight at fifteen that he might have passed for twelve. Having an Indian's warm, coppery coloring, he could not be said to be pale exactly, but his skin did appear thin to the point of transparency. The scrofula affected his tear ducts as well; when they were aggravated – as happened if he rubbed them too strenuously – his eyes watered so incessantly that his cheeks became chapped and had to be painted with a thick cold cream composed of boiled and strained Irish moss to which glycerin had been added. It was Sister Ann Brown who made most of our remedies and, if the truth be known, she had no little help in this from the mothers of our students who were always bringing her this root or that bark and saying, "Boil this with goat's milk and her diarrhea will disappear in two days," or, "If you let him eat freely of parched Indian corn, that jaundice will subside." And Charley had what Reverend Butrick referred to as a slight exophthalmia, which is to say, his eyes, always bright with the fluctuating fever that accompanies scrofula, bulged.

To discourage consumption, I used to rub a camphor salve on his thin chest and lay a piece of warm flannel over it. I warmed the flannel by wrapping it about a brick that had been placed on the hearthstone. There were four of these bricks in a constant rotation: two to warm the flannel cloths for his chest and two to place at the foot of his bed beneath the covers.

What picture of my boyish love have I drawn for you so far? A youth that looked like a child? Small, crooked and stooped as an old man? Thin as an animal starved over a long winter, who comes staggering on wobbly legs into the settlement to look for food with glazed eyes? His skin transparent, his eyes feverish and protruding, his greased cheeks flaming? Huddled among the feather pillows in Reverend Cornelius' garret room, smelling of camphor?

But there was something more, something I did not quite notice at first and then, later, once I had noticed it, did not dare to believe or, even later, to share with others, for it was something impossible, something that could not be true, that must mean that I was mad. It was this: regardless of whether the day was a cloudy one or the night moonless, regardless of whether the room was windowless or, later, when he had recovered somewhat and we took walks out of doors, I never once saw Charley Butler save in a pool of the most sparkling white light. And so I came to think of him as a kind of angel, whose radiance, apparently, only I could discern.

THREE

One of the stories that Charley told me as we whiled away the winter of 1824 in the Cornelius' garret was why his father had decided to send the two boys to school far away from their native village. There was a conservative movement afoot in Qualla and the surrounding region that rejected the ways of the white man and urged a return to the old ways. Because of his various business interests, George Butler was at odds with this movement. It was a source of further aggravation that it was the wheelwright Tsinawi, Snowbird's father, who headed it up. This, to the best of my recollection, was the story.

One day Tsinawi was fixing the wheel of a wagon belonging to a Moravian named Schmidt who had recently settled up around Sugarlands. The wheel had become bent when the wagon, driven by Schmidt's wife, had jumped the road into a field Schmidt had only half-cleared of trees and crashed headlong into a stump. According to neighbors, the woman had been screaming and had to be wrestled down from the wrecked wagon and sedated with laudanum. She was trying to get away from Schmidt and her five children, although it was not clear where she thought she might be able to escape to, out in the middle of the Back of Beyond on an afternoon in late July.

Schmidt, a big man with white blond hair and a massive skull, hunkered down in the yard next to the wheelwright and said, "You know, Tsinawi, your Great Spirit is the Father of Lies." He spoke with such great assurance that Tsinawi wondered how the white man could be so confident about matters that are difficult to understand – how the world began and who the moon and the sun are and how the people are to keep the world from growing so old that the cords which bind it to the sky vault snap and it falls into the Great Ocean. "Your legends are stories for children," he told him. "Your shamans consort with demons."

"Do you mind?" Tsinawi asked. "I am trying to fix your wheel."

"And I am trying to save your soul!"

Tsinawi sighed. He did not wish to point out that first Schmidt should see a healer about curing his wife's madness, for that was impolite. "I disagree with you," he said. "Our legends are how we know who we are and what has happened before us. Our medicine men act as guides at the points where different worlds converge."

"All you Cherokee are going to burn in the eternal fires of Hell if you do not forsake your heathen ways and follow the way of Christ," said Schmidt.

This exchange with the Moravian so upset Tsinawi that he decided to go hunting by himself away up north around Cold Mountain. His sons did not want him to go alone, for he was an old man by now and not so strong or nimble as he had once been and at times forgetful of eating and at others given to absences while still in the body – which is to say that he would appear to be someplace, but, upon closer examination, would be found to have gone somewhere else entirely – where, no one could say. But Tsinawi said there was no point in going away if he could not be by himself and would hear nothing of any company.

Cold Mountain is about a day and a half's journey from Qualla and separates the waters of Pigeon River from those flowing east into Tennessee Creek and Cany fork of the Tuckasegee; it is a sorter of waters. At its base lies Shining Rock or Datsuna-laskuh-i, "Where the tracks are," and at its crest the Tanasee Bald – the field the giant Tsulkaka cleared for his farm. About one hundred acres in all, a good-sized field for a giant, it can be reached only by climbing hand over hand up steep slopes covered with thickets of balsam and rhododendron, all grown together in a thick mass. This was where Tsinawi camped and where he saw the horsemen. And this is what he told the people who gathered in the council house to hear him upon his return to the village: "I had just made a fire when, all of a sudden, I heard a great noise coming from the sky. It is a storm! I thought, for all afternoon the sky had been filling up with clouds. I looked up and what did I see but the heavens opening up, and sun streaming through the opening so bright that it nearly blinded me and then Indians, thousands and thousands of Indians. So many I could not count. They were riding down to earth from the sky on black horses.

"Now this is something you don't see every day, I thought, but just then, their leader, a fine-looking man with long black hair drumming as he rode on a wooden drum, this man spotted me and rode over to where I was. His horse hovered about six feet above me but some feet away, which is good, for a man does not want to be directly under a horse, hovering or not. 'Don't be afraid, Tsinawi,' he said. 'We are your brothers and have been sent to tell you that the Great Spirit is displeased with the Cherokee for accepting the ways of the white people. You can see for yourself why. So much of the game which the Great Spirit put in these forests so that the Cherokee might hunt are now gone. Soon there will be no more. Also, you plant the corn of the white man in your fields – wheat, I mean, not the corn of the Indian. Hear this, Tsinawi. You must tell the Cherokee to plant Indian corn in their fields and to gather it according to the ways of our ancestors and to do away with these terrible grinding mills.'

"'Often we send Indian corn to be ground in the white man's mills,' I told him. 'When it is ground we call it grits or cornmeal. It is much easier to send it to the mill than it is for the women to pound it with a *ka no na.*'

"But the leader waved his hand impatiently. 'Don't you wonder why the Corn Mother has abandoned you?' he asked. 'It is because the grinding of the mills breaks Selu's bones! She wants to come back to you, but only if you drive the white men from the country and go back to your former ways.'

"'I agree with you,' I said. 'Tell me what we must do.'

"'You must put aside the white man's clothing,' explained the leader, 'and his beds that are off the floor and his books and, especially, you must put aside his cats. A cat does not make a fit companion for an Indian. A dog, on the other hand, that's a different story.'

"'Who can disagree with that?' I asked. I myself had long been clear on this point. 'But many Cherokee ask why can't they live like the whites? The whites appear to have many fine ways of doing things and goods the likes of which we have never seen before!'

"The leader shook his head. 'White people are different from us, Tsinawi,' he said. 'Surely they are the children of some evil spirit, fashioned from the scum of the Great Water. We, on the other hand, are the children of the Great Spirit, who fashioned us from red clay. Why else would we be red?'

"'I thought it was because old Sun burned us,' I said. 'Because we conspired to kill her daughter.'

"'That too,' he granted. 'There are many reasons for the redness of our skin, but you are not paying attention, Tsinawi, and this is a great matter I am sent on – a matter of life and death.'

"'Tell me your purpose,' I said. 'I will listen.'

"'Our people are in grave danger,' he told me. 'We have broken the road which was given to our fathers at the beginning of the world and, if we are to travel that road again, first we must fix it. The road is broken! It is broken!' And suddenly he threw back his head and began to wail, at which point the Indians accompanying him threw their heads back and began to wail as well."

Tsinawi had never heard such a terrible sound. He thought his eardrums might burst. It was as though he had been sucked up inside a thundercloud in the middle of a fierce storm. Clapping his hands over his ears, he cried out, "Stop! Desist! We have no argument, brother. The road is broken. I agree. Won't you tell me what must we do to fix it? I am a wheelwright. Perhaps I can help."

"Are you listening, old man?" the leader cried. "How many times do I have to tell you? Return to the old ways! Leave to the white man his flour mills and his talking leaves and his Jesus. They are not for you. What? Do you think that, just because you adopt the white man's ways, he will accept you?' He laughed a terrible laugh. ("I can hear it still, ringing in my still smarting ears," Tsinawi remembered.) "I tell you this,

Tsinawi, he will not accept you. He will never accept you, no matter what you do. The white man hates all Indians. He hates the Cherokee. It is our land he loves, not us. Despite what the missionaries say. Despite what the politicians in Washington say. They think nothing of us. They lie and they steal. They have no honor. Open your eyes. See what must be seen! Already the white man has taken much. Soon he will take it all. Tecumseh was right when he said the white man is like a hungry wolf, but the Cherokee chiefs would not listen to him when he came to them and so it has come to this. Our land! Our land that was given to us by the Great Spirit! What will we be without our land?" Once again he threw back his head and began to wail, a cue for his fellow riders to do the same.

Tsinawi fell to his knees and begged him to stop. "As for me, I will gladly foreswear the white man's ways but how am I to persuade others? I am not a chief or a rich man. Why would people listen to me?"

The leader held up his hand. "There will be a terrible storm. Tell everyone in Qualla what I have told you. Those who believe you must gather on top of Rattlesnake Mountain, for that will be the only safe place."

"Safe from what?"

"The Great Spirit's anger."

"But . . . ." Before he could ask how he would know that the storm in question was the correct one, storms being a frequent occurrence in these parts, the leader's black steed reared up and he wheeled around and galloped off after the other Indians from the sky. Tsinawi got up as quickly as his old, bandy legs would permit him and hobbled over to a big boulder onto which he crawled. From it he could see down into the shadowy valley where, in the gathering dusk, the Pigeon flowed dark, like a river of tar.

He watched as the Indians on black horses and their leader rode down, down, down through the mist that hung trapped in the valley and disappeared one after another into the river. "They probably went to visit the People Who Live Under the River," he deduced, for there was a man in our village named He Is Long-Winded who had fallen from his canoe into the very center of the Suck, a terrible whirlpool in the Oconaluftee, and had been swept first round and round and then down and down to the very bottom of the river. Then, just as his feet touched bottom, it seemed to open below him and he looked down as though through the roof beams of a house at a great crowd of people who all looked up and beckoned for He Is Long-Winded to join them. Only, as they put their hands up to seize his and draw him down to them, the swift current caught him once more and bore him upwards, out of their reach. This was one of the ways that the Cherokee know people lived under the river.

That night Tsinawi heard the sound of drumming and of voices singing and laughing, of gourd rattles and the rattles made of shells that women wear strapped about their ankles. The sound was very loud and it came from the north end of the Bald. However, as Tsinawi crept over towards the north to see who it was who was having such a fine time on the top of Cold Mountain, it seemed to him that the direction of the sound shifted from north to west, so he walked towards the place where the sun had set. No sooner than he had arrived at the westernmost portion of the Bald, however, but the direction of the sound shifted again, this time to the east. So Tsinawi walked east, only to find that the source of the sound had shifted again, this time to the south. At that, Tsinawi shook his head and returned to his camp and went to sleep, for he knew that it had been the Nuhnehi who lived inside the mountain that he had heard dancing and singing.

Needless to say, the people of Qualla were very excited when Tsinawi returned a day or two later and told them the story of his visit to Cold Mountain.

"I suspected this all along," said some.

"If this is true, what should we do?" others wondered.

"When will the storm be?" everyone asked.

George Butler, being three-quarters white and the owner of a mill as well as a trading post and tavern, was angry with Tsinawi. He didn't mind about the cats, but he did not want any Cherokee thinking that they might fire his mill and so win back the support of Selu or destroy the goods in his trading post and thereby mend a broken road. "Stop talking this foolishness in the council house!" he told Tsinawi. "You're giving people ideas!"

"I am just saying what I saw and heard," Tsinawi said.

"You're seeing things that aren't there, old man," objected George.

"Things that are . . . and *aren't* there," Tsinawi clarified. Then, after George had turned on his heel and stormed out, Tsinawi said to Charley, "Your father should not be so angry. Did you see how red his face was? One day he is going to fall over." He said this in a very bland tone of voice, but Charley knew that he hated his daughter's husband. For many years George had beaten Snowbird because she could bear him no more children – this was because Charley's grandmother had sawed her in half with the help of an old Granny Woman.

Soon afterwards a comet appeared in the night sky and it did not disappear for two whole weeks. You could even see it during the day. Then earthquakes shook the mountains. Finally one of Tsinawi's chief critics, a man called Duck, fell dead in the middle of the council house. Even more significant, he fell dead at the very moment when he was calling Tsinawi a fool and a troublemaker. There were people who argued that these were all signs and, since it had fallen to Tsinawi to save the Cherokee nation from extermination, that they had better pay attention to them and call to the people to come to Rattlesnake Mountain. Tsinawi was less sure. A comet, earthquakes, the death of an opponent . . . . Portents, yes, but the leader of the horsemen of the sky had told him that he would *know* when the time was at hand and he did not *know* anything. So he anguished and he vacillated until finally he succumbed to pressure and announced that the next time the Thunder Boys played in the mountains those who believed that the Cherokee should return to the old ways must repair to Rattlesnake Mountain to await the end of the world.

Everyone waited. They did not have to wait long, since it was summer by then and, in summer, storms are frequent events.

The day of the Terrible Storm broke clear. By mid-afternoon, clouds began to gather and the wind to blow. People looked up at the sky and sniffed the air and dampened fingers and held them up to determine which way the wind was blowing. It was blowing out of the East. This was agreed not to be a good sign, for the Darkening Land lies to the West. Hours passed. The sky became darker and took on a yellowish cast. The villagers became very nervous, even those who did not believe what Tsinawi said to be true. They ran from house to house, conferring. Finally, people began to pack food and clothing, even those who had laughed at Tsinawi. "Maybe the old man is right," they said. "Who knows? Look what happened to Duck!" Two and three families together, they set out up Tooni Branch and Owl Branch and Grassy Branch and up over Spray Ridge to Rattlesnake Mountain.

Back at the house at Ela, Snowbird pulled her calico dress off over her head. She removed the tortoiseshell combs from her hair and laid them on the table before the mirror. Then she braided her long black hair and put on a buckskin shirt which reached to her knees and, underneath it, deerskin leggings. She hobbled through the house, packing. "Snowbird! What are you doing?" George called. He had been sitting on the porch in the twig rocker all afternoon, a glass of whiskey in his hand, the Bucksmasher over his knees, watching the clouds build. The door to the house was open to let light and the breeze in and so that he could hear what Snowbird was doing. He did not trust her. He trusted no one.

"We are going to Rattlesnake Mountain," she told him.

"*What?*"

"I don't care what you say, George Butler! My father is right! Everyone is going to die!"

"Don't be stupid. It's just a summer storm."

"Maybe. Maybe not. I'm not taking any chances." Coming out onto the porch, she walked to its edge and called to us in the yard, "Charley! Joseph!"

"You're not taking the boys with you!" George objected.

"I'm not letting them die!" She turned on her heel and lurched back into the house.

George followed her. "I won't let you make a laughing stock of me, Snowbird!" He seized her roughly by the arm and turned her towards him. "No one will say that I can't control my own wife! And what are you dressed up as? You look like a Back of Beyond woman."

Snowbird stamped her foot and burst into tears. "I don't care what you say, George Butler! I don't care what you think! I don't want to die! I don't want my boys to die! We're going to Rattlesnake Mountain!"

But George only tightened his grip on her arm and pulled her closer. He was mean when he drank. "And how do you think you're going to get to Rattlesnake Mountain, Woman With No Middle? You can hardly walk across that door yard on your own!"

"And whose fault is it that I don't have a middle? Your mother Nancy Butler, that's who! Witch Woman! I will ride your horse to Rattlesnake Mountain and Charley will ride before me and Joseph will walk beside us and lead us."

"You'll not take my horse!"

"Yes, I will!"

He struck once her across the face, hard. *"No . . . you . . . won't!"* He enunciated each word, as if she were hard of hearing.

Snowbird stood for a moment, absorbing the blow. Charley could almost see it soak into her skin, leaving in its wake a broad red mark. Then she felt tentatively at her jaw, sliding it back and forth to see if it was not broken. "You know that you should not strike me, George," she said. "You've been told."

George raised one finger in warning. "I'll do what I want with my own wife."

At this Snowbird, feigning indifference, tossed her head and turned away. Not long ago her brothers had come to the door with rifles and asked for George. They did not like it that he had broke their sister's nose once and her collarbone and that she was always nursing bruises or black eyes. When George, in response to their call, appeared in the door, they had only showed him their guns and asked in low voices, "Do you understand how serious our warning is to you?"

A few moments later, there was a sound of horse hoofs in the door yard. To prevent Snowbird from going to Rattlesnake Mountain, he had taken his horse and ridden off to town.

❧

The storm, when it broke just before nightfall, was a terrible storm. There was lightning and loud claps of thunder, one right on top of the other, so that you knew the Thunder Boys were nearby, and strong, swirling winds and torrential rains. Trees struck by lightning burst into flame and fell onto other trees, starting fires, which, admittedly, the rain quickly put out. There were mud slides. One buried a house (and its luckless inhabitants) at the foot of Peggy Gap. The rivers and the creeks swelled. Cows were swept downstream along with bee hives and the shattered bits of wood and rope bridges. George's ferry was capsized with a lone traveler and a horse on it and dashed against the opposite shore, causing it to splinter into a thousand pieces. The horse and traveler were never found. For the space of half an hour hail fell – big as horse chestnuts and ruining the corn in the fields and the peaches in the orchards.

Unable to seek the haven of Rattlesnake Mountain, Joseph, Charley and Snowbird waited out the storm inside the house. Through the windows they could see big trees bend and sway like mourners at a burial while the wind shrieked an eerie, high-pitched whine. The roof leaked and the house trembled. "Your grandfather is right!" Snowbird kept crying. She clutched at the boys and rocked back and forth, sobbing, "The world is ending!"

The storm lasted most of the night. At some point during the End of the World, they fell asleep, huddled together on the parental bed, held tight in their mother's fervid, hysterical embrace. When they woke, the sun was shining. It was morning. Charley remembered how amazed he was to be alive. Joseph only asked scornfully, "Wh-wh-what did you expect?"

The boys made their way to the door and peered outside. The door yard was a big puddle of red clay full of branches and sticks and the corpses of three chickens who had drowned gaping up at the sky. They walked out onto the porch and surveyed the damage.

"What does it look like? Tell me?" Snowbird was so convinced of the totality of the destruction that she would not come out of the house but only cowered on the bed.

"The wind has torn some bark shingles off the roof."

"*Eu!*" she wailed. "It is as I feared! The place is destroyed! Everything broken!"

"Look!" Joseph pointed. "The w-w-ind has knocked the outhouse over!"

"No outhouse? What could be worse?" Snowbird tore at her hair. "The roof and the outhouse too! Destroyed?"

"W-w-ell, no," Joseph said. "It needs to be set upright again is all." Dropping down the porch steps, he crossed the yard to inspect the damage. "Hey!" He hunkered down and poked at the debris with a stick. "There's s-s-omething under it."

"What?"

"A c-cat. The one that belonged to Yellowman's wife. The black and w-white one."

"What is he saying now?" Snowbird pleaded.

"A cat! The outhouse fell on Yellowman's wife's black and white cat."

"How is the cat?" Snowbird demanded.

"D-d-dead." Standing, Joseph crossed back to the porch.

"You see! Your grandfather was right about everything! All the cats have been killed." She fell silent for a moment, musing on what the implications of Tsinawi's prophecy having come true might be. Her face brightened. "Your father. . ." she breathed. "Your father is probably dead too!" She clapped her hands.

At this the boys glanced at one another uncomfortably. Although they knew that the love that had once bound Father and Mother together had frayed like an old rope until both yearned to break it, they nevertheless experienced their various proclamations of disaffection as painful.

"Mother?"

"Yes?" Her pretty face was naked in its eagerness.

"It looks like there was a storm . . . ."

"A terrible storm! The end of the world!"

"No. It looks like the storm was a bad one, but it doesn't look as though the world has come to an end."

"What makes you say that?"

"It's just not . . . that bad, Mother."

"You're telling me that your father . . . is alive?"

"Probably. In fact, likely."

"He often stays the night in one of the rooms over the t-t-tavern," Joseph pointed out and, indeed, George frequently did stay over, particularly on nights when there was no moon. Although he would not admit to it, he was very frightened lest he meet a shape-shifting Utluhtu who would thrust her long, bony spearfinger into him and extract his liver while he was too drunk to notice. Such things are known to befall lone, inebriated travelers through the dark places of the Back of Beyond.

Snowbird stood shakily and pushed her disheveled hair back out of her face. There was still a red mark where he had struck her and a yellow slick swelling around one eye. "Oh, well," she said, hanging her head sadly. "We'd better start cleaning up then." She hobbled out to the porch and surveyed the yard. "Three chickens!" she exclaimed softly. "Such stupid creatures! Can't they learn to close their beaks when they look upwards? Well, nothing for it but to cook them! Anyway, accidents *do* happen to people, even when it's not the end of the world." Her voice sounded hopeful. "People on their way to and from places like town get struck by lightning, trees fall on them, their horses are spooked and throw them . . . ." Then she paused.

In the distance they could hear the muffled sound of horse hoofs popping against wet ground. It would appear that George Butler was returning home intact after his night in town.

All told, about sixty people spent the night that the world was supposed to end huddled together in hastily thrown up shelters of timber and brush on top of Rattlesnake Mountain. The encampment was just due south of Grassy Branch at that point where the bumpy ridge levels out. When they came down a few hours before noon, they were tired and wet and cold.

"Your grandfather is one crazy old man," they told the boys. "We will never believe another thing he says even if he lives to be one hundred years old and says a thousand things." They did not have to worry, however, because Tsinawi was very embarrassed by the incident and, from that time on, retreated into himself and had little to say to anyone other than small talk to pass the time and comments about the weather.

These events confirmed George Butler in his belief that, were his boys to succeed in the white man's world, they must be removed from the influence of their grandfather and similarly minded Cherokee and sent away to the new school recently established by the American Board outside Spring Place. Three short weeks after the debacle, therefore, he ordered Snowbird to pack a valise for Charley and Joseph. Less than an hour later, he loaded the entire family into the coach and told Lehi to drive up the Wachesa Trail to the Hiwasee, then down the New Echota Road into Georgia, then, heading north again (for there were few roads in the Cherokee Nation that were wide enough to accommodate a coach and no direct route to Brainerd) up the Federal Road past Spring Place, where they were abandoned like adolescent foundlings on the school's doorstep.

Remembering, Charley laughed. "You seemed almost as bewildered by our parents' unseemly haste at disposing of us as we ourselves had been," he told me.

FOUR

We were together all that winter in Reverend Cornelius' little garret, Charley Butler and I. I taught the boy letters and numbers and read him Bible stories and, when we wearied of that (as we soon did, for Charley picked at white man's learning the way someone sick picks at food), then I would take up my cross-stitch and listen as he told me old stories heard from the village elders or his grandfather or a woman named Toineeta who was the village's medicine woman. For all his inability to master the Lord's Prayer, Charley had a most remarkable memory for these stories and told them in an accomplished manner – like a professional storyteller, aware of just where their magic lay. Over that winter he may have told me a hundred different stories, and when, at times and at my request, he would repeat a story, he did not deviate by scarcely so much as a word or an inflection from the first time he had told me the tale. Then I realized that he was not simply repeating what he had heard but what he had learned – for up until a very few years before I arrived in Brainerd when the MB Sequoyah had invented the Cherokee syllabary, this was how the Cherokee learned everything – by listening and remembering.

I must confess that sometimes, sitting in that still, close, camphor-reeking hole beneath the eaves, Charley's strange stories so disoriented me that I became quite giddy and lost all sense of where I was and who I was and at what point in history I had come, like some poor bird in the midst of a confused migration, to light down. . . that is to say, I lost my place in time, for, unlike white man's stories, the stories of the Cherokee, no matter how ancient their origin (and those which told of the beginning of things must have been very ancient indeed) always seemed to have taken place in the very recent past.

Perhaps it is because the Cherokee have no distant event like the Cru-cifixion on which to hang their history that their past seemed to stretch behind them in an unbroken line. I could not then see that very soon my own people would provide them with such a central event.

I must also confess that, beginning that winter and growing thereafter, the Crucifixion had begun to seem to me increasingly distant, so distant, in fact, that it began to fade in the memory I had of believing in it and to take on the aspect of an unconfirmed report from a remote and barbarous land made by hysterical witnesses.

Charley and I sometimes discussed what I called religion and he called The Way It Is. He cited some of his objections to Christianity. "If I become a Christian, I will have to give up the sacred places."

"What sacred places?"

"We have ours just as you have your Jerusalem and your Mount of Olives," he explained. "There are many. There is the Place of the Lizard Monster and Ambush Place, where a nest of giant yellow jackets was destroyed by the Little People. There is Cold Mountain and Shining Rock and Turtle Place."

"Those are just the names of places, Charley. Like Jump Off Point up around Newfound Gap or Roundtop or the Chimneys. Those are not sacred places. Just . . . places."

"What are sacred places then?"

"Places where God has caused something to happen."

"Presumably the Great Provider made the giant yellow jackets and the Little People . . . ."

"No," I corrected him. "That is just a story. There are no giant yellow jackets or Little People. They are not real."

"And Christ really walked upon the water? Made water of wine?"

"Yes. And died on the cross and after three days rose from the dead."

Charley frowned and shook his head. "Sun sent men to fetch her daughter back from the Darkening Land, but her spirit escaped and became a redbird. After that no one has ever returned from the dead."

"That is just a story."

"It's no less probable than your story."

"What the Bible says is true."

"How do you know?" He sat forward in the bed so that his covers slipped away from him and his nightshirt fell a little open at his neck. His face was flushed, his dark eyes bright as mica with fever.

"Charley!" I laughed, for by this time his skepticism dismayed me less perhaps than it should have. "Sit back! Let me cover you up. You know what my answer will be! I *believe* the Bible to be true."

"Well. . ." He fell back among the pillows and allowed me to rub fresh camphor salve on his thin chest and replace the flannel with a fresh, warm one and button his nightshirt over it. "*I* believe that the giant yellow jackets and the Little People are real and *I* have been to Ambush Place with my grandfather and seen it and *I* have visited the–" He stopped abruptly in mid-sentence.

"Yes?" I prompted him, resuming my seat and picking up my needlework again. "What fairy folk have you visited?"

But he looked down and away. "Oh, none," he replied and shrugged.

"Charley, are you all right?" I could see that he trembled.

"Yes, yes, dear Miss Sophia. It is only that I would prefer a sacred place I may visit to a Garden of Gethsemane in which I may never sit or a Golgotha I will never climb."

But now his teeth chattered and sweat beaded his forehead. Rising, I leaned over and laid my hand on his brow. "Your fever has shot up!"

"Some creature has caused it," speculated Charley. "A bird or rabbit or perhaps a deer. They are the cause of most illness – long ago they held a council and hit upon disease as a way of keeping mankind in check lest we hunt and kill them all."

"Nonsense! Your fever arises from some corporeal humor that is out of balance . . . or the noxious night air. We live in a scientific age and must not cling to superstition."

He allowed me to arrange Mrs. Cornelius' quilt up around his chin. The name of the quilt's pattern was Tennessee Trouble. I remember because Charley had asked her. He was very interested in the names of quilt patterns.

Later I was to learn that, although visiting the Underworld was a common enough event among the Cherokee, it was nevertheless considered bad form to speak of such crossings. Those who were too casual in this regard tended to die a short time afterwards under mysterious circumstances. Charley, as it turned out, was only being circumspect in not revealing to me his acquaintance with those worlds beyond my poor, white understanding.

FIVE

When spring arrived and green buds hung on all the trees and the Brainerd orchard was a mass of white and the palest of pink blooms, then my beloved Charley grew stronger. This was the pattern of his illness – to suffer terribly during the cold, damp months of the year only to revive with the coming of spring and its attendant warmth.

Unfortunately, the tumor in his hip had ulcerated. This was according to Reverend Butrick, who, at regular intervals throughout the long winter, had duly palpitated the boy's hip and groin region. "Now it will gnaw at the bone like a dog," he confided in me. "And what it destroys cannot grow back. He will be lame for life."

That sweet spring, however, Charley could still get about with the help of his silver-headed cane and so he was able at last to leave Reverend Cornelius' garret for the boys' dormitory and to sit in the schoolhouse with the other students.

Naturally I did not see him so much now as before, and I found that I missed him terribly, so terribly that, in truth, I wondered at myself. I told myself that I felt towards him the way an older sister might – I was close to ten years his senior – and yet that was not entirely true, for at night I would dream strange dreams in which the boy I knew had become a man and whole. I cannot tell you what took place in those dreams, for they slipped from me the moment I attempted to grasp their meaning – quick fish in a swift river. But a song that my pretty sister Harriet used to coax out of the old parlor piano back in Portsmouth often played through my mind:

> Black is the color of my true love's hair.
> His lips are something wondrous fair.
> The purest eyes and the bravest hands . . . .

I would catch myself humming it . . . and be hot with shame. But not too ashamed, for who knew this secret longing of my heart besides myself? If no man was ever to want me – as I had often been assured they would not – what harm was there in keeping this secret love for myself? My heart is a hidden place, I thought, a room to which access is forbidden, to which I alone hold the key. And I was right, of course. No one has ever known about my feelings for Charley, except, perhaps, God, and I was beginning to doubt that He much cared.

During that strange, heady spring, we sometimes went walking, Charley and I, down into the woods that hugged in its vast green embrace our few log buildings, our field and garden and our little orchard. He walked slowly, of course, because of a limp now so pronounced that it might better be described as a lurch. I remember what a chore it was matching my stride to his, I with my ridiculously long legs.

One day when we were out walking in the farthest reaches of the orchard, we spied a young Cherokee girl up ahead dancing underneath the flowering trees. Arms raised over her head, she swayed gracefully this way and that, then, with an exceedingly light step, whirled round and round. Spotting us, she stopped and, lowering her arms to her sides, gazed at us in a steady way that suggested that she was neither frightened nor surprised but, rather, had been expecting us. She looked to be perhaps twelve or thirteen years old and was slight and very pretty, an FB, with black, shiny hair that hung to her waist in two long braids. I noted that she wore a traditional shirt of deerskin, while her legs and feet were bare. This in itself indicated that she was not a student at Brainerd – all the children at the missionary school wore English-style clothing – and, besides, neither I nor Charley recognized her as one of our Brainerd girls.

Charley took the initiative. "Hello!" he called in his native tongue. "*Si yu!*"

"*Si yu!*"

"Who are you?"

She tilted her head to one side and looked at him steadily. I remember thinking that she blinked very little. "I live not far away."

"No," he corrected her. "I asked what your *name* was."

Either she did not understand or she did not choose to say. "Down this trail," she said by way of reply and, turning, pointed to a clearly marked trail I'd had never before noticed, though I often walked here and believed I knew it well. "Come with me if you'd like. My mother is expecting you, and it is beautiful where I live."

We looked in the direction in which she pointed. Wildflowers everywhere – bloodroot and trillium, may apple and white trout lily peeping through the ground cover – and a little brook to which the trail she indicated led and then, apparently, followed in a southerly direction.

I remember being quite surprised at finding a brook in this part of the mission's holdings. The orchard lay to the southeast of the mission buildings. The stream that fed the spring house and provided us with our water, however, ran to the west of the school, perhaps a quarter of a mile from where we stood. I had not known that there was another stream on the property, nor had I heard anyone mention such a thing . . . and ours was a small, circumscribed world in which all features of the immediate landscape were as well known as one another's facial features. "Yes, Charley!" I cried eagerly. "Let's follow her and see where the path goes."

But Charley placed a restraining hand upon my arm. "It is not easy for me to walk where the path may be rough," he reminded me and, looking at the girl, he shook his head.

The girl shrugged. Turning on her heel, she walked jauntily down the trail towards the brook. However, just as she came to the point where the path turned to follow the brook, she disappeared from sight.

I blinked. "Wherever did she go?" I took a step forward, intending to pursue her, but Charley did not loosen his grip on my arm. Indeed, he tightened it. "Don't follow her, Miss Sophia."

"Why not? She must have ducked into a cave. How else could she suddenly vanish like that?"

"It's better that you not concern yourself."

"Charley! Why?"

"There are things it is not comfortable for you to know."

"What are you talking about?"

But he would say no more. He could be stubborn when he chose.

Later, towards evening when I was alone, I returned to the orchard, determined to find the path and the brook I had seen earlier that afternoon. Search as I might, I could find no trace of either.

SIX

"Are you eager to see your grandfather again?" I asked, for, in the summer, the parents came to fetch their children back home and Charley had received a letter from his father stating that he would arrive within the fortnight to pick him up – Joseph would be returning separately from Cornwall together with the Ridge and the Hicks boy. It tore at my heart to think of Charley gone for those few months, but after that he would return to me and once again we would have the cozy days and nights locked away in the Cornelius' garret together. The sweet certainty that his illness would render him invalid was surely God's gift to me, I thought.

Earnestly I poured over the fates assigned us – him to be crippled, me to be plain and un-prized; the disposition of Christians to proselytize, the inclination of the Cherokee to find interesting new ways of thinking and doing – as though these fates were a hand of cards dealt me. I sought in the myriad of their possible combinations a way in which I might finally win.

But Charley only shrugged. "I will not see my grandfather in Qualla," he said with a trace of sadness.

"But why? He has not died over the winter, has he?"

"No," replied Charley. "He is nevertheless . . . gone."

"Gone where?" I persisted. "To another village?"

"I'm sure there is a village there."

"Where?"

Charley appeared uneasy. He would not meet my eyes but glanced away. After a moment he said, "Under the river."

"Do you mean . . . he has drowned, Charley? Why didn't you tell me?"

But Charley shook his head. "No, no. Not drowned. He went to *live* under the water."

There was a moment of silence while I tried to decide if I had heard him properly. Then I asked. "How can he do that, Charley? *Live* . . . under the water?"

"After the night on Rattlesnake Mountain, he was very upset. He had picked the wrong time and made a mess of things. He felt sorry and ashamed; he believed that he had let the leader of the horsemen from the sky down, that he had let the people of Qualla down. He knew that the world was going to end. He just didn't know when, and he had acted too quickly, under pressure from others. He was not a natural leader. So he built himself a shelter of brush and timber on the banks of the Oconaluftee and went to live there. He prayed and fasted for seven days and on the seventh day, the Nuhnehi came and took him away to live under water with them."

"The Nuhnehi? You have spoken of them before. Who are they?"

"The Immortals. They are like us except that they are never unhappy and they live forever."

"And they live . . . under the water?"

"Sometimes they live inside mountains."

"But how do you know your grandfather is with them? Did you actually see them come and take him?"

Charley shook his head. "I went to see him by the river one day and he was not there. But I knew where he had gone. It is nothing strange, Miss Sophia. Others have gone before him. Later I heard him talking beneath the surface of the water, when it was quiet. I couldn't make out what he was saying, but I recognized his voice, and once, when I was dragging the river for fish, the net caught, even though the water was deep and there was nothing for it to catch on. It was my grandfather who caught it."

"How do you know?"

"He tugged at the drag three times. That was the signal we had agreed upon."

"Why would he want to signal you?" I asked.

Charley looked at me as if surprised. "Naturally he does not want me to forget him."

જ્ર

The day before his father was to arrive at Brainerd, Charley went out into the orchard alone. I know, because I saw him leave the boys' dormitory by himself and head in that southeasterly direction. I was helping Sister Ann Brown with the girls' sewing at the time; we were teaching them how to make shifts from flour sacks. I placed my hand upon my forehead, closed my eyes and made my excuses; I was well known at Brainerd for my headaches, which were epic.

I started for my quarters but, as soon as I was out of Sister Ann Brown's sight, doubled back and followed Charley at a slight distance. Normally, I would have caught up with him and kept him company, but that day I had a strange feeling of foreboding, twisted up in a knot with fear inside my belly. I needed to see where he would go and whom he would meet . . . . That he would meet someone I did not question. That much I knew for certain.

Just as I had suspected, he met the little Cherokee girl whom we had seen earlier that spring in that same, far part of the orchard. I dropped down to a crouch behind a gnarled peach tree and peered around its trunk at the two young people. Beyond the girl I could just make out the trailhead which I had sought in vain so many times. It seemed very clearly marked to me now, a dark arched opening in the dense foliage. There was no way I could have overlooked it had it, in fact, been there when I had come seeking it.

After exchanging a few words in Cherokee, which I could not make out, the girl turned and started down the path. Charley followed slowly. I could see from the set expression on his face that he was in pain.

I followed as well, again at a distance, noting with surprise how well worn the path was, almost bare of vegetation, as though it were quite often used. Yet we had no near neighbors at Brainerd. Beside the trail grew a plethora of wildflowers. In addition to those I had earlier spotted, I recognized dwarf iris, galax and the delicate strangeness of orchis.

By now the girl and Charley had come to the little brook we had previously glimpsed. Without so much as breaking her stride, the girl stepped off the path into the water and proceeded to wade downstream. The water was not deep; it rose to perhaps the middle of her calf. Charley, however, did not wade into the brook. He stood on the bank and looked after her. After a moment she paused and turned around. "Are you coming?"

"You are walking in water," he pointed out. "I should not get wet. The damp is very bad for my hip."

But the girl only smiled and shook her head, laughing. "This is not water. It is only the road to my house."

Charley still made no move to follow her. It was difficult for him to walk on uneven surfaces, since he couldn't place weight on his left foot and was therefore likely to stumble and fall. "The bottom will be slippery, the rocks slick with moss. It is too treacherous for me."

"It is only a level trail. Smooth. Step onto it and you will see."

Tentatively Charley bent over and thrust the tip of his walking stick into the sandy bottom of the stream until it seemed to grind down upon something solid. Then, leaning his weight on the stick, he swung himself down over the bank and into the brook. The water lapped mildly about his shins. He gazed down at it with an expression of extreme surprise. "You are right," he breathed, looking up at the girl. "Though it appears to be water, it is really soft grass. It is a fine, level trail. I shall have no difficulty walking on this."

"Throw away your cane," she said. "You will not need it where we are going."

Charley did as he was told, tossing the cane on the bank. The girl smiled and, turning around once more, began wading downstream, followed by Charley. When they had gone a little ways downstream, I ran to the point where they had entered the stream and, kneeling down, thrust my fingers into the water. My eyes had not deceived me. It was wet and very cold, water and no smooth trail covered with soft grass. His cane lay a few feet distant on the bank. I seized it and, standing, followed the bank, keeping some distance between myself and them so that I might continue unobserved. After a quarter of a mile, the brook joined a larger stream, which looked by its dark color to be deeper than the first and swifter. As before, the Cherokee girl did not hesitate, but plunged boldly into this larger stream. To my alarm, the water was up to her chin. Charley hung back, as he had on the bank. "Come!" the girl shouted over the rush of the current.

But Charley shook his head adamantly. "It is too deep and fast. The current will sweep me away and I will drown."

The girl only laughed. "Don't be silly. This is the main road that leads to my house. My house is very near now and my mother is waiting."

Now I became very frightened, for I knew that Charley was right. He could not long maintain his footing in such a swift stream. I stepped forward, intending to call out to him to stop and turn back, but, before I could so much as open my mouth, he had wobbled tentatively out into the deeper water. At once it was up to his chest. "You are right," he cried to the girl, lifting his elbows and hands up above the water's roiling surface and turning this way and that. "It appears to be water, but it is only tall waving grass . . . see! . . . that brushes me gently as I walk."

"I told you so!" the girl laughed. "But come now, for my mother expects me and will grow impatient if we do not come soon."

Crouching down, Charley's cane held under one arm, I crept along the bank beside this new, deeper, swifter stream for perhaps another quarter of a mile before a roar of water rushing over distant rocks and an opening in the forest up ahead warned me that this stream must soon empty into a larger body of water. Suddenly I was stricken by a terrible, overwhelming fear. It knocked the wind out of me as surely as if it had picked up me up and heaved me against a stone wall with big, invisible hands. I stopped dead in my tracks and bent double, resting my hands on my thighs to steady me, and breathing deeply. My head was spinning so that I could hardly untangle my thoughts one from the other: Charley would have found it difficult to keep his footing even in the little brook. How could he walk on an uneven streambed slippery with rocks in water up to his chest? Why were he and the girl pretending that the water was a road? And where had this child come from in the first place? Who was she and who were her people? Why this brook and this path and this stream when no map of the countryside around Brainerd showed such features? Where was she taking him and what in heaven's name was I thinking of? That I would steal after the two of them like it was a child's game and I the biggest child of all? That I could put an end to it simply by popping out of the bushes and shouting, "I see you!"?

No. The truth was that she was taking him away to a place from which he would not return and I . . . I was letting him go.

I straightened up then and made my way along the bank as quickly as I could. By now the trail running beside the stream had dwindled away to nothing and the mixed hardwood forest that prevailed in that part of Tennessee – basswood, magnolia, silver bell and buckeye – had gradually given way to a kind of vegetation typical of more mountainous regions . . . .

An evergreen forest had sprung up about me, dark and cool. The slender trunks of pine trees and hemlocks were sheathed in velvety moss the bright color of uncut emeralds; their bark yielded pale, lichenous extrusions. Beneath their drooping boughs, rhododendrons, laurels and doghobbles grew in a tangled, woody profusion, spangled with robust blooms of purple and white, and so dense as to be at points impenetrable. At times these huge shrubs – half again as tall as me – grew to the stream's very bank and then arched over its surface to form a kind of tunnel. At those points there was no forcing my way through them and I had to veer away from the bank and go around them. I cannot remember any other journey in my life so prolonged as that one seemed.

Finally I arrived at the point where the stream emptied, as I had suspected that it must, into a sizable river perhaps thirty feet across. To my astonishment, my arrival at this point, which had seemed to me so protracted, turned out to be, in fact, a few moments in advance of that of Charley and the Cherokee girl. They had, after all, been wading through deep water along a streambed and that, taken together with Charley's lameness, had made their progress slow. From where I stood, I could see them laboring towards me at a distance of perhaps twenty feet.

"Charley!" I called, but my words were lost in the roar of rushing water – there were rapids along the far side of the river and big rocks. "Charley!"

This time the girl was perhaps ten feet from me. She glanced at me with an air of indifference. She did not look surprised to see me, nor, I surmised, did she intend to acknowledge me. Instead she turned in the direction of the river. "We are home, Mother!" she cried in a loud voice. "I've brought someone to see you!"

I rushed forward and knelt beside the stream, extending my hand. "Charley! Take my hand! I will pull you ashore."

He looked at me. He did not seem surprised to see me either. Had they known I was following them all along? "Don't worry, Miss Sophia. It is only a road and I am going to a place that I might live."

"She has bewitched you, Charley! It is water and you will drown."

"No, no," Charley assured me. "Things are not as they seem. For months I have heard voices . . . invisible spirits in the air calling and warning me of wars and misfortunes . . . the same kind of disasters that the leader of the horsemen of the sky warned my grandfather about. I do not want to leave this land for another that I cannot love and so I will go where they will not think to look for me."

"What are you talking about, my dearest? Who are they?"

"Why, Miss Sophia!" Charley paused. Then a look of great kindness came upon his poor, haggard face and he said quite softly, "They are *you*, Miss Sophia!"

"Why do you dawdle, boy?" the girl demanded. "Come along!" And, with that, she plunged into the river.

"Charley!" I cried once more, but he too had dived into the river's swift current. For a moment I could track his passage through the dark water by that wondrous brightness he always wore. Then, nothing. He was gone.

I did not tell the others what I saw that day. I never said where it was that I had been. Indeed, I did not know, and I certainly have no idea how I managed to get back to Brainerd. No, nor memory of it either or, indeed, of how I could have managed to live for so many long, long years with so great and terrible a secret grief.

When Charley did not return to the dormitory that evening, the boys and the men were sent out to search for him.

The following day they searched again.

"What shall we tell his father when he comes?" they worried. "We can't tell him that he simply . . . disappeared."

Finally, they decided that they would tell George Butler that the boy had taken ill a few days before – when it was too late to send a message – and that he had died. They would say that heat had compelled them to bury him hastily, in the little graveyard behind the chapel. "He was a sickly lad," Reverend Cornelius pointed out. "That he should have died would not be entirely unexpected."

Everyone agreed that this was so.

SEVEN

For the remainder of that spring and summer, I looked for the river into which I had seen Charley plunge. I visited the orchard soon after his disappearance. As I had suspected, there was no sign of the trail we had followed or the little brook. I asked the local Cherokee mothers whose children attended the school what rivers there were in that region and how I might come to them. I thought I would recognize the river when I saw it . . . . I could picture it so clearly in my mind that the image seemed to have been a leftover fragment of a dream – it was gibbous as a moon.

As it turned out, there were two rivers within a day's ride of Brainerd Academy – the Tennessee and the Ocoee – and one farther north, the Hiwasee. I asked Reverend Butrick to take me to them, as he owned both a horse and a mule upon which I could uncomfortably ride; I am but an indifferent horsewoman. First we traveled east to the Tennessee, but that is a very big river, much bigger than the river into which Charley had disappeared. Then we went west to the Ocoee, but the forest that flanked it was of mixed hardwoods. It was not the hemlock forest with tangled shrubs that I recalled so clearly. That left the Hiwasee.

"I cannot take you to the Hiwasee," Reverend Butrick informed me.

"Why not?"

"We would have to spend a night on the trail."

"Surely you do not suppose that anyone could imagine that a man such as yourself might have designs upon my poor person, Reverend Butrick!"

He seemed taken aback. "Nevertheless," he said stiffly, not meeting my gaze. His face was scarlet. "It would be improper."

I was quite mad with grief. I had only one thought in my head – to find the river. I am not certain what I intended to do once I had found it, but this much I knew: it existed and I would know no peace until I had stood once more upon its bank.

As fortune would have it, it was just about that time that the mother of one of our pupils – an MB called Polly Duffy – died while giving birth to a second child. Polly's father, a well-to-do Scots trader, was overcome with grief and, quite likely, whiskey and, not wishing to leave his newborn son in a stranger's care (or so he claimed), wrote Reverend Cornelius to say that he was extremely hard put at present to pick Polly up. Might she perhaps stay the summer? Such a solution was frowned upon at Brainerd, and so it was determined that Reverend Butrick, being the traveler among us, should escort the child home and that, as the child was female, it might be more appropriate were the party to include a sober and amiable Christian gentlewoman, which description I was thought to fit.

When I found out the news, I was thrown into the maddest kind of excitement, for Mr. Duffy lived in a small Cherokee village at the forks of the Valley River and the Hiwasee, not fifty miles southwest of Charley's home village of Qualla.

It was upon that trip that I first saw my mountains. Blue cloud catchers, immense and endless, a smooth undulation of stone and forest lapping towards a distant horizon, a sound like the sea that was the wind blowing down the long valleys. Those forests were of hemlock and pine, of course . . . and rhododendron, laurel and doghobble all in a tangle. I recognized them at once and the river, when later I came to stand upon its bank, as well.

Polly told me that the place was called *Tlanusiyi* or Leech Place. "See that deep hole in the river? A giant leech used to lie on the ledge above that hole and, whenever it was hungry, it would fall off the ledge into the hole and wriggle about the way a leech will. But this was a giant leech, so, when it wriggled, it made a big wave. That wave would sweep anyone who happened to be crossing the stream off the ledge and into the pool, and then the leech would catch him and eat him. It was a terrible death to be eaten by the giant leech."

Later I said to her. "Let's fish a while, to pass the time."

She laughed. "But we have nothing to fish with, Miss Sophia!"

I laughed back and, reaching into my satchel, I produced a fish drag, which one of the Brainerd boys had fashioned for me at my request. "We can use this."

"Let me, Miss Sophia. My mother taught me how. If you throw it into the shallows, it will catch on the rocks. Perhaps you will wake the Giant Leech and we don't want that. No. You must throw it into the center of the river, where it is deep and will not catch." Taking the drag from me, she threw it into the center of the river and began to walk along the shore, drawing the drag after her. Suddenly she stopped short. "That's strange." She looked puzzled. "The drag must have caught on a rock at the bottom of the river. I thought that it was deeper there."

My heart began to beat wildly. Blood rushed to my head. I could hear it roaring in my ears. "Here, Polly," I said eagerly. "Give it to me."

She handed the drag to me. I held it still for a moment, scarcely daring to so much as breathe, and then I felt it – three tugs. Three distinct tugs.

EIGHT

Shortly after our return from Hiwasee, Reverend Cornelius called me
into the little front room of his house and offered me a seat opposite his.
As there was scarcely room for two people in the room and, as we were
both tall, thin persons, we were obliged to sit very straight and draw our
limbs up towards us to avoid unseemly knocking of bones. "Dear
Sister!" he began, leaning forward, his hands clasped between his knees.
He frowned, then smiled, then sighed. "We are all so very worried about
you."

"We?" I was wary.

"The entire Christian family here at Brainerd and, of course, the
Directors of the American Board as well. We wrote them, naturally."

"Naturally," I repeated. Then, because I didn't understand, "Why
would you write the Directors about me?"

"Well, we couldn't help but notice that lately you have become
somewhat . . . distraught. Not yourself. You know what I mean."

"No," I said flatly. "I don't know what you mean. If I am not myself,
then who am I?"

"Exactly!" cried Reverend Cornelius, as though he had made a
point.

I didn't understand. I waited.

"The life of a missionary is not for everyone . . . ." he began.

"What are you saying, Reverend Cornelius?"

"I'm just saying that the Directors do not doubt your faith and
commitment, but they feel . . . and we here at Brainerd feel too . . . that
your nerves are perhaps not quite strong enough to withstand the rigors
of working in this, one of Our Lord's more demanding vineyards. Consequently, the American Board wishes you to return to New England to
continue your good work there."

"My place is here . . . with the Cherokee!"

"I understand how you feel, Sister," Reverend Cornelius said. "Your dedication is truly exemplary. But you have become . . . well, frankly, too *involved*."

"What do you mean?"

"You are very susceptible, Sister. I know it's because you are tender-hearted, but I can't tell you the number of times we've noticed and never said . . . . Frankly, we didn't know how to tell you."

"What do you mean – 'susceptible'?"

"We thought perhaps you'd realize it on your own. With time. With experience. For this vocation, you must be . . . well, more detached."

I leapt from my chair, knocking it backwards. "I am *not* too involved! I am *not* susceptible! I *am* detached!"

"Sister, please, lower your voice!"

"I cannot go home! I cannot go back there again. My mother despairing. My sisters laughing. There is nothing for me there. I belong here."

"When we give our lives to God, He disposes of us according to His wishes!"

"And what of my wishes? Have I no say in this? Please!" I knelt before him, clasping my hands together as if in prayer. My face was wet and tight with tears; my throat ached as though someone had tried to strangle me with fierce hands. "Give me one more chance!"

Reverend Cornelius leaned back in the chair. He closed his eyes and dangled his thin fingers upon his forehead as though his head ached. "What do you want me to do, Sophia? After what happened in North Carolina, we cannot trust you out of our sight for a moment. We cannot be your nurses. We have other charges to take care of. We cannot take care of you too."

I breathed in sharply. "What do you mean? What happened at Hiwasee?"

Reverend Cornelius opened one eye and peered at me from it. "You don't remember?"

I shook my head. Strangely I remembered nothing of that trip from the moment I had felt Charley tug at the drag I had thrown into the river. I had been ill, I think, delirious perhaps. I was prone to sudden agues that lasted for days. Yes! An ague! That must have been it!

"You jumped into the river, Sophia," Reverend Cornelius told me. "You tried to drown yourself in the river. It was all poor David Butrick could do to fish you out! You struggled like a madwoman, he said. He said he had never seen anything like it. Sophia, what were you thinking? What has been going on?"

NINE

I escaped from Mr. Hiram Mayhew just the other side of Blythe's Ferry. Mr. Mayhew had been passing by Brainerd on his way north from Creek country in upstate Alabama when Reverend Cornelius prevailed upon him to escort me back to New England and deliver me into the hands of the American Board of Commissioners for Foreign Missions in Boston. The wretched man had fairly collapsed under the weight of the missionary's entreaties; in addition, if I am not mistaken, some money exchanged hands.

My escape was, if I might say so myself, a somewhat daring one which I effected under the cover of extreme darkness – the night was moonless. I was aided in this enterprise by the fact that Mr. Mayhew was burdened with the sin of habitual drunkenness and thus would fall, every evening, into a sleep that resembled death in the completeness of its stupor. The Final Day of Judgment with all its attendant trumpets and lamentations would not, I fear, have caused Mr. Mayhew to so much as stir in his bedroll once he had laid himself down to sleep upon it. In truth, the wonder was that he was able to rouse himself sufficiently in the morning to get onto a horse at all and remain upright in the saddle for the several hours at a stretch that he did. Mind you, our progress up to the time of my escape had been maddeningly slow, as Mr. Mayhew was given, at frequent intervals, to falling from his horse.

I must add that in the matter of my escape, I did avail myself of a horse belonging to the Mission, but, in truth, it was a very old horse and lame and might conceivably not have survived the journey north in any case. Upon its bowed back I headed up river to Hiwasee and thence to the little village of Qualla on the banks of the Oconaluftee.

Why I chose this course, why I turned my back on the only life that I had up to that point known, I know not, or, to be more accurate,

I elected not to question. After all, it was a rather poor sort of life, consisting, as it did, of scraps and tatters. Why not leave it at the crossroads? I had no husband, no suitor, nor was I likely to, given the plainness of my face and my ridiculous figure, and, now, no decent profession from which to derive a living and validation. My superiors had deemed me of unsound mind. Where could I go? Home to New Hampshire? Not likely. My family had ever been quarrelsome, divisive and difficult. I lacked the stomach to return to that roiling fold, where the best I might hope for would be to be taken in by a tiresome sibling or second cousin with an available garret and a half-dozen spoiled children, whose care I would undoubtedly be expected to assume in exchange for room and board. It was, when I paused to consider it, unthinkable.

In Cherokee country, on the other hand, I would be a free agent or so I imagined. I would leave my past behind, sloughing it like a snake sloughs its skin. No one would expect anything of me; I would therefore disappoint no one. Why not? I thought. I had a little money and a smattering of Cherokee. I could teach English to children. Judging from what my Brainerd pupils had told me, there was a great demand for English teachers within the Nation, as the Cherokees, one of the so-called "Civilized Tribes," sought to emulate in all ways their white neighbors. I would be an outsider, yes, but had I not always been an outsider? Besides, my time at Brainerd had taught me that the Cherokee were tolerant of those who were unlike them, curious but kind. No doubt I would be thought odd, but not shunned nor overly pitied and I reckoned I could live with that.

And, of course, there was Charley, always Charley. I can't deny that. The truth was this: I came to Qualla to find Charley. I was always looking for Charley. I would look for him the rest of my life.

But there was something else as well. Just before going to water, Charley had told me, "I do not want to leave this land for another that I cannot love and so I will go where they will not think to look for me." I had responded to this by asking him who 'they' were. "Why, Miss

Sophia," he had said, "they are you." I cannot tell you how much his reply has haunted me. Did he not understand that I in no way wanted any part of 'they,' that I sought to break free of that identity, those ties to race and culture? That I despised 'they' and what 'they' stood for – the greed and the carelessness, the condescension and the overweening sense of entitlement? Because I did. I fervently did. I wanted it with all my heart. Going to live in Qualla was, as much as anything, the next, most logical step on my chosen road.

๛

I gained entrance to the Butlers' house at Ela on the strength of having been their deceased son's tutor. Although George Butler took little note of me, Snowbird took great solace in the stories I told her about Charley's last year at Brainerd, asking me to repeat them over and over again so that she could laugh or cry as required. She became quite attached to me, so much so that, within a month of my arrival, she asked if I wouldn't prefer to lodge at Ela, rather than in the room over the tavern I had taken upon my arrival. I immediately took her up on this offer and, for the remainder of my life, the house at Ela was my home. I'm not certain that George ever understood this arrangement, for he always seemed surprised to see me on his return home; he did, nevertheless, accept without hesitation the small purse I gave him each month for room and board, derived from the money I made teaching a kind of rudimentary and occasional school to a dozen or more Cherokee and white pupils from the village and surrounding farms in Qualla's curious seven-sided council house.

As for the unfortunate Mr. Mayhew, he was never heard from again. Perhaps he died on his journey north. I could easily envisage him striking his head against a rock on one of those occasions on which he toppled from his horse. Lest my former colleagues think me similarly disposed of, I sought to allay their consciences by writing both Reverend Cornelius and the Board a letter:

Dear Sirs:

Upon consideration, I have decided to go into private service and so will require your attention (and need elicit your kindly concern) no longer. On the matter of the horse provided me for my journey northward, I regret to inform you that the poor creature died of exhaustion soon after I parted company with the regrettable Mr. Mayhew. I feel obliged to tell you that some persons, upon hearing of the circumstances surrounding my departure from the Brainerd Academy, might be inclined to reproach you for not providing a lady embarked upon a long and arduous journey with a somewhat heartier mount, as well as a more salubrious escort.

Sincerely,
Sophia Sawyer

I received a courteous, if stiff reply from both parties and thereafter heard nothing further from the missionaries. (In fact, on the matter of the horse, I had stretched the truth somewhat. She lived for several more years in the comfortable stable of the Butlers and continued to bear me in my daily treks to the village and back towards Ela. Her name was Jenny and a sweeter creature has yet to draw breath.)

Then on a soft Saturday evening in 1826, just after Easter, George Butler returned home to beat his wife. He was drunk, of course. He usually was. He struck her across the face so hard that she fell to the floor, rolling herself into a ball and shrieking hysterically. Blood streamed from her nose in a torrent.

I lunged at the cruel man, but he pushed me to one side and began to kick Snowbird in her back where her kidneys were. "Stop that!" I shouted and, grabbing the Bucksmasher from the pine gun rack, I proceeded to wield it like a cudgel: I struck him once across the back of the knees with the rifle, then, holding it with both hands above my head, brought it down as hard as I could across one of his broad shoulders. He seized the rifle and, twisting it from my weak grasp, flung it to one side. George Butler was an uncommonly strong man, built tall and heavy and lumbering as a bear. He scarcely seemed capable of pain. Indeed, his lack of feeling was uncanny. I had seen him burn himself on hot metal and take no notice; I had seen him cut himself and bleed with no change of expression. Of course, I did not know that it was the ulunsuti that made him impervious to pain. Now he said to me, "Sophia Sawyer, what are you doing in my house all this time? What are we to you? Is my wife your sister that you protect her?"

"I am your lodger and your wife has done nothing wrong!" I retorted. "You are too cruel to her!"

"*Ehh!*" Curtly he brushed my protest aside and half turned from me. His rage, however, appeared spent. This was not unusual. With him, rage erupted and then, as quickly as it had flared up, departed from him – the ulunsuti's effect. He stood in the middle of the room for a moment. An expression of pained puzzlement overtook his features. He seemed confused as to what had just taken place; he appeared to be grasping at fragments of a memory in disarray. Then he shook his big head as if to clear it and, without looking either down at Snowbird or in my direction, he stepped over his wife's prostrate body and lurched off to bed. We listened until we heard the heavy door slam shut behind him.

I looked about me. The floor was covered with broken crockery, the yellow floorboards smeared with blood from Snowbird's nose. Furniture was thrown here and there. Snowbird began to bawl, open-mouthed, like a cow.

"Quiet!" I warned her. "We mustn't provoke him!" I helped her to her feet, handed her a walking stick and a handkerchief for her nose and set straight two of the toppled chairs so that we could sit at the table. We waited in silence for perhaps ten minutes. Then I crept close to the door of their room and laid my ear against it. I returned to Snowbird at the table. "He is asleep. I can hear him snoring."

Hastily, we collected a few belongings, along with the Bucksmasher, and loaded them into the buggy – this was not the first time we had fled George Butler's presence. Taking the reins – for Snowbird's injuries required her attention – I drove her to her brothers' home in town.

"I am afraid to sleep at that house," she told me. She must have repeated this five or six times. Snowbird repeated herself endlessly; she seemed unaware that she did. "Oh, Sophia Sawyer! I am afraid that George Butler will kill me while I sleep. He was not like this when we were first married. What has happened to make him such a crazy man?" Later she told her brothers the same thing.

As it fell out, the bridge of her nose was broken.

The following day was Sunday. The tavern was closed on Sundays out of deference to the small but vocal group of Christians who lived in Qualla's immediate vicinity. By noon, George had recovered enough from his drinking bout to rise shakily from his bed and ride the three miles into town. As was his custom of a Sunday afternoon, he seated himself at a table in the darkened tavern and had just begun to reckon the week's take when the barrel of a rifle nudged open the door, which he had left a little ajar – the tavern's few windows were covered in sooty oilcloth and let in only a little light. Surprised at the intrusion, George half turned in his seat – his back had been to the door – and opened his mouth to speak. "What. . . ?"

The rifle discharged, blowing half of George's face away. It looked as though his face had exploded from inside; the range was that close, eight feet perhaps, no more.

I Tried Two Times, Old Tobacco's successor as conjure man, saw the body afterwards. He said, "What was left of his face looked surprised."

Everyone knew that one of Snowbird's brothers had murdered the tavern keeper. They had made no secret of their distaste for the way he had treated their sister all these years. They had warned him, it was felt, often enough. Nor was any action taken by the council. It was generally agreed that George deserved his death and it was considered particularly fitting that it had been his own Kentucky rifle that had dispatched him thither. There was, however, some discussion as to what to do with the curious and obviously very old buckskin pouch that the tavern keeper wore around his neck.

"It was his amulet," Snowbird remembered, when I Tried Two Times consulted her. "From the first time I met him, he wore it around his neck. He rarely took it off."

Others also recalled that the pouch . . . or one very like it . . . had once been worn by George Butler's uncle, Young Squirrel. "I am certain of it," said Toineeta. She had been blind for a quarter of a century, but no one questioned her assurance.

I Tried Two Times reflected long upon the disposition of the amulet. He set tobacco leaves on fire and, holding the smoldering leaves by their stems, observed which way the smoke blew. "Ordinarily I would say that an amulet should be buried with its owner, for an amulet is a very personal thing and a man may have need of its power in the Darkening Land, which is a land like any other land, and full of dangers. However, this particular amulet seems to have passed down the generations . . . from hand to hand. That, therefore, must be its nature and so I think that we must not bury it beneath the earth or it might dig its way out and come by night to carry off our chickens and our newborn babies. Such things have been known to happen." In the end it was determined that Snowbird should keep the pouch and present it to George's son, Joseph Butler, upon his next visit to Qualla. "But do not open the pouch," I Tried Two Times warned the widow. "Once an amulet has been prepared for a man by a conjure man, its power must be contained or terrible things will occur."

"Like what?" Snowbird was as curious as a child. What was in her husband's pouch? The feather of an eagle? A magic stone? Perhaps there was a jewel. Snowbird had always wanted a jewel.

"Well, for one, your husband's shadow spirit will most certainly return to torment you," the conjure man told her.

That was enough for Snowbird. She placed the amulet in a wooden box and slid the box under her bed against the day Joseph would return from Connecticut to Qualla.

She would not have to wait long to give her son the keepsake. Following hard on the heels of George Butler's death, scandal caused the

Mission School in Cornwall to close its doors for good; it seems that certain of the town's young ladies, all daughters of prominent families and the flower of Cornwall's womanhood, had eloped with students from the school, causing great distress and outrage. This I learned from Sister Ann Brown from Brainerd, with whom I maintained a desultory kind of occasional correspondence, despite the fact that she considered me quite mad. As for Joseph, he did not mention the scandal in his letter, but only wrote to say that he was returning from New England and that he would not be traveling alone. I know because I read Snowbird the letter; she, of course, could not read.

"But who?" she puzzled. "Whoever could Joseph be traveling with?"

SOPHIA SAWYER

ONE

Snowbird and I were seated on the porch when they arrived. As usual, she was nattering on like the careless, little bird she was, half in broken English and half in a rapid, emphatic Cherokee that I was at considerable pain to follow. She spoke of this and that, the past and present, George and her brothers, her sons and her father, the weather, tribal ancestors, rabbits and their evil intentions, all the while stroking Wesa, the fat calico cat that George had forced upon her as a kitten after the incident on Rattlesnake Mountain; rather than reject it as un-Indian, she had taken to the creature at once and had it always with her. Snowbird's mind was like a barrel full of bright tatters the contents of which she regularly rifled with splendid energy but to no apparent effect. I had ceased to listen to her long before and now merely nodded and murmured encouragement. Not knowing that my sister Eugenia had died two months before of rheumatic fever – for mail service was sporadic that far back in the woods – and despite the failing light, I was busy needlepointing a fire screen for her and her husband, newly wed when last I had heard. I had just held the canvas close to my face, squinting in an attempt to see the little holes through which my needle must pass, when Waya, the bloodhound puppy lying in a heap of liver and tan skin at my feet, struggled to his feet, wobbled his jowls and made a low preemptive sound – a kind of gargle that generally escalated into a howl. That was when I heard the rusty wheels of the buckboard turning over in the deeply rutted road. Lowering my canvas, I peered in the direction in which the sound had come. Snowbird followed my gaze, her mouth forming an 'O' of surprise. Then, as the buckboard lurched into view and Waya sprang across the porch and down the stairs in a tumble of legs and ears and tail, "Joseph!" she called. Putting Wesa down and seizing her walking stick, she pitched her weight forward and pushed herself tremulously to a standing position. The cat, not liking commotion, skulked away into the laurel flanking the porch.

"*E tsi!*" Joseph pulled up on the horse and brought the buckboard, piled high with boxes and parcels, to a halt. "Mother! But who is this little f-f-fellow?" He leapt off the wagon and bent down to greet the clamorous puppy, before coming towards us, arms outstretched. He was bigger than when I had seen him last – taller and heavier. His rumpled black suit looked too small for him; it seemed to bind him under the arms and across the back. His pants were too short, as were the sleeves of his clay-stained jacket. Truly, he had grown from boy to man in Cornwall. I was astounded by the transformation. I laid my needlepoint in my lap and stared at him, heart pounding. I thought this: Charley, had he remained above water and grown healthy and put on flesh where there had only ever been bone, might have been expected to look like this, for Joseph was his identical twin. Then, for one brief second, no longer than the thud of my heart, I willed myself to believe that it was my boy. But then you see, I always half-expected Charley to come walking across that door yard, dripping water.

In the meantime, Joseph had leapt up the steps to the porch and folded his tiny mother in his arms.

"Joseph! Joseph!" she wept, patting him on the back with both of her little hands.

Then "Miss Sawyer," he greeted me. "Hello." He extended his hand to me. I took it. "We m-m-meet again." He knew I had been living with his mother, of course, from the letters I had written him on her behalf.

"Hello, Joseph. Your mother has been looking forward to your arrival. But . . ." I cast a questioning look towards the buckboard. A young girl sat stiffly on the box, wringing gloved hands and looking terribly frightened. She appeared to be no more than seventeen or eighteen years old. "Do we have a guest?" I asked gently.

"Eh?" Snowbird demanded.

"Oh, yes!" Joseph appeared flustered. "Yes, Miss Sawyer! We do, indeed!" He crossed back to the buckboard, and handed the girl down from the conveyance. Waya pounced on her straightaway and she let out a little scream. "Don't be frightened," Joseph told her. "He's just a puppy. See." And he seized either tip of Waya's long, pendulous ears and held them up and to the side, so that the dog was standing on his hind legs, nearly suspended by his ears. For some unaccountable reason, Waya seemed to relish this. Perhaps it was the stretch. He grinned and slobbered. "See, Mary. That's what you do. They like it. Don't you like it?" He glanced up. "What's his name, Mother?"

"Waya," Snowbird replied. "Your father wanted a good hunting dog." She snorted. "A lot of good it did him! He bought him and three days later he died. Still, it is a safe house that has a dog."

"There, Waya! Good Waya!" Joseph released the dog's ears, patted his wrinkly head and gave his backside a little shove. Then he encircled the girl's waist with his arm and half-led, half-pulled her towards us, Waya crowding their heels the whole way. The girl was small and slight and moved quickly, with an efficient grace and downcast eyes – pretty in a pale, insipid way, with long, light brown hair and light gray eyes and skin so translucent that one could see the blue veins pulse beneath. "Miss Sawyer . . . . And Mother, of course, please allow me to introduce you to my wife. My wife, M-M-Mary."

Snowbird, who had never been encumbered by manners, gasped audibly and clapped her hand over her mouth.

Joseph, at a loss as to how to handle this awkward situation, forged ahead. "Mary, this is my mother." And he pulled the poor, terrified child forward and thrust her towards Snowbird.

Snowbird reared back, staring at the girl, wide-eyed, her eyebrows hiked up, as though she half-expected her new daughter-in-law to begin pummeling her with her fists. She cringed elaborately.

"Oh, Snowbird, stop that," I cried, exasperated by this childish performance.

"Aren't you going to say hello to M-M-Mary, M-Mother?" Joseph urged. "Please!"

But Snowbird only scowled and shook her head "*Tla no,*" she told her son shortly. "*U ne ga.*"

"*E tsi!*"

The conversation continued in such rapid Cherokee that it was all I could do to pick out the gist of it. This is, more or less, what they said to one another:

"Of course she is white, Mother. Did you think I would marry a Cherokee girl? Father sent me to the white man to be educated. Well, I am like them now."

"She will not like to live with an Indian woman."

"You are wrong. She w-w-wants to live with us. That's why she m-married me."

"She will not respect an Indian mother-in-law!"

"She will do as her mother-in-law tells her."

"*Heu!* Did *I* do what my mother-in-law told me?" Snowbird rolled her eyes.

"She will have Miss Sawyer to talk to. Miss Sawyer will advise her on how to b-b-behave so that we can all get along."

"Tskwayi?" Snowbird exclaimed, for that is how the Cherokee referred to me among themselves – the Heron, because of my attenuated limbs. "Do you know what your Miss Sawyer does? She asks everyone to tell her stories and, when they do, she writes them down as though they might be forgotten. Can you imagine? When she isn't playing with children, she's in the woods doing I don't know what. And sometimes she talks to the river. If you ask me, Tskwayi is a crazy woman." Joseph's eyes cut quickly to me to determine how much of their conversation, if any, I understood. "Don't worry," Snowbird told him in Cherokee. "Heron cannot understand a word we are saying. I talk to her all the time and do you think she understands a thing I say?"

I felt a tug on my sleeve. It was Mary. "What are they saying?" Her head came only to the level of my collarbone – she was miniature. With her slight figure and little hands and her narrow, small feet in their trim black boots, she looked like a tidy child swept far from home in a strange boat. My heart went out to her. She looked so tired.

"They are saying how pretty you are," I lied. "So you and Joseph . . . married, did you? In Cornwall?"

"We eloped." Her face fell, as though this fact overwhelmed her. "Two weeks ago today." It was then that I put two and two together – Miss Ann Brown's account of the scandal that had led to the closure of the school in Cornwall and Joseph's sudden appearance at Ela with this young girl. Joseph must have been one of the students to elope with a daughter of the town. I was astounded, impressed. He had always seemed so thick, cloddish almost. I didn't know he had it in him to pull something like this off.

"Why didn't Joseph let us know?" I asked.

"Oh, we didn't tell anyone, Miss Sawyer," Mary hastened to assure me. "Not a soul! There was no telling what might have happened had anyone known. Poor Papa! The fuss everyone made over us all . . . . It was so unchristian. We feared for our very lives! We did not travel from my hometown so much as flee it!"

"Well!" Snowbird put an end to our conversation with a snort. Glaring at Mary, she tossed her head proudly. Then she said in her broken English, "Let this white wife of yours come into my house, Joseph . . . so she can see what she is *not* and never will be boss of."

TWO

Dawn had just broken on the day after Joseph and Mary had arrived at the house at Ela, when Snowbird shook me awake.

"What?" I protested sleepily. "What do you want?"

"The amulet," she hissed in my ear. "George Butler's amulet!"

"What about it?"

"It left the house last night. In the shape of a ball of fire! About the size of a fist. It flew out from under the bed and out the door. It just flew back inside . . . just a few minutes ago."

"But . . . that's not possible!"

"I saw it!" she insisted.

"Did you dream it?"

"See, dream . . . . What does it matter? It happened, Heron!"

"Why didn't you wake me when you first saw it?"

"*Heu!* I don't know. I fell asleep!" She tugged at my arm. "Come on, Tskwayi, get up! You've got to get the amulet out from under my bed so I can give it to Joseph. You know I can't bend down myself, not since my mother-in-law and Toineeta sawed me in half – a woman with no middle cannot bend! Don't you see, Tskwayi, it's a sign!"

"A sign of what?"

"A sign of whatever it is a sign of! Don't you remember what I Tried Two Times said – that, if you bury such an amulet, one that has been handed down through the generations, it might dig its way out and come by night to carry off chickens and newborn babies? Well, we didn't bury it, but clearly, that's what it's been up to. Who knows what damage it has inflicted! We must give the terrible thing to Joseph at once and be done with it."

And so the buckskin pouch was retrieved from its hiding place under Snowbird's bed and, an hour later, presented to a blurry-eyed Joseph at the breakfast table.

"I remember this," he said, testing the heft of it in his hand. "Of course. Father used to wear this around his neck." He winced slightly; not even his son remembered George Butler with kindness.

"And your great-uncle Young Squirrel and his grandfather before him, the great Dayunisi" said Snowbird, "and all the men of your father's family all the way back to the Groundhog's Mother, who lived a very long time ago."

Joseph started to loosen the sinews that held the pouch closed.

"*Ayeh! Ayeh!*" Snowbird's brown eyes widened with terror. This set off Waya, who began to bay and to run around in circles. In the ensuing commotion Snowbird snatched the pouch from Joseph and scurried around the table, clutching the pouch to her bosom and panting elaborately.

"*E tsi!*" objected Joseph.

Mary leapt to her feet. "What's wrong with her?"

"Waya! Quiet!" I grabbed the puppy by his collar and pulled him towards me. "It's all right," I reassured Joseph and Mary. "She's just frightened. I Tried Two Times told her that, once an amulet has been prepared for a man by a conjure man, its power must be contained or terrible things will happen."

"What terrible things?" cried Mary. "Who is I Tried Two Times?"

"He's the local conjure man," I replied. Then, to Joseph, "She's afraid your father's shadow spirit will return to torment her, if you open the pouch."

"*Ayeh! Ayeh!*" Snowbird confirmed this. "I am not dead yet and I do not wish to meet your father in this or any other lifetime!"

Waya started up again.

"Enough!" I declared. I scooped him up, walked to the door, opened it and put the dog outside on the porch.

"What is this, Joseph?" Mary blanched. "Is your mother not a Christian?"

"Mary, p-p-please."

"I thought you said . . . ."

"Not now!" Joseph turned to his mother. He held out his hand. "Very well, Mother. I promise you that I will not open the pouch."

"You saw how your father treated me in life," she reminded him, cringing.

"I did."

"Then do not provoke his spirit."

"I won't," said Joseph. "I promise."

"And you will keep it safe?" she asked.

"I will."

"Because it is a terrible thing and terrible things must be kept safe."

"I understand."

Snowbird handed over the pouch, which he put in his breast pocket. As he did, I detected a slight wrinkling of his nose, as if in disgust. "There," he said. "That is done. Sit down, M-M-Mother. Eat your breakfast. Everything is all right."

Later, when Snowbird was out of earshot, but in Mary's hearing and for her sake, he said to me, "What shall I do, Miss Sawyer? I don't want the dirty thing. My father was a superstitious man, little better than a heathen, but I have been saved through the good auspices of the missionaries. What shall I do with this amulet?"

"Perhaps you could give it to me for my collection," I suggested.

During the first months I was in Qualla, I had attempted to write down some of the stories Charley had told me in Reverend Cornelius' garret while they were still fresh in my memory. These I read aloud to Snowbird or the village elders to determine whether I had gotten them right. They, in turn, told me new stories or other versions of the same stories. I wrote these down as well – stories about the Moon and the Thunders and the Origins of the Pleiades and the Pine; Why the Possum's Tail is Bare and the Rabbit and the Tar Wolf; Why the Turkey Gobbles and the Eagle's Revenge; the Bullfrog's Lover and the Katydid's Revenge. The history of creation in snippets, passed on from generation to generation – that became my subject, one in which I was keenly interested and much invested. An alternative view of the universe from the one I had been vouchsafed, one in which the whole of creation, and not merely man, or, to be more accurate still, not merely select members of the white race, was sacred and of consequence. In tandem with this archival endeavor, I had also embarked upon a small collection of Cherokee artifacts – a bone tooth comb used to scratch the naked skin of ball players before they went to water, ankle rattles made of shell, a peace pipe carved from white stone with seven stem-holes, so that seven men could sit around and smoke from it at once in a council . . . . Objects that, given the rapid rate of acculturation, might become obsolete and would prove, therefore, of historical interest.

"Take it." He handed the pouch to me. "It is of no use to me. Just make sure that M-M-Mother never knows."

"But, of course," I assured him.

Mary reached out and took his hand. "I am so very proud of you, Joseph. Something that belonged to your father and your great-uncle before him. Yet you chose to give it away rather than succumb to superstition!"

As I tucked the pouch into my pocket, I thought I detected a faint odor emanating from it – metallic, like fresh blood. Given the fact that the house, since Waya's advent, had come to smell powerfully of hound, this, in itself, was noteworthy.

THREE

Poor Mary! No sooner had she set foot in the house than Snowbird undertook to make her life as wretched as possible. Not only did she refuse to speak English in Mary's presence, she also pretended not to understand it when Mary spoke. Moreover, she guarded Joseph like a small, vicious dog defends some prize and complained loudly and incessantly about Mary's utter uselessness while not allowing her to do anything. She would not even let her stroke or hold Wesa, whom she snatched away whenever Mary, who was fond of cats, reached for her.

As for Joseph, he faced the daunting task of learning how to run the family's various business ventures in a short period of time – they were in some disarray, several months having elapsed between George Butler's death and Joseph's return from Connecticut – and the truth was that he was neither as bright nor as ruthless as either Young Squirrel or George Butler. Moreover, he lacked spine and Snowbird so monopolized and browbeat him when home that he could provide neither solace nor support to his young wife.

So it was that, over the next few weeks, in fits and starts, I came to learn in some detail the story of how Mary and Joseph had come to be married. She could speak to me and I would respond and people must communicate, particularly if they are young and alone in a strange, wild place. And our backgrounds were not dissimilar. Although I was fifteen years her senior, both of us hailed from small New England towns; both of us had been raised in Protestant households characterized by righteous rigor when it came to thorny moral issues such as the Indian Problem and Abolition. Both of our fathers favored the Whigs, who vehemently opposed Andrew Jackson's Frontier Party and its extravagant, scurrilous claims of Manifest Destiny, the belief that God intended that the United States extend from sea to sea. Don't misunderstand me. I am not saying that I was *like* Mary, just that I knew who Mary was. I recognized her. She, on the other hand, did not know who I was, but that was to be expected. I had many more secrets than Mary; I played my cards closer to the chest. And then there was the ulunsuti.

This was Mary's story.

⋘⋙

Born and raised in Cornwall, Connecticut, Mary lived until her seventeenth year with her father and mother and a housekeeper, Mrs. Bennett – for her mother was never well enough to tend house and her father, being a minister, required order and a semblance, at least, of harmony. They lived in the rectory behind her father's church – the First Presbyterian Church on Mason Street. I imagine the house to have been gray clapboard, quite small with white trim and very tidy, but I may be thinking of the house in which I was brought up. This I know, for I remember being struck by it when she told me: her bedroom window looked out over the old graveyard where all her siblings were buried – three boys and two girls. Little white headstones all in a row with lambs carved into them or angels. Poor babies, every one of them a stillborn. Her mother always knew of their death the moment it transpired. Apparently she was very sensitive to death. "The baby isn't moving, Mr. Sutter!" she would cry out to Mary's father. "Yes! It has definitely stopped moving!" Then she would take to her bed and weep for hours on end and, if Mary came to her (as she must to bring her food and see to her various needs), she would seize her by the wrist, drag her near, and whisper in a voice worn hoarse from jagged weeping, "Mary, Mary, the Lord God has made your mother's body a crypt from which none may rise! Why has God done this? Have I sinned, Mary? Do you think it is because I have sinned?"

Her mother frightened Mary at these times. "She looked as though she herself might have just risen from the dead, Miss Sawyer – gaunt, hollow-eyed, deathly pale, like I imagine Lazarus must have looked,

255

divested of his winding sheet, and smelling of tightly closed places underground." Mary hated going to her room at these times, but her father insisted. "Someone has to look after her while I prepare my sermons and Mrs. Bennett cannot do everything." He would shake his head sadly. "Your mother is not the helpmate I'd hoped for."

Then, as time passed and Mary grew older and her mother got no better, he started to say things like, "Thank God I have a daughter to help me! I hope you are not planning to marry and leave me, Mary, for I don't know how I would take care of your mother without your assistance!" And he would laugh as though it were a joke. And she would laugh too, despite the fact that, whenever he said things like this, her asthma would act up and she would have difficulty breathing.

As the years went on and the number of headstones in the churchyard bearing the name of Sutter increased . . . as the periods during which her mother could be described as "well" grew more and more infrequent until she rarely rose from her bed and was considered by all to be an invalid and, by many, to be all but mad, Mary's father spent more and more of his time sitting in his book-lined study, writing fiery abolitionist tracts. Like so many New England ministers, he had caught abolition fever and was an outspoken advocate for a forced end to slavery and freedom and equality for all men. He also regularly denounced from the pulpit the expansionist policy of the Frontier Party, which advanced the case for removing the so-called Civilized Tribes of the Southeast, including the Cherokee, to Indian Territory west of the Mississippi. "Surely it would be more benevolent to allow these tribes to continue to live and farm some portion of their ancestral homes than to banish them! What have they done to deserve exile except to adopt the habits of civilized man and emulate us in almost every respect?"

Cornwall differed from surrounding hamlets in that a school had been established in that town by the American Board for Commissioners of Foreign Missions. To this school, promising youths from many heathen parts were sent by the missionaries then at work in those faraway locales. The thought was that these savage youths, once educated in a civilized and Christian setting and made to see the virtues of both culture and religion, might return to their peoples as native missionaries. Students came from all over the world, from as far away as Malaysia and the Fiji Islands, but there were a number of American Indians as well.

In general, the Indians at the mission school, particularly those from the southern regions, came from quite affluent families who were themselves desirous of living in accordance with European standards. They were familiar with these through living close by white men; some, indeed, were children of mixed marriages. Because of their command of English and the high degree of acculturation they already boasted, these southern Indians moved more easily among Cornwall society than did those rough, wool-headed natives from other continents who spoke with peculiar accents and displayed an almost childlike wonder and terror at the most commonplace items, like guns and pipe organs (and, if the truth be told, often smelled rather rancid, like milk that has gone off).

Of particular interest to the more enlightened citizens of Cornwall were the handful of Cherokee Indians who attended the school, to such an extent that these youths were sometimes invited into the homes of Cornwall's more prominent citizens, not so much as guests as exotic specimens, and also, of course, so that their presence there might attest to those citizens' generosity of spirit, while at no point endangering the china.

Mary's father was frequently invited to these social functions to ensure perhaps that God was watching . . . and taking note.

She was sixteen when she and her father were invited to tea at the home of Dr. Northrup, one of her father's parishioners. (Her mother had been invited to the Northrups as well, but, as usual, she was indisposed, either recovering from some loss or girding herself for a fresh one – an effort that enlisted all the invalid's powers of concentration.)

A light snow was falling, salting their shoulders white as they walked towards the big house on Elm Street and the frozen ground squeaked under the pressure of their footfalls. It was going onto Christmas time, already dark though it was only four o'clock in the afternoon. Harness bells jingled on passing horses – a silvery sound – and a smell of pitch and fire snaked through the air like a slow river.

The tea had been arranged so that others in the Northrups' circle might meet the family's new boarder, Johnny Ridge. Dr. Northrup, it seemed, was very proud of this boarder, a Cherokee student at the Mission School. As the school's physician, he had been called in a few days before to advise the missionaries on Johnny's condition. The boy suffered from a mild respiratory malaise, a kind of wetness that appeared chronic. After examining him, Dr. Northrup had advised that his place of residence be changed from the school's notoriously under-ventilated dormitory to a more salubrious abode. Then, Dr. Northrup, whom the invalid had evidently charmed, suggested that Johnny live with his own family for the duration of the winter. (When Mary told me this, I must confess to having experienced a sudden dislocation of the heart. How close her tale was, in this particular, to mine! For you will recall that Charley spent his winters at Brainerd in the Cornelius' garret because of a similar kind of indisposition and that this is how I came to know him.)

"This young man, Ridge . . . he really is quite extraordinary," Dr. Northrup confided in low tones to Mary's father, as the servant took his coat. Turning to Mary, he said, "Miss Mary, please allow me introduce you to our special guests." Taking her by the elbow, he led her into the bright, hot parlor and steered her over to a compact Cherokee who stood beside the fireplace, gripping a china teacup in two hands. His suit, cut in the finest English manner and of excellent cloth, was nevertheless outlandish – the coat was a brilliant robin's egg blue, the vest a bright yellow. Was this the famed Johnny Ridge, she wondered. It wasn't.

"Elias Boudinot, allow me to introduce you to Reverend Sutter's daughter Mary. Mary, Elias Boudinot."

"Charmed!" Elias placed his teacup carefully on the oak mantelpiece and seized the hand Mary offered him, inclining deferentially over it. He was spare, wiry and as poised as a fox on the point of flight. His head was somewhat too big for his small body, giving him a look at once childish and intelligent.

"Mr. Boudinot!" she murmured, but Dr. Northrup was already drawing her away to meet a second student, a big, bear-like boy, clad completely in white, including white boots. "And this is Joseph Butler."

Joseph fumbled awkwardly for her hand and gulped a greeting. He was tall and of a quite stocky build – thick-necked, barrel-chested with large, muscular thighs and big hands and feet. His white suit, though dashing, seemed not to fit so much as bind him. She also noticed that his skin was not so coppery as Elias'; rather, it was olive in cast and there was that about his features that suggested mixed blood. Nor were his eyes as dark as Elias'; instead, they were a curious hazel color, and his hair, which he wore long and clubbed at the back of his neck, was dull brown rather than shiny black.

Dr. Northrup then led her to a black horsehair settee before the fireplace where a third youth languished, clad in an elegant dressing gown of a vivid emerald hue. A wool plaid lap rug, woven in vibrant reds and blues, was tucked up about his knees. "And, finally, Mary, this . . . *this* is our new boarder. Johnny Ridge, Miss Mary Sutter."

Slender to the point of litheness, tall and languid, John Ridge possessed huge, solemn eyes and a precisely cut, almost feminine mouth that was a shade too small for his long face. There was a kind of softness to all his features, a fleshy quality that imparted to his person a kind of indeterminate and restless sensuousness. He appeared slightly fretful, exotic, hybrid and delicate and his smile, which he bestowed on Mary now, was unspeakably radiant. Hesitantly and tremulously – for his beauty quite took her aback – she extended her hand to the attractive invalid. He seized it with cool fingers and gave it the gentlest of squeezes.

"Please! Please, everybody!" Dr. Northrup pleaded jovially. "Do sit! Martha!" He called to the servant. "Tea, please!"

With the kind of urgency that characterizes a game of musical chairs, Dr. and Mrs. Northrup, Colonel and Mrs. Gold, and Mary's father all promptly deposited themselves in chairs drawn up close to the fire, while Sarah Northrup, a year ahead of Mary at Normal School, bolted across the parlor to perch upon the right arm of the settee on which Johnny lay, and Harriet Gold, Sarah's classmate and best chum, lay claim to the left arm of that same settee. Mary plunked herself down on the piano bench and Elias slid quickly into the wing chair to one side of the fireplace. Only Joseph, looking somewhat stunned, remained standing.

"It was so awkward," Mary remembered. "Like the cheese standing alone."

It was only then that Dr. Northrup realized that they were short a chair. "Martha!" he called out to the servant. "Another chair, please, for Mr. Butler!"

Mary's father initiated the conversation. "You do not grow too bored, Mr. Ridge, lying in bed all day?"

"Heavens, no!" Johnny protested. "For Miss Northrup brings me the finest meals on a tray and reads to me by the hour."

"We are presently reading *A Pilgrim's Progress*, Mr. Sutter," said Sarah. She was an over-large girl, according to Mary, with rather a thick waist and a dull complexion, who nevertheless gave an impression of beauty because of masses of thick, curly auburn hair that extended to the middle of her back.

"A judicious choice!" Mary's father caught Dr. Northrup's eye and nodded approvingly.

By this time Martha had arrived with a spindly chair that was clearly far too delicate for one of Joseph's bulk. No one took any note of the disparity; they were too beguiled by Johnny Ridge to notice Joseph's discomfiture. He sat down gingerly, but kept shifting this way and that, as if concerned the chair might break were he to rest all of his weight on it. As a result of this activity, the chair squeaked dolefully.

"Ridge! Isn't it a funny name?" cried Sarah, then to the company at large, "Johnny, do tell Mary and Harriet where it comes from."

Johnny smiled his radiant smile. "My father is named Kahnung-dat-lageh, He Who Walks Upon The Mountaintop. He fought with General Jackson against the Creeks and the white soldiers called him Major Ridge for short."

"And what does your father think of Andy Jackson these days?" Colonel Gold asked. Jackson was a keen proponent of moving the five Southeastern Tribes to Indian Territory.

"We have an Indian name for General Jackson," replied Johnny. "It is not a nice name. We call him Chicken Snake."

"Isn't that quaint?" asked Sarah. "Chicken Snake! And Johnny writes the most wonderful sonnets! Just as good as Mr. Keats. Johnny, recite one of your sonnets for our guests. The one about the rose! I do love it so!"

"Do, John. There's a lad!" Dr. Northrup added his encouragement.

Johnny cleared his throat and, sitting up a bit on the settee, folded soft, manicured hands in his lap and recited carefully:

> "Like as the damask rose you see,
> Or like the blossom on the trees,
> Or like the morning to the day,
> Or like the Sun, or like the shade,
> Or like the gourd that Jonas had:
> Even such is MAN. . . !"

According to Mary, the effect of this recitation was nothing less than profound. "Of course I was still a child and so still given to extreme reactions to rather commonplace events," she told me. "However, up to that moment . . . or so it seemed to me . . . my life had been a small one, trickling its slow course down narrow channels – confined, restrained. I had lived riddled with small fears the way others live riddled with worms. I had been a child, bent on play and pleasing, at home in a sad place, with God in all the cupboards. Now it occurred to me that I might be in the process of becoming a woman and, with that thought, everything around me became suddenly amplified – the clatter of silver on the tray, the chink of china saucer meeting china plate. Glancing about myself, I saw everything with the most wonderful and ruthless clarity. Most particularly, I saw the way Sarah Northrup gazed at her family's boarder. As everyone put their hands together in polite applause, desire slashed my heart into bleeding ribbons. I had fallen in love with Johnny Ridge, you see. There! I confess it freely! How I came to be married to Joseph Butler . . . . Well, that is a story of a different kind."

๛

A week after the party at the Northrups, Sarah had invited Harriet and Mary over for tea and proposed a game of cards.

"Don't worry, silly," Sarah had assured her. "Not a *wicked* card game. Only cutting and shuffling and dealing. We're not playing for money. We're playing for hearts!" The rules of the game were this: whoever drew the King of Hearts, got first pick – whichever of the Indian boys she wished; whoever drew the Jack of Hearts got her first choice of the two remaining; and whoever drew the Ace of Hearts got whoever was left over.

Mary was hesitant to play, but, "I reckon this is your only hope of marrying at all," Hattie told her. "I mean, your Pa told my Pa that he couldn't possibly allow you to marry because who else would there be to look after your Ma. He said that Mrs. Bennett couldn't possibly do it all. He said you were a sensible girl and he didn't expect you to make any fuss. Think of it, Mary! You'll be nothing but a lonely old maid carrying bedpans for your Ma and taking care of your doddering old Pa!"

"And they're rich," Sarah chimed in. "Johnny's told me all about his father's plantation. Did you know that Major Ridge has two hundred and fifty acres of cleared land, with eight fields for crops – corn, tobacco, indigo, potatoes, oats . . . . Oh, I don't know what all! Did you know that he has a ferry and a store and an orchard with over a thousand peach trees and four hundred apple trees and a big white house and lots of slaves to work the fields . . . Well, owning slaves is a terrible thing, but never mind that. We shall just have to free them. And that there are peacocks . . . peacocks, Mary. . . just walking around on the lawn?"

"But our parents would never let us!" Mary objected.

"Oh, yes they will! We shall make them. If they refuse to let us marry our red Indian lovers, we shall refuse to eat and say we are dying of love."

Mary was skeptical. "And if they still say no?"

"We shall waste away! It won't be easy. We must be extraordinarily brave and committed."

"I don't know how long I could go without eating," Mary worried.

"Oh, don't worry," Harriet assured her. "Your asthma can become so aggravated that your death by suffocation is almost certain. Think of it, Mary! They won't hold out for long. Besides, they will not want to be seen as hypocrites."

"After all, your father is forever preaching sermons on how all men are created equal in the sight of the Lord," said Sarah. "He would look a complete hypocrite if he refused to allow you to marry an Indian."

So they drew. To Sarah went the King of Hearts; to Harriet, the Jack of Hearts; while Mary drew the Ace of Hearts. Sarah picked Johnny Ridge; Harriet, Elias Boudinot; Mary had no choice but to go with Joseph.

"I'm pretty sure Sarah cheated," Mary told me. "Hattie, too."

Later the three girls swore a compact, no matter what, to adhere to the plan which they had that day made. Further, they pronounced themselves blood sisters after a painful and drawn-out operation involving puncture wounds made in the tip of the ring finger of their left hands – where they would one day wear a wedding band – with a rather dull tapestry needle. This transpired only with the utmost trepidation and much muffled shrieking.

Then, as it was close to the dinner hour, Harriet and Mary took their leave of Sarah. As they were walking down Elm Street towards the Square, Harriet said, "You know Sarah cheated. She had the King of

Hearts up her sleeve all the time. I saw it poking out from under her lace."

What Harriet did not say was that she had had the Jack of Hearts up her sleeve all the time. Mary had seen it tucked under her wristband.

The wound in Mary's finger became septic and had to be lanced and drained. For days the finger throbbed painfully, like a second, inflamed heart attached to her hand and then the swelling diminished and the pain all but disappeared. The pact, however, was made.

"My course was set," she told me dolefully, dabbing at her swollen eyes with a sodden handkerchief, "and, as Papa so often reminds his congregation, God writes in the book of our lives in indelible ink."

I shook my head. "No, He doesn't, Mary."

"Miss Sawyer?"

"It is not God who determines the course of your life," I told her. "That is your responsibility."

She was clearly aghast. "Miss Sawyer," she stammered, "please tell me that you do not believe in Free Will? For then you would be . . ." She lowered her voice. "A *Papist!*"

I laughed. "Do not fret, Mary," I reassured her. "I am not a Papist." Nor, I thought, am I a Protestant. In fact, I was no longer a Christian. What I was, what I had become in the months that intervened between the end of my time at Brainerd and this day on the porch at Ela with Mary was something altogether different – a Pantheist, I suppose, someone who believes that everything is part of an all-encompassing, that God is the same thing as the Universe or Nature. I had suspected my apostasy for quite some time, beginning at Brainerd, when Charley had first challenged my assumptions. I certainly hadn't prayed for a very long time, except to the individual spirits of things and the cosmos in general. That seemed reasonable. The idea of a personal god, on the other hand, one who, in the distant past in a faraway land, was made flesh and sacrificed himself for our sins, a father who was also a son, a vengeful god who was also a merciful god . . . . That, I'm afraid, did not. Still, learning of my heretical views would have only served to upset and alarm Mary further and there was no point in that. She would have doubtless felt honor bound to save me from certain perdition and that would have proved tedious in the extreme.

FOUR

The next near decade was the most remarkable period in my life. I did not know it at the time. I certainly did not know why. Only through death and dissolution have I been able, at last, to see clearly what is and was, to know the contents of that pouch and understand its import. One thing I have found: you cannot see much if all you see with is your eyes.

I kept the pouch always on my person, tucked away in a pocket, so that Snowbird would not know Joseph had given it to me, and I obeyed the conjure man's stricture never to open it – not because I feared that George Butler would come back to torment Snowbird, but because what I Tried Two Times had said made a kind sense to me: the amulet, if that was what it was (of course, it wasn't), had not been handed down to me by my ancestors and I knew somehow both that it would only be in my possession a short time and that I would ungrudgingly pass it on to its next rightful owner, when that period of transition had ended. And I would know when that time came. Somehow I would know. My task, in hindsight, must have been to preserve the ulunsuti until its next, more rightful owner might be found. I don't know how I knew this, but I did. There was so much I did not know then, yet did. It is a mystery to me still, for in eternity secrets stand exposed, but magic . . . . Magic remains magic.

And, besides, even if I had opened the pouch, I might not have known what to call the stone within or what its powers were. Like George Kinnahan before me, I might not have seen the magic. But I felt it. I certainly felt it. And it changed me.

What was it like to possess the ulunsuti?

I will tell you: I felt well. For the first time in my life, I felt well. I had always been somewhat sickly, prone to headaches and dyspepsia and neuralgia, and suddenly . . . suddenly I was bursting with health. My energy was boundless. I needed little sleep and what I needed, I easily found. My digestion was excellent and my constitution hearty. Throughout those years I carried the ulunsuti about with me I suffered not one whit of illness – not a sniffle, not a cough, not a stomach ache.

But there was more.

In those years, three things happened that, for the life of me, I couldn't explain, yet somehow never thought to question.

The first was this: I became, in a matter of months, fluent in Cherokee, both in the dialect spoken in the Lower Towns in the vicinity of the South Carolina-Georgia border – a dialect to which I had virtually no exposure – and the Anikutani dialect spoken in Qualla. Not only was I able to speak this slippery language, I could both read and write it, using Sequoyah's syllabary. This from a woman whose French and Latin teachers had despaired of in Normal School; a woman with no ear for language; a woman whose command of Cherokee up to that point could only be described as patchy.

The second was that I became a tolerably good shot – useful, given the fact that Joseph's aim was poor. In any case, he spent most of his days in town; had we required protection, he would not have been around to provide it. (The Negroes were never entrusted with guns, of course, lest they turn them upon us.) I did not hunt, as I have always had a weak spot for woodland creatures and would not like to kill or injure them, but I have scared off many a bear in my day, not to mention wild boar, panther and raccoon, and would while away long summer afternoons shooting at targets set on a log. My favorite gun was the Bucksmasher, George Kinnahan's fine Kentucky rifle, made of walnut with a hand-rubbed oil finish. It had a very long barrel, as it was designed to be used in dense forest, but was lighter weight than many of its counterparts with a slender stock and a deep, curved butt plate. The trigger guard, patch box cover, side plate, thimble and nose cap were solid brass, while the lock plate was case-hardened steel. Firing it was the sheerest pleasure. I don't know how to describe it. With a proper prime in the tray (just a dash) and a clean touch hole, it would fire with almost no perceptible delay. The deep curve in the butt plate was surprisingly comfortable and the stock, once shouldered, stayed in place nicely, particularly if one leaned a hand upon a tree or wall and rested the barrel on one's hand. I became very fond of that gun and took it with me on my and Waya's frequent forays into the forest, lest we encounter some danger.

The third was this: I became an accomplished basket weaver. How I did this, I cannot begin to know. Certainly no one taught me. Rather, I saw the baskets that other women made elsewhere – either waking, in my mind's eye, or dreaming – and I *knew* how to make them. I just *knew*. I knew how to weave a slew and a French slew and a wale and a randing, how to chase with two colors and double weave. I became expert at the pairing weave, but after the local fashion, with the top wearer twisted counter rather than clockwise. I saw designs in my dreams and wove them into my baskets and called them by their traditional names, which, again, I *knew*: Noon Day Sun, Chief's Daughter, Double Peace Pipe, Arrowhead, Mountain Peaks and Lightning. I knew what woods to use (white oak is best) and that hickory makes excellent handles and rims. I knew that it is best to hunt river cane and mulberry and red maple either early in the year – before the snakes awake in the wood – or in the autumn, when the vines are longest. I knew what roots and leaves to gather to make my own dyes and how to set those dyes so that I could weave colored baskets.

Clearly there was a mystery here. Nancy Butler had worn out the cold moons at Gall Place by quilting, this despite the fact that there were no women about to show her the patterns they made and handed down to their daughters or shared with the woman on the next farmstead, no, or the names by which they called these patterns. Like Nancy, who could not have known, but did, so I, who could not have known, did. Again, I did not question it; it seemed so natural as to be inevitable.

I see now that these abilities were the effect of the ulunsuti, which affects different people differently and imparts different kinds of knowledge to those who possessed it. As it had with Nancy, the ulunsuti gave me what I must have needed. And I took it with both hands and reached for more.

But my newfound exuberance had to it a ragged edge. Dark passions stirred in me that I had hitherto not experienced, at least not to such extent: desire and possessiveness and envy all in a stew. And there was something else. I didn't see it at the time. It was this: I was less kind. The ulunsuti renders one less kind. Not unkind, for that is not my nature and an ulunsuti will not alter its owner's essential nature, but not so kind as I might otherwise have been. Please understand, it was not that I was cruel. Rather I was self-absorbed and single-minded, always placing myself and my interests first. Perhaps if I had not had the ulunsuti, I would have taken better note of the dreadful conditions in which the Butlers' slaves lived and done something to improve their lives.

Perhaps I would have paid more attention to what was going on in the outside world. After all, it was during this period that the Indian Removal Act was promulgated and passed in Congress, despite fierce opposition from the same Christian missionaries in whose ranks I had once counted myself. I could have joined my voice with theirs to defend the Cherokees' right to their ancestral lands and yet . . . . And yet I barely took notice and this despite the fact that I read Snowbird every issue of the *Cherokee Phoenix* that came into the trading post. This was a newspaper out of New Echota that provided an ongoing account of the government's various and increasingly heavy-handed attempts to coerce leaders of the Five Civilized Tribes to sign treaties that would oblige them to give up their land and move to Indian Territory west of the Mississippi. I knew what was going on and, yet, at the time, it never occurred to me to speak out against it.

And perhaps, just perhaps, Mary's life would have been easier.

FIVE

As far as her daughter-in-law went, Snowbird continued to be perfectly, maddeningly impossible, refusing to speak with her in English, while continuing to flaunt her own ability to speak English (albeit a very ungrammatical English) when conversing with anyone else. Of course, Mary asked Joseph to speak with his mother. Of course, he did. Numerous times. And, of course, Snowbird remained obdurate. Finally we settled on the following means of communication:

Mary would tell me something to tell Snowbird in English.

I would tell Snowbird what Mary had said in English.

Snowbird would respond to me in English.

I would relay the response to Mary in English.

If Mary attempted to speak directly to Snowbird in English, Snowbird would respond in Cherokee.

And that was how we managed conversations. It was awkward, unpleasant and tiresome.

Given Snowbird's intransigence, Joseph's involvement in the family's various business ventures and the demands placed upon me by my little school, coupled with my feverish forays into basket weaving, I do not know what Mary would have done had it not been for the Negroes. There were four of them living in a decrepit lean-to out back of the stable, something between a shed and a dog run – if living it could be called that, so squalid were the conditions.

Lean, leathery, grizzled and toothless, Lehi was in charge of the horses; it was Lehi who had driven the same fine white coach that now moldered in the stable, roads in these parts being too rough and narrow to easily accommodate so elegant a conveyance, that had delivered Charley and Joseph to Brainerd.

Ned took care of the livestock – two cows, a variable number of chickens and several pigs. Squat, broad-shouldered and thick with a flat nose and filed teeth, he was a harrowing sight, moody and belligerent.

Isaiah was a lanky young man – all long legs and arms and lolling head – who did odd jobs about the place when he could be persuaded to.

And finally there was Nettie, who resembled nothing so much as a boiled chicken. She was the cook.

As for their ages, it was impossible to pinpoint exactly – they certainly did not know how old they were – but I would have put Lehi at fifty, Ned in his early thirties, Isaiah in his late teens or early twenties and Nettie anywhere in her thirties.

Their well-being and improvement became Mary's great project.

The acquisition of these slaves had been driven less by utility than by the desire for status – many prominent Cherokees owned slaves and George had not wanted to be seen to be less successful than the Ridges or the Rosses or others of their ilk. In truth, however, there was really very little for the poor creatures to do, and what tasks were allotted them, they performed indifferently and with an air of great confusion. This was in large part due to Snowbird's complete disinclination to train them or, indeed, to deal with them in any way at all. For her, their principal function seemed to be decorative, like peacocks on the lawn. More often, for they annoyed her utterly and she had the greatest contempt for them, she treated them as though they were mangy dogs underfoot. Nettie was the only one she would allow in the house and then only to deliver food from the kitchen – the kitchen was housed in a cabin separate from the house and connected to the main house by a covered walkway; this was quite common in the southern states. Being filthy and, except in the colder months, almost naked, Nettie was neither expected nor allowed to clean, despite the fact that the house was, by Cherokee standards, quite large – for the simple cabin that Young Squirrel had built so many years ago for his half-sister had been added onto until, by the time of George Butler's death, it consisted of seven big rooms, spread over two stories.

Mary devoted herself utterly to the Negroes' welfare and improvement. It was a formidable task, for, with the exception of Lehi, whom George Butler bought off a white man on one of his trips to Charleston, the slaves at Ela had been purchased at market directly off the boat from Africa and behaved as I imagined they would back on that dark continent – singing and dancing in a highly uncouth manner and going about quite naked. Mary undertook first to urge a Christian modesty upon them by providing them with suitable clothing. She instituted a regular Saturday night bath. Distressed by the impropriety that resulted from Nettie sharing the same squalid quarters as the male slaves, she commandeered Ned, Isaiah and Lehi to build another, separate shed for the cook. She undertook to teach them English (for they spoke the strangest, must guttural language I have ever heard and had but a smattering of Cherokee and English at the time she commenced their education). She also endeavored as best she could to convert them to Christianity, which, given their tenuous grasp of English, was slow going to say the least.

After the passage of a year and much under-requited toil on her part, the poor child ventured to write her father, with whom she had not communicated since her elopement and whom she clearly revered, begging his forgiveness for having gone against his wishes in the matter of her marriage and asking how she might accomplish the liberty of the slaves in her charge. She read the letter out loud to me before sending it: "You see, Papa, this marriage has provided me with noble work to do, far nobler than might have been my lot in Cornwall. I pray that you will see in time that I have not been selfish in marrying Joseph, that I have not run away, but, indeed, that I have sacrificed myself upon the altar of equal rights for all mankind. This I vow to you!"

Six weeks later she received his sober reply and learned for the first time that, upon word of her marriage to Joseph Butler, her father's parishioners had hurled rotten eggs and vegetables at him while in the pulpit and that some malcontent had actually gone so far as to set the church afire – "Thank God the sexton discovered the blaze in time and was able to extinguish the flames before they did any real damage." Mary was aghast. "Are we not Christians and has God not created us all equal?" she cried, then, ravaged by guilt, "How my father has suffered on my account! It is clear that I must repay him by a life of constant sacrifice!"

SIX

Shortly after hearing from her father, Mary sought me out. "Dear Miss Sawyer," she said, "my monthlies are past due these three months. Does this mean that I am in the family way?"

I was not versed in these matter, being a maiden lady, so I undertook to ask Snowbird, who immediately pronounced that Mary was too small to have a baby and that, if she were, in fact, pregnant, it was an absolute certainty that the baby would get stuck up inside of her and die and that Mary would probably die too. Snowbird seemed exhilarated at this prospect and went about the rest of her day gloating.

"What about Nettie?" I asked. The cook had apparently produced several children in the past; George had sold them off as soon as they were weaned, which might have accounted for her somewhat stricken air. "Who attended on her?"

"Nobody." Snowbird shrugged. "She shat those babies out like they were turds. She is an animal."

So I consulted with the parents of my students who recommended the services of Toineeta.

Upon hearing this, Snowbird cried, "*Ayeh!* Tell my daughter-in-law that it was Toineeta who cut Joseph and his twin brother out of my stomach when they wouldn't be born and that is why I have no middle."

"Is it true, Miss Sawyer?" Mary looked distraught. She wrung her hands.

"From what I understand, Toineeta has birthed hundreds and hundreds of babies," I assured her, glaring at Snowbird, who ignored me.

"Tell my daughter-in-law that Toineeta is a blind woman and a witch and one hundred years old! Tell her that she will surely die in childbed!" She consulted the cat, her familiar. "Won't she, Wesa? Won't she die in childbed?"

A high-pitched sound – a kind of dire squeak – emerged from Mary's upper airway, followed by a protracted expiration, signaling the onslaught of an asthma attack. "My chest!" she gasped. "I . . . can't . . !" Suddenly red-faced, her chest over-inflated and the muscles of her neck straining, she rose from her chair and staggered, weaving, towards the door, trying, evidently, to escape Snowbird. Despite the daily dose of mustard seeds, quicksilver and cinnabar prescribed long ago by Dr. Northrup, she had frequent bouts of this acute breathlessness, no doubt exacerbated by isolation and her unhappy situation.

I took her firmly by the shoulders and escorted her from Snowbird's gleeful presence to her and Joseph's bed. Suppressing my own irritation at having been cast once more in the role of comforter, when what I really wanted was to go into the woods with Waya to hunt honeysuckle and blackberry canes while he treed raccoons, I sat her down, wrapping one arm around her and remaining thus until her panic subdued and she began to breathe in a more regular fashion. "You're not going to die in childbed," I told her then. "Don't listen to Snowbird. She is a kind of monster."

"I don't understand. I don't understand why she hates me . . . why she torments me . . . why she wishes me dead! No, I don't understand anything! Anything at all!" She erupted in tears.

"Now, now, Mary!" I patted her on the back – ham-handed, awkward. I had never been very good in these sorts of situations and my reserves of sympathy were, at that time, low. It was the snake in me. "What is there to understand?"

She groped about her for a handkerchief, found one, blew her red nose and dabbed at her eyes. Clearly she had glimpsed an opportunity. "The death of my father-in-law, to begin with. What happened there? Whenever I raise the subject, everyone becomes very quiet and looks everywhere but at me. Then they start talking about something else entirely, as if the question had never been raised. And Joseph's grandmother . . . she just up and disappeared one day. And his grandfather – same thing. And his twin brother. People seem to just vanish in this family and nobody thinks it the least peculiar! It seems that half of Joseph's relations have simply fallen off the face of the earth!"

I didn't know what to tell her. She was right, of course. "Ah, well . . ." I began.

"And you, Miss Sawyer, you!" She seized my hands and held them tight, her eyes perilously large, her face ashen. "You are the most confounding of the lot. Not for the life of me can I figure out how you came to be in this place and why you stay? How did that happen?"

I must have inadvertently flinched, for she immediately cried, "Oh, will you tell me, Miss Sawyer? Will you at least tell me your story? May I at least have that?"

"There's nothing to tell," I said stiffly. I could not tell her about Charley, about what had happened to him. I had tried that once and been dismissed for my efforts and thought mad. I was not going to do that again. Besides, she wouldn't have believed me. How could she have? As to the rest, how I had changed, what I had become, what I still strove to become – one with him and his people – how could I tell her that? I barely understood it myself and she . . . . She was one of Charley's "they." "There's nothing to tell," I repeated.

She stared at me for a moment, unblinking, then turned her head to one side and contemplated her lap mournfully. "Then I'm all alone," she said.

SEVEN

Contrary to what Snowbird maintained, there seemed to be more room inside of Mary than any of us had counted on – any of us, that is, except Toineeta, who guided her through her pregnancy and delivered her rather small baby without incident. Mary named him Jonathon after the first of her little stillborn brothers. "All the time I was growing up, I would visit my brothers and sisters quite regularly in the graveyard," she told me, "and every night I would whisper goodnight to each of them by name through the bowed glass of my bedroom window – Jonathon, James, Ezra, Louise, Henrietta . . . ." She had felt tenderly towards them, sweet, dead babies, but, like her mother, they had frightened her. They were, after all, ghosts; tiny ghosts cheated of life. Of all her parents' six children, she alone had drawn breath and lived and she reckoned they might resent her for it. "I used to tell them that, if ever I had children, I would call them by their names that they might live," she confided in me. "I like to think that Jonathon is that brother reborn, though that thought also frightens me and I suspect Papa might consider it blasphemous."

A year later, she gave birth to James and a year after that to Ezra. To her astonishment, all three boys thrived. Mary could scarcely believe it. Her mother's sad experience had not prepared her for reproductive success; she did not trust her body not to betray her and was weighed down always by a terrible sense of foreboding that hung about the house like a miasma.

Sadly, the advent of children did not bring Mary and Joseph any closer. At first their conversations had tended towards the general – as newlyweds they might have discussed the Evils of Slavery, for example, or the Broadening Benefits of Travel – speaking their parts as though they had rehearsed them, stiltedly, without conviction, as though they were bad actors in a bad play. Later, however, their discourse became more of a monologue, which is to say, Mary complained and Joseph, for his part, found himself at a loss for words.

"In truth, before we were married, we spent very little time alone," she confided in me, "or I might have discovered how plodding and wholly unoriginal he is. Sadly, he has neither the grace of a Johnny Ridge nor the wit of an Elias Boudinot." (As time went on she became increasingly candid about her disappointment and chagrin at the way her life had turned out.)

Another time she told me, "I sometimes catch him looking at me out of the corner of his eye, and the look on his face is one of perturbed bewilderment, as if he were trying very hard to figure out who and what I am. He does not know what to make of me apart from the fact that I am some kind of human trophy – the White Wife, proof that he is as good as any white man. As for me, Joseph is as much my trophy as I am his – my proof that I am more noble, more self-sacrificing, more right-eous, indeed, more Christian than other women, that I am an exemplar. The new Ruth. *Whither thou goest, I shall go, and thy people shall be my people and thy God my God.* Only none of it is true, Miss Sawyer. None of it. I am no exemplar. I have played my life as though it were a card game, and it isn't, and if Sarah and Hattie are happy, then I rejoice for then, but I . . . I am utterly ruined!"

Did I mention that she had grown bitter?

As for Snowbird, the arrival of grandchildren altered her attitude to her daughter-in-law not one wit; she was no more inclined to speak to Mary than previously, nor would she allow her to do anything her way. However, she doted on the children and her preoccupation with them gave her less time and inclination to torment her daughter-in-law than previously.

"Often I catch myself wishing that she would die," Mary confessed to me. "It's a terrible sin, I know, but I can't help myself. If only Joseph would not spend so much time in town . . . . But I am scarcely happy when he is here either. Were it not for my boys . . . . But such specula-tion is useless. It is I who have nailed myself onto this cross."

Flush with the terrible energy that came from the ulunsuti, I never rose to her bait (for bait it was; Mary was fishing for salvation, casting her line in the hopes of freeing herself from the life in which she found herself). But I had willow to split and wood to trim and plane and soak and cedar bark to burn for its ashes and dyes to make out of sassafras and indigo and madder and cochineal. I had the mountains, cloaked in whispering forest, and all that dwelt within them, an animate universe that held me tight in its thrall and Mary . . . well, Mary was not so interesting as all that.

Following the birth of his third son, Joseph's fortunes declined markedly. More and more he found himself pulling up a chair and joining in on the card games that ran more or less continuously at the tavern. He discovered a liking for poker, but it was an obsessive, desperate liking, not friendly at all – the dark and exasperated longing a man might feel for a woman who will never love him or, indeed, show him any interest whatsoever. Joseph played cards badly and never became any better at them. Over the years he had grown very stout. ("*Eu!* He is eating for the two of them!" Snowbird explained his prodigious appetite. "For him and his brother Charley that is gone, both!") When he was under pressure, he broke into a visible sweat; his breathing became labored and his hands trembled. His anxiety invariably betrayed his hand to more experienced players.

Then, in 1833, he made the tactical error of putting the trading post and tavern down as collateral in a big game. Within the time it took to play a couple of hands, Joseph had lost half of Young Squirrel and his father's legacy to a white farmer with an inscrutable expression named Marshbanks.

Joseph was distraught at the loss. After signing over his deeds, he found that he could hardly bear to go into the village any longer, for the sight of the trading post and the tavern only reminded him of what he so ardently wished to forget – that they were no longer his.

He sent Isaiah to buy whiskey and sat on the porch doggedly drinking glass after glass of it. Perched on one of the old twig rockers, he looked like a treed bear in autumn – fat, sleepy, unwieldy, baffled, precariously balanced. Waya lay at his feet in a pool of slobber, his expression doleful – the bloodhound had decided at some point that Joseph was his responsibility and rarely left the drunkard's side.

The rocker Joseph favored soon broke under his weight. He ordered it hauled away and sat in the other one until it broke. Then he ordered another rocker made – a bigger, stronger one.

Mary despaired. She was just twenty-three and the mother of four children – Louise Butler had been born on November 6, 1832, the same day that Andrew Jackson won the Presidency for the second time in a landslide victory. There had been no liquor in the Sutter house. She had never seen anyone drunk save at a distance and now they had financial worries to contend with as well. While the mill still did a good business, the ferry had never brought in a great deal of revenue. Their income was reduced by almost two thirds.

Mary begged Joseph to stop drinking, but he said he could not. He wept a good deal, sitting in his chair. Sometimes he would rear up, stride the length of the porch, and lumber off into the woods, flailing his arms and crying out loud to those who had gone before him – his father, his brother, his grandmother and his grandfather – to help him find peace. Waya accompanied him on these desperate and melancholy rambles; his baying provided a melancholy counterpoint to his master's doleful lamentations.

"He is lost," Mary told me. "I fear that I cannot help him find his way. I don't think he wishes to find it."

Snowbird took a different view of the situation. "Joseph's crazy," she said flatly. She shook her head. "Crazy like all the Butlers are crazy. I'm the only one around here who isn't crazy, but then I am not a Butler. Of course, my father was crazy, but that was a different matter."

For a time Mary hit upon the idea of hiding Joseph's whiskey. Joseph simply sent Isaiah out for more. She took the slave aside and instructed him to ignore her husband's orders in this regard. He did and Joseph, in a tremendous rage, ordered him whipped. Everyone was horrified, even Snowbird. Joseph had always been an extremely mild man and, even in his cups, inclined more to despondency than to violence. Now, however, he was in a towering rage. Ned, who, as it turned out, had a bone to pick with Isaiah, fulfilled his duty with excessive zeal, taking most of the skin off Isaiah's back. Infection set in and the boy took sick and died. Joseph then asked Lehi to fetch him whiskey from town; Lehi did as he was told and Mary said nothing further.

Instead, she decided to leave.

Accordingly, in the spring of 1835, Mary announced that she intended to visit her old school friends Sarah and Hattie in New Echota, Georgia. She had not seen them for nine years nor had she left Qualla in all that time. She took the children with her along with Nettie. Nettie was to help Mary look after the children. There were five now, Baby Henrietta having been born the winter before.

Snowbird did not mind seeing Mary go – she would like the house to herself, as it had been in the old days – but she did not want her daughter-in-law to take the children.

"You listen to me, Joseph Butler," she advised her son. "If you let her take them, you'll never see them again!"

"Nonsense," Joseph said blearily. "She's only going to see Sarah and Hattie. She'll be gone six weeks." And he poured himself another glass of whiskey.

Snowbird was right. After a stay of some two weeks in New Echota at the pleasant clapboard colonial home of the Ridges, Mary traveled by coach to Augusta and then up the eastern seaboard. The children went with her. She had received word that her mother was ill, she wrote her husband (when was her mother not ill?) and had returned to New England to see her for perhaps the last time.

It was a perhaps that was to last forever. Mary Butler never returned to Qualla. Her asthma, she wrote, had become too aggravated, her mother was too ill; her father had aged so that she had scarcely recognized him . . . .

I cannot help you, Joseph, she wrote, *so I must help myself.*

EIGHT

"I always knew she would leave," said Snowbird. She and Joseph sat on the porch of the house at Ela, Wesa on Snowbird's lap and Waya at their feet. "She was not suited to this place. She was not like us, nor could she have ever become like us. That was because she was a Christian. Christians are not very adaptable. The Heron is adaptable . . . but I don't think she is a Christian. Not really."

Joseph stared out into the forest with unfocussed eyes, a look of dumb anguish on his face. What was his mother talking about? Oh, yes. His wife had left him and taken all of his many children with her. How many were there? Four, five, six? No, less than six.

The memory was like a knife slashing through cotton batting. It slashed and slashed and most of the time he felt nothing, but sometimes he did feel something – a sharp, searing point press into his soft brain somewhere between his eyes. There was a terrible roaring in his ears, a rushing as of water or blood, and his vision was so blurred – it was like when he had been a boy playing with Charley on the river bank. There were grapevines there that a boy could swing over the water on and then twist back and forth, back and forth, growing dizzier and dizzier . . . .

Snowbird sighed and patted her son on one stout knee. "There was a story that Toineeta told me once. She called it, The Bride from the South. It goes like this: "The North became restless and so went traveling to see new places and, after going far and wide and meeting many different tribes, he came to the land of the South and fell in love with that chief's daughter, so much so that he expressed a wish to marry her.

"Now the girl was willing, but her parents rejected the North's suit. 'Ever since you came to our land, the weather has been so cold, and, if you stay here, we may all freeze to death,' they said.

"But the North redoubled his efforts and promised that, if they would give their blessing to the marriage, he would take her back to his own country and so they at last consented. The two were married and the North carried his bride away to his own land and, when they arrived there, she found all the people living in ice houses.

"The next day when the sun came up, those ice houses began to melt and, as it climbed higher and higher, they melted more and more and it grew warmer and warmer until finally the people came to the young husband and told him that he must send his wife home again or the weather would grow so warm that the entire village would melt away. The North loved his wife and so held out against the entreaties of his people as long as he reasonably could. However, as the sun grew hotter, the people became more and more urgent, and at last he was forced to send her home to her parents.

"The people of the North spoke about this matter at great length and decided that, as the bride had been born in the South and nourished all her life upon food that grew in the South, her entire nature was warm and so unfit for life in the North."

"I don't miss Mary," muttered Joseph.

Snowbird only sighed and rocked some more. "I just wish she hadn't taken the children."

What had happened to her life? Once she had been young and small and bright, a little bird that her parents had called lovingly Snowbird. Once she had tended house for her father and brothers and ruled the roost. Then a handsome nearly white man had come along and married her. She had succeeded in driving her hated mother-in-law away. When George had turned mean and beat and abused her, she had outwitted and then outlived him, with the help of her brothers. She had even succeeded in bringing her own daughter-in-law to heel and keeping her there for nearly a decade before she had escaped. Snowbird could not understand how so many victories could add up to this heap of failure. Her fat, drunken, middle-aged son put his big face in his big hands and began noisily, in gulps, to weep. "Oh, hush!" she said unsympathetically. "Hush, Joseph! That's enough!"

༚ঌ৩

A New England poet named Silas H. McAlpine, moved by the marriages spawned in the fecund pool of the school for Foreign Missions in Cornwall, Connecticut, sat down one evening and put his vision of these happy interracial unions down in verse:

O, come with me, my white girl fair,
O, come where Mobile's sources flow;
With me my Indian blanket share,
And share with me my bark canoe:
We'll build our cabin in the wild,
Beneath the forest's lofty shade,
With logs on logs transversely piled,
And barks on bark obliquely laid.

O, come with me my white girl fair,
Come, seek with me the southern clime,
And dwell with me securely there,
For there my arm shall round thee twine;
The olive is thy favorite hue,
But sweet to me thy lily face;
O, sweet to both, when both shall view
These colors mingled in our race . . . .

Then come with me, my white girl fair,
And thou a hunter's bride shalt be;
For thee I'll chase the roebuck there,
And thou shalt dress the feast for me:
O, wild and sweet our feast shall be,

The feast of love and joy is ours;
Then come, my white girl fair, with me,
O, come and bless my sylvan bowers.

NINE

One day shortly after Mary had left for New Echota, I visited Toineeta up on Madcap Branch. I had made many calls on Toineeta over the years, enough that I think she grew rather tired of me. However, she was indisputably the oldest person in Qualla, an herbalist whose match I have yet to find, and a rich source of the Cherokee myths and legends I had begun to collect many years before. In this instance, I wanted to determine what three items I had recently added to my collection of artifacts, in fact, were. Although Toineeta's sight was limited by cataracts, her sense of touch was exquisite and I knew she would be able to identify objects simply by feeling them. I was not to be disappointed. After she had identified a feathered dance wand, a booger mask, and a fringed medicine bag and explained their function, I remembered the old buckskin pouch given to me by Joseph.

"What is the difference between this medicine bag and this pouch?" I asked, taking the buckskin pouch from my pocket, and handing it to Toineeta. (Remember that Joseph had asked only that his mother not know what he had done with the pouch, and since Snowbird refused to speak to Toineeta, I thought that there was no harm in discussing the pouch with the old woman.)

As her crabbed fingers closed, claw-like, around the pouch, a faint smile lit up her face, which she quickly suppressed. "It's old."

"Very old," I said. "It belonged to George Butler and his uncle before him. Snowbird said that it had been handed down over the generations—"

"From Dayunisi, did she say?" Toineeta interrupted me. "From the Beaver's Grandchild?"

"I think that was the name she mentioned."

"Ah! I see." Her expression clouded over and she shook her head. "Pardon me for saying so, Tskwayi, but I am offended that a Cherokee man should give away something that belonged to his father and that has been in his family for so long to a white woman. Not that you're so very white, but still. You see what I mean?" Then she shrugged. "Joseph Butler has chosen his path. He walks beside the white man. Let us see how long they permit him to do so and how he fares."

Later, when we were having tea made from burrs, she hit upon a plan.

"Seeing that the son has no respect, I will trade you something wonderful for that old amulet," she told me. "You can only benefit from the trade, for the amulet is ugly and smells bad, but what I will give you has great magic."

"What is it?" I was, in fact, keenly interested, for, the buckskin pouch was very pedestrian looking and did give off a sharp odor; I sometimes worried that people thought my personal hygiene was less than adequate.

Toineeta stood haltingly and, hobbling over to her bed, stood on tiptoe to remove an object which hung from a nail driven into the logs. Slowly, for her arthritis had encased her in a crust of pain through which she could not break and which she must be careful not to strain against, she returned to me and extended the object towards me with a gnarled hand that looked more like it belonged to an old tree than an old woman – as brown and twisted as the stunted branch of a yaupon.

I took the thing from her and, turning in my chair, held it to the light coming through the open door – a clumsy circle of sorts, like a rustic embroidery hoop. It looked very old.

"What is it?" I asked.

"It is a dream catcher."

"What does it do?"

"Ah, well, you see, it lets the good dreams slip through the center and down along the feather into the head of the dreamer . . . but the bad dreams it traps and holds in the web until dawn – the dawn kills those bad dreams so that the dreamer is never troubled by them. I have found it very useful over the years."

"Where did you get such a thing?" I turned the hoop slowly, peering through the center.

"A famous conjure man who lived long ago. A Shawano by birth. Back then the people ranged wide, west and south and north. Not like today when there is so little land to walk on that is ours. This was his dream catcher." She did not say the Shawano's name; it was, of course, the Groundhog's Mother.

"Are you certain you want to give this up?" I was trying to be fair. Truly it did seem an uneven exchange to me, a battered old pouch for this primitive, but clearly magical object.

Toineeta shrugged again. "Bad dreams are scared of old women. They never come to Madcap Branch anymore."

"All right," I said, desire for the dream catcher washing over me. Was this truly desire for the dream catcher or the ulunsuti wishing to be passed on to Toineeta? I think the latter. "If you're sure."

"I am very sure," Toineeta assured me.

Later, after I left the cabin at Madcap Branch, Toineeta loosened the rawhide sinews that held the amulet closed with fingers that shook from apprehension and excitement. Carefully she tipped the pouch, letting its content slide onto the wooden table. Then she settled herself before the crystal and stared hard at it. Though cataracts rendered her sightless, she could still perceive the flashing light of the ulunsuti. Finally she spoke aloud, but softly, in a hushed voice: "I thought so," she said to no one in particular. "Yes. That is what I have thought all these years. And now it is mine."

Halfway down the trail to Ela I felt woozy and had to sit down on a log. I was exhausted, spent. Suddenly the six-mile hike, never an issue given my long legs and boundless energy, seemed impossibly long. Would I make it? Did I have the strength? A wave of nausea swept over me and I bent over and spewed an evil mess onto a black clump of Deadman's

Fingers growing on the rotted wood. My joints ached and my ears rang and my head swam. What is happening to me? I thought in a panic. Then I fainted. Some time later, I regained consciousness and stumbled back to Ela.

Thus began my own swift decline.

TEN

When Joseph Butler died suddenly of apoplexy in 1836, Snowbird keened, wailed, tore at her hair, beat her breast and generally carried on, but, in the end, seemed to absorb the death of her son with a surprising degree of equanimity. There was one problem: the house was so isolated, so far from the village that she did not feel safe at Ela without a man, despite my prowess with the Bucksmasher.

"What are we to do, Tskwayi, if some danger presents itself? I, a woman with no middle, and you . . . ." Her voice trailed off; clearly she was trying to spare my feelings, while, at the same time, making it perfectly clear that she considered my abilities in this regard insufficient. And, in truth, since my visit to Toineeta, I had not been myself, or, to be more accurate, I had been more like the woman I was before Joseph had given me the ulunsuti.

"It's not as if Joseph furnished much in the way of protection," I pointed out.

"True," Snowbird reflected, idly stroking the cat coiled sleek and fat in her lap, "but he was very large and of a bear-like nature. And he spent most of his time on the porch, so anyone coming would see him and be frightened off."

"There's Waya." I pointed to the despondent puddle of bones and loose skin at my feet. Of all of us, the bloodhound seemed to have taken Joseph's death the hardest. Ever since his master's enormous carcass had been manhandled into an oversized coffin and taken by wagon to the cemetery at Yellow Hill, the dog had seemed listless and depressed.

Snowbird snorted. "Wesa offers more protection than he does! She, at least, will hiss and scratch, while he only lies and drools."

Later she hit upon a solution. "I will ask my brother's son Ammoneta to come and live with us. He is a man."

"But Ammoneta has a family and a house," I protested.

"*Pah!* He lives with his father-in-law. There is more room here. Besides, this is a better house. He will be happy to come."

She was right. Ammoneta, once summoned and advised of the plan, promptly accepted her offer. He was a farmer and had his eye on that piece of land down by the river that the Wild Boy had cultivated so successfully. It had not been worked for many years, but it seemed to him a fine spot for a cornfield.

Inviting Ammoneta's family to live with us was a good thing. The house had been lonely since Mary and the children had left and Joseph's extravagant, almost operatic decline had rendered it a deeply melancholy place, full of shadows. Moreover, both Snowbird and I were grateful to have the extra hands; not only were we both feeling our age by this time, but shortly after Joseph's death, Lehi and Ned had mysteriously disappeared, leaving no one to care for the animals and outbuildings, much less the house. (I've often wondered if Mary had been in communication with Lehi and Ned and had taken the opportunity of Joseph's death to effect their escape, but they may have just glimpsed an opportunity and disappeared into the mountains. As Mary had pointed out, people in these parts did tend to disappear.)

Ammoneta's family consisted of his wife Nundayeli, their son Suyeta, his widowed sister-in-law Walini and her daughter Adsila. Snowbird, in her characteristic way, lorded it over the two younger women – although she did not treat them as unkindly as she had treated Mary – and she doted on the two little children, spoiling them shamelessly with stories and games and candy from the trading post. The truth was that it did both our hearts good to hear Adsila and Suyeta's laughter ring throughout the house, to be surrounded by all the commotion and disorder that comes from having young children underfoot. Even Waya took heart and, after a very short time, became entirely smitten with Suyeta. He was the boy's constant and loyal companion, trotting along behind him everywhere he went, all skin and droopy eyelids and pendulous dewlaps and stiffly wagging tail.

I only vaguely remember this period of my life, the two years after Ammoneta moved his family into Snowbird's house. Undoubtedly this was because I was by then no longer in possession of the ulunsuti, which lends to everything a kind of terrible and urgent clarity . . . . Or maybe because the events that followed were so overwhelming that, in their wake, my memory of the friendly domesticity that we enjoyed, that lull, cannot help but pale.

Oh, I can describe Ammoneta to you well enough – he was a square, blocky fellow, as broad as he was tall, with big, competent hands and an elaborate nose that occupied a disproportionate amount of his face. I can describe Nundayeli too – a pliant beauty, slender and clear-eyed, but born with a twisted and misshapen foot, which joined her leg at a strange angle and curled piteously inwards – what we would have called a club foot. Walini I remember less clearly. That was because she was stricken and bestride worlds when I knew her. The epidemic of smallpox that had but recently carried off her husband had also killed her two older children and she was terrified of losing Adsila, a not unreasonable fear: the child was small for her age and fragile, prone to respiratory disorders. When I think of Walini, I cannot bring her face or shape to mind; only a kind of palpable anxiety.

I can describe them, but I cannot call them to me the way I can the rest – not whole, not who they actually were. And this puzzles and saddens me – that I have lost them in this way. That, though they may have lived on, they became as ghosts to me.

Snowbird told me a story once. It was this:

"A long time ago a man had a dog who began to go down to the river every day and howl. At last the man was angry and scolded the dog, who spoke to him and said, 'Very soon there is going to be a great freshet and the water will come so high that everybody will be drowned; but if you make a raft to get upon when the rain comes you may be saved, but you must first throw me into the water.'

"The man did not believe that this would happen and the dog said, 'If you want a sign that I speak the truth, look at the back of my neck.'

He looked and saw that the dog's neck had the skin worn off so that the bones stuck out. Then he believed the dog and began to build a raft. Soon the rain came and he took his family, with plenty of provisions and they all got upon it. It rained for a long time and the water rose until the mountains were covered and all the people in the world were drowned.

"Then the rain stopped and the waters went down again, until at last it was safe to come off the raft. Now there was no one alive except the man and his family, but one day they heard a sound of dancing and shouting on the other side of the ridge. The man climbed to the top and looked over; everything was still, but all along the valley he saw great piles of bones of the people who had been drowned, and then he knew that the ghosts had been dancing."

"There is a story like that in the Bible," I remarked at the time. "About a great flood. Only there was no dog or dancing ghosts."

Snowbird was not impressed. "*Heu!* What kind of a story is that?"

Waya, why didn't you warn us?

TOINEETA

ONE

It was just before mid-day on August 16, 1838, when Nundayeli arrived at Toineeta's door yard up on Madcap Branch. She had come to fetch a tonic for Adsila, who had fallen ill with a bad case of croup the previous evening. "Big Granny?" she called out. "Big Granny, are you home?"

No response.

Nundayeli slid off Spotted Horse – it was the red spots on his white coat and his red mane that gave the pony his name. Ammoneta had paid a great deal of money for him, but what could he do? His beautiful wife found walking painful and scarcely practical since, lurching and dragging the way she did, it took so long for her to get from one place to the other. "Big Granny!" she called again before spotting the old, bent-double woman – Toineeta was sitting on a log way a long way off over by the bean field smoking a corncob pipe. Nundayeli waved broadly – Toineeta's cataracts were not so bad that she could not discern movement.

This time the old woman turned in Nundayeli's direction and, taking her pipe from her mouth, called out, "Who comes here? Answer me now! I'm an old woman, but I'm friends with the Devil!"

"It is only Nundayeli from down in Ela. I've come to fetch medicine for Walini's daughter. She's taken bad with the croup!"

Toineeta stood and hobbled towards her with a kind of rolling gait. Every year she seemed to get smaller and smaller; now she was no taller than a ten-year-old child. "The croup, you say?" Toineeta asked. "Not soldiers?"

Nundayeli was confused. "What? No. It's Adsila I'm talking about. Walini's daughter. My niece. She has the croup."

"I thought they might have come already," Toineeta said. Then, "Never mind. Adsila, you say?" She shook her head. The old woman had scarcely enough white hair to yank into a bun underneath the blue kerchief she wore tied around her head and only a random scattering of teeth. "Gone for sure, poor little thing. If she's the one I'm thinking on, there weren't but a speck of life in her to start out with. Still I'll get you something you can fetch back. That's what you come for."

Nundayeli followed the old woman into the little, one-room cabin, which had been built in the old, correct way – that is to say, the logs had been stripped of their bark, not like the white man builds his cabins – and the walls were plastered thick with red clay. There were no windows, the floor was dirt and the smoke hole was at the center of the roof just above the round open hearth. Toineeta went to her ramshackle pine shelves and fumbled about the bottles and jars, removing corks or lids and sniffing at the contents until she found the right one. "Ah! This here's the best remedy for croup there is. Equal parts blood root, lobelia, garlic, skunk's cabbage, elecampane, sage and thorough wort. Don't give her too much, girl. She'll only fetch it up again. Don't sit well on the stomach, this decoction. You bought something to carry it in? I'm not a bottle maker."

Nundayeli produced a treated pig's bladder. Toineeta poured a small measure of the thick, greenish-brown liquid into it. "I'm not giving you too much. Lobelia's as rare as hen's teeth these days and the child won't live long enough to take a full draught."

"Yes, Big Granny," murmured Nundayeli. She was a little frightened of the old woman – everyone was, even the village elders who seemed, compared to her, a gaggle of reckless youths, despite their long white hair and stooped shoulders and wrinkled faces.

Toineeta frowned. "Perhaps Adsila's upcoming death is what has been disturbing me. All day long, this sense of foreboding, as if the ropes that hold the world up are fraying . . . ."

Before Nundayeli could ask what she meant, the old woman suddenly lifted her chin and turned her face in the direction of the open door. "What?" she demanded. "What is that sound?"

"What, Big Granny? I don't hear anything."

"I do." Toineeta sniffed the air. "Yes," she said. "And I can smell them too. They're coming this way. It's as I thought."

"What are you talking about?"

"Come!" Toineeta took Nundayeli by the wrist. "We will sit on the porch and wait for them."

"Wait for who?"

"For those who are coming."

"But I can't wait . . . ."

"You cannot go. Not now. Besides, there is no point. Adsila has already taken her first steps towards the Darkening Land. Mark my words. You cannot save her now. You cannot save anyone. You cannot even save yourself."

"Big Granny!"

"Sit!"

"But what . . . . ?"

"You'll know soon enough."

Ulunsutis confer upon their owners success in many things, but particularly in prophecy. When an ulunsuti is consulted for the purpose of divining the future, it mirrors what is to pass the same way a quiet stream reflects the image of a tree standing on its bank. It reflects recovery from illness, return from battle, old age achieved. It reflects upheaval and death and exile – images that lie folded in the arms of the future. This was how Toineeta knew what was going to happen on August 16, 1838, when nobody else did. I did not know this at the time, or at least I didn't think I did; at some level, however, I must have. Once you have dreamed the uktena's dream, you are fundamentally altered. No matter what happens, you keep dreaming that dream. No one who has carried the baleful boon of an ulunsuti forward in time is ever quite the same, no, not even when one has passed it on. A mere drop of the poison blood of the uktena of the Cohutta range had caused a snake the length of a man's little finger to grow from the Groundhog's Mother's forehead; he had to endure its hissing all his life, for to kill it he must kill himself. There was no snake growing from my forehead. Instead it lay within, coiled around my heart. That is the way it works with these things.

☙☙

Nundayeli and Toineeta were sitting on the porch when two white soldiers straggled into the dooryard. One was fat and one was thin. The thin one was tall. He squinted at a list. "Which of you is called Toineeta?"

Nundayeli looked at the conjure woman. Toineeta's face was impassive. She understood English only when she chose. Nundayeli could see that on this occasion she must act as the old woman's interpreter. "She is."

"Who are you?"

"Nundayeli Tuskateeski."

"Where do you live?"

"Down in Ela."

The soldier tipped his cap back on his head and wiped his forehead. "Bad day to go visiting."

"Why?" Nundayeli felt suddenly very nervous.

Eight years earlier, Andrew Jackson had signed the Indian Removal Act into law. Five years after that, a handful of Cherokee in Red Clay, Tennessee, signed the Treaty of New Echota, ceding the Cherokee Nation's holdings to the U.S. government in exchange for lands out west in the Oklahoma territory. But Red Clay was an Overhill town; no one from the Middle Towns had signed the treaty, so how could it be binding on people of the Middle Towns? This is what we all had reasoned. Then Chicken Snake had issued an ultimatum: the Cherokee had until May 23, 1838, to move to Oklahoma. If they did not go voluntarily, they would be forcibly removed. And now it was mid-August, three months past the deadline.

"We're rounding up all the Cherokee in this region," explained the fat soldier. "Got to get you folks to Fort Lindsay by nightfall. Murphy and me's a detachment. Sent up here to get backwoodsers out."

Nundayeli panicked. "What do you mean? Today? But we've had no warning!"

"From what I hear, Government's been warning you Indians for the last ten years. You people have had your chance. As for today . . . . Didn't want the half of you taking off and hiding in the mountains. Hard enough to round you as it is, but this way we at least got surprise on our side. Now you tell Grandma there that she'd better pack up her things. We got a couple of other of you backwoodsers we got to bring in and you're the first on the list."

"But what about my family?" Nundayeli wrung her hands. "I must go to them."

"They're probably long gone by now. You come with us. You can meet up with them at Fort Lindsay."

Nundayeli turned to Toineeta. "Big Granny. . ." she began in Cherokee.

"I heard what they said," Toineeta replied, also in Cherokee. "I am not going."

"She says she is not going," Nundayeli told the white soldier.

"That's what she thinks. Tell her to pack. If she doesn't want to pack, then she can go with nothing. That's the only choice she has. And tell her to be quick about it. One half hour."

"She's lived here all her life," Nundayeli protested. "How can she figure out what to pack in one half-hour?"

"Better be something she can carry," observed the tall soldier called Murphy. Spotted Horse had caught his attention. "Hey, Kimball. Look at this pony! Ain't he a nice one though?"

"Big Granny, what shall I say to them?" Nundayeli asked Toineeta in Cherokee.

"Tell them this," said Toineeta. "In my language there is a word for the land – *eloheh*. It means many things – land, the story of my people on the land, the way of my people on the land, the gods that inhabit places . . . . *Eloheh! Eloheh!* I cannot tear out my heart and live. In the same way, I cannot leave my land and live."

"But, Granny, they will not listen."

Toineeta shrugged. "Then let them shoot me. I have lived longer than most people."

"She refuses to go," Nundayeli told the soldiers.

Murphy turned to his companion. "Hell, Kimball. That old woman couldn't walk from here to the stockade, let alone to Oklahoma. Leave her here. She'll die soon enough."

Kimball scowled. Then he made a gesture of dismissal. "We could say she's too sick to walk. They said we could make exceptions if they was too sick. You're right. Let's leave her here."

"As for me, I think I'm going to requisition this pony," said Murphy, stroking Spotted Horse's mane admiringly. "I could use me a good pony."

"You can't do that," Nundayeli protested. "That's my pony."

"Not anymore it ain't," Murphy replied. Spotted Horse's reins were looped over the porch rail. He untied them. "I expect you can walk to Oklahoma, Missy."

"No, you don't understand," said Nundayeli. Holding onto one of the porch's posts she swung off the porch and limped a few steps towards the soldiers.

"Well, look at that!" Kimball laughed. "The squaw's a cripple! A cripple can't walk all the way to Oklahoma." He pointed at her twisted foot. "Look, she's got her a club foot."

"I need the pony," Nundayeli said, reaching for the reins which Murphy held in his hands. He twisted to one side, holding the reins beyond her reach, laughing.

"Please!" she pleaded. "I can't walk far with my foot."

"You'd best stay here then, seeing how you're a cripple." Kimball stepped between her and the other soldier. "Take care of Old Granny here. Murphy! Let's head out."

Murphy swung up onto Spotted Horse.

"But what about my family . . . my husband and my son? I must get to Fort Lindsay!"

"Look at it this way, Little Lady," said Kimball. "We're doing you a favor. There's no way you'd get to ride all the way to Oklahoma, so you might as well separate from your family now as later. Get it over with."

"No, please!" Nundayeli pleaded. "Let me ride just to Fort Lindsay. Then I promise you can have the pony. I have to see my son and my husband."

"Well, Missy, it's this way," said Kimball. "Our sergeant, he's a stickler. Do you know that he probably wouldn't let Murphy keep that little pony if he knew it was yours? And I expect Murphy don't want to risk that."

"You're out of luck, Missy," agreed Murphy. "I've taken a shine to this little feller and I plan to keep him." He goaded Spotted Horse in the ribs and started the pony down the path that led to Fox Knob at a brisk trot.

Nundayeli picked up her skirts and started after him, but Kimball moved to bar her way. "No point trying to follow him. You couldn't keep up if you tried. Why not give up now before you've gone and worn yourself out?"

"You don't understand. It's my family! I must be with my family!" Nundayeli clung to him, weeping.

He pushed her away. He looked embarrassed. "It's hard. I warrant that. Still, you people had your chance . . . ." Turning, he started up the path after Spotted Horse and the man named Murphy.

Nundayeli stood for a moment, looking after him. She started to follow him, but he was right. She would not be able to catch up or even keep up. She sank down onto her hands and knees in the door yard and wept. "Big Granny. What am I to do?"

Toineeta continued to sit stone-faced on the porch, rocking slowly back and forth, back and forth. "It has finally happened," she said at last.

"What?" sobbed Nundayeli.

"The ropes have broken," Toineeta explained and then, reading in Nundayeli's silence that the woman did not understand, she said, "The earth is a great island afloat in a vast sea of water. It is suspended at each of the four cardinal points by a rope, which hangs down from the sky vault. This vault is made of solid rock. When the world grows old and wears out, well, that's it! The ropes snap, and the earth sinks down into the ocean. Then it will be as it was before: all water. For a long time the Cherokee have been very afraid of this happening. Now, I think, it has."

TWO

Not an hour after Nundayeli had left Ela for Madcap Branch, Adsila's larynx became so swollen that it blocked her air passage and the little girl noisily suffocated in her distraught mother's arms. When I pronounced her dead and drew blue eyelids over eyes that no longer had any light in them, Walini covered her mouth with her hands and shrieked and rushed crazily about, then out the door and down towards the river. Snowbird and I were convinced that she was going to hang herself down at Turtle Place and debated as to what we should do – Ammoneta had taken Suyeta out to the cornfield so that he would not have to watch his playmate die and neither of us could have hoped to catch up with Walini, what with Snowbird's lack of a middle and my bad hips – while bereft, Walini was many years our junior. Fortunately, the issue resolved itself shortly, for about a half an hour later Walini returned to help me and Snowbird wash and dress the little girl's body. "How sad she looks!" she kept saying, before breaking down in wrenching sobs.

With all this sorrow to occupy us, we did not know that the white soldier was there until a floorboard of the porch loudly creaked and, Snowbird, looking up to see if Ammoneta and Suyeta were returning, saw through the window a gleam off metal as the blade of a bayonet caught the sunlight. *"Heu!"* she hissed. "Tskwayi! Who is this?"

There was a sharp rap of metal on wood, followed by a gruff, "Open up! Do you hear me? Open up in there."

Walini, Snowbird and I exchanged glances.

"You!" Snowbird hissed. "Tskwayi! You are white. You talk."

"Who is it?" I called out.

"U.S. Army. Open the door."

Dread struck me to the heart, followed by an icy clarity – was it actually happening, the unthinkable, what we had always feared? Of course we were aware of the May 23 deadline set by Andrew Jackson, but the chiefs of the Middle Towns were still in Washington, working to set matters straight, to clear up the misunderstanding over a treaty they had, none of them, signed. Didn't we have strong allies in the Senate and Congress and the vehement and outspoken support of many Christian missionaries? Of course, there had been talk about a stockade being constructed down in Nantahala, but no one had worried overmuch about this. There was corn to be planted, fields to be tended, crops of beans and squash to put in. A mistake had been made and would soon be rectified. That's what we had thought, but now there was a soldier at the door.

I rose and, leaning on Charley's silver-headed cane, lurched over to the door – my hips were particularly troublesome that day, like rusty hinges on an old gate. I opened the door. "Yes?"

"Ma'am?" A tall, spare man, his grizzled cheeks and bulbous nose reddened and bumpy with rosacea, stood before me, clad in the dark blue frockcoat and slouch hat that, together with insignias and a red sash, comprised the uniform of a junior officer in the United States Army. Upon seeing me, he swiftly removed his hat. I got the distinct impression that I had startled him. (I was not what he had expected, but, then, I seldom was.)

"Sir?" With a downward glance, I took quick stock of his various weapons – a Springfield musket equipped with a nasty-looking bayonet, a dragoon saber and a holstered revolver.

The soldier stared at me for a moment, blinked, then cleared his throat. "And who might you be, ma'am?"

"I am Miss Sawyer, sir. And who might you be?"

"Lieutenant Perry of the United States Army, at your service." He made a nominal bow.

I did the same. "Lieutenant."

Perry replaced his hat on his head. "Excuse me, Miss Sawyer, but is this the domicile of . . . ." Retrieving a list from his breast pocket, he consulted it. "Ammoneta Tuskateeski?"

Snowbird bustled up behind me, combative as a badger. "It's the house of Snowbird Butler! That's whose house it is!"

Perry cast a quick, annoyed glance at her, but continued to address his questions to me. "But Ammoneta Tuskateeski lives here?"

"And what business is that of yours?" Snowbird demanded.

"Snowbird!" I warned in an undertone. Then, to Perry, "Yes, he does. He and his family. As does Mrs. Butler here." I paused, glancing over my shoulder to the cot on which Adsila's little body was laid out. "Lieutenant, excuse me," I said, "but there has been a death in the family—"

"A death?" Perry interrupted me. Once again he scrutinized his list. "Would that be . . . Walini Tuskateeski?"

"No," I replied. "Adsila, Walini's daughter. But . . . ."

Perry amended the list with a pencil and replaced it in his pocket. "Well, that's unfortunate, Miss Sawyer, it truly is, but orders are orders. These people are going to have to pack up their things and come with me." He doffed his hat. "Not you, Miss Sawyer. Of course."

"What?" I asked.

"I have orders from General Scott to move these folks out to Fort Lindsay preparatory to removing them to Indian Territory out in Oklahoma. I'd advise you to say your goodbyes, ma'am, and get yourself home."

"What is he talking about?" Snowbird tugged at my arm. "He talks like a bear, all muffled. I can't understand him."

"He's saying that we have to go with him," I told her in Cherokee. "To Fort Lindsay."

"You speak Cherokee?" Perry was impressed. "We could use somebody like you! All these Indians around here . . . people say that they're civilized, but half of them don't even speak English! What are you, anyway – a missionary?"

I was curt. "A schoolteacher. And speaking English does not make you civilized, Lieutenant Perry."

Snowbird was tugging at my sleeve. "That fort in Nantahala? *Heu!* I'm not going there. Spearfinger lives in the Nantahala Gorge! You've heard of Spearfinger, Heron. She will spear your liver on her long, claw-like finger and eat it."

"Tell her to speak English," Perry told me.

By now Walini, too, had come forward and was tugging on my sleeve, her voice shrill with anguish. "Tskwayi! Before we do anything, we must bury Adsila!"

I turned back to Perry. "We have to bury the child."

He shook his head. "Sorry, ma'am. No time for that."

"Lieutenant, are you not a Christian? This is a dead child! Her mother wants to bury her!"

Once again Perry removed his hat. He rubbed his bumpy forehead with the heel of his hand and sucked air sharply through his teeth. I was clearly testing the limits of his patience. That was all right. He was testing mine. "Will you please come out here, ma'am?"

"Where?"

"Outside. On the porch."

"What for?"

"If I may have a word, Miss Sawyer!" Taking my elbow rather more forcefully than necessary, he steered me out onto the porch and away from the door. This attempt to separate me from Walini and Snowbird, however, proved unsuccessful; the two women tumbled after me, hard on my heels and clung the one to my elbow and the other to my dress. Perry lowered his voice and leaned into me, his breath sour. "You've got to understand my situation here, Miss Sawyer. There are over three thousand Cherokee in these mountains and we've got to get them all rounded up in less than a month. It's a next to impossible task as it is, and I can't brook delays at this point."

"But it's all a mistake. . ." I began.

He cut me off. "Look, if these Indians had done what they were supposed to do and left back in May, none of this would be happening. But they didn't listen and now it's up to us to round them up and march them all the way to Oklahoma before winter sets in, if that's even possible at this stage. Do you know how many people will die on the trail if we don't make that deadline?"

"No one in the Middle Towns signed that treaty. The chiefs are in Washington right now, appealing the order."

"I'm sorry, ma'am, but I take my orders from General Scott, not some Indian chief. Anyway, what business is it of yours? You're a white woman."

Ammoneta appeared from around the spring house now, trailed by Suyeta. At the sight of her brother-in-law, Walini gave out a sharp cry and, rushing down the steps, hurled herself at him. "Ammoneta, Adsila has gone to the Darkening Land and this soldier says we can't bury her! He says we must leave this place and go to Nanatahla where Spearfinger lives, that we must hurry and there is no time to bury Adsila." All this in Cherokee. "We have to bury my poor child!" she sobbed. "Don't you see? I cannot leave her for the animals to eat."

Ammoneta was confused. "What's going on? Who is this soldier?"

"He comes from Chicken Snake. He says we must go to Oklahoma," Snowbird cried. "How can we go to Oklahoma? Our dead are buried here! We cannot leave our dead!"

"But I thought the chiefs . . . ."

"He says never mind the chiefs."

"What about Nundayeli? Where is my wife?"

"She has not yet returned from Toineeta's."

"We go nowhere without her!"

Everyone was talking at once. Perry turned to me. "What are they saying?"

"His wife is away," I told Perry. "He says we cannot go without her."

"There are soldiers fanned out all over these parts," said Perry. "Tell him that they will find his wife and bring her to the fort."

"I won't leave without her," insisted Ammoneta, speaking this time in English.

"You'll do what you're told," Perry said sharply. "Your family will be reunited at the stockade. Now, you people have a choice. You can go west with nothing or you can pack a few things now." He pulled a gold watch from his pocket. "You have half an hour to pack. That's all. After that, we're on the road."

"How do you expect us to pack our belongings in so little time?" Ammoneta demanded. "Why didn't you warn us?"

"Warn you!" Perry exploded. "The Indian Removal Act was signed in 1830. You were told that you had until May 23, 1838, to go voluntarily. Did you think that Old Hickory didn't mean it when he said he wanted all the Indians out of this country? You've had eight years and eight months to pack. Now, get started."

At that moment Waya loped around the corner of the spring house from the direction of the cornfield.

"Waya!" Suyeta clapped his hands. "Come here, boy! Come here!"

The dog started towards him. Then a shot rang out and another, hitting Waya squarely in his broad chest. The dog seemed to freeze in mid-air for a second. A moment later the puppy who had greeted Joseph and Mary upon their arrival in Ela, who had accompanied me on my forays into the wood to gather blackberry canes and honeysuckle vines, who had been Joseph's constant companion and who had become in his old age a child's best playmate, lay twisted in the door yard in a spreading pool of blood. I looked down to see Perry's drawn revolver smoking by his side.

"No dogs in the stockade," he explained, replacing the gun in its holster.

I stared at him. We all did. Then Snowbird and Walini started to wail and Suyeta began to sob convulsively. Ammoneta knelt in the clay and pulled the boy to him, but I. . . I just kept staring at Perry. That was when it struck me that the lieutenant had a cruel mouth and little eyes. That was when it struck me that all of the men of my race had cruel mouths and little eyes. The snake coiled around my heart stirred. I knew what I had to do. "I'd better start packing," I said flatly.

"Not you, Miss Sawyer. . ." Perry began.

"You don't understand," I cut him off. "I live here. I have things to pack."

I went into the house, but, instead of going directly to my bedroom, I crossed over to the gun rack and retrieved from it my beloved Buck-smasher and my powder horn. Then I went upstairs. There was a song ranging through my head all this time, fragments of melody intertwined with scraps of lyric . . . .

> *Away and away, we're bound for the mountain.*
> *Bound for the mountain, bound for the mountain.*
> *Over the mountain, the hills and the fountains,*
> *Away to the chase, away, away.*

I propped the Kentucky rifle against the wall of my room, upright, muzzle up. Then I poured powder into its muzzle and tapped its butt against the floor to settle the powder. Next I placed a scrap of oilcloth onto the end of the barrel and checked to ensure that the ball's sprue mark was centered and facing upwards. I picked up my bullet starter and pushed the bullet into the bore, then I rammed the ball down the bore until it contacted the powder charge.

> *We heed not the tempest, the toil nor the danger,*
> *As over the mountain, away goes Ranger,*
> *All night long, till the break of dawn,*
> *Merrily the chase goes on.*

Turning the rifle over, I tapped its muzzle smartly a few times against the floor to ensure that the bullet fit tight in the bore. Then I opened the frizzen, poured a small amount of priming powder into the pan and placed the gun at half-cock. My bedroom was over the porch. From my window I could see the lieutenant. He was standing over Waya's body. With the toe of his knee-flap boots he prodded the old bloodhound. I opened the window carefully, not wanting to make any sound that might alert him to my purpose.

Now we're set just right for the race,
The old hound dogs are ready for the chase,
The deer is a-bounding and the hounds are a-sounding,
Right on the trail that leads o'er the mountain.

The song I did not know, but knew, the song that had always been there, caught in the places between – the Bucksmasher's song. I shouldered the rifle and cocked the hammer. Silently I thanked Lieutenant Perry for the gift his death would bestow upon my people – the gift of *eloheh*, of the land. *For you see, Charley, I am not them. I was once, but now I am transformed. Now I am you.* I took careful aim. I squeezed the trigger. A second later the bullet struck its intended target: the jugular notch of Perry's sternum, exploding the bone and severing the artery. A torrent of blood arced from his neck. His hands flew to his throat as if to contain the outpour. He twisted to the left and fell to his knees, still clutching his throat, before pitching forward so that, in the end, he lay sprawled across Waya's body, his blood pooling with that of the bloodhound.

THREE

They all four stared up at me, mouths agape, eyes round. "What?" I said, through the lingering cloud of smoke exhaled by the Bucksmasher. "It had to be done. Now you must go. Quickly. Before any others come."

"But Tskwayi. . ." Snowbird began.

"I mean it," I insisted. "You must run. All of you. Run and hide."

But no one moved. It was as though they were paralyzed, as though they had woken up to find themselves suspended in a spider's web, hapless prey, incapable of action. They just stood there looking – at me, at the heap of slain dog and man, at each other – blinking and wordless.

I stomped my foot in frustration, remembering the chickens in Charley's story of the Terrible Storm, the ones that drowned because they hadn't the sense to close their beaks when they looked upwards. Didn't they see how urgent this was? How little time they had? There were soldiers all over our valley, going from farm to farm, rounding people up. That's what Perry had said. They must be taking them to some central holding place before marching them to Nantahala; it made sense that that would be in Qualla, which meant I had to get them out of here before Perry's failure to report was noticed. "Hold on!" I called. "I'm coming down!"

Negotiating stairs had been a trial for me ever since my hips had started to fail me; negotiating stairs while carrying the Bucksmasher and a powder horn was fraught with peril. By the time I made it out to the porch, I was done for. I collapsed onto Joseph's immense twig rocker, out of breath, my heart racing, and gestured for them to come to me. Then it was as if the spell that had immobilized them broke. Quickly they gathered round.

"This is your chance," I said. Charley's words came back to me: "For months I have heard voices . . . invisible spirits in the air calling and warning me of wars and misfortunes . . . I do not want to leave this land for another that I cannot love and so I will go where they will not think to look for me." How right he had been! How had he known? "You must go up into the mountains," I told them. "*You must go where they will not think to look for you.*" I glanced at the lieutenant's sprawled body and experienced a sudden, eviscerating horror. I had shot a man. A fellow human being. My stomach heaved. I felt dizzy, a creeping gray. I closed my eyes and doubled over at the waist, so that my head hung between my legs. It had to be done, I told myself. I had had no choice. Not if I was to be true.

"Tskwayi is right," Ammoneta said. "We must run. And quickly."

"Run?" Snowbird erupted. "How can I run? A woman with no middle cannot run!"

"Auntie will ride Ruby," Ammoneta decided. Ruby was an old roan mare, sway-backed, but reliable. "Suyeta, get Ruby from the stable."

"What about the other horses?" Suyeta asked. There were two more beside.

Ammoneta shook his head. "We must leave them. We will walk instead. It is hard to hide with a horse. They are too big; they make noises and leave tracks. We can't take the chance."

"But what about Tskwayi?" Snowbird cried. "With her bad hips, she can't walk either."

"I am not going," I said, not realizing until the moment I uttered the words that this had been my plan all along. Snowbird stared at me. "I will just slow you down," I explained.

Suyeta appeared, leading the swaybacked roan.

"What are you talking about, Tskwayi?" Snowbird demanded. "You must come. If it hadn't been for you, George Butler would have killed me a hundred different times, but you . . . you protected me. I cannot leave my old Heron behind." Wesa, driven into hiding by the recent commotion, emerged from a clump of mountain laurel at one end of the porch, stalked over to Snowbird and rubbed herself against her mistress' legs, mewing insistently, her tail held high. Snowbird scooped her up and held her tight to her breast.

"It's not forever," I assured her. "Once the soldiers are gone, I will find my way back to you. You'll see. This way I can find out what's going on. The white soldiers will not suspect me. They don't know my heart."

"But my baby girl . . . . What of her?" Walini pleaded.

"I will take care of her," I promised.

Walini clung to me. "You will bury her?"

"I will make sure no animal can get to her."

Ammoneta seized Snowbird in the general vicinity of what would have been her middle and swung her, cat and all, up on Ruby's back.

"But what about our things, Nephew! Surely we have time enough to—"

"No, Auntie." Urgency thickened his voice; he understood. "They will be here soon. We must leave right away."

"He's right," I said. "It will be worse for Ammoneta if they find you. They will blame him for the soldier's death. He will be an outlaw. They will not think to suspect me." *Things are not as they seem.* I thrust the Bucksmasher towards Ammoneta. "Take this."

Ammoneta took a step backwards and held up his hands. "Bucksmasher belongs to you."

I shook my head. "No, it doesn't," I said. "Nothing belongs to anyone. Things bide with us a while, then move on. You will need a good rifle."

He understood then and took the rifle and the powder horn from me.

"Suyeta," I called out. "Get the soldier's revolver."

Suyeta tiptoed into the darkening pool of blood, squatted down and pulled the revolver that had killed Waya from its holster. He brandished it in the air.

"We will go to Madcap Branch and find Nundayeli," Ammoneta told me. "We will go by the back ways, up Newton Bald, down Deep

Creek and, if we see anyone, we will hide until we know whether they are our friends or not."

I nodded. "I will seek you out," I promised. "When it's safe."

And then they were gone, not by the dusty road that connected Ela to Qualla, but away from the river, up past Birdtown and towards Newton Bald. I watched them so far as I could make them out. After that, it was as though the mountains had swallowed them whole.

I returned to the house and wrapped Adsila's body in one of Nancy Butler's quilts – Young Lady's Perplexity it was called and it was a pretty thing, made for a single bed, with scalloped edges, petal pink and mint green against a field of white. I was amazed when I hefted her at just how light she seemed, light as a feather, as though death had deprived her of substance, leaving only form behind. Unlucky Adsila, I thought, but, on the other hand, perhaps not so unfortunate as all that. After all, who knew what kind of hardships she might have had to endure had she lived?

I tucked a tinderbox into the pocket of my apron and carried her to the corncrib out back of the spring house. The floor of the crib was elevated so that mice could not plunder it. Stepping up into it and ducking my head (the crib was not over five feet tall and the door but four), I laid my bundle down in a heap of dry husks. Because the harvest was not yet in, the crib was empty save for these remnants of last year's crop. A fire started here would burn hot and fast – the husks were dry and the crib's walls slatted to allow air to circulate through the corn – fire feeds on oxygen and here would be aplenty. I would have buried her, but I doubted whether I had the strength to dig a hole deep enough to keep animals out and I had promised her mother that Adsila would not be food for vultures and wolves. I would not go back on my word.

Taking the tinderbox from my pocket, I laid a jute charcloth at her feet and struck the flint against the firesteel so that sparks fell upon the cloth. I used the fire started in this way to ignite, one by one, three wood splints dipped in sulfur. These I placed to the north, east and west of her. In moments a ring of fire crackled around the little girl, wreathing her with flame. Holding my sleeve over my mouth so as not to breathe in too much smoke, I retreated from the crib several yards, watching as the flames took hold. Then I sat down on a bench outside the spring house to wait; I told myself that I had to be certain that the conflagration would consume all of Adsila before I could proceed; that I owed her mother that vigilance. As I watched, the fire filled my head with a sound like a thousand whispers and I found myself imaging the scene which must have been unfolding up and down these valleys. It was as though I could hear them in the fire – the people and the soldiers.

"Wait! The cows! We can't leave the cows!"

"It's bad enough driving people, let alone livestock."

"But what will we do for milk?"

"I've got three hams and a side of bacon in the smokehouse."

"Take what you can eat right away. Leave the rest. A ham's as heavy as a baby once you've carried it ten miles."

"All my dried apples! That was a lot of work."

"The corn in the field! It'll be ready for picking in a month. What will we eat in Oklahoma without a harvest?"

"The peaches just ripe too . . . . I was fixing to pick some just this afternoon."

"Stop talking and start packing!"

"Blankets, pots and pans. That's the pot for bean bread. We have to take that."

"A pouch of tobacco . . . ."

"That piece of calico I never did do anything with . . . ."

"That round of butter in the spring house . . . ."

There must be others, too, like Snowbird and Ammoneta and Walini and Suyeta, who were able to elude capture and were even now making their way deep into the mountains to wait out this catastrophe. There would be many who would have preferred to die than leave their land. Apparently this included me.

When I saw that the fire had done my bidding, I returned to the house, but only to retrieve the dream catcher that Toineeta had given me in exchange for George Butler's amulet. Then I took Charley's old silver-headed cane and made my halting way down to the river beyond the cornfield, where I would fill my pockets with stones and walk into the slippery green water, there at Turtle Place where the Oconaluftee runs deep, where a monster turtle is said to live, where Salili, Dayunisi's wife and the mother of Tsikiki, hung herself, and where children swim on hot summer days.

FOUR

Take you my ulunsuti, for he who possesses such a stone is assured of success in hunting, love, rainmaking and anything else he might wish to undertake . . . .

It was by means of the ulunsuti that Toineeta saw the future of her people and through its power that she was able to help the many Cherokee who, over the course of the next month, came to her cabin by stealth, under cover of darkness, to seek her assistance. And come they did, a thousand strong, Snowbird and Ammoneta and Walini and Suyeta among them, for a rumor had spread through the mountains like fire on the wind that the Granny Woman at Madcap Branch could help those, who had thus far evaded capture, find refuge where the white soldiers could not track them down.

This is what she did.

She entered into negotiations with the Nuhnehi who make their homes under the balds found at the summit of mountains or along their narrow ridges, making her way on foot to Newton Bald and Hemphill Bald and Maddron Bald and Andrews Bald and Pilot Knob, to the Nuhnehi townhouses that lie beneath the old Nikwasi Mound and to Blood Mountain and Cold Mountain and Nugatsani.

She went to Hiwasee, as well, and spoke to the Water Dwellers there, and to the Suck, a terrible whirlpool in the Oconaluftee, below which lies a pleasant land.

She also contracted with the Yunwi Tsunsdi, a race of Little People no taller than a man's knee, but well-shaped and handsome, who live in caves or crevices high up the rocky cliffs or in grottoes under the waterfalls, to take in lost children.

No people were more accommodating than the Tsundige'wi, another race of Little People who live in nests scooped in the sand and covered with dried grass. Long ago flocks of wild geese and other birds had terrorized these queerly shaped people, swooping down on them and sticking their long bills into their nests, seizing and carrying them off, but the Cherokee had taught them to use sticks for clubs and where to hit the birds so as to slay them (on the neck) and the Tsundige'wi remembered this and were grateful. They took in many children and cared for them as though they were their own.

Toineeta also spoke to White Bear, the chief of the Bears, on Kuwahi, where the Bears congregate and hold dances every fall before retiring to their dens for the winter. She visited Rabbit Place, under Gregory Bald, and smoked a pipe with their chief, Great Rabbit, who is as big as a deer. She tracked the Panthers to their Under Mountain home and sat with their chief around the fire. And the Bears and the Rabbits and the Panthers all agreed to take in runaway Cherokees – not too many, for they had reason to distrust mankind – but a few at least.

She even visited the Thunders – not the great Thunder and his two sons, who live far to the west above the sky vault, but other, lesser Thunders who make their homes lower down in the cliffs and mountains and under waterfalls and who traveled invisible bridges from one high peak to another where they have their townhouses. These Thunders, too, took pity on the Cherokee and let them bide with them a while in their invisible fastnesses.

A few she escorted to Adagahi, Gall Place, where they joined Nancy Butler on the shores of the medicine lake until, after a period of some years, they could quietly creep home to build the haphazard cabins connected by a tangle of trails up high in the mountains that still pepper these peaks today – they were, after all, still outlaws. It was just that nobody was looking for them anymore.

All in all and in the span of scarcely more than a month, Toineeta managed to find hiding places for the thousand Cherokee who did not go to Oklahoma, but remained hiding in the mountains. These thousand Cherokee formed the basis of what would later become the Eastern Band of the Cherokee Nation.

As for the rest of the Cherokee Nation, fifteen thousand strong, by the time Toineeta had settled all the refugees, they had barely begun the thousand-mile journey that, through one of the worst winters on record, would take them from Tennessee to Kentucky, from Kentucky to Missouri, from Missouri to Arkansas, from Arkansas to the wide limestone plateau that is Oklahoma. Along the way, they would leave four thousand of their fellow tribesmen buried in shallow graves, casualties of an exercise the Government called The Removal and Cherokee call *Nunna daul Isunyi* – The Trail Where We Cried.

FIVE

When the summer of 1839 came, Toineeta took to her bed. "I am old," she explained to Walini, "and my journeys have worn me out." (Being terrified of heights and otherwise fragile, Walini had elected not to live with the precipitous Thunders who had taken in the rest of her family, but to bide instead with the Granny Woman at Madcap Branch.)

Needless to say this announcement on the part of Toineeta made Walini very nervous. The ostensible reason for her living with Toineeta (other than her acrophobia) had to do with education – she wished Toineeta to instruct her regarding the use of herbs and medicine. The real reason was that she wanted Toineeta's protection. It was clear to the widow that the Granny Woman possessed great magic and, given the current calamitous state of affairs, Walini judged it prudent for so timid a rabbit as herself to remain within the more powerful woman's purlieu. "You had better get up," she told the old woman. "You'll feel better, if you do. Lying about all day would make anyone feel sick."

"Walini! Do you know how old I am?"

Walini shook her head.

"When Hog Bite was a little baby not more than two years old, it was my job, as the oldest daughter in the house, to keep him from falling into the fire when his mother came to visit mine!"

Walini considered this. Hog Bite was ninety-three. "That is very old."

"Yes," Toineeta agreed. "Too old. Certainly old enough to take to my bed if I feel like it." Later that week she said. "I have been thinking it over and decided that things have changed too much for me to go on living."

Walini dropped the wooden bowl of beans she was snapping onto the floor, scattering the beans everywhere. "What do you mean?"

"What I said."

"Please!" Walini dropped to her knees and started to pick up the beans, but with trembling fingers. "Don't talk like this. You cannot die."

"Oh, yes I can! And I will! What is the matter, Walini? Are you a little tree toad that hops away at the sound of a footfall? At the sound an acorn makes, dropping from the tree to the ground? I didn't notice you were a tree toad. In any case, you must get over being so afraid all the time, for soon I will be gone and this blind old woman will no longer be able to protect you."

"Don't say that!"

"Don't worry," Toineeta said. "I shall leave you something to protect you, something so powerful that you need not ever worry."

"What is it, Big Granny? Is it some magic?"

"It is. It is some great magic, but, like all such great magic, it comes from a place we do not know and so is a thing of wonder and dread." Here the old woman's voice became stern. "You must handle it carefully, Walini," she warned the younger woman, "and mark my words: let no one know you possess this magic thing, not even those whom you love most, for sooner or later they will be obliged to kill you in order to possess it and that shall make their souls blue and they will live as dead men do, alive but full of despair. Know that I have seen this happen. Over and over again."

Walini shivered. "What is this terrible thing?"

Toineeta sighed. She sounded weary. "Look in the cupboard. An old buckskin pouch."

Wallini rose and crossed over to the cupboard. She rummaged about on the cluttered shelves. "I don't see it . . . ."

"If it was a snake, it would have bit you. On the left. Second shelf. In the corner."

Walini reached into the dark, cobwebby corner and pulled out the buckskin pouch. With age, it had grown even more brittle and discolored than before. It did not look like a thing man had fashioned from skin, but like something which had grown on its own accord – the blown, dehiscent seedpod of a plant or a long discarded and withered egg case. Walini stared down at it.

"Come along. Bring it here."

Walini crossed back to the bed and, handing the pouch to Toineeta, resumed her seat by the bed. The old woman felt at the pouch for a moment, then smiled a nearly toothless smile. "Yes!" She loosened the strings with crabbed fingers that trembled as she worked the rawhide, but only slightly, thrust three fingers inside the narrow opening and drew out a long, triangular piece of rutile quartz crystal. Upon exposure to air, the crystal began to pulse with a strange, yellow-green glow, like that emitted by fireflies. With each pulse, the light grew brighter.

Walini sat back in her chair. "What is it, Granny? Why does it pulse like that? Like a heart! Does it live?"

"It is an ulunsuti, child, the crystal that an uktena wears in the center of its forehead, which is the seat of its power and the cause of it. It is very rare. I have lived one hundred and six years by my best reckoning and this is the only one I have ever seen. It belonged to the great hunter Dayunisi and, after him, to Young Squirrel and, after him, to his nephew, George Butler and, after him, to his son, Joseph Butler, but he was a foolish man and did not know its worth. Now it is yours." Reaching out, she groped for Walini's hand and, finding it, pressed the crystal into her palm. To the young woman's surprise, the stone was as cold as ice is, but dry too. "As to whether it lives, it is said that the whole of the uktena is contained within a single drop of its blood or a single scale that drops from its body . . . or its ulunsuti."

"But . . . what am I to do with it?" Walini noted that its light pulsed with the beat of her own heart, which made the stone feel as though it were not separate from her, but a part of her being. Her fingers closed about it.

"Just keep it safe and in your possession. It will make of you what it will . . . not necessarily what you wish . . . but, in the end, you will survive."

And Walini took the ulunsuti and replaced it in the pouch and kept it safe and in her possession and told no one of this magic that was now hers. And, as time passed, she grew less and less timid until she became, in fact, fearless, even when it came to heights, and was widely considered the most renowned Granny Woman of her day, respected, but also feared, for she developed quite a temper and had a rare penchant for revenge. Or at least the snake in her did.

୧୨୭

Just before she died, Toineeta told Walini this: "The elders tell you stories when you are a child, or your grandmother, and all of them say to you, 'Now, child, remember this! This is important.' And so, out of deference and because you know that they are wise, you do remember the stories told over and over again by the fire, around the council house, but not the way you remember something which has happened. Rather, you remember them the way you remember strange, improbable dreams – as jumbled sequences of events that make little sense or as parts of some whole that escapes total recall, yet somehow preys upon the imagination, licking memory with a prickled tongue.

"Then, one day, you wake up and, out of nowhere, here comes the meaning of a story which you heard long, long ago, when you were a tiny child and everyone you knew was still alive, but which you never quite understood.

"So it was for me with the story of the Ice Man. One cold winter's morning after the Removal, I awoke early and suddenly I understood what it was about.

"This is the story of the Ice Man:

"Once, when the people were burning the woods in the fall, the blaze set fire to a poplar tree, which continued to burn until the fire went down into the roots and burned a great hole in the ground. It burned and burned, and the hole grew constantly larger until the people became frightened and were afraid it would burn the whole world.

320

They tried to put out the fire, but it had gone too deep, and they did not know what to do.

"At last some one said there was a man living in a house of ice far in the north who could put out the fire, so messengers were sent, and, after traveling a long distance, they came to the ice house and found the Ice Man at home. He was a little fellow with long hair hanging down to the ground in two plaits. The messengers told him their errand and he at once said, 'Oh, yes, I can help you,' and began to unbraid his hair. When it was all unbraided, he took it up in one hand and struck it once across his other hand, and the messengers felt a wind blow against their cheeks. A second time he struck his hair across his hand and a light rain began to fall. The third time he struck his hair across his open hand, there was sleet mixed with the raindrops and when he struck the fourth time great hailstones fell upon the ground, as if they had come out from the ends of his hair. 'Go back now,' said the Ice Man, 'and I shall be there tomorrow.' So the messengers returned to their people, whom they found still gathered helplessly about the great burning pit.

"The next day, while they were all watching about the fire, there came a wind from the north and they were afraid for they knew that it came from the Ice Man. But the wind only made the fire blaze up higher. Then a light rain began to fall, but the drops seemed only to make the fire hotter. Then the shower turned to a heavy rain, with sleet and hail that killed the blaze and made clouds of smoke and steam rise from the red coals.

The people fled to their homes for shelter, and the storm rose to a whirlwind that drove the rain into every burning crevice and piled great hailstones over the embers, until the fire was dead and the smoke ceased. When at last it was over and the people returned they found a lake where the burning pit had been, and from below the water came a sound as of embers still crackling.

"That is the story of the Ice Man.

"The meaning of this story is that sometimes the people do something that they have always done, that is a good thing, like burning the brush in the fall, a practice which allowed our people to travel the forest at will all year round, without having their way obstructed by new growth. However, sometimes something goes awry and what is good becomes bad and the people can't stop it without resorting to extreme measures and strange, chilling magic.

"This is how I interpret this story: When the white man came to this land, the Cherokee tried to be his friend. They showed him the rivers and the mountains and the best places to hunt. They helped him to kill his enemies. And, in return, the white man showed the Cherokee how to till their fields with ploughs, not hoes, and how to spin cloth from flax and shoot guns, not arrows, and the Cherokee liked the white man's way of doing things and so we did them that way too. When the white man asked us for our land, we gave him a piece of it . . . then another . . . then another, because the Cherokee had much land and the white man was his friend. Then, little by little, a fire started and burned out of control and finally there was nothing we could do to stop it. The fire ate the world and there was no Ice Man or anyone to blow it out."

EPILOGUE

Perhaps you think I was a suicide. Of course, that is what people think when you walk into a river with stones in all your pockets. But let me assure you: that was not the case. Sophia Sawyer's story, the story I find most difficult to recount even now, more than a century later, when so much of me that was her has fallen away and those things that used to tear at me – the rejection, the awkwardness, the unrequited longing – that story ended the moment my bullet connected with Lieutenant Perry's sternum. I had chosen the Cherokee over my own race, I had chosen *Eloheh*, and I sealed that covenant with his blood. As for the rest, Toineeta was right. The world was on fire and there was nothing we could do to blow it out. So I chose to go to water, as Charley and Tsinawi had so long before.

And that is how I came to be here, wherever "here" is – hung up, forever lingering on this periphery, waiting for a chance to reappear, for a dark that suffices to be seen, caught in the crucible of these mountains – blue cloud catchers, smooth undulation of stone and forests of hemlock and pine lapping towards a distant horizon, a sound like the sea that is the wind blowing down the long valleys, waiting, always waiting for Charley.

> *Gonna build me a castle*
> *On the mountains so high . . . .*
> *So I can see Charley*
> *As he goes on by.*

Here my story ends, but not *the* story, for the ulunsuti endures. Remember that it is compressed stone, hard as any diamond, and cannot be destroyed save by wind and water and the careful work of millennia and, even then, may only be broken down into pieces of itself. And this has not yet happened.

Suffice it to say that the stone has continued to be handed down over generations, but with a difference. From the time of the Removal on, no man has ever been in possession of the ulunsuti, only women. This is a good thing, because women are more likely to use power wisely than men and, though the ulunsuti might render them ill-tempered, it does not usually incline them to drunkenness and murder. As for the stone's current owner, I will not tell you her name or how she happened upon the stone, for then you might seek her out and try to steal it for yourself. This much I will tell you: she is, like me, a weaver of baskets. I know this, because she was my student. I came to her in dreams and taught her how to weave. For, if there is one thing I have learned, it's that there's no keeping ghosts out of dreams, no matter how many dream catchers one employs. Dreams are our very playground.

ACKNOWLEDGMENTS

I would like to thank the Ontario Arts Council for its ongoing support, Barry Callaghan for his generosity to me over many years, Michael Callaghan for cleaning up the mess, and my agents, Frances and Bill Hanna, for trying to do right by me no matter how hard I resisted. A special thanks to David Sobelman, whose keen insight and adroit guidance was simply invaluable – *Broken Road* is the book it is because of him. Finally, I would like to thank my wonderful husband, Ken Trevenna, for putting up with me and for so, so much more. I would also like to acknowledge James Mooney's *History, Myths and Sacred Formulas of the Cherokees*, my source for most of the old Cherokee stories that found a new home in these pages.